There's A Place **P9-BYM-470**
With A Need To Be Healed.
A Need To Be Saved.
A Need To Be Loved.

STEVIE KNIGHT

The Oasis' guiding spirit. Her mission is to help women in pain, the kind of pain she understands because she once shared it herself. But, in healing others, can she escape the demands of her own heart?

ANNE GARRETSON

The Senator's wife. As much as her husband's political life is ruled by pundits and pollsters, her personal life is controlled by the pill bottle.

LIVY WALSH

The media baroness. Her transformation into a female Citizen Kane took a lot of guts—and a large dose of "liquid courage," the kind that mixes well in a cocktail glass.

KANDA LYONS

The superstar singer. Her breathless climb from Chicago's black ghetto to the stratosphere of success was paved by the powerful white dust of cocaine.

DENI VICKERS

America's top TV anchorwoman. Though she makes the news as often as she reports it, she secretly and shamelessly uses sex, no matter how degrading, to take her where she hungers to go.

Also by Jessica March

ILLUSIONS

Published by
WARNER BOOKS

TEMPTATIONS

JESSICA MARCH

WARNER BOOKS

A Warner Communications Company

WARNER BOOKS EDITION

Cover design by Jackie Merri Meyer
Cover photograph by Karen Filter

Warner Books, Inc.
666 Fifth Avenue
New York, N.Y. 10103

W A Warner Communications Company

Printed in the United States of America

First Printing: May, 1989

10 9 8 7 6 5 4 3 2 1

#
Prologue

1

Hal Garretson reached across the bed and stroked his wife's bare shoulder, his touch tender yet inviting.

Anne stirred, her body tense with the hundred anxieties that filled her mind. She glanced surreptitiously at the bedside clock. Only two hours until they were due to keep the appointment that might change their lives. Send them rising to greater heights, to the pinnacle of their dreams ... or bring their hopes crashing to earth.

Hal's touch grew more insistent, and with a muffled sigh, Anne turned and kissed the man who had been her lover, her friend, her partner in life for almost twenty years. His strong hands caressed her firm back, then moved with an easy familiarity to touch her shoulders and slide down her arms to her breasts.

Always when they were together, Anne gave herself without reservation, finding comfort and renewal in their passion. But now she made love from memory, trying to give pleasure with her body while her thoughts were elsewhere, rehearsing what she would do and say later tonight. She moaned softly when he entered her, as she always did, contracting her inner muscles to hold him tightly, just the way he liked. Raising herself on the pillow he tucked under her buttocks, Anne wrapped her slender legs around Hal's back, drawing him close. And when he began his rhythmic stroking, penetrating her very core, Anne closed her eyes, willing herself to be with her husband, trying to conjure up fantasies of other times. But the harder she tried, the more distant she felt. And when she became aware of his body straining with the last push for release, she gave a small cry, a tiny shudder—and hoped she had been convincing.

"Oh, babe," he murmured, releasing her slowly, "that was so good. . . . You always give me just what I need."

Thank goodness, she thought, Hal hadn't noticed how preoccupied and distracted she was. She couldn't bear to disappoint him.

"So how does it feel to make love to the next President of the United States?" he asked sotto voce.

"Twice as good as making love to an ordinary senator," she countered with a brightness she didn't feel, trying to ignore the leaden weight of anxiety that seemed to plague her every waking moment. "Do you suppose it gets even better in the Lincoln Bedroom?"

Hal put his forefinger to his lips and pointed at a gloomy portrait of Lenin, a cautionary reminder that the room might be bugged. Anne felt a moment of panic. Had she carelessly said something that could hurt Hal, that could be used against him?

"Relax," he said, smiling. "I was just kidding. . . . Our boys from the Embassy swept the place this morning."

She tried to match his smile—and his confidence. "What the hell," she said, "even if Big Brother is listening, maybe we just set a good example for the comrades. Like in the old days . . . make love, not war, right?"

The ring of the telephone preempted Hal's answer. He sat up, and Anne studied his athletic frame as he picked up the phone. Still well muscled, not an ounce of fat. Presidential timber for sure, she reflected proudly.

From the brief phone conversation that followed, Anne knew that the caller was Phil McKinney, Hal's aide and all-around troubleshooter, putting in a reminder for Hal to start readying himself for the evening. It was time, Anne realized, to leave the safe shelter of her husband's arms and face her other wifely duties: to go and charm the man who had the power to send Hal to the White House—or to cripple any chance he had to win his party's nomination.

The thought of what lay ahead sent Anne racing into the old-fashioned bathroom of their enormous hotel suite, an opulent marble chamber that looked as if it had been lifted intact from one of the czar's palaces. The Russians certainly knew how to treat their guests, she reflected; it was only their own people who remained deprived. *Watch out,* she cautioned herself then, purge all those critical thoughts from your head; the last thing she wanted was to have some negative comment pop out of her mouth at dinner tonight. And calm down, for heaven's sake, calm down! You've got to be in control.

Automatically, she reached for her makeup bag and rummaged through it until she dug out a vial of green pills. Thank God for these, she thought as she shook one into her palm. She filled a cut-glass tumbler with water from a silver carafe and swallowed the pill, then stood by the sink, waiting—praying—for the magic to take effect. Looking into the mirror in front of her, intensely studying her own eyes, she saw the moment of arrival, a sudden sparkle, even as she felt herself refueled by the energy and confidence she desperately needed. Everything's going to be fine, she could assure herself now, everything's under control.

In the deep claw-footed tub, she bathed quickly in water that wasn't quite warm enough, then returned to the array of cosmetics she'd lined up in the order in which she'd use them. Planning and organization. She'd learned those lessons back in the congressional days, right along with the lesson that politics was an unforgiving arena that blessed winners and forgot losers.

Always sharply critical of her own appearance, Anne made up her face with a skill born of constant effort and reinforced by regular lessons with America's leading cosmeticians. Just enough artistry to enhance her wholesome cover-girl looks and no more. Her thick, black curly hair had been shaped a few days before. She ruffled it with her fingers, and as her hairdresser had promised, it framed her face like a soft Grecian cap.

"Hurry up, hon," Hal called out as he prepared to shower. "Phil will be here with the Embassy limo in half an hour."

Hurry up, Anne repeated to herself as she opened the massive, carved mahogany armoire that held the wardrobe she'd chosen so carefully for this trip. She rifled through the half-dozen gowns she'd packed in tissue and plastic wrap. The black velvet Norell sheath was her original choice, but now she wavered. Was it perhaps too dramatic, too obvious? Would the Premier's wife feel that Anne was trying to upstage her? From the briefing notes she had studied on the plane, Anne had noted that the Premier's wife was known for her capricious moods. She had the capacity to be generously warm and vivacious when she chose, but there were also times when she was cold and uncommunicative, or petty and vain. There had been well-publicized problems between her and a past First Lady. If only *I* can win her over, Anne thought, if we can really hit it off, that would be a real step toward helping Hal with his campaign, showing how he would bring the personal touch to the successful handling of foreign relations.

Pulling out a floor-length periwinkle blue silk gown with simple, draped lines, Anne held it against herself, frowning as she looked from one dress to the other. Look good, she told herself, but don't upstage the other woman. . . .

She was still standing in front of the mirror when Hal came into the bedroom to pick out a tie. "Darling, come on," he said, impatience edging his voice. "The car will be here soon, and you know we can't be late."

She turned questioning eyes toward him.

"Either dress will be fine," he said, reaching for his jacket. "You always look lovely, Anne. . . . But hurry."

She nodded, inwardly cursing the mire of pressure and indecision that had overtaken her. She wasn't in control, after all. Her eyes went to the makeup bag, wondering if she didn't need another pill. . . . No, she had to resist that. She had been a politician's wife for all her married life, and she had performed brilliantly—hadn't she heard that over and over again? Yet ever since Hal had said "I think I can be President," ever since she'd answered "Go for it," something had changed. The green pills didn't seem to be doing their job anymore.

For a long time Anne had thought of the pills as "emotional management." Hadn't her own brother, a respected physician, prescribed them to ease the strain of too much work in too little time during her last year in college? "Only when needed, of course," he cautioned, and Anne had understood and never broken that rule. Not then. But ever since Hal had decided to seek the destiny they both knew could be his, almost every day brought new anxieties. Now her need was daily. Sometimes two or three times a day.

No, Anne commanded herself as she slipped into the blue gown, not another. She had to manage on her own, never be a slave to the pills. She could take them or leave them; that was what made her different from women like Joan Kennedy and Betty Ford.

She was caught again in gazing at her reflection. A moment later, she took the dress off and put on the black velvet, studying her mirrored image. Did she look as if she belonged at the side of a future president . . . ?

Hal came back into the bedroom, slamming the door. "Time to go, Anne," he said, the sharper edge in his voice galvanizing her into action.

She tore her eyes from the mirror and reached for the small alligator jewel case that held her finest pieces. Without looking at her reflection, she accessorized her dress with diamond ear clips and a matching spray pin by Van Cleef and Arpels. She slipped on a pair of simple black evening pumps a second before a discreet knock signaled the arrival of Phil McKinney.

Hal opened the door and admitted his most trusted adviser, who was carrying a stack of newspapers.

"Have a look at these later," Phil said, dropping the papers on a chair. "This European swing has been a triumph. The Brits are saying you're the West's greatest hope for détente, the Germans like your slant on the economy—and the French love Anne's 'impeccable style.' By the way . . . you do look great, Anne. I don't know how you manage it, but keep up the good work."

Anne smiled her thanks, but Phil's words only fed her anxiety.

As Hal put on his topcoat, Phil helped Anne into her voluminous Black Willow mink. "I noticed the Premier's wife admiring your coat this morning at the airport," Phil remarked.

"I almost didn't bring it," Anne admitted. "Then I decided it would be hypocritical to freeze in a simple Republican cloth coat—as someone once called it."

"Yeah," Phil laughed, "especially when *their* first lady will show up wearing a sable that could be worth eighty grand."

"Do you suppose she loses any sleep over what she

should or shouldn't wear?" Anne mused ironically as they stepped out into the corridor, where they were joined by a pair of stolid men in dark overcoats, their KGB escort.

"I doubt it," Phil said. "According to my sources, anyone who criticizes *that* lady lives to regret it. Lucky for us, she's looking forward to spending time with you."

"Oh? How do you know?"

"Annie—we don't maintain a multibillion-dollar intelligence operation for nothing." After Anne's laugh, he went on. "She told the ambassador's wife that she likes what she's read about you in *her* briefing notes." He leaned closer. "I don't need to tell you what a break that could be, how important it is if you could be . . . friends."

No, she thought as they stepped into the old-fashioned European-style lift, you don't have to tell me. I know too well that everything I do these days is important, vital, crucial, a matter of win or lose, life and death. The litany of warnings seemed to pile up around her like heavy stones walling her into a narrow corridor, a perfect straight path she'd have to follow, or else risk losing Hal's respect— and, sooner or later, his love.

In the cavernous and ornate lobby, a few passing guests stopped to stare at the sleek, well-dressed Americans, but a word from the KGB escort quickly dispersed them. Outside, a black Zhiguli limousine awaited, its engine idling to warm the interior against the bitter cold of the Moscow night.

Phil helped Anne and Hal inside, then took a seat beside the driver in a front compartment separated by a glass partition. The KGB men followed in a small Moskva sedan.

"When I make my little speech tonight," she said, "should I mention anything about this being a historic moment? Implying . . . you know, that no one does international diplomacy the way Senator Hal Garretson does?"

"Don't overdo," Hal replied. "I'm only a potential nominee, remember. No matter how far ahead I am in the polls, I'm nowhere near President yet. And my party would prefer I didn't embarrass the man who holds that office."

"Why not?" Anne laughed nervously. "He embarrasses himself on a regular basis."

Hal frowned and touched her hand. It felt cool, too cool to match the flushed face and shiny eyes. His eyes narrowed as he turned and studied her. "Anne . . ." he began tentatively.

"Stop . . . stop right there," she said. "I've only taken one. Just enough to keep me on my toes. . . ."

His tone became harder. "I thought we'd agreed—"

"*You* agreed," she retorted. Then, more softly, "Listen, I'm fine, Hal, really. You don't think I'd mess up after we've come this far, after all we've sacrificed?"

The question hung in the air. It was more than mere rhetoric, though they'd both agreed long ago to put the past behind them, never to speak of how different their lives would be, if only . . .

Hal kissed his wife's forehead and looked into the eyes that reminded him sometimes of those in the great impressionist portraits of Renoir or Manet—big, and dark, and luminous . . . and somehow a bit hazy, not sharply defined. For a moment he put aside thoughts of his career, remembering the long-ago night when Anne had first declared her love—and then had taken him to bed with the virgin passion that had bound him to her forever. In love, she had become his partner, his soul mate, his alter ego. In the service of his career, they'd been like twin meteors blazing a single trail, with but a single noble purpose: to advance his career as a truly dedicated public servant. As his political goals had been realized one by one, Hal felt himself growing stronger, going sixteen or eighteen hours a day with little food and almost no rest, defying natural laws and running on the adrenaline of his ambition. Anne had been his greatest asset. With her beauty, her intelligence, and her background in international affairs, she shone on the campaign trail, and never failed to give him invaluable advice in their pillow talk. Now, in spite of the pills she used with increasing frequency, he believed she was fine. He had to believe that. . . .

But was she? Or was his wife a ticking time bomb that could shatter the dreams that now seemed within reach?

Flanked by their KGB escort, Hal's party pushed past the crowds who waited outside the Bolshoi pleading for an extra ticket with an eagerness Anne had rarely seen in the United States. They were hurried through the marble-and-gilt lobby and taken upstairs by one of the security guards to the private dressing room of prima ballerina, Natalia Simonova.

A uniformed maid welcomed the visitors in halting English, explaining that Madame Simonova would be with them soon.

The walls of the anteroom were red velour and the furnishings seemed to be French, though several pieces were covered with immaculate white sheeting, as in a summer house in a Chekhov play. On one wall hung an oval mirror, its ornately carved frame like a memory from the age of the czars.

Peeking into the dressing area, Anne could see a wall of mirrors. In their reflection, the ballerina—tall and unnaturally slender—was doing her warm-up exercises. She moved like a racehorse, her muscles stretching inside her skin, her thin face impassive, her almond-shaped eyes a study in concentration.

Performing in her own ballet of manners, feeling at times no less threatened than if she were whirling *en point* across a high wire, Anne felt a kinship with the Russian dancer. What is she feeling now? Anne wondered. Is she terrified as I am of making some humiliating mistake? Does every performance feel like life-and-death, no matter how many successful ones went before it? Or did it only get worse, every success making the possibility of failure loom even larger and more frightening?

Finally, Simonova appeared. Like a czarina holding court, she nodded graciously as the KGB man presented Hal and Anne. The ballerina held out an exquisitely tapered hand to each of them. "I will dance for you tonight," she said in English, "in tribute for your visit to my country."

"We are indeed honored," Anne replied in flawless Russian.

A flicker of surprise warmed the ballerina's expression. Anne had seen the look before; it recognized her years of hard work and study. But Anne knew only too well that, for politicians and performers alike, hard work wasn't always rewarded with success.

As Hal and Anne entered the Premier's box, the Russian leader, a heavyset man, and his wife, an attractive, elaborately made-up woman, rose to greet them. As mutual politenesses were exchanged, Anne felt herself being carefully scrutinized by her hostess, who was wearing a burgundy gown with a matching brocade jacket. "Your dress," said the Premier's wife, "it's an American design?"

"Yes," Anne replied, trying to decide if a discussion about fashion would be politic or merely frivolous.

"You have the figure for it. I cannot wear such severe lines."

Now what? Anne wondered. A diplomatic compliment or a murmur of commiseration? Before she could decide, the Russian woman filled the silence. "I bought mine in Paris," she said, preening slightly.

That was easier to deal with. "Lovely," Anne said. "It suits you perfectly."

The Premier's wife smiled. Then, fortunately, the house lights dimmed, and as the orchestra began to play the familiar music of *Swan Lake*, the theater was filled with a hum of anticipation.

The sound grew louder as the first dancers appeared, and Anne remembered to turn and give a smile of appreciation to her host and hostess. For a little while, she tried to lose herself in the lilting, melodic music, the graceful movement of the dancers. True to her word, Simonova glanced toward the Premier's box. Anne held her breath as the ballerina executed a special cadenza, legs and arms shooting backward, her body cutting the air like an arrow, soaring upward, as if defying the laws of physics.

"Beautiful," Hal whispered, laying his hand over Anne's. His touch came as a reminder that she, too, would have to perform tonight, in spite of the icy clutch of fear that held her in thrall.

The caviar was delicious, everyone said so—choice gray Beluga presented in delicate glass bowls nestled in mountains of shaved ice, served as this supreme delicacy was meant to be served, without such garnishes as chopped egg or onion. A magnificent intermission refreshment, but Anne hated the stuff. Still, she smiled and accepted the dish proffered by the Premier's wife, who said emphatically, "No one outside the Soviet Union has ever tasted caviar of this quality."

Anne bit into the gray eggs after popping them into her mouth. To help fight the powerful briny taste, she took a long swallow of the other national delicacy: superb 120-proof vodka, chilled almost to the consistency of syrup. The liquor was exhilarating, with its clean, icy taste, and Anne took another swallow, followed by a third.

"You are enjoying the ballet?" the Premier's wife asked.

"Very much," Anne replied, searching her mind for the cultural material she'd committed to memory—and finding nothing.

"Russian ballet is very different from American dance, don't you agree?"

"Different . . ." Anne stalled, feeling tiny beads of sweat forming on her upper lip. "Russian ballet is . . . more classical. American dance tends to be . . . experimental."

"But which is more creative, do you think?" The Premier's wife was smiling, but in Anne's eyes, she was looking more and more like the Grand Inquisitor.

"I don't think such comparisons are fair," Anne answered carefully. She glanced over at Hal, who was smiling and relaxed as he regaled his host with an anecdote about one of his Senate colleagues. How does he do it? Anne wondered. Why is it so easy for him?

The performance resumed, giving Anne a merciful respite from further conversation, but all she could think about was the state dinner ahead. What if I forget my speech? she asked herself. What if the Premier's wife hates me? And with those thoughts came an even more frightening possibility: What if I turn into a political liability— what happens to my marriage then?

Lost as she was in her private misery, Anne scarcely noticed either the dancers or the music. Startled by the thunderous applause that signaled the end of the performance, she rose mechanically from her seat to join in the ovation. With a smile fixed on her face, she allowed herself to be led out of the theater.

The air in the limousine seemed unbearably stuffy, and Anne longed for escape. She pressed a button that rolled down the nearest window, but the blast of arctic air that rushed in made her face feel as if it would suddenly freeze and turn hard enough to crack. She raised the window again.

But the feeling didn't go away; she still had the notion that she might shatter.

"You're doing great, hon," Hal was saying. "Just keep it up, and tomorrow we'll be home free."

Oh, but I'm not doing great, she wanted to say. My head hurts, my throat's as dry as sand, and I'm so damn scared I can hardly breathe. I'm on the brink of flying apart, my darling, losing it all, everything you've wanted. . . .

But she couldn't say a word of it without risking the very foundation of their love.

The magnificent St. Catherine's Palace was ablaze with light, from within and without, and as the limousine approached, the largest, grandest, and most brilliant summer residence of the czars looked like a child's fantasy. But to Anne the grandeur was yet another reminder of how much was at stake.

"Break a leg," Hal said jokingly as he helped Anne out of the car.

"I love you," she said in a whisper, as if she were already pleading for forgiveness.

The centuries-old palace was a relic of another age. The magnificent marble staircase, the rococo detail, all seemed strangely incongruous with the spartan Soviet state of today. In a formal gallery lit with glittering crystal chandeliers was a long receiving line of national and party officials and their wives, all dressed in their best finery. Anne gulped a breath of air and followed in Hal's wake, murmuring a phrase of greeting to each person on the line.

In the next room, an orchestra played classical music, and waiters in black tie circulated with great silver trays of canapés and champagne. Anne longed for a drink to quench her thirst, but before she could get one, the Premier's wife approached.

"Would you care to see some of the palace?" she offered.

The invitation was impossible to refuse. "Yes . . . thank you," Anne said. If only she could find a moment to take another pill, it would be so much easier then. . . .

"This palace was the summer residence of the czars since Catherine the Second."

"It's very beautiful," Anne said politely.

"Much more beautiful than anything we build today, don't you agree?"

Anxious as she was, Anne failed to see the mischievous gleam in her hostess's eye. All she saw was yet another trap into which she might fall, and so she said nothing. She followed silently through a great hall adorned with carved cupids, into a square room decorated with gold leaf and ebony, its walls hung with gilt-framed paintings, portraits of long-vanished Russian royalty.

"This is the so-called Chinese Salon. . . . And that painting, the nude . . ."

"Is the Czarina Elisabeth," Anne blurted out, finally remembering *something* she could use.

The Premier's wife smiled. "So," she said, "you do know something about our country. . . ."

Anne flushed deep red, fearful that she'd somehow offended. "I majored in Russian studies in college."

"An unusual choice. You were interested in a diplomatic career . . . or perhaps a career with the CIA?" The mischievous gleam reappeared, but Anne felt herself in danger.

"No," she answered firmly. "I . . . I've always felt it was important that our two countries truly know each other. I . . ." She faltered, silently cursing the fog that muddled her search for the right words. "I believed the . . . the biggest obstacle to peace was fear and misunderstanding. I wanted . . . to do something to make a change for the better."

The Premier's wife appraised her guest coolly. "I believe you might," she said noncommittally. "Shall we rejoin the party?"

Anne followed back, cursing herself for wasting an opportunity, for faltering when she should have been eloquent. All the knowledge she'd acquired over the years, all the pages of Russian literature she'd memorized, everything seemed lost or misplaced. When they returned to the main reception room, she took a glass of champagne from a passing waiter and sipped it slowly. Just enough to relax me, she told herself. Just enough so I can remember my speech.

The silvery tinkle of a dinner bell sent the assembled guests into the dining room, where a table for sixty had been laid, with sparkling white linen, heavy antique Russian silver, and fine French china.

When the guests were seated, the Premier introduced Hal. "Senator Garretson is a most welcome guest," he said, "not only for his views on world peace, but also for his beautiful wife."

Standing, Hal acknowledged the laughter and applause, as comfortably as if he were among friends in the Senate. "I'm reminded of our late president, John F. Kennedy, who also had a beautiful and intelligent wife—and was wise enough to share her accomplishments with the world. I give you Anne Garretson, who speaks for both of us tonight."

Anne rose from her chair, feeling as if she were all alone on a high wire, as if any misstep would be a mortal mistake. She cleared her throat and began to speak in Russian. "More than half a century has passed since a small radical party overthrew the czars and created the world's first socialist state." She paused and looked at Hal's face. He nodded encouragingly. When she had tried to show him the notes for her speech, he had declined to look, saying he wanted to respond spontaneously tonight—and affirming that he never had had any doubt she would always say exactly the right thing.

"We've had half a century of comparisons between your way of life and ours," she continued, "and still we're both here, still trying to coexist. And who are we to judge you? The American is both the best and worst observer of the Soviet Union. Best because we share the same grand scale in technology and resources. Worst because our history may leave us ill prepared to understand yours. And so too often our comparisons are unfair, comparing our best with your worst."

A flurry of applause interrupted, but Anne pressed on, afraid of forgetting the words she'd rehearsed so often.

"But our two great nations share a faith in progress," she said, "in believing that it is the fate of the human species —no, our responsibility—to go from worse to better. So let us join together to meet that responsibility. How much more successful we can be if we do it not just as neighbors in the community of nations, not merely as partners on this planet, but as true friends."

She bowed her head and sat down, shaking so hard she felt as if she'd break apart. As if from a distance, she heard the sounds of approval, clapping that died out only reluctantly when she merely nodded without standing again to acknowledge the applause. It's all right, she told herself, it's all right. But the trembling wouldn't stop.

"A wonderful speech," the Premier's wife said, placing her hand on Anne's arm. Then, no doubt aware of Anne's trembling, she added sympathetically, "You must be tired."

Anne demurred quickly, but the Russian woman persisted. "When I visited your country last year, I was exhausted by the second day. I told my husband I must have my rest, and he agreed."

Anne felt a pang of envy. And then she yawned openly.

She heard herself giggle. "Jet lag," she rushed to explain. "It can creep up on you just like *that*." She struck the table for emphasis, and to her horror, a crystal water goblet overturned.

Quickly a footman in military uniform produced a linen towel and began blotting up the mess. Though she knew she should keep silent, Anne heard herself babbling like a child, offering apology after apology.

The Premier's wife reached over and touched Anne's hand lightly. The gesture should have been reassuring, but across the table Anne could see Hal's worried expression. She began to tremble again. Oh, God, let me make it through this meal, she prayed over and over.

The smell of food seemed overpowering, but Anne forced herself to move it around on her plate, pretending to eat when the thought of eating filled her with nausea. By the time coffee was served, she felt as if she couldn't endure another moment.

"Please excuse me," she told her hostess. "I need to find a powder room." She rose from her chair.

The Premier's wife rose with her. "Let me show you the way."

Anne hesitated. She needed to be alone, but what excuse could she make? Without protest she fell in behind the Russian woman, who led the way to a spacious pink and gold boudoir. There were a half dozen white marble sinks with golden faucets in the shape of swans' heads, several toilet cabinets concealed behind gold-leafed doors, and a row of chairs upholstered in pink silk lined up before a huge mirror.

"My dear," said the Premier's wife as Anne sank into one of the chairs. "Can I get you a glass of water? You look so pale. Or some schnapps, perhaps . . . ?"

It was a chance for a solitary moment, unobserved. "Yes, I'd like some water," she said, then added quickly, "I feel fine, though. If I look pale, it's probably just that my makeup needs repair."

The Premier's wife gazed at her uncertainly before moving into an alcove to get the water.

Anne shifted to another chair, at a far corner of the mirror, and took from her purse a compact, a lipstick, and a comb. She laid them on the marble counter in front of her, then glanced over her shoulder to make sure her hostess was still out of sight. Now her hand darted back into the purse and grabbed the vial of pills. Fingers trembling, she fumbled with the cap. The effort to get at the pills seemed to go on forever. Suddenly the vial opened and the pills scattered across the marble countertop. Anne started to reach out and gather them.

"Do you know what my husband's secret service could do with those?"

The voice over her shoulder seemed as loud as a cannon shot. Lifting her eyes, Anne saw the image of the Premier's wife in the mirror, standing right behind her, her gaze directed down at the green pellets dotting the marble.

"I . . . I don't . . ." Anne tried to speak, to deny there was anything wrong, but the words wouldn't come. A Pandora's box of horrifying possibilities raced through her mind. Hal's chances were ruined now, weren't they? He would never forgive her. She would never forgive *herself*. Within the silver window of their reflected images, Anne's eyes locked with the Russian woman's, trying to read her intentions.

"Why?" the Premier's wife asked simply.

"Do you need to ask—you of all people? Don't you find it impossible sometimes? The demands . . . being everything he expects—everything the *world* expects . . ."

There was a long silence. The image in the mirror nodded at Anne, then sat down beside her.

"Does your husband know?"

Anne turned to her. "Not how bad it is. We have to be strong for them, don't we?" Tears stung the corners of her eyes. She glanced down, hiding her weakness.

The Russian woman reached over and clasped her hand. "I will not speak of this to anyone," she said. "You have my promise."

Anne looked up, startled by the gesture.

"But you must make me a promise in return," the Premier's wife went on. "That you will do something to solve this problem, to rid yourself of this . . . dependency."

Anne glanced down at the pills, wanting one more than she'd ever wanted anything.

"I think we can be friends, you and I," the Premier's wife continued. "One day, perhaps, we could even make the difference you spoke about. It would be a great pity if we did not have the chance. . . ."

Anne nodded, still not trusting herself to speak.

"May I have your promise?" the Russian woman persisted.

After a moment Anne swept the pills into her palm. Watched closely by the Premier's wife, she stood and walked to one of the toilet cabinets, threw the pills into the water, and flushed them away.

"You have my promise," Anne said when she returned.

"So. Shall we return . . . ?"

"Give me a moment alone . . . please."

"As you wish," the Premier's wife said. She turned to leave and then stopped. Abruptly, she threw an arm around Anne's shoulder and squeezed hard, as if sharing her own strength with one who needed it more.

And then Anne was alone—with the truth she could no longer deny. Somewhere along the line, she had lost her power of choice. She had become dangerous to herself and to Hal.

Weary of charades and pretenses, the senator's wife

looked at her reflection and saw herself as she was—as she had been seen through the eyes of a powerful stranger who had just declared herself a friend. Yes, something had to be done. "You have my promise," she said once more, whispering it now to the woman in the mirror.

And she knew the only way—and the only place—the promise could be kept.

2

From the outside, The Oasis looked like a resort or country club. Set amidst the blue-black mountains of New Mexico, its sprawling Spanish-style adobe buildings were bordered by native wildflowers and carefully tended grounds dotted with picnic tables and benches.

Inside were a thousand heartbreaks and shattered lives —and Stevie Knight had shared them all.

The Oasis was quiet now. All the staff and "Travelers," as Stevie called them—she detested the word *patients*— were asleep, and she stood alone in her office. It was a cozy room, decorated in the warm, inviting style of the American Southwest, with a stone fireplace and a Navajo rug on the wideboard floor. By day the wide picture window framed the red-gold mountains and the azure sky.

But now, in the dark hours that preceded the dawn, the office felt cold and lonely. A shaft of moonlight fell across the array of photographs covering one wall—film and television stars, corporate executives, well-known newspaper columnists who peddled everything from political comment to gossip, and one of the world's leading opera stars, not to mention the many ordinary housewives and mothers— every picture signed to Stevie with a heartfelt message of gratitude and affection. Two things these former Travelers had in common: they'd all been in desperate trouble, virtually fighting for their lives; and they were all women. They had brought their problems to The Oasis and they had gone away healed. Over and over Stevie had taken despair and turned it to hope, planted seeds of new beginnings in the ashes of defeat. For more than fifteen years, since she had passed through the fires of her own troubled youth, word of mouth had spread Stevie's fame, and she had been lauded as a worker of miracles.

Tonight, however, as she sat alone in the darkened room, Stevie knew she was no worker of miracles, for if she had that power she would invoke one for herself—take the love that had eluded her for so long—and damn the consequences. But instead all she had left of him was the memory of that last bittersweet embrace, the hollow echo of that last good-bye.

Why had it taken so long? Why, when they finally knew they were right for each other, why did it have to be too late? Her heart cried out in protest—against logic, against duty, against the principles that conspired to steal him away. Why, oh why, did she have to sacrifice her own happiness for the sake of another woman?

Because, she reminded herself just before she surrendered to sleep, because without that sacrifice you lose the deepest part of your self. In the past twenty years, she had clawed herself up from hopelessness only by discovering that she could help others.

She opened her eyes again to bright rays of sun splintering over the mountain's horizon. She looked at the clock on her desk—a few minutes before six. Though she had slept, her body felt achey and unrested. A shower and a cup of coffee, she decided, would revive her enough to face the heavy workday ahead.

The sharp ring of the telephone made her jump. She picked up the receiver. "Stevie Knight . . ."

At first, there was only silence, then the sound of quick shallow breaths. Stevie waited patiently. She knew the meaning of this sound from a thousand other phone calls. Someone was struggling to find the words.

At last the voice came through. "This is Anne Garretson, Miss Knight. My husband is Senator Hal Garretson."

"I know who you are," Stevie said gently. "How can I help?"

There was still a struggle, but this time the pause was shorter. "Will this be—"

Stevie didn't need to hear the whole question; it was always their first. "Whatever you tell me, Mrs. Garretson, will remain confidential. Unless, of course, a time comes when you want it to be known."

The words rushed out then in a desperate jumble. "I need your help, but I just don't know what to do—the newspapers, my husband's campaign, the expectations. So much is riding on all of this, you see."

"I understand. You're worried if word gets out that you're here. Let me assure you again, it would never come from me. But I can't make any guarantees about the news media, whether or not they'd be able to get the story. But is that the determining factor? You wouldn't call me unless you were in need—in pain. Isn't your health—your life— more important than any other consideration?"

"I don't know." Anne's voice was barely a whisper. "To me, Hal's career is the most important thing in the world. What he wants is . . . what I want. I'm just afraid that if I don't get some help, I'll ruin everything."

"Mrs. Garretson," Stevie cut in gently, "Anne . . . if you want my help, it's yours."

"When?" Anne asked, as if even a day's delay would be too long.

Stevie glanced at the schematic chart that covered one wall, then punched up a series of commands on a computer that sat blinking on her Spanish mission desk. "Be here Tuesday, the twenty-second," she said. "You'll stay for six weeks."

"Six weeks!" Anne protested. "But Hal has obligations, party functions and fund-raisers to go to all over the country. I should be with him. If I'm not, there are bound to be questions—"

"Anne, I don't know yet what your problem is. But please believe me . . . in fighting any addiction, time is one of the biggest weapons you have—time to give yourself relief from the pressures, to make an all-out commitment to get straight. If you can't make that commitment, then I'm powerless to help." Though the speech sounded harsh, Stevie knew that the only way she could start out on the journey with any of her Travelers was to tell the truth—and have them know she always did. She had seen all too many vibrant, seemingly intelligent people cling to whatever was destroying them by degrees, embrace it with more unshakable fidelity than they'd offered any human being or cause—and go on in their fatal illusion because some of the people who loved them most were afraid to tell them the truth. Stevie had learned from bitter experience that no treatment worked until everyone—the person with the problem and all who suffered along with them—accepted that getting straight must be the number-one priority.

Stevie let her words sink in, then asked: "Shall I put you down for the twenty-second?"

"I'll be there." The voice was low yet resolute.

"One more thing. After the first three weeks, we expect spouses to take some part in the treatment. Will the Senator be available?"

"I can't speak for my husband," Anne replied. "But I can promise I'll do anything you tell me, anything I—"

"Okay, let's just take it one day at a time," Stevie said, knowing how painfully Anne's promise would be tested. Stevie Knight's greatest weapon in helping to fight the battles of those at the knife edge of self-destruction was in knowing everything they would feel—because she had been there herself.

For a moment after cradling the phone she reflected on Anne Garretson's final answer, her inability to promise her husband's support. Was Hal Garretson not the devoted husband he seemed to be in public? Stevie wondered. Or was he part of Anne's problem?

The answers would come in time. Right now, another day at The Oasis had begun. Using all the experience gathered from her own years of being lost in a nightmare, of doing battle with the ugliest and most vicious demons within the human spirit, she would be expected to guide her Travelers to safety, away from the dangers of their own worst temptations. She did it well, better than anybody, many said. She failed no one—not if they were ready for what she could give them.

But she wondered, as she headed out the door, if her greatest failure wasn't still with herself. Or was it true that love was just one more temptation that had to be denied?

Book One

Book One

1

Newport News, Virginia. Spring 1969

The great gray leviathan stood proud and erect under the
blazing Virginia sun. The nuclear submarine *Neptune*, 447
feet long, could maintain a surface speed of 27 knots, 20
knots submerged, and remain at sea for 200,000 miles before its plutonium reactors had to be "refueled." Though its
sophisticated sonar and radar detection devices were said to
be defensive in nature, the *Neptune* was also armed with
sixteen Polaris missiles, each fitted with a nuclear warhead
that could be launched from 1,400 miles at sea, and was
powerful enough to reduce a city the size of Philadelphia to
rubble. The sub carried a crew of 172 of the Navy's finest
men.

In America's cities and college campuses, many men
were marching to a different drummer, protesting the war
in Southeast Asia, shouting, "Hell, no, we won't go," as
they filled the television airwaves with images of burning
draft cards, desecrated flags, and tarnished innocence.

But none of that would interfere today with the proud
moment of the *Neptune*'s launching. The United States
Navy had outdone itself with an almost defiant show of

military splendor. A reviewing stand and stadium seats had been set up to overlook the new submarine's launch slide. Scores of American flags fluttered in the breeze. The guest list included the Secretary of the Navy and assorted senators and congressmen—all pro-war "hawks"—along with prominent businessmen and members of the national press.

And the man who would christen the *Neptune* was none other than the movie star Luke James, who had risen to become the number-one box-office draw by playing an assortment of fast-shooting lonesome cowboys and tough renegade cops. Indeed, the only species of distinctly American hero he had yet to play in any film was a soldier.

The guests had not yet assembled for the christening ceremony, but already two fresh-faced sailors in dress whites stood proudly at attention, their brass buttons gleaming in the sun, rifles off to the side in angled precision.

And I'm ready, too, Stevie Knight thought as she walked toward the launching dock. Her streaked blond hair had been teased into a bouffant cap, a single lock falling seductively over one eye. Her prominent cheekbones had been artfully blushed, her enormous thick-lashed green eyes had been outlined with charcoal. The black silk suit she wore —a short-cropped jacket over a pencil-thin miniskirt— clung so tightly it looked almost as if it had been sewn onto her skin. Her long slender legs were encased in sheer black stockings, shod in spike-heeled sandals.

As she showed her pass and strolled through the gate, Stevie noted the way the two stared at her. Walking on, she smiled with satisfaction. Her clothes and makeup were calculated to provoke any man who saw her; she liked all of them to sit up and take notice. She accentuated the movement of her hips provocatively as she sauntered away, enjoying the idea of the two overheated sailors she was leaving in her wake on this warm spring day.

But as she passed the reviewing stand, Stevie's expression darkened. All this flag-waving bullshit made her sick. Bad enough young soldiers and sailors were being killed by the thousands in some dinky country on the other side of the world that no one really cared about. Now the Navy brass had the nerve to pretend they had something to celebrate—just because they'd built another death-dealing machine. Bastards, she thought. Maybe she hadn't gone out to join the kids who marched and protested against the war in Vietnam. Still, she mused slyly, I'm making my own little protest, in my own way. . . .

Approaching what was normally a parking lot, Stevie could see a huge red-and-white-striped tent. Inside, a reception was in progress, dignitaries mixing with naval officers in dress uniforms and wives in Sunday best.

To the left, on a portable platform, a grand piano had been set up, and a young man played classical music. To the right, there was a linen-covered buffet table laden with silver serving platters heaped with cold meats and salads. There was a sprawling open bar tended by Annapolis cadets on special assignment. In the center of the bar was a fountain bubbling with California champagne surrounded by arrangements of flowers in red, white, and blue. Even the goddamn flowers, Stevie thought, were being made to perform their patriotic duty. *Made* to do it, she reflected bitterly, by the Admiral. Of course, in these quarters, he could get anything done with a snap of his finger. Or a slap of his hand.

Pausing under the shaded fringe of the tent, Stevie wondered if she should go in, watch his cold eyes blaze to life as she showed her stuff. No, she decided, she wasn't ready to face him, not quite yet.

"Hi, gorgeous."

She whirled to find Lieutenant Commander Sanford Graystone standing at her shoulder. A trim six-footer with chestnut hair and a clean-cut Jack Armstrong face marred only by spectacles, Sandy was the principal aide to Admiral Custer ("Cus") Knight, base commander.

"Hi yourself," Stevie said passively. "I suppose you're like the rest of them—got a big hard-on for the Navy's new toy?"

"Not when you're around," Sandy said huskily, devouring her with his eyes. "I've missed you, Stevie. Can't tell you how much. Why haven't you called in a week? It's been driving me crazy. . . ."

She hated making explanations. "You shouldn't be talking to me," she said flatly. "You know, if the Admiral ever guessed what you'd been doing with me, you could kiss these good-bye." She flicked the gold bars on his dress uniform with a fingertip.

Sandy retreated a step, as if the mere mention of Admiral Knight's wrath were enough to cool his ardor. "You wouldn't ever—"

"Say anything? Hell, he'd kill me, too."

"Then meet me later, Stevie, please. At the usual place . . ."

She half closed her green eyes in a way that she knew would excite him. "Maybe. But I'm not making any promises." She saw the hunger in his face give way to hope, an expression that reminded Stevie of the way her mother looked when the Admiral was around—weak and kind of childlike. It was a look she vowed she'd never wear herself, not for anyone. And, seeing it on this man's face, it turned her off. Once it had been exciting to toy with Sandy and with others like him, to use the raw power of her sex to turn them into little boys begging for her favors. But lately the sport had gone out of toying with the Admiral's slaves. Much as she loved pulling the wool over his eyes, it had become all too easy. "Don't you have something to do?" she asked Sandy, suddenly cool.

The naval officer nodded obediently, ready to be dismissed.

But she wasn't quite ready to let him go, not when she might still have some use for him. She wet her crimson lips and blew him a kiss, watched his face light up before he hurried away. How easy it was to control them, she thought. Just as long as you had something they wanted, they could all be made to act like fools.

Turning back toward the tent, she scanned the assembled guests until she spotted her quarry. In the flesh, she thought, Luke James was even better looking than in his films, tall and lean, his ruggedly handsome face deeply tanned, so that his famous blue eyes seemed even more startlingly clear and icy. She could remember seeing a movie of his when she was twelve or thirteen—still a virgin, but already given to the wildest fantasies. No doubt about it, Stevie thought, this was a trophy worth having. Making her fantasies with Luke James come true would be her biggest conquest ever.

She pulled the seductive lick of hair slightly farther down over her eyes and set off to make her entrance, moving slowly, sinuously, walking the thin line between trash and allure, knowing that none of the dowdy Navy wives in the tent could hold a candle to her.

The crowd seemed to part as Stevie approached, and with no trouble at all she managed to position herself just where she wanted to be, leaving no more than a couple of adoring fans between her and Luke James. I've got him in my sights, she thought, now let him find me.

Within seconds, one of the sailors serving as waiters materialized at her elbow. "Something from the bar?" he asked, trying to sound diffident while his eyes did a radar sweep over Stevie.

"Just a Shirley Temple," she said demurely.

She felt no need to make conversation with anyone

around her. She simply stood her ground and watched Luke James hold court, lowering her eyes when he glanced in her direction.

He signed a couple of autographs and then, just as she'd hoped, he inched over to where she was standing. "Hi, I'm Luke James," he said, just as if his face wasn't enough introduction. "Who are you?"

"I'm Stevie," she said softly, giving him her shyest smile.

"Stevie?" He laughed, the famous blue eyes crinkling. "You sure don't look like a Stevie to me."

"Stephanie's my real name," she explained, "but nobody calls me that. The old story—my father wanted a boy." She searched Luke's face for a clue to what her strategy should be. She had never stalked a movie star before, and she didn't have time to make a mistake.

"He ought to be happy with what he got," Luke said.

"He's not the type to be happy with anything."

"So what are you doing here?" Luke asked.

Stevie thought it might be fun to try snaring Luke James with his own politics, much as she disagreed with them. "Well, I wouldn't miss this launch for the world. I think it's so important to stand up for what you believe, especially now, when everyone's so down on the military. And America too, for that matter."

Luke gave Stevie an appreciative nod. "Well, well. I didn't think there were any young women around who felt that way. Most of the ones I know are either burning flags or bras."

She met his eyes boldly. "If you were to get to know me, Mr. James, it wouldn't take you long to find out I'm different from other young women . . . in a lot of ways."

"Oh?"

Stevie could see that he had caught her meaning, that the pictures in his head had started to play. But then, as he started to undress her with his eyes, his gaze clouded as though to close down on his imaginings. It was the age thing, she thought. It had occurred to him she might be too young for him. What could she say to get him over that hump?

"Did I hear someone say you'd been in some movies?" she asked abruptly.

Luke James frowned. Yes, that had done the trick, she saw—getting the hook into his vanity.

"You're not going to tell me you haven't seen any—"

"I told you about my father. He's very strict. The only movie stars I'd recognize are Mickey Mouse and Fred Astaire."

"Is that a fact . . . ?" he said lightly. It seemed he had seen through her. Yet he was still enjoying the game. Changing the subject—the best way to soothe his wounded vanity—he said, "You still haven't told me how you got to be here. You don't look like a politician or a sailor. . . ."

Stevie smiled. "I live on the base . . . with my family," she said.

"A Navy brat," Luke remarked, and Stevie thought he might start fishing for her age again.

But before he could say anything else, Admiral Custer Knight materialized at his side. Tall and ramrod straight, the Admiral had a stern, sharply chiseled face with the creased leathery skin that testified to many years spent standing on an open command bridge, staring into strong winds and salt spray. His hair was the same shade of gray the Navy painted on the hulls of its warships.

Shit, Stevie thought. Damn the old bastard for butting in now.

Luke turned from one to the other, apparently on the brink of making polite introductions.

But Admiral Knight spoke first. "I see, Mr. James, that you've made the acquaintance of my daughter. Or," he added with an icy glance toward Stevie, "would I be more correct to say she's made yours. . . .?"

Luke stared speechlessly at Stevie. And again, always taking the high ground before others could act, Custer Knight filled the silence. "But I'm afraid it will have to be a brief acquaintance. We're ready to begin the ceremony. We've got a ship to launch, Mr. James." And, as if he had taken the movie star prisoner in battle, the Admiral grasped his elbow and pulled him away.

But Stevie caught the glance that James threw at her just before being led into captivity, and it left her smiling. A ship, she thought, was not the only thing that would be launched today.

She waited until the first few rows of the reviewing stand were filled, and then she took a seat well behind the Admiral and her mother, the genteel and dainty Irene. Irene looked every inch the lady today, dressed in lavender chiffon, with matching picture hat and gloves, but Stevie wasn't fooled for a minute. No doubt her mother had already used up a pack of Sen-Sen, disguising the smell of her breakfast of bourbon pick-me-ups.

A Navy band struck up a medley of Sousa marches, and a group of Annapolis cadets broke ranks with the group and marched smartly in a precision drill. As they passed the reviewing stand, they turned eyes right and snapped a smart salute. Admiral Custer Knight, decorated six times in war and peace, holder of the Navy Cross, vice-commander of the Pacific fleet—and likely candidate for promotion someday to the Joint Chiefs—stood straight as an arrow as he returned their salute. Exactly, thought Stevie, as if he had a hot poker up his ass.

Desperate for some distraction to get her through the ceremony, Stevie foraged in her purse and found a piece of Bazooka bubble gum. In the middle of "Stars and Stripes

Forever," she blew a great big pink bubble and popped it with a long, red-tipped finger. Someone giggled nearby, and, just as she hoped, Luke James turned around and favored her with a sly grin as she plucked the strands of sticky stuff from her face and wound them back into her mouth with the languorous workings of her tongue.

When the music ended, the politicians started their long-winded speeches about how we were winning the war and how all the protests were the work of professional agitators and misguided idealists. The Admiral came next, blowing long and hard like the rest, talking about freedom and liberty, just as though he knew what that meant. Funny, Stevie thought, from a distance and in his dress uniform, he could almost pass for somebody's idea of a hero. But she knew better. If she'd been a boy, she had no doubt whatever that he'd have shipped her off to be killed, just so he could pride himself on being a real patriot.

When the Admiral finally finished, the band played a fanfare, and two officers' wives stepped forward and handed Luke James a champagne bottle decorated with red-white-and-blue ribbons.

Luke stood at attention, his craggy features as familiar as an American monument, his blond hair streaked by the California sun, pale blue eyes squinting against the sunlight. "I'm real proud to be here," he drawled in that way that made the eyes of the assembled Navy wives shine with desire, "and I'm proud to be an American. Some folks think that's out of style these days, but I think we'd all be making a bad mistake if we forgot that we live in freedom because we've always had the guts to fight for our country and for the ideals it stands for. God bless America," he concluded reverently to the accompaniment of hearty applause, then hefted the champagne bottle. "I christen this submarine *Neptune* in the name of all loyal Americans."

He swung the bottle against the sleek narrow hull . . . but it bounced off, unbroken, with an ignominious *clunk*.

The officers' wives giggled, and the television cameras moved in closer as Luke gave his trademark "aw shucks" grin and ad-libbed: "I take this as a good sign, folks—and I predict that this vessel will last forever." He swung the bottle again, harder, and this time it shattered with a satisfying noise into a hundred tiny pieces.

The ceremony was over. As the fans closed in on Luke, seeking a touch, a word, an autograph, his eyes were searching the crowd. Finding out that the beautiful, sexy young blonde was the Admiral's daughter had been a shock, but he'd gotten over that pretty quickly. There was something in the green eyes, something in the way she used her body, that told him she might be worth taking a risk for. All kinds of risks . . . because it was even possible she was a minor. Yet when you were getting paid three million bucks a picture, and women of all ages and shapes and colors were always throwing themselves at you, when everything got to be too damn easy, how in hell could you feel *really* alive without taking a few chances? Fast motorcycles and fast women—his manager was against both, but Luke knew best what kept his juices flowing.

Long legs crossed, skirt pulled up high, Stevie perched atop the fender of the long, red Cadillac convertible waiting for Luke James. With first a pout and then a promise, she'd cajoled Sandy Graystone into revealing that the movie star's car was parked in one of the motor-pool garages. Then she'd sent Sandy back to his wife.

As soon as Luke entered, his tan face creased into a grin. "So this is where you went," he said. "I was looking for you."

"I figured you might be," Stevie said. She slid off the

car, hiking the skirt even higher up her long legs. "So here I am. Isn't it nicer to meet here?"

"Nicer?"

"Private. Less trouble for you—with your fans . . . and my Admiral."

Luke shook his head and smiled, plainly marveling at her brazen confidence. "Tell me, Stevie . . . how old are you?"

So he still hadn't thrown caution to the winds. "Maybe you're better off not knowing."

"Maybe?" he echoed.

"Isn't it enough to say I'm . . . an old soul?"

"Not if you're jailbait," he said, letting toughness come through in his abrasive tone. He had to show this little girl that she couldn't completely lead him around like a schoolboy.

He was slipping off the hook, Stevie felt, her biggest trophy ever. Time to pull out all the guns. She walked across the gap of cement floor that separated them, put a finger up to his cheek, and ran three of her long red nails very lightly down the line of his jaw, then rested her hand across his shoulder. She felt she'd won when he didn't make a move to stop her.

"Why don't we say this, cowboy? This whole thing will be our little secret. I'll make sure you don't get locked up. In fact, if you fuck me, I may even—in some way—set you free."

The fire flared higher in Luke's eyes. He grinned again, "You're some piece of work, Stephanie."

"Stevie," she said.

Luke had made up his mind. He wasn't going to be frightened off, not just because of her father. In his own world, after all, he outranked an admiral—he was a god. "Hop in," Luke said, holding the car door open. Stevie did, flashing a generous expanse of calf and thigh, a provocative peek of black garter.

"Where to?" he asked.

"Let's have a picnic," she said, wanting to be different from the other women Luke had known. "Outside . . . on the grass."

As he turned the car out of the garage, Stevie switched on the car radio. The Wonders, a hot new black group, were singing "Look What Love Has Done to Me," and Stevie snapped her fingers to the beat, humming along with the silken voice of the lead singer.

When they had left the base behind, Stevie directed Luke to a general store on the highway. She waited in the car while he shopped, her head thrown back on the white leather seat, her eyes closed, a tiny anticipatory smile on her lips.

He returned with a picnic basket, a plaid blanket—and the same kind of smile. "Now where do we go?" he asked.

She gave him directions to a deserted estate outside of town. "It's supposed to be closed up, but I know where there's a break in the fence."

"Is that where you take your boyfriends?" Luke asked as he restarted the car.

"Only the good ones."

When they reached a long, winding driveway overgrown with weeds, Stevie instructed him to park behind the tree-high hedges, out of sight and away from the main road. She picked up the blanket from the back seat and led Luke past the gate of the deserted mansion, to a spot where the elaborate wrought-iron fence had rotted away with rust. "Follow me," she said, gingerly making her way through the opening.

They walked through a landscape of overgrown flowers and shrubbery, until they came to a small clearing overlooking a secluded pond. Stevie spread the blanket under a tree, kicked off her sandals, and sat down. "Let's eat," she said, "all that stupid flag-waving made me hungry."

Luke set down the picnic basket. "Stupid flag-waving?" he echoed. "But I thought you said—"

"What did I say?" she asked, mugging a look of wide-eyed innocence, then helping herself to a sandwich.

Luke shook his head as he opened a bottle of wine. "Well, this is quite a scoop. Is the Admiral's daughter really one of those down-with-America pinkos?"

"I like America fine," she countered breezily. "It's the people who pretend to speak for America I can't stand."

He filled two plastic tumblers, then paused as he was handing her one. "I forget; is Stevie old enough to drink?"

"I didn't say." She plucked the wine from his hand. They sipped, exchanging glances over the rim of their cups.

"And what does your father think about your politics?"

"I don't much give a damn what he thinks."

Luke smiled tolerantly at Stevie's rebellious talk. Hadn't he been accused of the same attitude a dozen times? "Grow up, Luke," his manager pleaded with monotonous regularity. "The studios think you wanna be James Dean." Luke didn't care what they thought either. As long as he was box-office gold, he could do what he pleased. He liked it that this luscious young woman was a rebel too.

They finished the wine and stretched out on the grass in the shade of a big maple tree.

"When do you go back to California?" Stevie asked.

"I'm not going to California. I'm shooting a picture in Washington; figured I'd drive up tomorrow. Relax, take my time . . ."

"Speaking of relaxing," Stevie said lazily, "why don't we go for a swim?"

"Sounds good to me." Nonchalant as he tried to sound, Luke felt a pleasant buzz of anticipation. He pulled off his shirt first, thinking to ease any embarrassment Stevie might feel. Women were funny that way, he'd found. Getting them out of their clothes was hard, yet once they'd shed them, it was like they threw off their inhibitions too.

But Stevie didn't seem to be embarrassed in the least. She got to her feet gracefully, like a young lioness, and began humming "Look What Love Has Done to Me" again, as she unbuttoned her silk jacket.

There was no blouse underneath, just a black lace strapless bra that displayed a creamy curve of breasts. Swaying to her own music, she unzipped her skirt. It fell with a tantalizing whoosh to her ankles, and with a single easy motion, she kicked it away. With the same easy grace, she peeled off her stockings and garter belt, then raced to the pond, looking very much like a blond wood nymph.

It was Luke who felt clumsy and inexperienced as he followed her lead. Yet he found the feeling curiously refreshing. Stevie was the first woman in years who hadn't come on like a fan, who seemed unimpressed by his celebrity. She dove into the water and began to swim a lazy sidestroke. When Luke dashed into the water behind her, she took a deep breath and ducked below the surface, swimming quickly until she saw his muscular legs. She grabbed his right toe with her mouth and pulled hard, grazing his calves with her long fingernails.

Caught by surprise, Luke went down sputtering, but he soon recovered his balance, shaking Stevie off. His strong arms circled her waist, and he pulled her close, pressing her firm white breasts against him. He tried to kiss her, but she struggled out of his grip and swam to shore.

There she waited, savoring the warmth of the sun drying the droplets of water that clung to bare flesh. When Luke rose out of the water, Stevie held out her hand. Once again the movie star was bemused by the incongruity of this kid's being the one who set the pace, made all the first moves.

He took the proffered hand and jumped onto the grassy bank.

Without preamble Stevie moved into Luke's body, thrusting boldly against him, searching for the erection that would tell her she had won. When she felt only a slight hardness, she pulled away, swaying suggestively, as she ran her hands along the contours of her own body, imitating a lover's caress. Her eyes were closed, but she knew he was watching, heard his breath quicken. This was always the best part for her, being in control. In the middle of the most heated lovemaking, she never lost awareness of a secret voice within her claiming victory. This was her own form of protest against all of them—men, with their wars and weapons and certainty that they would always have it their way. Or was it only a battle against the Admiral that she was fighting—determined to prove again and again that she could win . . . ?

She felt Luke growing rough with her, but it didn't matter. She was the winner, she assured herself, even as she submitted when he grabbed her arm and pulled her back to the blanket. She wet her lips and knelt between his long, muscular legs, noticing the deep, serrated scar on his thigh. Then she took him into her mouth, teasing with her lips and tongue, running her fingernails along his lean, hard flanks. For a while he lay still, surrendering to Stevie's ministrations. Then he began to move, thrusting deep against her throat.

But when he grabbed her hair and tried to force her to his rhythm, she moved away again. Straddling his body, she pushed herself down on his erect penis; squeezing his thighs with her knees, she rode him like a rodeo queen on a bucking bronco, pushing him harder and harder until he came with a husky groan.

At once, she rolled off to one side and propped herself on one elbow, watching Luke's face as she traced delicate little circles on his chest. "Are you all done, cowboy?" she teased, her words a challenge along with the feathery touch of her fingertips.

Luke would have sworn he was done, at least for now, but before he could say anything, she began licking the sweat from his body—first his chest, then under his arms, and then his legs. Her hands cupped his buttocks, her fingers probed inside his body, massaging him, and before he knew what was happening, he was beginning to get hard again.

Smiling smugly, Stevie knelt on all fours, thrusting her firm white buttocks into his face. "Let's see if you can really ride, cowboy. . . ."

Luke laughed as he mounted her. She was tight and hot; she took him completely inside her—and then reared up, daring him to stay on for the ride.

He grabbed her breasts and squeezed hard, his excitement growing as he pushed and pounded her lithe, young body, wanting to dominate her, if only for a moment. He hadn't experienced this kind of raw, driving sexuality since he was a teenager. Feverishly, his hands roamed her body, his fingers touching and probing until she began to tremble and moan. He wanted to go on forever, to make her come over and over until she screamed for mercy. But no matter what he did, she seemed to want more, and Luke felt a twinge of regret as he exploded in a great, roaring rush.

They lay together in a sweaty tangle of arms and legs, Luke wearing an expression that was part satisfied grin, part sweet surprise. If Stevie wanted more, he might even get it up again. He hadn't been so hot since the first flush of his Hollywood success, when he couldn't get enough of what girls were offering. The tough part about being a sex symbol was that sex got to be so routine and predictable, but something about this girl had totally captured him. He even thought: Who knows where things might go?

"You do this often?" he asked, only half kidding.

"Only when I'm bored," she replied, and he couldn't tell if she meant it or not.

Just as casually as she'd stripped, Stevie began pulling on her clothes.

Luke tried to hide his disappointment. He'd wanted to lie around a while, try for one more time. "Like I told you," he said, "I'll be shooting in Washington for three weeks. I'll be staying at the Mayflower. Why don't you come down for a visit?"

The invitation capped Stevie's feeling of triumph. She had bedded the great Luke James and, even better, she had him wanting more. "No need for that," she said flatly. "I got what I came for."

The shock on Luke's face was almost laughable. No woman had ever kissed him off, and so coolly at that. "You're one in a million, Stevie," he said. "What in hell made you this way?"

She met his eyes for just a moment. "Ask the Admiral," she said, and then turned away.

It was very late when Stevie got out of Luke's convertible down the road from the base's main gate. She passed the two sentries easily, receiving a knowing sign from both, and made her way back to the house on 128 Shady Lane. Quickly she ran across the gravel driveway, then took the three steps leading to the front door, her heart pounding. The Admiral was supposed to have gone up to Washington after the launch, yet dread and foreboding had become a habit whenever Stevie approached the place where she lived.

She knocked over the umbrella stand as she let herself in, and stood paralyzed in the entrance hall for a long moment, listening.

Finally, she exhaled with relief. He wasn't at home. In

the living room, the television set was on, tuned to a late movie. A cut-glass tumbler smeared with pink lipstick sat on the coffee table, and Stevie noticed the damp puddle that would certainly leave yet another ring she'd have to scrub away. There was no bottle in sight. No matter how drunk she was, Irene usually managed to remove the evidence of how much she'd put away. Not that the Admiral seemed to care. Stevie thought it suited him fine to have a wife who was off on another planet half the time.

Almost from habit, Stevie tiptoed upstairs, and as she passed the master bedroom, she looked in. Irene lay on the double bed she often occupied alone, what with the Admiral's frequent absences. She was dressed in a frilly nightgown with lace around the neck, hands folded across her chest, looking almost like a corpse except for the rising and falling of her chest and the delicate little snoring sounds.

Stevie shook her head in disgust and went to her room. It was furnished with military simplicity, almost cell-like: a single bed, made up barracks-style, sheets tightly tucked around the mattress; a night table and a small clock radio; a dresser bare of objects, except for a comb and brush. Only the wallpaper—incongruous pink rosebuds against a white background—suggested the place was occupied by a young woman.

She hung up her clothes and lay on the bed. The dark night air was still and warm, and Stevie found it oppressively hard to breathe, as if a heavy weight were pressing on her chest. She let her mind replay the memory of her conquest over Luke James—in its way, one more triumph over the Admiral.

Theirs was an underground war, just like the one being fought in Vietnam. Guerrilla warfare, wasn't that the term? Stevie had learned the hard way that she couldn't defeat Cus Knight's superior power on the home front, so she waged war on her own terms, undermining the authority he had over her any way she could. Hers were secret victories, yet they were no less real to her. Sooner or later, she thought, she'd wear him down—if only she could last long enough herself. It was the only way she knew to survive.

2

It was a year ago that Stevie had said good-bye to her last hope of salvaging any scrap of a reasonably normal childhood.

She had awakened early that morning, feeling an odd sense of expectancy, an unaccustomed optimism. Yet, she cautioned herself, she ought to be careful: there was little enough reason to think any day would turn out well. When she got out of bed, however, she was reassured that her hopes weren't misplaced. Hanging on her closet door was a brand-new dress, a birthday gift from Irene. It was pink cotton—and all wrong with its sugar-and-spice lacy trim. But as Stevie put it on, she was overcome by affection for her mother. Not only had Irene remembered her birthday this year, she had also insisted on giving her a party. This year *would* be different from others. Irene would certainly try . . . if only the Admiral wouldn't ruin it.

For a moment, a flood of memories threatened Stevie's bright mood. There was the time when she'd been five years old and she had spilled a glass of milk on the living-room carpet. Seeing the frightened look on her mother's face, Stevie had started to cry. "That's it," the Admiral had said in his cold, steely voice, "go to the brig and stay there." Irene had tried to intervene, to mop the spill with the lace handkerchief she always carried in her sleeve, but the Admiral had pulled her away. And Stevie had learned that her room was "the brig"—and that her mother was powerless against the Admiral's anger.

Once, when she was ten, she had been made to stand at attention for four hours under a burning August sun because she had forgotten to put her toys away. When she cheated, and ran inside for a glass of water before the time was up, the Admiral made her repeat the punishment the following day. Then, at thirteen, she had been forbidden to attend her own elementary-school graduation party because he had found balls of dust under her bed during his weekly "inspection tour."

In time, Stevie had come to know her father as a sadistic tyrant, her mother as well-intentioned but weak. And her home as a prison—the brig. She had tried to find refuge in her schoolwork, comfort among her classmates, but the Admiral's reach proved to be as long as it was powerful. The base teachers were harder on Stevie than on anyone else, because the Admiral insisted on it. The kids her own age—children of other officers—often kept their distance. Stevie always had the feeling she was being judged and found to be—worst of all sins—"different," and so she had developed the habit of rejecting others her age before they could turn away.

But if she could pull off this party today, maybe it wasn't too late. Looking in the mirror this morning, Stevie saw a younger, more innocent-looking reflection than the one she'd become used to. Seeing herself without all the makeup she'd begun wearing to spite the Admiral, Stevie thought the dress looked nice on her, after all. Was it possible, she wondered, was it really possible for her to be "sweet sixteen"?

When she went downstairs to prepare her usual solitary

breakfast, she was struck at once by the sense of something different—the sweet, lingering aroma of the cake Irene had baked last night—fluffy white angel food, frosted in pink and decorated with sixteen candy rosettes. It was such a change from the usual stale smell of liquor and cigarettes that Stevie felt it could be a sign.

She walked through the dining room and then the living room, trying to see the place as her classmates would see it tonight.

There were some handsome furnishings, mostly from her dead grandparents' home in Atlanta—a mahogany table and Queen Anne chairs with tapestry cushions, a carved sideboard and enormous gilt mirror. Everything gleamed with a rich patina, thanks to Stevie's constant dusting and polishing.

But for as long as she could remember, no one had thought to rearrange the furniture, to hang a picture or to buy anything new—not even to replace the china that had become scarred and chipped after years of Irene's drunken accidents.

Still, she thought, the kids from school would probably think it was a nice enough house, as befitted the Admiral's status; in fact, it was like her parents, fine on the surface, if you didn't look too carefully.

Yet today the Knight house did seem more than usually cheerful. Maybe it was the rolls of pink and white crepe paper that sat on the dining-room table, waiting to be twined and hung. Or the untidy pile of party hats and favors, the bag of colored balloons. It all seemed so young, so innocent, yet for once Stevie didn't feel the urge to mock these things.

Even the atmosphere at the base high school struck Stevie as warmer and friendlier today. Her homeroom teacher and a boy she scarcely knew complimented Stevie on her new dress. Usually she attended classes like a stranger, isolated by her own sense of being different. But today she accepted the friendly gestures and tried to return them.

When she picked up her lunch tray at the cafeteria, a group of three girls—Tammy Forrester's clique—followed in her wake. "Hey, Stevie," Tammy herself called out, beckoning her to an empty seat, "come and eat with us."

Stevie did as she was asked, feeling cautious and tentative, as she took a place at the coveted Forrester table. Could it be that the girls who usually seemed so aloof had changed their minds—and all because Irene had pushed her into inviting them to a party? Though Stevie didn't quite trust the sudden welcome, there was a part of her that longed so much for a normal teenager's life. She overcame her usual decision to remain standoffish.

"We've just been talking about your party," Tammy said, to the accompaniment of nods from the other girls. She leaned forward conspiratorially and whispered, "Are you going to spike the punch?"

Stevie almost laughed aloud. In her house, getting hold of liquor was the easiest thing in the world. "No problem," she said breezily, and was rewarded with smiles of approval.

"What about chaperones?" Tammy inquired. "Is your father . . . I mean, will your parents be around all night?"

Stevie understood the question. Everyone on the base knew about Admiral Custer Knight, and everyone was afraid of him. "He's in Washington," she said, "and my mother goes to bed early."

Tammy beamed. "Super," she approved. The conspiratorial tone returned. "Do you have a date for the party?"

"No . . . no, I don't."

"That's great! Not about your not having a date, I mean," she added hastily, "but my cousin Tim from Richmond is staying with us, and I'd so much like to bring him along tonight. He's six feet tall and so good-looking. He's a freshman at William and Mary, and he even has an Italian sports car. I bet you'd adore him, Stevie. Is it okay if I bring him along?"

"Sure." Stevie nodded agreeably. "The more the merrier." Spiked punch, blind dates . . . they all were part of a world she'd never known. Could she fit in? she wondered.

The question still preyed on Stevie's mind as she walked up the driveway of her house, accompanied by Tammy and Eve, Tammy's friend. With the air of a monarch granting an enormous favor, Tammy had volunteered to help Stevie with the decorations and to make sure that everything was "just right" for the party. As she turned the key in the door, Stevie thought how strange it had felt to be with girls her own age instead of making her usual solitary walk home.

She stepped inside and the girls followed, frankly curious in their inspection of her house. For although Admiral "Cus" Knight was a virtual legend, none of Stevie's classmates had ever been inside his home; in fact, all they knew about him was what they'd heard from their parents.

Even before she'd walked into the living room, Stevie picked up the awful signs of something gone wrong—the sour smell, and the sound of the television set blaring one of Irene's favorite soap operas at ear-splitting volume.

There was a collective intake of breath as the girls took in a scene that was all too horribly familiar to Stevie: Irene passed out on the sofa, surrounded by a half dozen inflated balloons, her hair disheveled, her dressing gown falling open, a bottle of Wild Turkey and a tumbler sitting in a damp puddle on the coffee table.

From the chandelier hung a few limp streamers of crepe paper, and where they hit the carpet, there began a trail of vomit that led toward the powder room.

In the space of a moment, Stevie said good-bye to her

fantasy of being "sweet sixteen." Without a word to her companions, she ran into the kitchen and returned with a roll of paper towels, a bucket of soapy water, and a brush.

Tammy and Eve fled without a word, almost as if they were afraid of being contaminated by the ugliness they'd seen. As they raced down the walk outside, Stevie could hear their excited chattering. Of course, the story would be all over school by tomorrow.

Stevie got down on her hands and knees and scrubbed the carpet until her knuckles were red. Slowly the stain faded, but the rancid smell lingered. Though it nauseated her to breathe, Stevie inhaled deeply, as if to punish herself even more for daring to dream.

When she finished, she half dragged, half carried Irene up the stairs and maneuvered her onto her bed. Then Stevie tore off the pink and white birthday dress and ripped it into shreds, leaving the tattered remnants on the floor of Irene's room.

She put on a pair of jeans and a man's shirt and went back downstairs. With grim determination, she gathered up the rubble of the party she'd never had, the balloons and party hats and favors, and stuffed them into a trash bag. She pummeled the pink and white birthday cake with her fists, dumped it in the bag, and flung the mess out the back door with the rest of the garbage.

The next part was harder. Choking with hate and humiliation, Stevie picked up the telephone and made eleven phone calls, informing each of her invited guests that the birthday party had been canceled. She gave no reason, knowing all too well that Eve and Tammy had probably begun to spread the word about the scene they'd witnessed.

All too briefly she had tasted what other girls took for granted—and all too quickly, Irene had sent her back to being the outcast Stevie Knight.

She vowed never to expose herself in that way, not ever again.

When, after several hours, Irene had still not come downstairs, Stevie felt a twinge of worry. Though she hated her mother today more than ever before, the habit of responsibility was strong and deep in Stevie. Long years of picking up the slack, of making sure that Irene was all right during the Admiral's frequent absences, had made Stevie more like a mother to Irene than a child. And though she often wished both parents dead, Stevie couldn't bring herself to abandon her mother completely, not even now. Knowing how Irene forgot to eat when she was drinking, she poked around the refrigerator, trying to find the remnants of a meal. She took some limp vegetables from the crisper and a few pieces of chicken from the freezer, put them in a big pot, added seasonings and water, and set the pot to simmer while she cleaned up the last traces of Irene's alcoholic binge.

After an hour or so, she heard a thud from upstairs, as if something or someone had fallen on the floor. Shaking her head, she tasted the concoction on the stove and decided it was good enough to eat. She prepared a tray and took it upstairs. At the door, she knocked loudly, giving her mother time to compose herself.

Irene was fluffing up her hair and adjusting her housecoat as Stevie entered. "I have the most blinding headache," she complained, as if it were unusual for her to be so indisposed. Stevie waited for some mention of the ruined party, but Irene didn't seem to remember. Or perhaps she was simply running true to form and ignoring anything that might tarnish her ladylike pretensions.

"I thought you might want something to eat," Stevie said, offering the tray.

Irene sniffed at the soup, then tasted a tiny spoonful, as

if she were measuring it against some higher standard. "Stephanie, dear," she murmured, "I see a paper napkin here, and a luncheon-size one at that. I don't mean to criticize, but a young lady should know that these are appropriate only for picnic lunches. Will you try to remember, dear?"

Rage rose in Stevie's throat, dark and wild and consuming. She tossed over the tray and bolted to her own room, slamming doors behind her.

It was nearly nine o'clock when the ringing of the doorbell woke Stevie. After hours of crying, she had dozed off. She let the ring echo again through the house. She decided Irene must have had another drink or two and descended back into a stupor. She rubbed at her face and went downstairs.

At the door was her father's principal aide, Lieutenant Sanford Graystone. "Happy sixteenth, Stevie," he said, handing over a florist's box. Nestled in the green tissue was a corsage of pink camellias. "This is from your father," the officer explained. "He was sorry he couldn't be here, but he said to wish you a special happy birthday from him." He looked past Stevie into the house. "I figured your party would be in full swing by now," he said.

"The party's over," she said harshly, her tone making it clear that there were to be no questions. She picked the card out of the box and read the simple message: "To my beautiful daughter, Stevie. Happy Birthday. Love, Dad." For a wild moment, Stevie's need to be loved almost pushed aside her hatred of the Admiral. But as she studied the words, she remembered how many times she'd been fooled before. "Love, Dad"? It wasn't his style. . . .

Her glance switched to Sandy's eager face. In the course of his duties—bringing documents to the house for the Admiral, or coming to escort him to a staff meeting—she'd often seen him eyeing her appreciatively. Now the realization came clear. "The old tyrant didn't send these," she said, and tossed the flowers onto the ground. "You did."

Sandy flushed with embarrassment. "It was on his calendar," he protested. "He would have, but—"

"Nice try," Stevie said bitterly. "And thanks. At least *you* cared enough to bother."

Sandy shrugged awkwardly.

Suddenly, with forced brightness, Stevie said, "What the hell. Why don't I celebrate my sweet sixteenth? I'll do it with you. A real party, not just some dumb kid stuff. Whattaya say?"

The officer hesitated, working it all out in his head—her meanings, the chances. Maybe if he didn't hate the Admiral so much, his answer would have been different. But after a moment he said, "Okay, Stevie, what would you like to do?"

As she weighed the possibilities, Stevie's face underwent a transformation. Banished were all traces of the girl who had awakened this morning believing she could be a normal teenager. In her place was a cynical woman who knew too much about life and far too little about love.

"What I want," she said, her voice redolent with hidden suggestions, "is for you to take me to the Dreamland Motel."

3

The barbecues at Admiral Custer Knight's home were a base tradition. Held on the afternoon of the second Sunday of each month, they were planned as carefully as a naval operation—commencing at 1300 hours, over at 1700, precisely. The guest lists consisted of naval officers and their wives—and lately included the Washington politicians and ranking military men Cus Knight had been romancing in his quest for a fleet promotion that might give him an eventual crack at the Joint Chiefs.

A dozen sailors were assigned to the Knight house to cook, serve, tend bar, and clean up when the function was over. There had been a time when Stevie flirted with them all behind the Admiral's back, but that particular war game had palled. This afternoon, she sat on a step leading down from the rear terrace to the lawn, idly squishing the damp, warm grass through her bare toes as she watched the Admiral's minions scurrying around.

"Stevie, what the hell do you think you're doing?"

The Admiral sprang from the living room's French doors, his face red with anger as he took in her shorts and halter top. "We're expecting guests, and you look like a goddamn hippie!"

Stevie smiled to herself. Of course, she had been waiting for him to see her and explode. Then she rose to her feet slowly, insolently, fully aware of how crazy he got when she didn't leap to attention the way everyone else did.

"You know what's expected of you," he barked. "Get upstairs and make yourself presentable. That's an order."

Stevie drifted into the house. Yes, she knew exactly what he expected—for her to make herself beautiful so he could show her off to his cronies. What he didn't know was that she played that particular game only because it suited her too.

She went up to her room and began rifling through her closet. One thing the Admiral had never been stingy about was her clothes. He bought many of her dresses himself, intent on guaranteeing that she looked like an asset. She pulled out two, and when she turned to hold them up in front of the mirror, she saw with a shock that he had entered quietly behind her, a curiously intent expression on his face.

"The green dress," he said. "Put the green one on." For a long moment, he remained where he was, almost as if he expected her to change clothes in his presence. Stevie found the thought strangely exciting, and she wondered how he'd react if she pulled off the halter, if she let the brief shorts drop to the floor.

But he turned on his heel and left the room as abruptly as he'd appeared. Stevie slipped the green linen strapless dress over her head. Then she applied makeup—a pale apricot lipstick, a gray-green shadow that matched her eyes, and lots of mascara.

When she presented herself downstairs for inspection, the Admiral studied her from head to toe without comment. Then he rewarded her efforts with another order. "See what's keeping your mother. Senator Harper will be here at thirteen hundred hours sharp."

Once again, she walked away slowly, testing the Admiral's patience. She returned upstairs and found Irene in her bedroom, fussing over an imagined spot on her peach chiffon. She seemed tense but reasonably sober. Stevie had often seen her mother bombed out of her mind, but almost always when the Admiral was away. Fear was part of it, Stevie assumed, but also habit. Her mother had started drinking during the years when Cus Knight was away at sea, captain of a PT boat fighting the Japanese. Of course, he knew now that she drank, but it was rare for her to flaunt it in his presence.

"He wants you out there," Stevie said.

"Do I look all right?" Irene asked, pleading for reassurance that she would pass muster.

"Ask him," Stevie said. "Only his opinion matters." Perhaps she'd been cruel, she thought as she left her mother's room, but she still hadn't forgiven her for the birthday-party disaster.

She went down to the foyer, where the Admiral stood at ease, hands clasped lightly behind his back, keeping watch over the sweating sailors who ran back and forth in the kitchen, on the front lawn, and in the other rooms, preparing for the meal that would soon begin.

"Well?" he demanded.

"She's almost ready."

"Is she . . . shipshape?" he asked.

"She'll stay afloat," Stevie retorted, mocking the Admiral's tiresome habit of putting everything in naval terms.

He cleared his throat. "Your mother's . . . problem," he said evenly. "It's difficult on all of us. But if we pull together like a strong fighting unit, we'll be fine."

He paused, waiting for a response. But what could she say? They would never be "fine," Stevie knew. When she remained silent, he put a hand on Stevie's shoulder. His touch on her bare flesh made her skin crawl; she never imagined him as her father anymore, only as a stranger who had acquired power over her. Yet she endured his touch, refusing to retreat. Forcing herself to meet his icy blue eyes, she returned a look that was as penetrating as his own.

Suddenly he shifted ground. "You've grown into a lovely young woman," he said softly. "Even more lovely than your mother was. . . ."

The complimentary words and the soft tone were as unnerving as his anger, but before Stevie could summon a response, a sailor appeared to announce that the senator's car had just turned into the driveway. The Admiral went to greet his guests.

A moment later, Irene came rushing down the stairs. Passing her, Stevie felt she almost resembled the young bride captured for posterity in the silver picture frame on her dresser. She was still slender, her fair skin smooth and unmarked by wrinkles, her light-brown baby-fine hair curled weekly and tinted monthly by the base beautician. But Stevie knew better than anyone else that Irene wasn't anything like the smiling young woman in the photograph. Just as she knew it was the Admiral who had made her change, who had beaten her down and robbed Stevie of a mother.

"I've traveled to military installations all over the country," said Senator Albert Harper, the portly majority leader and chairman of the budget committee. "Morale seems to be at an all-time low. But here, Cus, you've accomplished miracles . . . no Section Eight discharges, no disciplinary problems. You run a tight ship, Cus. We could use more of that in the Navy. What's your secret weapon—or is that classified?" The senator chuckled.

"It's no secret, Al," the Admiral said earnestly. "My philosophy is the same as Harry Truman's: the buck stops here. And when a commander at any level takes that responsibility seriously, he solves the problems . . . no, dammit, he *anticipates* them, and he takes care of them before they reflect on him and his command."

There was an appreciative murmur from the senator and the other bigwigs from the Pentagon, standing around on the lawn with their drinks in hand. Hidden from sight by a huge hydrangea bush, Stevie frowned scornfully as she eavesdropped on the Admiral's sales pitch. Why didn't anyone see through him? she wondered. Was she the only one who knew what kind of man he was? That "tight ship" of his was run purely by terror and intimidation, the same way the Admiral ran his home. As for morale, Stevie had overheard the threatening phone call he'd made to the new base psychiatrist, dictating in no uncertain terms that there were to be no Section Eights under his command. "Let any man try to shirk his duty by pretending to be crazy, and he'll go straight to the brig." To whatever protest the doctor had made on the other end of the line, the Admiral had countered. "Maybe you can have things your way in civilian life, Doctor, but here you'll do it my way. I think you'll find that ninety days in the brig can cure mental illness a lot better than all your fancy pills and mollycoddling." That had ended the argument.

The idea that he might soon succeed to a position of even greater power made Stevie hate him even more. She wished she could find the courage to step out from her hiding place and denounce the Admiral as the liar he was. But would anything she said make a difference? Or would she only succeed in bringing down some terrible reprisal upon herself?

Unable to speak up or to listen in silence any longer, she moved to the refreshment table. She took a plate of barbecue and watched Irene make small talk with two officers' wives, holding on to her tumbler of Wild Turkey for dear life, desperately trying to make it last. Before each of these gatherings, the Admiral gave his flunkies clear instructions: "Mrs. Knight is to have one cocktail—understood?" It was.

Suddenly Stevie smiled, thinking of how she might rock her father's tight ship. She took a whiskey sour, lifted it to her mother, and downed it defiantly. Then she took a second.

Stevie was reaching for yet another drink when her mother materialized at her side. She put a restraining hand on Stevie's arm. "Stephanie, dear," she whispered, "I think you've had enough. . . ."

Stevie shook off her mother's hand and turned to her with a withering stare. She didn't bother to whisper. "Enough? Tell me, Irene, since you're the expert, what *is* enough booze? How do you tell? When you're still standing up . . . or when you're flat on your back?"

The broadside struck home. Irene gasped and flushed deep red. The lace handkerchief came out and was pressed to quivering lips, as the women around her diplomatically moved away.

Emboldened by the alcohol and still brimming with spite, Stevie turned from her immobilized mother and sauntered over to the men's circle. The Admiral eyed her fiercely as she approached, but before he could protest, Stevie slipped her arm through Senator Harper's. The elderly politician beamed at her.

"My dear Stephanie," he said, "I can't believe how much you've grown. You get more beautiful each time I see you."

"And you get more handsome," she said sweetly. "I hope your wife knows what a lucky woman she is."

The old man blushed and laughed. "You have the makings of a politician, my dear. Do you have any ambitions in that direction?"

"Oh, I'll leave that to the men." She lowered her eyes in a parody of feminine modesty.

But the senator took the gesture as sincere. "Never mind, Stephanie. These days, young women can do anything. Why, I believe you could even follow in your father's footsteps."

She looked at the Admiral, who had been holding his breath, hoping that Stevie might actually score some points for him with the senator. "Be like the Admiral?" Stevie said at last. Then, in a tone of the utmost pleasantness, she added, "I'd rather be dead."

The group froze with embarrassment. But before Stevie could savor it, her stomach gave a terrible lurch. She dropped her plate of barbecue and ran, oblivious of the stares she left in her wake. Speeding to the nearest bathroom, she bent over the toilet and surrendered to the racking spasms that emptied her stomach. And in between the retching, she laughed. She'd never dared so much before, never gotten him quite so good. . . .

Suddenly the bathroom door flew open, and he stood there, hands balled into fists, his face white with anger. "How dare you," he raved through clenched teeth. "You're confined to quarters for a month. And that's just the beginning. You're not so old that you couldn't do with a whipping, Stevie. I'll deal with you later, you can be damn sure of that!" With that parting threat, he slammed the door.

Weak and queasy as she was, Stevie could feel a thrill of satisfaction at spoiling the Admiral's day. One for my side, she thought just before her stomach began to heave again.

Two weeks and two days after the barbecue, Stevie was on a bus bound for Richmond—violating the Admiral's order to "remain in quarters" except when she was in school. After counting and recounting the days since her last period, she had realized she was late, very late. The

tenderness in her breasts, the spells of nausea, and the recollection that she'd gone to bed with Luke James "unpro-
tected" added to the fear that she might be pregnant.

For the past week, Stevie had clung to the superstitious
hope that her predicament might somehow not be real.
That slim possibility had all but vanished during a physi-
cal-education class, when she'd bent over to touch her toes
—and instead crumpled to the floor in a sudden loss of
consciousness. Irene had been summoned to take her
home, and though Stevie had fended off her mother's questions with a plea of overexertion—Irene still believed
strenuous exercise was both unladylike and potentially dangerous—she could no longer pretend there was no cause
for worry.

Slipping away to the local offices of the telephone company, she had pored over the yellow pages of out-of-town
directories till she found the name of a clinic.

Arriving at the Richmond address, Stevie found herself
standing before a run-down building in the town's black
ghetto. Inside, up a pair of unswept stairs, Stevie entered a
crowded waiting room. She was given a number by a harried black receptionist and told to wait her turn. Seating
herself on one of the hard benches that lined the walls, she
studied the faces around her, trying not to think ahead. The
other women all looked sad or tired or worried. Strange,
Stevie thought, the way people pretended that having a
baby was so great; no one here seemed the slightest bit
happy.

The time passed slowly. Stevie was too nervous to read
any of the tattered magazines tossed carelessly around the
room. In all her seventeen years, she had seen a doctor
only once, at age seven, when a neglected cold had turned
into pneumonia. She'd been terrified then, as she was now,

of putting herself in the hands of people who could inflict pain.

The doctor who called out Stevie's name seemed harried and impatient, but not unpleasant. He was thin and short, with skin of pale pink that made him seem too young to have already graduated from medical school. Oddly, that made her feel better—gave her a sense of kinship.

The doctor fired a series of questions at her, then swabbed her arm with alcohol and took a blood sample.

The next part was harder. Feeling as if she were shedding her last vestige of protection, Stevie stepped behind a screen and took off her clothes, covering herself with a paper gown. It took all the willpower she could muster to climb up on the examining table and lift her legs into the stirrups.

"This may be uncomfortable," the doctor said mechanically as his gloved fingers began to probe inside her. Only Stevie's pride kept her from crying out.

"It's difficult to say," he murmured finally. "The cervix is a little tender. . . . Some changes here that might indicate pregnancy . . . or they might not. The blood test will tell us for sure. You can get dressed now," he said, snapping off the rubber gloves. "Call tomorrow for the results."

"Tomorrow?" Stevie repeated, sitting upright, shocked by the realization that her ordeal was not yet over. "Please," she said, forgetting her pride, "can't you tell me today? I'll wait. I really have to know. . . ."

The doctor looked into Stevie's face, and then, as if he'd just noticed how young she was, became kinder. "Our lab is always jammed up," he said, "but if a day makes that much of a difference . . . wait outside, and I'll see what I can do."

Two hours later, Stevie was on the bus going back to Newport News. She stared out the window as the miles unfolded, but she saw nothing. All she could do was ask herself the same question, over and over. What am I going to do? The doctor had suggested "termination," but no matter how much easier that would have made some things, Stevie recoiled from the idea. Something was alive in her; she couldn't begin to think of killing it. Perhaps it was because she'd heard so many of the men around her talk of killing and destroying as something good—as connected to winning. That might be true for the Admiral, but then, it was all the more reason for her to resist the temptation.

So the only hope she could find lay in a fantasy of going far away, of having the baby, and starting a real family of her own. But how would we live? she asked herself, remembering the tired, beaten women at the clinic.

Would Luke James help? He had seemed interested in her. Maybe he'd be pleased at the idea of having a daughter or son. She was realistic; he couldn't be expected to marry her. But he had plenty of money, and he could help her get away from here, find a job. Maybe he'd even come and see the baby once in a while. Lots of Hollywood people did that kind of thing these days.

She got off the bus in the center of town, and went into the Buy-Rite pharmacy. After getting change for a five-dollar bill, she went into the phone booth and called the Mayflower Hotel in Washington.

A desk clerk answered, and she asked for Luke James's room.

"I'm sorry," the voice said mechanically, "but Mr. James is not taking any calls."

"This is Stephanie Knight," she persisted. "I'm a good friend of Mr. . . . of Luke's."

A pause of a few seconds raised her hopes. Then the clerk came on again. "I'm sorry. But you're not on the list. . . ."

"What list?' she asked. But the connection was broken abruptly before she received any answer.

She sat a while in the stuffy phone booth and then tried again. Disguising her voice, she asked for Luke. "This is the overseas operator. I have an urgent person-to-person call from Mr. Foster of Paramount Pictures, on location in Rome. . . ." She held her breath, praying the deception would work.

A moment later, Luke was on the line.

"Thank goodness," she said, weak with relief, "thank goodness it's you. . . ."

"Who the hell is this?" Luke demanded.

"It's Stevie, Stevie Knight. . . ." There was no acknowledgment, no sign that he recognized her name. Fearful he might hang up, she added quickly, "The day you launched the *Neptune*—remember?"

"Oh," he said.

Oh. That was all. So he was paying her back for the way she'd played with him. All right, maybe she deserved it. She forced herself to press on. "Listen," she said, "I've just found out that I'm pregnant. It's your baby, and I—"

"Mine?" he cut in. Then he laughed, but there was no merriment in the sound. "That's a pretty old-fashioned trick, little girl, for someone as smart as you are."

"It's no trick," she protested. "I've just gone for the tests. Look, I don't expect anything but a little help. Enough so I can go away and have the baby."

"And once I fall for this—act as if this really could be mine—what then? You'll have me by the short and curlies."

"No, I wouldn't—"

He came right back, his voice cold and cutting. "Listen, Stevie, I don't give a shit whether you're pregnant or not. As far as I'm concerned, you knew what you were doing, knew so damn well that it's far from sure that baby is mine.

So don't push me, little girl, or I'll bet I can prove you've had enough guys to crew the next sub they launch down there."

The phone went dead.

Stevie was left with the echo of satisfaction she'd heard in his voice. His pride was redeemed, his perfect record with women restored.

The walk back to her house on Shady Lane seemed to take forever—and yet it wasn't long enough. She had no strategy, and without that, she could see only defeat.

Inside, Irene reclined on the sofa watching television, enthralled by one of her favorite soap operas.

"Stephanie . . . ?" she called at the sound of the front door closing.

"Yes." Stevie walked into the living room. At least she isn't drunk, Stevie thought, studying her mother.

Irene turned from the television program. "You weren't supposed to be out," she said quietly—not to scold, obviously, but as a reminder of their common interests, to keep secrets from the Admiral.

Stevie said nothing, half hoping her mother might ask why she had breached the rules. "You look tired, darling," Irene said. "Why don't you sit down next to me and have a nice cup of tea?" Irene pointed to the china service she'd put out, placed where the tumbler of Wild Turkey usually sat. "My program's almost over, and we could have a visit. We haven't talked in such a long time."

Intrigued, Stevie sat down. It had been a long time since Irene had made such an effort on an ordinary weekday. She was even dressed in her normal clothes, rather than the lace-trimmed wrapper she favored for late-day lounging. Stevie poured a cup of tea and took an arrowroot biscuit to quiet her stomach—and wondered what Irene's metamorphosis might be signaling.

Maybe her mother could help. Weren't mothers supposed to help their daughters—not just the other way around? Stevie waited in patient silence until the soap opera ended.

Then Irene turned to the tea set and began pouring a cup for herself.

"Uh . . . Mama," Stevie said hesitantly, "I'm . . . in trouble."

Her mother kept her gaze straight ahead. Blandly, she said, "Nothing we can't solve, dear. Is it the Admiral . . . ?"

"No. *That* I could handle."

Now Irene looked up. For the first time her face clouded with concern.

"What is it, Stephanie?"

"I'm pregnant." With the confession, Stevie suddenly felt reduced to a child herself—a child in need of comfort. "Mama," she said desperately, "I don't know what to do. . . ."

Irene looked blank, as if Stevie had spoken a foreign language. Then she frowned again, as though she were reaching deep inside herself to meet the challenge. "Nonsense," she said finally. "You're worried about nothing, I'm sure. Girls your age are always so fanciful. I remember when I was sixteen. I necked for *hours* with Freddy Baker, and then I was sure I was pregnant because it was all so . . . so thrilling. I worried for days, but of course my mother saw how pale I'd become. Before you knew it, she had set me straight. We had such a good laugh together. . . . Imagine. . . ." Irene trailed off, losing herself in memories of a happier time.

"Mama, it isn't like that with me," Stevie said, her stomach knotting up again. "I've been to see a doctor. I took a test. It's Luke James's baby. We . . . I was with him when he was here for the launch. But now he doesn't want anything to do with me."

Irene was quiet for a long time. Then her face crumpled and, pulling her tiny lace handkerchief from the sleeve of her dressing gown, she began to sob into it. "How could this happen?" she wailed plaintively. "How could you do this to me and your father, Stephanie? My God, I made this tea just for you....I wanted so much to have a nice mother-and-daughter talk, but you . . . you. . . ."

"Mama!" Stevie shouted, rising from her chair to shake her mother by the shoulders, "listen to me, for God's sake. I'm in trouble, and I need help." Then, in a quieter voice, "Please. Be my mother—just for once. Help me. . . ."

Irene stared back with sad eyes at her daughter's anguished face. Her voice cracked with pain as she answered, "I can't help you, Stephanie....I can't even help myself." Overcome with emotion, she bolted from the sofa and ran upstairs.

The sound of her mother's bedroom door closing had a crushing finality for Stevie. Why did I think it could be different? she asked herself. She had made the same mistake so many times, whenever she'd dared to hope for a miracle, for something that would show her she had a family in more than name only.

She was still sitting in the darkness, in exactly the same spot, when the Admiral came home. He switched on the light. "What the hell?" he exclaimed, startled by the sight of Stevie, rigid as a statue, scarcely seeming to breathe. "What's the meaning of this, Stephanie?" he demanded, indicating the tea set still on the table. "KP is your responsibility. If you can't remember that and act in a mature, responsible way, then you'll be confined to quarters for another two weeks."

A cold fury filled Stevie. She rose from the couch and faced him. "I'm a lot more mature than you think, *Father*," she spat out. "Mature enough to have a baby! What do you think of *that*?"

The Admiral's face drained of blood, his body went rigid, and his jaw worked soundlessly. Finally he summoned a couple of words. "Explain yourself at once," he commanded hoarsely.

"That great American hero you brought down here a month ago—Mr. Luke James—he launched your ship, and then he knocked me up. What else is there to explain?"

The Admiral's openhanded slap caught Stevie by surprise, knocking her off balance and into the wall. As she clawed at the surface to keep from falling, she felt both sheer terror—and a rare exhilaration. Never had his control failed so completely, never had her victory been greater.

Before she could right herself, Custer Knight's fists began to flail at her savagely. "Whore!" he screamed, his face contorted with rage. "Slut!" he shouted as he brought an arcing blow sinking into her abdomen.

The pain was blinding. Doubled over, she whimpered, "Daddy . . . please. . . ." The street-tough wisecracking girl was gone, leaving only a pain-wracked child pleading with her father.

But Custer Knight didn't seem to hear. Eyes glazed, he went on savagely beating his only child with clenched fists and words of hate. "You've been screwing some sailor! Admit it, you little liar! No movie stars. You're no better than a common whore! After all I've done for you." Bringing his arm back once more over his shoulder, he paused before delivering his final shouted condemnation. "Traitor —dirty little traitor!" Then he sent his fist flying into Stevie's head, a blow that mercifully sent her into unconsciousness.

Opening her eyes, Stevie saw nothing but a white haze. For one moment, it occurred to her that she had died. There is a heaven, she thought. But then she became aware of the dull throbbing pain in her head. After she blinked a few times, the hospital room came into focus. Walls of institutional green, and a white curtain around her bed.

Stevie tried to turn her head, but nothing happened. Her body felt as if it had been broken in a thousand places.

From somewhere a woman's voice spoke gently. "Glad to see you awake. You had us worried for a while. . . ."

It wasn't Irene's voice, she realized. But the sound of genuine concern brought tears to Stevie's eyes. "I . . ." she croaked, her voice sounding ragged and unfamiliar.

"Don't try to talk." The voice moved around the bed, and then Stevie saw the nurse, a Navy nurse, judging by her uniform. "That was a nasty accident, dear. We've given you something to ease the pain, but let me know any time it gets bad again. For now, just lie still and let the medicine do its job. Before you know it, you'll be on your feet again."

Now Stevie's last moments of consciousness rushed back into her mind, the terrible look on the Admiral's face, his fists driving into her. . . . She began to tremble.

"Take it easy, Stephanie. Easy, now," the nurse soothed. "You'll be fine, I promise. Just give it time. The kind of accident you've had is a real shock to the system. But you're young. You'll heal quickly."

Accident?

The nurse leaned closer. "Don't you remember?" she asked.

Until then, Stevie wasn't even aware she'd spoken. "I didn't have any accident," she murmured.

The nurse nodded, but not in full comprehension, only the professional recognition of a patient's confusion. "Of course you did, Stephanie. But it's normal not to remember. You're still in shock. You fell down the stairs and your father brought you in. Lucky he was home when you took that tumble. Who knows what might have happened...."

Slowly, through the narcotic haze, Stevie realized what she was hearing. The Admiral had almost killed her—and then he had lied, as he always did. And now no one would believe her. He was the Admiral, and she was nothing. He could do anything he wanted and get away with it, just the way he always had.

Stevie felt even sicker, thinking that all her little battles, her little victories, had added up to nothing. The Admiral had shown her that no matter what she did, he had the power of life and death over her. Tears began coursing down her cheeks.

The nurse stroked Stevie's brow with more than professional care. "Poor baby," she cooed.

Baby... Stevie had all but forgotten the child she was carrying. "Is it okay?" she asked, forcing the words from her throat. "The baby...?"

The nurse's face closed up, as if Stevie had said a bad word. "In your condition... well, it couldn't be saved. But that's behind you now, dear. At your age, you can hardly be sorry...." The nurse hesitated, as if waiting for a response, and when there was none, she continued with her soothing words. "Once you get back to school and get on with your life, you'll be just fine. Now... I have to look in on my other patients, and you need your rest. Press this buzzer if you need anything."

She left the room, but the echo of her words and the horror of her revelation hung in the air. The beating had cost her the baby. As dead inside as she had felt for years, there had been a stirring of life with the idea—the fantasy —that she would have this child, someone of her own to love. But he'd beaten it out of her. A cry broke from her lips, but then she choked it down. She'd never give him the satisfaction of letting him know it mattered. She buried her face in the pillow, and willed herself into oblivion.

Stevie woke up and looked at the bedside clock. Three in the morning. The last sedative had worn off, and she felt too restless to sleep.

With difficulty Stevie raised herself up on the pillow and looked at her reflection in the shiny chrome water pitcher. The face that stared back at her was frighteningly swollen and discolored, distorted even more by the contours of the pitcher. She fell back on the pillow, wanting to summon a nurse, to beg for enough pills that she could sleep forever. But she knew the routine. The nurse would say it was too soon for another sedative, and she would have to wait.

To pass the time, Stevie turned on the little radio one of the interns had lent her. She found a music station and lowered the volume. Closing her eyes, she tried to lose herself in the music, in lyrics that told of longing and disappointment, of despair and pain and loneliness without end. Soon the Number One song came on; the silky voice of Kanda Lyons, lead singer of the Wonders, belted out "Look What Love Has Done to Me." The irony of the title brought a smile to Stevie's lips. Look, indeed. Stevie folded her hands across her chest in an unconscious imitation of Irene—and thought about death. Could there really be a heaven, a second chance for happiness? She would never have it here on earth, she felt.

Help, she cried out silently. Won't someone help me?

But no one came.

4

It was Sandy Graystone who arrived to take Stevie home from the hospital, just as it had been Sandy who'd made the only visit she'd had during the ten days of her confinement.

When he came, she was sitting on the single chair in her room, dressed in an oversize T-shirt and an old pair of dungarees. Her face was bare of makeup, and her blond hair, washed early this morning by the nurse, fell in a straight line to her chin. Except for her hollow, haunted stare, she looked like a little girl.

"Hi, kid," Sandy said awkwardly, his face creased with concern. "You okay? You look kinda thin. . . ."

Stevie didn't need a mirror to tell her that she wasn't the same person she'd been before the Admiral had savaged her body so badly her baby had been killed. "Part of me is gone," she said quietly.

Sandy nodded with his head bowed, almost like a guilty man accepting punishment. Did he know what the Admiral had done? Stevie wondered. Did he blame himself for doing nothing to stop him?

Quietly the naval officer gathered up Stevie's belongings—a small suitcase and the wilted flowers he'd brought

on his earlier visit. He stood by while the nurse settled
Stevie into the wheelchair that would transport her to the
front entrance of the base hospital.

Once outside, he took Stevie's elbow and helped her to
his car. As the reality of returning to the house on Shady
Lane sank in, she hesitated by the door Sandy opened for
her. Icy fingers of dread knotted her stomach and con-
stricted her throat. Her heart was pounding furiously, and
for an awful moment, she felt she might faint.

Sandy was looking at her. "Are you feeling sick again,
Stevie? I can call the nurse. . . ."

Holding on to Sandy's arm, she steadied herself. "I'll be
all right," she said at last, though her voice trembled. "But
I can't let you take me . . . back there." She couldn't bring
herself to utter the word *home*. It had never been that. Only
a shelter—a barracks.

"Listen, Stevie," Sandy protested. "The Admiral told me
to come and get you. He could be there, waiting. It's an
order, you see. . . ."

A shudder ran through Stevie, and her anxiety escalated
to panic. "Help me get away," she pleaded wildly, gripping
Sandy's hand so hard that he winced. "Lend me some
money. I'll pay you back, I promise. The Admiral doesn't
have to know. Please, Sandy, please. Say . . . I ran from
you, escaped." A desperate little laugh mingled with her
plea. "Like a prisoner of war . . ."

He looked down at the ground as he loosened her fingers
from his hand. "He's got me outranked," Sandy said
quietly. "I have my orders."

Stevie's body slumped in an attitude of defeat. She accepted the rules . . . knew, at least, how hard they were for
Sandy to break. But where else could she turn?

"So that's it," she said wearily. "You'll just do what the
Admiral commands, no matter what. Your leader, right or

wrong. Do you know what he did to me, Sandy? Do you even—"

"Stevie, I'm sorry. I know he's a shit. But whatever he did, whatever he does . . ." Sandy trailed off.

Stevie could finish it for herself—the military oath of allegiance. There was nothing more to say on the subject of her escape. They made the drive to Shady Lane in silence.

When they pulled up in front of the house, Irene stepped out of the front door, as if on cue. Stevie guessed that her mother, too, had been given orders about this "homecoming."

She rushed forward as Sandy helped Stevie from the car. "Stephanie, darling," Irene said, attempting a motherly embrace. But Stevie pushed her away and walked straight up the path. As soon as she crossed the threshold, the air seemed to close in around her. The familiar furnishings inside seemed to have taken on a sinister look. Where once the Admiral's house had been oppressive and suffocating, now it seemed poisonous and threatening.

Following Irene's rather unsteady footsteps, Sandy helped Stevie up the stairs to her bedroom. He waited until she was under the covers, then departed with an empty-sounding "Feel better soon."

Irene fussed around Stevie for a while, dusting surfaces foolishly with her little lace handkerchief. Finally, she sat down on the bed.

"Would you like . . . ?"

Stevie waited for the perennial offer of tea or cookies— but it died on her mother's lips. Then Irene's chest began to heave, and a flood of tears burst forth. "I'm so sorry I didn't help you, Stephanie." She bent forward, touching her daughter's cheek. "But your father . . . If I had, he'd never have forgiven me."

Irene's watery eyes pleaded for understanding, but Stevie continued to stare, unable to respond. Her mother had just confessed to whose forgiveness really mattered. Now Irene seemed to be crying to her from beyond a glass wall. It was as if Stevie had already moved outside the world she'd once inhabited.

Finally, Stevie turned her face to the wall, screening out her mother's presence. She concentrated hard on the wallpaper, and wondered if her parents had actually chosen it just for her—these tiny pink rosebuds against the white background—or whether it had been there when they moved into the house. She began counting the little flowers, trying very hard not to miss a single one, and soon she was asleep.

She had no sense of waking up, except that suddenly she felt his presence. Her room was pervaded by the gloomy light of afternoon. Face still to the wall, she listened to his footsteps approaching. The hair on the back of her neck rose, and she had a premonition that if she turned around, if she actually looked at him, something horrible would happen. And so she lay very, very still, scarcely daring to breathe, as she felt him looking down at her.

But then he switched on the bedside lamp, clearly determined to speak with her—to make his speech. She turned over, and they stared at each other like two enemies encountering each other in a no-man's-land. He was dressed in his formal white uniform, apparently on the way out to some official function.

"I hope you've learned something, Stevie," he said at last. "If you want to fight a war with me, you can never win. War is my business. I'm trained to fight. So you'd better make peace. Now."

Looking up at him, she rolled her head slowly from side to side. "No surrender," she said.

"Then get out. I won't have you in my house."

She pulled herself up. Was it freedom he was offering . . .or the threat of total defeat? Could she survive on her own?

"Just give me enough money to go somewhere," she bargained.

He shook his head. "If you want to be a whore, you can earn your way fast enough."

The spark of rage was extinguished in her by a greater need to cling to control. She got out of bed, holding the covers around her. "All right, have it your way. But just 'cause I'm going, don't think I won't go on fighting." She stood in the middle of the room, glaring through the shadows thrown by the small lamp.

It seemed to reach him, throw him just a little. "How do you think you can do that?"

"I don't know yet. Maybe by telling people what you did to me."

He shrugged. "That's all been taken care of."

And it had, she knew. "Then maybe I'll just hang around the base . . . and get pregnant again."

His hand flew up, fingers curling into a fist, but then he relaxed and brought the arm down to his side. He understood her game strategy; keep to the high ground. "By God," he said quietly, "I guess I let you off too easy. . . ."

"Should have killed me, you mean."

"Should have had you fixed—ordered the doctors to take everything. Not just deal with the baby, but make sure you could never do it again."

"Ordered them . . . ?" Stevie murmured in a disbelieving hush.

Now the realization came over her, and she was filled with a horror and loathing that surpassed any past feelings she'd ever had about the Admiral. Losing the baby hadn't been just an unfortunate side effect of the beating. He had *told* them to take it—"ordered" them, as he put it. Whether, in fact, he could have actually commanded such

an act, there was no doubt that the baby might have been
saved but for his power and position.

For a second, there was the impulse to rush at him, to
attack. But his warning came back to her. In that kind of
fight, he would always win.

Regarding him now with absolute hatred, her first impulse was to ask one simple question: why? Why had he
even let her come into the world? If he could kill her baby
so heartlessly, if he was so incapable of love, why had he
bothered to have his own child? But she was able to provide the answer for herself. She just wasn't what he'd expected—what his battle plan had called for.

"I'll go," she said at last.

"You have until morning," he said plainly. Then he
strode from the room. His one human touch, Stevie mused,
was not to say "six hundred hours." In a minute, she heard
the front door close as he left the house.

Already drained of tears, she went into action. From a
shoe box in her closet she retrieved a small secret cache of
personal savings. She'd received only the most meager al-
lowance, starting when she was thirteen. And often
enough, the Admiral had withdrawn it for weeks at a time
to punish some minor infraction. Most of the rest had gone
for makeup, an occasional treat, or obligatory Christmas
and birthday presents to Irene and the Admiral. But, desperate for some symbol of independence, she had nevertheless managed to save fifty-five dollars. How far would it
take her? she wondered as she dressed and packed a valise
with some clothes. For there was no reason to wait until
morning. There had been no reason, she realized bitterly,
not to run long before now.

On her way downstairs, she paused to look into the master bedroom. As Stevie had anticipated, Irene lay on the
bed, taking her usual late-afternoon nap. Looking at her
mother, Stevie affirmed to herself that there was no need to

wake her, no need even to leave a note. She felt no sense of connection at all. It was as if she had actually been an orphan for as long as she could remember, placed into the home of two people unfit to act as parents. Away from them, things might finally be better.

When she burst from the house, she ran, not stopping for even a single backward look—like a prisoner of war escaping. But her war wasn't over, she thought when she finally paused for breath just outside the base gates. Wherever she was headed, it was only to a new battleground.

Book Two

Book Two

1

Anne Garretson ran down the long corridor like a child afraid to be late for school. But arriving outside Day Room Number Three—also known as the Eldorado Room—the habits of a public life took over. She stopped to compose herself before opening the door to walk calmly inside.

No one else was there. Checking the wall clock over the door, she saw that the hands stood at six minutes before ten. Her headlong race had been needless. After all, though, wasn't that her problem? Always running too fast, trying to stay out front—even when no one was chasing her.

Anne sat down in one of the chairs that were arranged in a semicircle and took a breath as she looked around. The walls were painted a bright golden yellow; the rustic wood and rawhide furnishings were made by local craftsmen. Bouquets of desert wildflowers splashed the room with orange and red, and in the corner, growing from earthenware pots, stood a quartet of graceful pine palms. With the desert sun streaming through the arched windows, the Eldorado Room had an atmosphere of optimism.

Yet after two weeks at The Oasis, Anne still felt as anxious as she was hopeful. There had been, at first, a curious kind of relief in dropping out, simply leaving behind the pressures that had overwhelmed and disabled her. It had even been a blessing to give up making her own decisions, to do as she was told. Mopping floors, washing dishes, making beds . . . the chores routinely assigned to Travelers seemed easy, even soothing, compared to the never-ending perfection demanded of a political wife. Nourished by simple, healthy meals and regular exercise, aided by medication to ease her withdrawal from amphetamines, Anne felt more healthy than she had in years.

Yet underneath it all was the same confusion and self-doubt that had brought her here. What would happen when she left the cushioned isolation of The Oasis and returned to the real world? The public spotlight might be brighter and harsher, more unforgiving than ever before—if her addiction became a matter of public record. For now, she had been able to retreat from sight easily, without question. She had come to The Oasis by way of a stopover at her summer house in New England—"a chance to relax with the Garretsons' college-age children," said the press release they'd given out. With the attention of the media focused on Hal, who remained abroad, acquainting himself with European leaders—part of building up his presidential image—she'd been able to travel incognito to New Mexico. So far, so good. Stevie Knight had proven as good as her word in protecting the names of all of her guests from exposure.

But could the secret be kept long enough? She and Hal had agreed on the game plan. It would be impossible, of course, to conceal her trip to The Oasis forever. But if she could only cleanse herself of the drugs before announcing her success to the press, her courage would be applauded, her example praised. The problem would be relegated to the dustbin of "old news."

What worried Anne daily was the possibility that the

news would leak too soon. There was an implied oath of secrecy among all who worked at The Oasis; and the Travelers naturally protected each other. Still . . . one weak link was all it took. If the news got out, then she and Hal would both be destroyed. How could she withstand the pressure of public attention that would result if her addiction became known before she had been able to conquer it?

As the chairs around her filled up, Anne smiled a hello to each arrival, nervously fingering the spiral notebook that held her daily "homework" assignments. She had labored long into last night, trying to fill but a few lines under the assigned heading: "A Truth I Have Learned About Myself." After two decades spent polishing and refining the role she played in public, it was excruciatingly difficult to peel away the polish and refinements, to expose herself before a roomful of strangers.

Precisely at ten, Stevie Knight walked into the room, her tall, curvaceous figure moving with a confident grace that seemed incongruous with the unmasked vulnerability in her eyes. Unconsciously, Anne sat up straighter in her chair, as a pupil might when a teacher enters the room. Though she prided herself on being a good judge of character, Anne still hadn't made up her mind about Stevie. She had seen enough to know that the rigorous discipline and positive spirit of The Oasis seemed to derive solely from Stevie's energy and determination. But Anne didn't trust what she didn't understand—and she had yet to understand what was behind Stevie Knight's drill-sergeant methods, what indeed had given Stevie the mission of rescuing so many women in trouble.

"Good morning to you all," Stevie said with a smile. "Today you'll each take a turn in the hot seat. You can talk for just one minute . . . or ten. The only rule is that you stick to your assignment: tell us the truth you learned about yourself. Who'll start?"

A skinny arm shot up. It belonged to Francie Evers, a bespectacled heroin-addicted teenager, one of The Oasis's "scholarship" assignees. "I'll be first," she said, and took the chair in the center of the semicircle. "You're not gonna like what I say, so I might as well get it over with." She faced Stevie squarely. "My truth is that I don't ever want to change. I like to get high, see. I love my drugs, and I'm not afraid to die for them."

Several of the women in the circle inhaled sharply. The girl's admission struck a chord in some of them. Sure, they wanted to be free of their cravings. But sometimes the goal didn't seem worth the torture they had to go through; sometimes they couldn't remember ever being happier than when they were lost in a narcotic or alcoholic fog.

"That's it, Francie?" Stevie said incredulously. "That's your big flash of truth? Why don't you tell us something we don't already know? Sure, you're in love with your drugs. If we weren't all hooked on something, we wouldn't be here." Stevie leaned forward, challenging the teenager with her fierce gaze. "But your truth is mixed up with a lie, Francie—a big fat lie. Because you say you're not afraid to die for your junk."

"That *is* the truth," Francie shot back.

"Then maybe you don't know shit about living," Stevie snapped, her own voice rising. "You're just a dumb kid."

"I've seen more than you ever will!"

Stevie said nothing, merely smiled contemptuously.

Francie's face twisted with anger and confusion. "I'm no goddamn liar," she insisted, as if the whole of her dignity was anchored in the claim.

"Sure you are," Stevie said evenly. "All addicts are liars . . . masters of deception. You know why that is, Francie? Because once you look in the mirror and see what's really there, you have only two choices—to go straight to hell, or go through hell to get straight."

"I've been in hell," Francie muttered. "And now I'm here, with nothing to help me get high, and I still can't see what's so goddamn terrific about being straight. Can you tell me?"

Stevie shook her head. "That's not my job, kiddo, that's yours. But you can learn it only one way. There is one thing I will do to help, though. I'm going to round out your education with a field trip. Just you and me. We'll take a trip down memory lane . . . visit a bunch of other junkies who loved their habits too much to give them up. See me after lunch, and we'll make plans."

Francie was silent, her brow furrowed as she puzzled out what Stevie had in store.

"Now, who's next?" Stevie went on briskly. "Anne . . . we haven't heard from you in a while. Take the hot seat, please."

Anne did as she was told. She cleared her throat. "I had a lot of trouble with this assignment," she said, her voice tremulous and low. "My truth is that nothing seems to change. . . ."

"That's not a truth," Stevie remarked. "That's a fortune cookie. Tell us about you, not about the vast mysteries of life."

Anne couldn't fight back at Stevie's sniping the way she had seen the teenager do. Ingrained with the lessons of politics, she automatically throttled down the resentment that could lead her to say something damaging. Flushed deep red with embarrassment, she replied, "I meant that I feel better physically, but I know that the same pressures are still out there waiting for me. The minute I get out, Hal's enemies—even his friends—they're all going to be watching, to see if I slip. It . . . it scares me."

There was a derisive burst of laughter from Francie.

"Did you have something to add?" Stevie asked pointedly.

"Yeah," the girl replied. "I'm sick and tired of listening to all this bullshit about Mrs. Garretson's tough life. If you ask me, she doesn't know how good she's got it. I'd like to take *her* on a goddamn field trip—let her change places with me for a couple of days ... living in three crummy rooms, doing all the shit for my brothers and sisters, while my old man hauls off on us anytime he feels like it, and at night sometimes ... at night crawls in with me and ..." Her voice caught, and she turned to Anne with an almost vengeful glare. "Just live like that, lady, try it for a day, and then you'll know what pressure is all about. So what if you get out of here and people know you pop a few pills whenever you run out of gas? Big fucking deal!"

Anne swallowed hard, fighting back tears. She still wasn't used to the way people talked to each other in group; no one had ever attacked her like this, not even in the hottest fit of anger.

Before she could offer any defense, Jane Peters, a veteran of three different alcohol-treatment centers, spoke up. "Suppose you put a lid on it, Francie. According to you, nobody else *but* you has real problems. Maybe if you could sit back and listen, you'd learn something for a change."

"Sorry, Jane, but I'm with Francie on this one," Stevie chimed in. "I *have* been listening, and I still haven't heard anything but whining and self-pity from Anne. What's the big tragedy? If she doesn't like being a senator's wife, why hang on to it? What's so special about it—or being a senator, for that matter? The ones I've met didn't give a damn about anything but their own careers and getting their pictures in the papers. So why should we give a damn if they run into a couple of rough spots here and there?"

"That isn't fair," Jane argued. "Are we only supposed to care about poor people's problems? Isn't someone like Anne allowed to have problems, too?"

"Gosh, I don't know," Stevie said ingenuously. "What do you think, Francie?"

"I think you have a big mouth and a mean attitude," Francie snapped. "Maybe it wouldn't hurt me to shut up and listen to *Miz* Garretson talk about her *problems*. But you know, Stevie, it wouldn't hurt you, either."

Stevie threw up her hands. "Hey, I want to hear about the problems. But all I keep getting is bullshit about 'pressure' and 'image' and . . ."

"Stop it!" Anne shouted, her voice trembling with anger. "Stop talking about me like I'm some kind of idiot! And don't you dare get Hal Garretson lumped in with any cheap politicans you know! He's decent and smart, he really wants to do something for this country . . . and he'd make one hell of a fine president!"

"Excuse me?" Stevie said with exaggerated politeness. "I didn't know this was about electing presidents. I thought this was about you."

"It is about me," Anne said, her voice falling. "I've been trying to tell you . . . I'm proud to be Hal's wife, and I want to help him any way I can. Do his job, get elected if he can. I know he . . . I know *we* can make a difference. . . . It's what we've worked for all our lives."

"So let me get this straight," Stevie said matter-of-factly. "You're proud to be a senator's wife . . . but you hate what it takes to be a good one? Does that make sense to you, Anne? You made yourself into a kind of cripple—hooked on speed—because you hate the pressure of being out there all the time, having to be *good*? Hell, being on is a fact of life for you, my friend, and if you can't hack it without drugs, why don't you do yourself a favor and get out? Get out and let somebody else do the job."

Now Anne was sobbing, her head bowed.

"Hey, lighten up, Stevie," Jane Peters called out.

"Yeah, leave the poor bitch alone," Francie seconded.

Stevie ignored them. "I want an answer, Anne," she demanded. "Why do you make yourself do things you hate?"

It was half a minute before Anne raised her head and met Stevie's eyes. "Because it's necessary," she answered, strength coming into her voice. "It's just part of the job . . . and I don't *want* to do anything else."

Stevie's eyes locked into Anne's in a final challenge. "Then why are you here?"

There was a long quiet, broken only by the whisper of breathing. Anne sat very still in her chair, feeling strangely at peace, as if she had finally stopped running a desperate race with no beginning and no end. But before she could reply, a rhythmic beating noise came through the open window, rapidly rising from loud to nearly deafening.

Stevie recognized the sound first, not unfamiliar to her ears. A helicopter was landing. She could guess, too, who it must be. There were a number of Travelers who arrived by helicopter—often their private craft—but they landed on a pad that had been provided farther away from the main buildings. This lady was different, though. Livy, dear Livy . . . she did what she pleased, sailed in here almost as if she owned the place. Which, in a way, Stevie mused, Livy had a right to do.

Normally, Stevie would have let herself be pulled out of a group session only by an emergency. But this, too, was a case of extreme need. Livy Walsh was coming back to The Oasis after an absence of fifteen years. Stevie knew how much it would mean to her to be received with an embrace and a promise of personal help.

With a glance around the Eldorado Room, Stevie assured herself she wouldn't be missed if she left now. She could sense that Anne was on the right track. Leaving the others to polish the rough edges off Anne's realizations would help them as much as her.

Stevie rose from her chair. "Would it be all right if I left you on your own for a while . . . ?"

Anne Garretson looked up, and for just a second, alarm flared in her eyes. Then a slight smile touched her lips. "We'll be fine," she said.

The others looked to Anne and then nodded, none even thinking to object that she had spoken for all of them, had automatically taken the role of their representative.

The dust of the earth swirled like a golden cloud as the helicopter floated slowly down to settle on the ground. The door opened, a short ramp swung outward, and Livy Walsh descended, her regal carriage befitting a woman *Fortune* magazine had once described as one of the ten most powerful shapers of public opinion in the world. On a good day, the chief executive officer of Walsh Communications looked at least a decade younger than her fifty-eight years; the day-to-day effort of running a billion-dollar media empire—publisher of the *Washington Chronicle, NOW* newsmagazine, owner of the second-largest independent chain of television stations in America—none of that had drained Livy of her youthful energy. But today her face showed every bit of the tension and strain that had brought her here.

Am I crazy to leave Washington now? she had asked herself over and over as her private jet had flown across the country to the planned rendezvous with the helicopter. Livy Walsh had a reputation as a fighter, yet now she was in for the fight of her life—and she had chosen to retreat from the business front to battle instead the alcohol that had been her constant companion for more years than she cared to remember. Was it only Dr. Trumbull's latest and most dire warning that had brought her again to The Oasis? Or was her journey a flight from the shambles her personal life had become, a silent admission that she had used up her spiritual reserves and was teetering on the brink of emotional bankruptcy?

As the dust settled, Livy saw Stevie coming toward her. Her arms opened wide, inviting her into an embrace. If she could have had a daughter, Livy thought—and then caught herself. It was just such fruitless wishes that had once eroded her strength, made her reach too quickly for a quick way to forget their futility. Holding back her emotions, Livy didn't let her arms go around Stevie but simply clasped her shoulders.

"Thank you," she said.

"For what?" Stevie responded lightly.

"For being here. . . ."

Stevie gave a slight smile. "I owe *you* for that."

They regarded each other with affection for another second.

And then the dam Livy had tried to erect against her feelings broke. "Oh God, Stevie," she sighed hopelessly, "can I do it again? I thought I'd beaten it before. . . . I stayed on top for so long . . . but—"

Stevie cut in. "No buts. If you want it badly enough, Livy, you'll do it. And you'll make it stick."

Livy searched Stevie's face with the practiced eye of a reporter looking for signs of insincerity, of an unpleasant truth hidden by easy assurances. The determination she saw in Stevie mirrored her own.

"Good," she said. "Because everything's riding on it now. More than before. They want to get rid of me, Stevie. *He* wants to get rid of me."

For a moment, Stevie weighed the words against the rest of the story she'd heard when Livy had phoned from Washington. Then she put her arm around the older woman and began guiding her toward the nearest door. Knowing the battles that lay ahead of Livy Walsh—and the battles she'd fought in the past—Stevie suspected winning wouldn't be easy. Right away wasn't too soon to get started.

Livy stared at the valise that had been brought to her room and asked herself again if she was in the right place. The simple, homely task of unpacking clothes from a suitcase was something that she hadn't done for herself in years. Now she was always surrounded by servants who handled such minor tasks so that she could be free to attend to the constant demands of running Walsh Communications, making decisions, giving orders, taking phone calls from business and political leaders—exercising her power.

It was the desire to hold on to that power that had brought her back to The Oasis. But where had that desire come from? There had been so many other things in life she wanted more, so many kinder virtues she had been raised to cherish. "True power belongs only in the hands of God," she could remember her staunchly Catholic father saying long ago. "Any time men try to use it, they just mess up the world." Of course, the idea that women should make the same attempt was not even deemed worthy of comment. And she had happily gone along with the prevailing wisdom in her household. The fourth child in a family of eight, she had wanted as a girl only what was summed up in a single phrase quoted in her grade-school yearbook: "As happy a marriage as Mom and Dad, and a big house full of children."

Her father had been superintendent of schools in Riverdale, an affluent section of the Bronx. His position afforded the Callahans a comfortable stone house overlooking the Hudson River and earned them the respect of the community. Snug and secure, cushioned by her family and her faith against hardship and cynicism, Livy had grown up with a curiously circumscribed worldview, a sublime confidence in Jesus as her personal protector. She knew there were "others" less fortunate to whom she must respond with compassion, yet Livy had a secret suspicion that being less fortunate somehow went hand in hand with being less worthy or less good.

"A little shy is our Olivia," her mother would explain to strangers, though in fact Livy thought of herself as "deep" and "reserved"—selective in her enthusiasms, yet dedicated once committed. When an aunt had teased her once about being so quiet in comparison to her gregarious little brother, Frank, Livy had drawn herself up to her full three feet and declared primly: "It's an empty walnut that makes the most noise."

At Holy Rosary Academy, where conformity was prized more highly than imagination, she had been an A student. And it was also there, at a Halloween dance, that Livy learned that being kissed was an interesting and not unpleasant feeling. It was her first inkling that the temptations of the flesh might be more subtle and more difficult to avoid than she'd previously imagined.

A firm believer in the value of education, James Callahan, Sr. believed equally that teaching was an eminently suitable career for young women of good families. "Teaching is an honorable calling," he told his eldest daughter, Livy, on her seventeeth birthday. "The hours are civilized, the benefits are excellent, and it's a career you can fall back on during hard times. Your mother and I won't be here forever, and it would be a comfort to know our girls will always be taken care of. . . ."

Though she had no quarrel with teaching, Livy bridled at the suggestion that God might not send her a husband. "I'm getting married, Dad," she said firmly, confident that God's design matched her own. "There won't be any hard times, because my husband will take care of me."

Jim Callahan was startled by his daughter's line of reasoning. "I hope so. . . . Livy, your mother and I want nothing less for all our girls. But none of us can know God's will. Take your education degree. Even if you never teach a day in your life, it will make you a better wife and mother."

This last argument appealed to Livy, and in the end, she agreed to major in education and home economics. She could imagine—as a prelude to the joy of teaching her own children—guiding eager young hands as they stitched their first apron or sifted flour to make their first batch of buttermilk biscuits.

She was in her junior year at Marymount College when her brother, Jim Junior, brought home Kenneth Walsh for the Christmas holidays. A senior at Notre Dame, Jim had written his family about the tragic auto accident that had orphaned his friend at the age of eighteen. "Ken's a great guy," he went on, "but the Walshes don't have any close relatives (not like us Callahans!), and I think it's a damn shame that he has to spend his holidays with people he hardly knows. I figured I had family enough for two, so I'm counting on you all to show Ken a good time."

When the two young men arrived, the Callahans were already in high gear for Christmas. The house was decked with evergreen wreaths and handmade garlands, the walls decorated with hundreds of Christmas cards, the stone fireplace hung with an assortment of brightly colored stockings. The aroma of holiday cakes and puddings permeated all of the twelve rooms with the promise of feasting yet to come. A ten-foot Scotch pine stood bare in the living room, awaiting the traditional trimming party on December twenty-third.

As Jim introduced his friend to the family, Livy studied the young man she'd heard so much about. His parents, she'd been told, had owned and operated one of the biggest newspapers in Washington, D.C., and several radio stations in the south. After their car had crashed on an Alpine road while they were vacationing in Switzerland, senators and congressmen and even the President himself had attended the funeral. Yet Ken Walsh had no airs about him, and within minutes of his arrival was laughing and joking with Livy's parents as if he'd known them all his life.

"Ken's the most eligible bachelor I know," Jim laughingly announced at dinner that night, "so I thought I'd better let him see our crop of beauties before some other desperate Irish family takes advantage of him."

Mrs. Callahan flashed a glance at her eldest son, reproving his indiscreet banter. But to the astonishment of her family, Livy piped up:

"And what would be your requirements in a wife, Mr. Walsh?"

"Big brown eyes would be my preference," Ken answered, his own dark-blue eyes sparkling with mischief, "and chestnut hair with a dash of red here and there. A turned-up nose would be nice, too. . . ."

The brothers Callahan hooted as Ken went on describing their sister Livy, but she simply smiled and looked down at her plate, for once not minding the boisterous teasing. It simply reinforced the thought that had crossed her mind the moment that Ken walked through the door: that God had finally showed His hand and revealed the design for the fate they had both agreed upon.

Later that evening, Livy went up to her room—and reappeared half an hour later, carrying an oversize gym sock with the name "Ken" hastily embroidered in red. Solemnly she hung it over the fireplace beside her own stocking, then turned to Ken. "We don't want Santa to forget our guest on Christmas Eve."

"Santa's already taken care of me," he said, looking into Livy's eyes so there could be no mistake about his meaning.

Thus their courtship began. Disproving once and for all her family's assumption that she was shy, Livy adopted a proprietary air toward Ken, making sure she sat next to him at mealtime, taking care that the choicest morsels of chicken or roast beef found their way to his plate. Ignoring her brothers' winks and nudges, she suggested walks along the snow-covered cliffs overlooking the Hudson River. Away from the distractions of her loving but noisy family, Livy drew Ken out about his future plans.

"I'm luckier than most," he said. "Most guys my age still don't know what they want to do when they grow up. I've worked at the *Chronicle* every summer since I was a kid. I always knew I'd be a publisher someday. I just didn't expect it to . . . to fall on me like this." His voice cracked and trailed off. Livy took his hand and squeezed it tight. Ken was good and decent. She couldn't understand why God would take away his parents—and not understanding made her uneasy.

He returned the pressure of her hand and they walked for a while in silence. As they turned toward home, Ken stopped and took Livy's face in his hands, kissed her gently on the lips. "I am lucky," he said, "now that I've found you. I've been so lonely, Liv. . . . Maybe you don't know what that's like, but it's the worst feeling in the world . . . worse than being sick, maybe worse than dying. . . ."

Livy kissed him back, long and hard. His arms drew her close, and through the heavy winter coats their bodies pressed together. Livy felt first a flutter and then a weakness in her knees, a warmth so exciting that she was shaken to the core. Ken seemed to know what she was feeling and drew away, laughing gently, not at her, but at the secret she had revealed. "Sweet Livy," he said tenderly, "I'm so glad you waited for me. . . ." She began to cry softly, feeling like the basest kind of sinner, for rubbing up against him so wantonly, for hungering after the thrill of his touch.

"It's all right, Livy luv," he whispered, "it's all right. There's nothing wrong with wanting each other. I wouldn't do anything to hurt you, not ever."

That night Livy had a nightmare. She was walking the streets of Riverdale, pregnant and alone. Disembodied voices whispered her shame, fingers pointed at her swollen belly. She woke up feeling the threat of punishment looming over her like a dark cloud, and she could scarcely wait until afternoon for the relief of absolution.

She spoke softly in the confessional, clumsily trying to explain what she'd felt when Ken held her close, how hungry she'd been for more, how it had been Ken who had shown restraint. For her penance, she'd been given ten Hail Marys and ten Our Fathers. "Avoid the occasion of sin, my child," the priest cautioned. "If you love this man, commit yourself to one another, and sanctify your love as soon as possible." Livy understood that the dream had been a warning: being with child was a punishment for girls who sinned, but within the holy bonds of matrimony, it was a woman's highest privilege and blessing.

A week later, Ken sat in the front parlor with the elder

Callahans. They asked just two questions. "Do you take the sacraments regularly?"

"I do," Ken replied, looking so strong and handsome that Livy's heart almost burst with love and pride.

"How many children do you plan to have?"

"At least eight, God willing." There was a hint of mischief in his smile, but Livy knew he meant every word.

They were formally engaged on St. Valentine's Day. As soon as Ken graduated from Notre Dame, he enrolled in a master's program at the Columbia School of Journalism and found a small apartment on Riverside Drive. It was Livy who made the place a home away from home, filling it with plants and pictures and the warmth of her presence. Had she started mothering Ken even then? she often wondered. Though when he held her in his arms and kissed her until she was breathless, Livy felt anything but motherly. In spite of her determination to wait until their love was blessed by the church, it took every ounce of willpower she had to fight the desires of her young, healthy body.

After they received their diplomas, Livy took a position in the Riverdale school system and Ken went back to Washington to fulfill the training program at the newspaper set down by the trustees of his father's estate. He would spend three months in each department of the *Chronicle*—and then he would sit in the publisher's chair that had once been occupied by his father.

For Livy, the separations between their weekend visits were bittersweet. She had her work, her family, but most important, the delicious myriad of plans for her upcoming wedding. There was a trousseau to purchase, bridesmaids to outfit, a wedding gown to choose, and invitations to address.

It was Ken who seemed to suffer more from being alone, and though his weekdays were consumed with work, he called Livy almost every night, as if the sound of her voice would give him strength and sustenance. Often she would feel guilty about her own busy contentment when she heard the loneliness and insecurity in his voice. Then she would remember to pause in her happy recitations and listen instead to the details of Ken's work—to reassure him that when the time came, he would be capable of filling the position that awaited him.

"I don't know, Liv," he said once. "There are guys here who know a hundred times more than I do about running a paper."

"And you can learn everything they know," she reassured him. "Don't be afraid to ask questions, Ken. . . . My father says only the truly ignorant refuse to ask."

"Your father's right," he laughed, "but there will come a time—soon—when I can't do that, when I'll have to start making decisions, important ones, Liv. Then I'll be on my own."

"No, you won't," she said softly. "When that time comes, I'll be right there with you."

When at last their wedding day approached, Livy was sure the hard part was behind them. Now they would be partners in all that life had to offer, joined forever in the sacrament of marriage.

The wedding of Olivia Callahan and Kenneth Walsh took place in June, their union blessed in a high mass at St. Aloysius by Father Patrick McBride, who had seen Livy through her First Communion and her Confirmation. The reception afterward, at Riverdale Country Club, was attended by more than three hundred guests. Among the friends of Ken's parents who came were Averell Harriman and Bob Hope and a former secretary of state. As she and Ken danced to the strains of "The Girl That I Marry," Livy made a conscious effort to capture forever the memory of this most perfect of days: the beauty of her silk organza gown trimmed with old Belgian lace, the fragrance of her bridal bouquet, the intense concentration on her handsome husband's face when he'd repeated his wedding vows. Still, as great as her joy was at this moment, she felt it would be surpassed by all that lay ahead. At last they could possess each other body and soul . . . without sin.

The bridal suite at the Plaza Hotel was filled with flowers—long-stemmed apricot roses, pink-and-white lilies, exotic birds of paradise, and delicate camellias. An enormous basket of fresh fruit awaited the newlyweds, along with a bottle of champagne chilling in a silver cooler.

"You look like an angel," Ken said when his wife appeared in her white crepe de chine nightgown embroidered with tiny silk roses. "Now close your eyes, Livy luv." Around her slender neck, he fastened his wedding gift—a perfect two-carat diamond on a platinum chain. "This is just the first," he said tenderly. "I plan to give you one on each anniversary . . . and," he added with a laugh, "maybe one for every baby if that doesn't bankrupt me."

When all the rituals had been done, it was time for them to become man and wife. Ken held out his arms and Livy surrendered herself to his embrace, to his gentle kisses and tender caresses. Yet, though she loved him with all her heart, there were no melting flames of passion and no undeniable longing. And when he tried to consummate their union, her maidenhead resisted stubbornly, refusing to yield the virginity she'd held so dearly. "It's okay," Ken assured her, "I figure we have at least fifty years of making love ahead. . . . We'll just wait until you're ready, Livy luv."

Silently she thanked God for giving her a man so patient and understanding, pushing aside the disappointment that threatened to mar the most beautiful day of her life. Tomorrow they would fly to Paris for a two-week honeymoon.

There she would yield herself completely, make her body belong to him. . . .

They arrived at the Hotel Lotti on the Rue De Castiglione at eleven in the morning. Livy exclaimed over the rococo elegance of the grand old hotel with its gilt-and-marble lobby, its ornate towering ceilings, the spacious antique-filled suite in which they would spend the next two weeks. As soon as the bellman deposited their bags, she threw herself on the canopied featherbed, exhausted from the long overnight flight. Suddenly she wondered: did Ken want to make love right now, when she was tired and grimy and wanted nothing more than to rest? As if he knew what she was thinking, he patted her face and said, "Let's just sleep for now."

Curiously she felt shamed by Ken's understanding, and though she'd been married for less than two days, the first tiny seed of doubt was planted in her mind. What's wrong with me? she asked herself as she drifted off to sleep.

It wasn't until the third day of their marriage that Ken took away her virginity, asking forgiveness for the terrible pain he'd caused and promising that it would get easier in time. But Livy wasn't at all sure. Something had changed, something for which she had neither explanation nor solution. Had she been wrong in believing that marriage would mean the same thrilling excitement of courtship—only better for being sanctified? Something mysterious had happened to take the excitement away. Were those hungry kisses and guilty embraces all she'd ever know of carnal pleasure?

She couldn't ask Ken; she couldn't admit she felt no passion, but only pain when they made love. It was wrong to make him apologize or feel guilty for just wanting to love her.

Yet if the physical part of their love was imperfect, the

honeymoon was sublime, everything a young woman might imagine in her romantic fantasies. Ken completed her; he was everything she was not—outgoing, gregarious, interested in all kinds of people. He struck up conversations with street vendors and tour guides, asked in his elementary French about their families, and, without seeming to notice Livy's blushes, he told everyone they were on their honeymoon.

Free from parental supervision for the first time in her life, Livy gloried in her new status as wife. She scribbled "Mrs. Ken Walsh" on cocktail napkins, and wrote postcards to everyone she knew, just so she could sign them "Mr. and Mrs." They rode the *bateaux mouches* on the Seine; they posed for pictures in front of the Palais de Versailles. They visited the Louvre and Notre Dame, ate pommes frites in a corner café, and they kissed in the back of taxicabs. But while their days were filled with lovely variety, for Livy the nights held a painful sameness.

When the newlyweds took up residence at Greenhills, the Walsh estate in Middleburg, Virginia, Livy's confidence revived. Rising majestically from the rolling verdant hills for which it was named, surrounded by century-old oaks and graceful beeches that sheltered it from the changes of season, Greenhills was rich with history and tradition. Here was a place where Livy felt she could be a perfect wife and a gracious hostess, a place where she could excel.

Her only past experience with domestic help had been with the Callahans' once-a-week cleaning woman, but Livy put on a convincing managerial air for the large Greenhills staff. "I'll be preparing most of our meals, Mrs. Sheridan," she told the housekeeper, "and I'll be serving them myself. There will be times—when we entertain—that I'll require your help, of course. But for our quiet evenings at home, I'll look after Mr. Walsh. . . ."

Young and inexperienced though Livy was, her manner convinced the venerable Mrs. Sheridan to alter the routine she had followed when Ken's parents were alive.

As mistress of a beautiful and established home, Livy's days flew by in a flurry of pleasurable activity. She polished and rearranged the antique furniture, then attacked the cupboards and drawers, storing silver and china and linen in ways that were convenient and efficient. She refinished the handmade cabinetry in the sprawling old-fashioned kitchen, and ordered new, more efficient appliances.

She enjoyed nothing more, however, than the simple ritual of planning and cooking dinner every evening for Ken. From her growing collection of elaborate recipes, she prepared exquisite dinners for two and served them on antique lace cloths in the glow of candlelight. Determined to be a helpmeet in every way, to supply the reassurance and support he seemed to need, she drew her young husband out, listening attentively to his problems, eager to ease the burden of responsibility he carried.

"But why don't you fire Briggs if he keeps making mistakes?" she asked one evening, after Ken described the most recent of his city editor's mishaps.

"I'm trying to be fair, Liv. It isn't like Briggs to make dumb mistakes," Ken explained. "Briggs and the *Chronicle* have a lot of years invested in one another. The man is obviously in the midst of some personal crisis. I'm hoping he'll talk to me about it. Meanwhile . . . you don't throw good people away when they get damaged or broken. . . . It's bad business and it's wrong. What you do is fill the gaps. For now, maybe it's up to me and the rest of the staff to look for solutions."

She loved Ken for his fairness. But were there solutions to every problem? she wondered, thinking of the one place where all her best efforts had failed—the bedroom. She powdered and she perfumed herself, filled vases with fresh flowers, and put soft music on the radio—all to create the most romantic of settings. Still she failed to recapture the magic of courtship, that time before she had been obligated to perform sexually. Sometimes she felt Ken was remote and uninterested because he was so preoccupied by the problems of running the paper, not yet comfortable with filling his father's shoes. But more often she blamed herself for failing to arouse him.

On the morning after their two-month anniversary, Livy told Ken she was flying to New York for the day. "I'll be back before dinner," she added hastily, "so you won't miss me at all."

"Homesick already, Livy luv?" Ken teased.

"Never!" she replied fiercely. "You're my home, Ken, you're my family. I just need to...to do some special shopping."

Arriving in the city, she traveled first to the church where she had arranged an appointment with Father McBride. "How can a wife know," she asked him, "if she loves her husband...in every way?"

The priest looked surprised. "We covered that in your instruction for marriage, Livy dear. Have you forgotten?"

"I remember," she said hastily. "I should love my husband as...as Christ loves his church, with all my heart and soul. But, Father..." She faltered.

"Yes, child?" he prompted.

"The feelings," she blurted out. "I want to know about feelings, Father. Not in my soul, but..." She clutched her hands to her breasts, slid them down. "In here. How can I *give* to my husband?"

Father McBride nodded understandingly, and Livy felt a rush of relief—dashed a moment later by his words. "Some feelings," he said, "are not to be trusted. Particularly carnal feelings. What you can trust, Olivia, is the teaching of the church. Obey your husband, give him comfort and sustenance, be faithful to him. That is the core of conjugal love. It is an active role, you understand, not a passive one. Follow the teachings of the church, and there can be no confusion."

But when she retreated from her audience with the priest, Livy's confusion was greater than ever.

After searching the yellow pages of the telephone directory, she cajoled an appointment with a Dr. Emily Saunders. Perhaps it would be easier to talk to a stranger, Livy reasoned.

But when she was shown into the office of the gynecologist, a pleasant motherly woman, she felt tongue-tied and foolish. In an agony of embarrassment, she tried to explain that making love with her husband was painful, and that it had been so since the first time. She uttered the dread word *frigid*—and waited, holding her breath.

Dr. Saunders examined her gently, pausing frequently to assure her that all was as it should be. After Livy dressed, the doctor sat down with her. "I can't be certain," she said, "but the problem could be your husband's, not yours. Perhaps he attempts penetration too quickly. Have you asked him to wait?"

Livy blushed furiously, her fair complexion splotched with bright patches of pink. "No," she said, "it isn't Ken. He's very patient. It's my fault. It has to be me." Haltingly she explained how, when they were courting, her body was wracked with longing and how she'd say good night in an agony of self-denial.

"Then you aren't frigid, Livy," Dr. Saunders said with a smile. "What you felt before, you can feel again." She noted the worry in her young patient's face, the tension in her body. "It may be," she said, "that your problem has to do with anxiety. Are you perhaps afraid of pregnancy?"

"No! I want to become pregnant, right away. Ken wants that, too, Dr. Saunders."

"Perhaps you're just trying too hard, Livy," she suggested. "You can't *will* a pregnancy, any more than you can will sexual pleasure. Maybe you just need to relax and let nature take its course."

Livy's disappointment was obvious. "Isn't there something you can do? Something you can give me?" she asked, gripping her handbag so tightly that her knuckles were white.

Dr. Saunders toyed with her prescription pad, then put it down. "You're a perfectly healthy young woman," she said gently. "It's you who must give yourself permission to enjoy the physical side of your marriage."

"I want to, really I do," Livy replied in bewilderment. She had always wanted Ken so much. . . .

"I have an idea," Dr. Saunders said. "Before you go to bed, try a glass or two of white wine, or perhaps a cocktail. A little alcohol might relax you . . . loosen up your inhibitions."

At last, Livy thought, jumping up from her chair, at last a tangible answer to what ailed her. "Thank you, Doctor," she said, "thank you so much."

She paid the receptionist in cash, not wanting any record of her visit, and bolted from the office in her eagerness to catch the next plane home.

She was home in time to prepare dinner, bathe and dress, and meet Ken at the door by seven. In the kitchen she had had a glass of vermouth, then another while lying in her bath. A bottle of good red Bordeaux was already open on the dining-room table.

"Hey," Ken laughed when she ran to meet him and smothered him with hugs and kisses, "if I get a welcome like this every time you go on a shopping spree, it's worth every penny."

"I didn't see anything I wanted to buy," Livy murmured

against her husband's chest. "I . . . I just missed you, that's all."

"Even better."

By the time the bottle of wine was empty and dinner was over—topped off by the chocolate layer cake she'd spiked with a quarter bottle of rum—Livy could only wobble as she rose from her chair. Ken, who'd had only a couple of glasses, did his chivalrous duty and carried her up the stairs. Looking down at her in his arms, he dropped a kiss on her nose. "You're adorable, do you know that? Smashed, but adorable. . . ."

When he placed her on the bed, she opened her arms wide and he fell into them eagerly. Warmed by the liquor, too giddy to think or worry, Livy discovered at last the delicious sensations that had eluded her. Joyfully she kissed and caressed her handsome husband, losing all sense of where her own eager flesh ended and his began.

"Oh, my love, my darling Livy luv, I've waited so long . . . so long to have this," he said, his voice ragged with passion.

"Me, too." She sighed.

Later, as they lay intertwined in the marital bed that now seemed blissfully cozy, Ken propped himself up on one elbow. "I was so worried," he said softly, smoothing Livy's hair away from her face. "I thought I couldn't make you happy, luv. . . . I was so afraid I'd never make you happy."

Ken's confession shocked and frightened Livy. Caught up as she'd been in her own worries and doubts, she hadn't realized how hurt and frustrated her husband had been. Thank goodness she had found a remedy before it was too late. Amazing, she thought, how a few drinks could make easy what had seemed impossible.

Only two months later, Livy missed her period. The pregnancy was difficult almost from the beginning, but she celebrated her condition, symptoms and all. Happy and complete at last, undaunted by morning sickness and swollen ankles, she redecorated the old nursery in bright yellow and white. Together they shopped for a layette, buying dozens of tiny sleepers and sweaters and blankets in every available color.

When Livy's first contractions came, Ken left his office immediately. "It isn't time yet," she protested as he bundled her into the car. "Dr. Fenniman said—"

"I don't care what he said," Ken cut in, his face tender with worry. "This is my wife and my baby and he'd damn well better take care of you both!"

In the hospital, he stationed himself at her bedside. "Squeeze my hand when it gets bad, Livy luv," he said. "Squeeze tight and let me share the hurt."

Never had Livy loved her husband more than at this moment. The pain that had begun as a nagging kind of cramping grew worse, and Ken's face became ashen and taut each time Livy dug her nails into his palms. "God, this is terrible," he said hoarsely. "I didn't know it would be like this. . . ."

"I guess the Bible wasn't kidding," she said, trying to smile, "when it promised children would be brought forth in pain."

When Dr. Fenniman examined her, Livy could tell that something was wrong. A bolt of fear went through her. "Is my baby all right?"

"The baby's fine. . . . We just have a little problem with position, that's all. It's called a breech."

"What's going to happen?" Livy demanded.

"Calm down, Olivia. We'll try a normal birth, which of course would be best for the baby, but if it gets too rough for you, we'll do a caesarean. Everything will be—"

"No caesarean," Livy broke in. "I've got to have it the normal way, Dr. Fenniman." She looked beseechingly to Ken. "I've got to. . . ." Ken nodded.

In the long hours that followed, Fenniman pressed Livy to change her mind. Though the pain became excruciating, though she felt as if the contractions would rend her body in two, she refused the surgery. Finally, at four-thirty in the morning, Carey James Walsh was born. Ten minutes later, Livy was wheeled into the recovery room. "Get a little sleep, Mrs. Walsh," the nurse said, "and then you can have a little visit with your husband. Poor man's been waiting all night."

Exhausted and drained, Livy retreated into sleep. The room was quiet and dark, but she was awakened later by a sensation of cold. She touched the sheets that covered her. They were wet, and as she brought her hand closer to her face, she saw to her horror that it was red and sticky with her own blood.

"Nurse . . . nurse," she cried out, but her voice was weak and faltering. I'm dying, she thought, stricken with fear she'd never know her own child, never watch him grow up.

With enormous difficulty, she turned on one side. The room began to spin; black haze closed in around her. Just before she lost consciousness, she reached the call button and pressed it, whispering the Act of Contrition: "Oh, my God, I am heartily sorry. . . ."

When she came to, the light was on in her room and Ken was sitting in the chair beside her, haggard and unshaven, his eyes bloodshot and glazed with pain.

As soon as she opened her eyes, he stroked her face and began to cry. "God, you scared me, Livy luv. Oh, God, you scared me. Don't ever do that again. Please, don't ever do that again."

She had never seen her husband cry. "What happened to me?" she asked.

"You . . . you had some hemorrhaging. . . . They had to do an operation."

"The baby?" she blurted anxiously. "Is he all right?"

"He's wonderful . . . six pounds, eleven ounces, healthy and beautiful and yelling his head off for his mama."

Livy smiled—and then remembered the terrifying moments before she'd blacked out. "What about me? What did they do to me, Ken?"

"They just stopped the bleeding. Dr. Fenniman says you'll be fine. You need a good rest, sweetheart, and you'll be fine."

"Good." She smiled, relaxing completely. "Then we can work on a little brother and lots of little sisters."

Ken began to cry again. "Oh, God, Livy luv, no. . . . Fenniman said it was too dangerous, that if you tried to have another baby, it might . . . it might . . . I can't lose you, Livy, I just can't. . . ."

In the first few years that followed, Livy refused to give up hope of a large family. She saw one specialist after another, but all agreed that another pregnancy would put her in mortal danger. Ken wore condoms when they made love, though she protested against them as mortal sin. "Married love is to have children," she cried, spouting the teachings that had been drummed into her at church.

At last, he yielded to her objections—but only by getting a vasectomy. Livy's dream of a large family, a house teeming with children whom she could tend and love, was shattered. Their lovemaking diminished, and Ken and Livy became more like brother and sister, each in mourning for the children they would never have.

And yet in some ways her marriage appeared to flourish. They bound themselves together in a hundred thoughtful, considerate gestures, and found satisfaction in community service and in their individual interests and hobbies.

Livy busied herself with dinner parties for the *Chronicle* staff, charity bazaars, weekend visits to the Callahan home in Riverdale. Ken resumed his flying, a hobby he had all but given up when they were married. He bought a World War II P-51 and set about restoring it to mint condition.

And, of course, they were bound together in loving their son. Carey was a beautiful child, quiet and stubborn like Livy, though he had his father's dark hair, his facial expressions, and his blue eyes. As soon as the boy was able to walk, Ken began taking him to the newspaper office, as his own father had done before him, taking him to see the giant presses, letting him sit at his desk.

Livy doted on Carey. She listened to his stories of school, helped with his homework, answered the questions he raised—performed all the requisite motherly rituals. Yet she often wondered if she was failing to give him something she had taken for granted while she was growing up herself—a real sense of family. In a restless search for her own fulfillment—filling the days she had expected to devote to the raising of a large family—she had involved herself with so many volunteer activities. And yet none ever seemed right, and she moved from one organization to another, searching for something she couldn't quite name.

But the search ended when she discovered the Mother Cabrini Shelter for Unwed Mothers. In the home's pink and blue nursery, she found a task that gave her purpose and assuaged her own aching need. As she held the tiny babies, soothing their fretful cries and giving the love and care they so badly needed, Livy felt at peace. Her volunteer work grew from one day to two and then to three; she let it be known that she was always ready to stay an extra hour or two if needed.

"Where were you?" Carey demanded late one afternoon, his blue eyes hurt and accusing. "I was the only one in the play whose mother didn't come. You didn't come,

Mommy. Everyone said I was the best Easter bunny, but you didn't see me—and now it's too late!"

Stricken with guilt, Livy apologized. "Oh, sweetheart, I'm so sorry. I meant to come, honestly I did, but there was so much work and so many babies to take care of, I just lost track of the time. . . ."

"But they're somebody else's babies," he said, his face still set against her, "and you're supposed to be *my* mother. You promised me . . . you promised."

"I'm sorry, Carey. I'm very sorry I let you down. I'll try never to do it again." How could she tell her son that other people's babies gave her a tiny bit of forgetfulness? How could she explain how it made her feel to hold an infant against her breast and pretend for a little while that it belonged to her?

"Daddy wouldn't forget. He wouldn't let me down."

No, Livy thought, Daddy wouldn't. Somehow Ken had put behind them the dream of a big, boisterous family like the Callahans. Somehow Ken had made peace with all their lost hopes and promises.

Or so she thought until the day she came home early from the Mother Cabrini Shelter to see Ken's car already in the driveway. In all the years they had been together, he had never left the paper this early. Was he ill? She hurried into the house.

He was in the study, sitting at his desk, his head in his hands. The sound of his sobs filled the room.

"What's wrong, darling? Oh, Ken, please tell me what's wrong?"

He looked up, his face contorted with pain. "What happened to us, Livy luv? Where did it all go wrong? We loved each other so much, so very much. . . . How did we get lost, Livy? How did it happen?" He buried his face in his hands, and Livy felt the cold knot of dread forming in her stomach.

He's in love with another woman, she thought, remembering now what she had willfully ignored—nights he'd stayed late at the office, the times she had tried to reach him, only to be told he had left to attend some function. Had she known even then? Had she been too cowardly to question him, to hear that he'd found a woman who could heal the pain she'd inflicted?

But as Ken went on in a voice choked with sorrow, Livy snapped to attention. It wasn't another woman he was talking about—it was a man! What she was hearing was impossible, ugly and sordid and impossible! And yet her darling Ken was saying it was so.

"...It's all my fault," he continued. "I wasn't strong enough to bear the cross we'd been given, Livy luv. I was so damn lonely, so...cut off. Maybe I never wanted to be unfaithful to you," he said, attempting a smile that nearly broke her heart.

Even as she recoiled from the terrible details, her conscience tried to defend Ken. It was against all her beliefs—a cardinal sin against man and God, as she'd learned from her catechism. Yet wasn't it her fault he'd been lonely, her fault he'd been tempted? She sank to her knees by his chair and took his hand, silently vowing that she would be there, that they would fight this thing together.

"There's more," he said with an expression that heightened her fear into terror. "The man...he...he's with the White House."

"Who?" she asked, as if the name would make a difference.

"Fred Williamson," he said, naming the President's chief of staff.

Then he took a deep breath and let the other shoe drop. "I've just had an anonymous note. Someone who knows ...about Fred and me. He...he says he has pictures...

dates. He says they'll be given to . . . to the media next week."

"Oh, my God!" Livy tried to take in the magnitude of this disaster—the shame that would not only dirty her beloved Ken, but ruin their families and even scandalize the White House. "What does he want?" she asked, reaching desperately for hope. "Money?"

Ken shook his head, his face a study in agony. "It's the President he's after, not me. He's planning to break the story the day before the convention. I guess the note was to . . . to give me fair warning," he finished with a strangled sob.

Livy threw her arms around him, and they clung together like shipwrecks, trying to stay afloat for a few precious moments when there was no hope of survival in sight.

Curiously enough, they were closer in the next few days than they had been for years. Livy called the *Chronicle* to say that Ken had the flu; she notified the Shelter that she was needed at home. Neither of them left the grounds of Greenhills. They shared sleepless nights, they ate together, they walked for hours under the canopy of leafy trees, oblivious to the richness of nature's green spring as they talked with measured calm and tried to prepare for what was ahead. "We'll have to talk to Carey—and soon," Livy said. "My family, too. . . . I don't care about anyone else."

"I can't face your family," Ken said grimly. "God only knows how they'll feel about me." He clutched her. "Don't let them turn you against me, Livy. You're my rock."

"I won't leave you," she said.

"God, Liv, I never meant to hurt you, to make you suffer. . . ."

"We'll think of something. We still have some time."

* * *

The next morning, he told her he had to fly to Boston. There was some business to attend to—things to put in order before the terrible deadline came and the scandal forced him to step down at the *Chronicle*.

It seemed so sudden to Livy. There was so much still to plan. She needed to discuss how they could spare Carey. . . .

But he assured her he would be back by evening—just as she had once promised him when she'd spent an unexpected day away. He moved to kiss her then, and in spite of herself she shied away. He stepped back, and smiled as if to show that he didn't blame her. Then he left the room.

Only after he was gone did she remember, too, that the explanation she had given for her one-day trip had been a lie. She ran after him, her mind changed about the kiss. . . . But he was gone.

She was called in midafternoon by a captain of the Massachusetts State Police. In a gentle voice, he told her about the accident: what remained of the P-51 he had been flying alone was scattered along the Berkshire Mountains. It was too soon to be sure, but the cause seemed to be the old plane's faulty instrument panel. She had barely hung up before the question began echoing through her mind: Was it an accident, my love, or did you sacrifice yourself? Oh, my darling, my dearest love, forgive me, forgive me for failing you so badly.

The phone was silent only a minute before the next call came—from Matthew Frame, editor of the *Chronicle*. "Mrs. Walsh, I'm sorry to bother you. But there's some new—"

"I've heard it, Mr. Frame."

He shifted gears at once. "You must know that everyone at the paper shares your loss. Ken was a wonderful man, the best."

"Yes . . . yes, he was," she answered, thinking how terrible it was—the past tense, how final and irrevocable.

"Mrs. Walsh, I hope you won't mind—but there is a paper to get out, and I wanted to discuss the obituary, to ask if there was anything you'd like to add . . . any family material we might not have on file."

She thought for a moment. Then the words came—almost by themselves it seemed, like dictation taken from a ghost. "Since you ask, Mr. Frame, I'll tell you exactly how I want this handled. Run the story of Ken's death on page one, with a black border. I want you to mention every one of my husband's charitable works, and I want you to call the chairmen of both parties, get quotes from both men on what a loyal and patriotic American Ken was. Any problem with that, Mr. Frame?"

A silence indicated that the editor was taken aback by her commanding tone. But then he gave his obedient reply. "No problem, Mrs. Walsh."

It was Livy Walsh's first tiny taste of power, and even in the bitter ashes of her grief, she noticed the sweetness of it, never dreaming then that it would become her food and drink. "Thank you, Mr. Frame," she said. "And I'll have some further instructions, later."

The editor said good-bye without objection.

Is that right, Ken? she asked the presence that seemed to be hovering close by. Will that do the trick? Will that shame the bastard into keeping his silence?

Good work, Livy luv, his ghost whispered, but there's something else. . . .

She nodded, just as if she could see the presence, picked up the telephone, and called the White House. "Fred Williamson, please. Tell him it's Mrs. Kenneth Walsh. I'm sure he'll take my call."

The voice that answered was deep and masculine—and, Livy detected, utterly frightened. "Mrs. Walsh," he said, "my deepest sympathy on your loss. All of Washington . . ."

For a moment Livy's attention lapsed, as she tried to imagine the man to whom Ken had turned in his loneliness. Stop it, she told herself, this isn't the time. "Mr. Williamson . . . Fred," she said with her newfound calm. "I think you ought to resign immediately . . . before the convention begins. If you don't . . . if you don't," and here her voice cracked, "then I'm not sure you can count on Ken's death to protect you from the consequences."

There was only a silence from the other end, then the click of the call disconnecting. But Livy didn't try to call back. The second taste of power had been even sweeter than the first.

A week after Ken was buried, Livy marched into the *Chronicle* and summoned all the editors to his office. Standing behind Ken's desk, she made her announcement. "I've called you together because I don't want to make this speech more than once. No doubt you've all been wondering who will be the new publisher. You're looking at her." She waited a moment as the members of her editorial staff exchanged surprised glances. "I know what you're thinking: Livy Walsh isn't qualified, Livy Walsh knows next to nothing about running a newspaper." Her glance went from one man to the next. "Except Ken Walsh knew—and I think I know better than anyone on this earth how Ken would want things done. So don't give me any arguments. Give me your help and your patience. No doubt I'll be asking many foolish questions at first, but I will expect answers, and I'll expect—no, I demand your support and loyalty. These will be my foremost considerations when your contracts come up for renewal. I hope we understand each other. That's all for now." And with that, Livy dismissed a stunned and disillusioned staff.

For the next six months, she lived on her own adrenaline. She took up smoking, and kept her energy high and her butterflies subdued with endless mugs of bitter coffee laced with bourbon. Sitting in Ken's chair at the *Chronicle* —swimming in the space she was so far from being able to fill—she swore to learn.

And then, miraculously, the bits and pieces of information began to form a coherent picture. Livy's questions became fewer, her directives stronger and more confident. The bourbon became her ally, her source of courage, and, when she needed it, her supplier of rest.

Her newest reporter, hired away from the *Boston Globe*, won a Pulitzer Prize for a series on drug addiction in Washington's black ghettos—and then Livy herself was asked to sit on the Pulitzer nominating committee for the following year.

She tried to make Carey a part of her mission, to keep alive his memory of Ken and his pride in the *Chronicle*. But Carey had become distant and unforgiving, blaming Livy first for her absence from home, then for replacing his father—and finally, for everything that had gone wrong with his young life. She tried to reason with her son, but he had erected an impenetrable wall against her. Do something, her conscience nagged. He's only a boy. You can't let him go on like this. But she had no idea of what she might do—and there were so many demands on her time and energy at the *Chronicle*.

She was relieved when Carey began spending more time away in Riverdale with her parents—first an occasional weekend, then every other weekend, and finally most of his school holidays. The doting of grandparents was just what he needed, she told herself, remembering with fondness and regret the noisy bustle, the warmth and energy of the Callahan household. A boy needs to be around men, she thought, especially a boy who's lost his father.

It never occurred to Livy that she might one day provide Carey with a stepfather or even the semblance of a family, now that Ken was gone. It was as if her own dreams had been so badly damaged, so mutilated beyond recognition that she could no longer bear to contemplate what was left.

I'm doing this for Ken, she told herself when work became both family and friend. Yet there was more to her absolute dedication than a mission to preserve and enhance Walsh Communications. Somehow Livy's first taste of power created an appetite that grew in direct proportion to her lost faith. As she lost the ability to pray, Livy found a new kind of security in her ability to bring others to their knees.

And the whiskey was always there, not only to calm the doubts, but to fuel new dreams. Fearlessly, Livy tightened her reins on the paper, building circulation and then using the inflow of new money to acquire more papers and begin the newsmagazine. She sold off the small radio operations and bought into major television stations. The Chronicle Company became Walsh Communications. Ken's business became *hers*. She didn't think the drinking slowed her down at all. Now, when she drank she could sometimes feel Ken near; his ghost came to her like a genie emerging out of the bottle, bringing promises of forgiveness and loving encouragement.

But one morning, the *Chronicle*'s night editor, Sam Conover, found Livy slumped over her desk, wearing the rumpled suit she had worn the day before. "Mrs. Walsh," he shook her awake, "Mrs. Walsh . . . are you all right?"

Livy's head ached; her eyes blurred as she struggled for a sense of time and place. She saw that Sam was looking down, and she followed his gaze—to the empty bottle that sat atop the crumpled papers in her wastebasket. "I'm fine," Livy said, struggling to overcome her shame. Pride made her smooth her rumpled suit and add an explanation.

"I worked late last night . . . and sometimes . . . the memories, you know . . ."

The editor nodded sympathetically and left her office. Livy searched her memory for the missing hours. She *had* decided to work late; the untidy stack of papers before her proved that she had done so. Yet the notes—in her handwriting—were unfamiliar, and she couldn't remember making any of them. Where had the last twelve hours gone? My God, she thought then, what if something had happened to Carey? What if no one had been able to reach her?

And then the realization hit—a truth concealed through years of nips of kitchen sherry before sex with Ken, and cocktails before dinner, and the shots for courage, and the late-night whiskey to help her sleep.

It was then that her mind tossed up the memory of an article that had appeared in the newspaper a year before—a tiny place in New Mexico that had helped some woman film star whose career had been destroyed by alcohol.

Livy ran down the three flights of stairs to the *Chronicle*'s morgue. Ignoring the curious stares of the clerks who were busy filing and cross-referencing the stories of the past week, Livy made her way through the narrow corridors of steel-gray file cabinets and stopped at the letter *H*. Here it was, under Halloran, Brenda—an article headlined "Star Credits Comeback to Miracle." Livy scanned the article, her eyes resting at last on Brenda Halloran's final quote. "I tried everything, but I still couldn't stop drinking. Then I heard about The Oasis. My whole life changed. It was a miracle."

She had been taught to believe in miracles once, Livy remembered. She had prayed for others in the past—like another child—and there had been no answer.

But maybe it wasn't too late to believe in one more.

* * *

The Oasis had not been as she expected. In those days, it was a single cream-colored adobe building that, flanked by craggy mountains and surrounded with miles of desert, looked from a distance like an Indian pueblo. Livy's first impression was of a religious retreat, yet the resemblance evoked not the comfort of familiarity but rather an instant sense of loneliness. For the first time in years, away from the demanding routine she'd established, away from the cushioning trappings of power, Livy noticed how isolated she had become.

How can she possibly help me? Livy thought when Stevie had first come to her room, only minutes after Livy's arrival. She's hardly more than a child! A bossy child at that, Livy amended as Stevie started searching suitcases, then instructed an assistant to take away most of the excess clothes, along with Livy's perfumes and aspirin and work papers. Finally, Stevie handed Livy a mimeographed list of rules that was as all-encompassing as it was long.

"Is all this really necessary?" Livy asked, feeling as if she'd been catapulted back into childhood.

"Yes." Stevie's reply was unadorned with explanations.

Livy persisted. "No explanations? You just expect adults to . . . to follow orders like little children—just because you say so?"

"We don't have any adults here," Stevie replied, her hazel eyes meeting Livy's challenge. "We only have children who got lost. If you could find that lost child inside yourself, you wouldn't need The Oasis . . . or the rules."

"You seem awfully sure of yourself, Stevie Knight. How old are you, anyway? Or is that classified information?"

"I'm twenty-five." A moment later, she added, "Would it make a difference if I told you I've made enough mistakes for two lifetimes—and that I'll probably make a lot more before I'm through? Would it make a difference if I said I was sure I could help you, regardless of my own mistakes?"

"A confession . . . right up front," Livy said mischievously. "It might make me think you're very clever. Telling me you're fallible . . . is that supposed to inspire trust? Because if it is, I'll tell you now that I don't trust easily."

"But you came here anyway," Stevie said pointedly.

"You should have been a Jesuit," Livy observed dryly.

Now Stevie smiled. "I'll take that as a compliment." She held out her hand, and when Livy shook it, she felt a warmth and strength unusual in one so young. Could it be that this child had something to teach her after all?

In spite of her professed skepticism, Livy fell quickly into the Oasis routine. While some of the other two dozen Travelers grumbled that the place was more like a boot camp than a place of healing, the child in Livy found order and comfort—not tedium—in the regulations. And while others fumbled for words, trying to bare their innermost secrets to a group of strangers, Livy found that years of practice had made it easy to peel off a variety of sins without digging too far past the surface. Willingly and without prodding, she confessed to her group all the ways in which she had failed her husband, her marriage, and her child.

After three weeks at The Oasis, with her system cleansed of alcohol, Livy felt fit and strong. The regimen of good food and regular exercise had restored her body; the daily sessions of yoga and meditation had restored her sense of control. She had done everything right, yet in the time she'd been here, Livy had yet to hear anything of her progress from Stevie Knight. The youthful director of The Oasis was as generous with encouragement as she was with her rules, yet with Livy she seemed always to be watching and observing—like the nuns at St. Aloysius.

"I'm thinking of leaving The Oasis," Livy announced during a morning group session, then looked directly at

Stevie. "I feel fine, and I think it would do me good to get back to work."

There was a collective grumble—and then a challenge. "Where do you get off making your own rules?" demanded Tanya Snow, an artist who, like Livy, was an abuser of alcohol. "Do you think you can just drop in and check out . . . like this was a hotel? You don't drink for a few weeks . . . and just like that, you think you're cured? You're dreaming, lady. . . . Take it from somebody who knows!"

"Maybe Livy knows something we don't," Stevie interjected mildly. "Maybe Livy has her own secret formula. I don't know about the rest of you, but I've sat in this room day after day, waiting for Livy to tell us why she's here, and all I've been hearing is a neat, tidy story. I'll bet you wouldn't print a story like that in the *Chronicle*, Livy. And you know why? It stinks to high heaven . . . it's just a cover-up, start to finish!"

Unnerved by the suddenness and accuracy of Stevie's attack, Livy went blank. She looked around at the other women and saw that they, too, were surprised by Stevie's accusation.

"I . . . I don't know what you mean," she stalled, suddenly feeling trapped.

"No?" Stevie challenged. She rose from her seat at the center of the semicircle and walked straight over to Livy, confronting her almost as one of Livy's reporters might when trying to crack a story. "Let me ask you this. If your life had turned out fine and dandy . . . if Ken had turned out to be a tin god instead of a human being with problems, if you had a dozen perfect kids instead of just one imperfect son, what then?"

Livy shook her head in bewilderment as Stevie described the dream that had eluded her.

"I'm waiting for an answer, Livy!"

"I . . . I can't. . . ."

"I say you wouldn't," Stevie cut in. "Maybe . . . just maybe you might have felt a little smug and self-righteous —but you would have given God the credit. So how come, when your perfect life turns to shit, you beat your breast and say 'mea culpa, mea culpa'? How can that be, Livy? How can it be that God does all the good stuff and you do all the bad?"

"But you haven't been listening!" Livy shouted, pounding her fists against her chair in frustration. "I told you, Ken and I loved each other, dammit! So he wasn't a tin god, but he was my husband, and we should have been happy together!"

"And I say bullshit! You know what your problem is, Livy? You've invented your own little Catch-22! First you make yourself out to be more important than you are . . . so you can take credit for everyone else's lousy choices. You didn't create Ken's problems; he did that for himself. But you go ahead and wallow in useless guilt . . . like a little kid. When are you going to stop doing that, Livy? When are you going to grow up and take responsibility for your own shit? Instead of hiding in a bottle every time the going gets rough."

Livy sat stiffly in her chair, confused and immobilized by Stevie's barrage, and angry that her feeling of well-being had gone up in smoke so quickly. "I'm not saying another word," she choked out.

"Then don't. Not until you're ready to be honest with yourself. But don't wait too long, Livy. And don't expect me or anyone else to do the job for you. You don't get any neat little penances here, and you don't get any nice little absolution. All you get is a second chance . . . if you really want it."

Feeling naked and humiliated, Livy had spent the remainder of the day wondering if she should leave The Oasis, no matter what Stevie Knight said. Livy Walsh wasn't a stupid child, she was the head of a powerful empire, and she had the willpower to drink in moderation. Hadn't she already proved she could go without? Wasn't that what she had come here for? Certainly it wasn't to be badgered and insulted . . . and unfairly, at that.

Still undecided, she went into the dining room for her evening meal. As if to prove to herself that she was fine, she loaded her tray with a generous portion of chicken, two vegetables, and a salad, then found a small corner table where she could consider her future in peace.

As Livy picked at her food, she became aware of a presence behind her. She turned around quickly and caught Stevie watching her with an odd mixture of concern and wistfulness. She could scarcely believe it was the same woman—the same girl—who had attacked her so vehemently. Livy turned away.

But Stevie wouldn't be ignored. Without waiting for an invitation, she sat down at Livy's table. "I know you're angry with me, but you can't leave. Not now, not when you're so close."

"Watch me," Livy said, her mind suddenly made up. "Tomorrow morning, I'm out of here."

Stevie reached across the table and took Livy's hand. "You can't. It would be such a waste, Livy, such a terrible waste."

Putting aside her anger, Livy studied the young woman. Gone was the abrasive manner of this morning; in its place was a strong, yet gentle, plea. "You told me to take responsibility for my own choices, and I'm doing just that. I've spent enough time away from my business . . . and I've already paid for my treatment. I won't ask for a refund, if that's what you're worried about."

Livy felt she had scored a hit. But Stevie shook her head sadly. "I don't care about the money."

"Then what?" Livy asked, now certain the advantage

was hers. "Is it your ego? Are you afraid I'll give you a bad press when I leave?"

Now it was Stevie who struggled for control. "That's fair," she said. "That's a fair question. You could hurt The Oasis if you chose to. . . . But I swear I didn't think of that until you just mentioned it."

"Then what?" Livy repeated, closing in hard. "If honesty is so damn important, let's have some, right here and now. I've felt you gunning for me since I got here. There's something personal behind it. What is it, Stevie? Do you have a problem with Catholics? Or maybe I'm too Establishment? Am I getting warmer? Come on, Stevie, it's my turn to demand answers!"

Stevie's eyes filled with tears. "It is personal, Livy," she answered softly, "but it's not what you think." She looked down. "My . . . my mother's a drunk," she went on brokenly. "I never could help her. I know now . . . I know we both tried, but we just never connected. You . . . you remind me of her."

So that was it. A stand-in for her mother. But her confession had touched that part of Livy that needed another child. "And you think you've been helping by . . . insulting me, acting like a one-woman Inquisition?"

Stevie smiled apologetically. "I'm trying to make you think. You haven't been doing that, Livy. . . . all you've been doing is playing old tapes in your head over and over. Boxing yourself in, blaming yourself, and using the booze for anaesthesia. Dammit, Livy, just forgive yourself. Please . . ."

Livy had stayed.

A month later, she had gone home, resolved to succeed in a new way. She had left Stevie with an enormous donation to The Oasis, a check that had been the first of many. But Livy's help extended beyond money alone. She assigned the *Chronicle*'s Sunday magazine to do a special feature on Stevie Knight—and personally saw to it that The Oasis received glowing publicity on a regular basis.

Hoping it wasn't too late to mend her relationship with Carey, she invited him to dinner. She acknowledged the breach that had made them more than strangers yet less than mother and son—and described her drinking problem frankly and without excuses. "I know I've neglected you emotionally," she said. "I can't blame that on the alcohol. . . . I don't even know that I can blame myself. I thought I was being a good wife and mother. . . . I followed all the rules. They just didn't apply, Carey. I'm sorry. I hope you'll . . ."

"That's a nice speech, Livy," he said, using her first name in a way that sounded casual but wasn't. "I'd say it took—what? A few minutes to deliver, maybe a little longer if you rehearsed? And now everything is supposed to be swell?" Carey's face was impassive, but the blue eyes were so cool, so judgmental. It was as if his father had come back to haunt her.

"No," she said, "I didn't imagine it would be that easy. I thought . . . well, I thought we might try some family counseling."

Carey smiled, but only with his mouth. "I don't get it, Livy. You tell me that you messed up . . . and now you want *me* to see some kind of shrink?"

"Not a shrink, Carey. I just want us to be able to talk, to clear the air. . . ."

"We're talking now, aren't we?"

"I'm trying, Carey. I want to know what's on your mind, how you feel about—"

"Okay," he cut in. "If you really want to know what's on my mind, I'll tell you. I want to go to school in New York. I'll live with Grandma."

"Are you sure, Carey?" she asked softly. "I mean, if you

want to go away . . . there are some excellent schools right here in Virginia."

"I'm sure," he said flatly.

Livy felt a hollowness in the pit of her stomach. All right, she told herself, it was good for Carey to be close to family. . . . It didn't mean he'd never have room in his heart for her. She gave her consent, trying to see it as a positive choice for Carey and not a slap in the face for her.

Silently she said the prayer that had been part of every day at The Oasis: Grant me the serenity to accept things I cannot change, the courage to change the things I can, and the wisdom to know the difference.

When Carey asked for a summer job at the *Chronicle*, she got him one gladly—in the mailroom. "It's where your father started," she said when Carey expressed disappointment. "Ken said it was the best place to get a handle on the entire organization."

"He said that?" Carey asked with a strange smile. "Then it must be true. Okay, Livy . . . you've got yourself a new mailroom clerk."

To celebrate his first day at work, Livy invited her son to lunch in her private dining room—a magnificent glass-walled suite atop the *Chronicle* building with a panoramic view of the city. Looking heartbreakingly like his father, he arrived wearing his best suit. He surveyed the room and the view as if he'd never seen either before. He helped Livy into her chair, then sat down across the burnished mahogany table. At lunch, he remarked politely on the vichyssoise and the cold poached salmon, and she asked polite questions about the job. How did this happen to us? she asked herself, echoing Ken's words—and then caught herself. No self-pity, no useless guilt. Give the boy time, Livy, she told herself. Show him you care and then give him time. And don't have any wine with the fish.

"Let's make it a weekly thing," she said when lunch was

over and Carey had thanked her. "I'd like to keep you briefed on what's happening at the paper."

"No," Carey said. "If I'm going to be working in the mailroom, I don't belong in the publisher's dining room. Not yet. We'll do this again when I really belong here."

She felt something at that moment—but the sensation was unclear. Was it just motherly pride . . . or was it mingled with fear?

Each summer she moved Carey up, but only a single notch in the *Chronicle* hierarchy. When he entered the Columbia School of Journalism, she put him to work in Matt Frame's office. "Matt's a good teacher," she said. "You'll learn more with him in one summer than you'll get in four years at Columbia."

"About the editorial side of things," Carey said. And Livy agreed. The "other side" was her own domain, and Carey wasn't ready for that, not just yet.

"That girl of Carey's is a peach," said Livy's mother during their regular Sunday-morning phone call. "Your dad and I are betting this one is serious."

What girl? Livy thought, while pride made her say, "Yes, she's lovely. When did you meet her?"

There was a brief silence, then a hasty reply. "Why, Carey's been bringing her when he visits. He said it was all right with you. . . ."

"Yes, of course it's all right with me."

"I'm glad," her mother said. "When he told me what a difference Sharon made in his life, I could tell he's been very lonely for a very long time." Livy's mother had said no more, but the reproach was implicit. Livy had abandoned Carey, chosen to fill Ken's shoes herself—and live closer to his ghost than to her living son. She hung up wondering if Carey had slipped forever into the realm of things she could not change.

Her remedy for that was more of what she could change. Livy computerized the *Chronicle*'s operations with state-of-the-art machines, and then she launched an ambitious expansion program for Walsh Communications. She acquired more magazines and television stations. But when she revealed to Matt Frame plans to add an ailing wire service to the Walsh empire, her chief executive intervened. "Don't do it, Livy. Even if you can make the buy at bargain-basement prices you'll still get stuck in the end."

"Acquisition is the only way to grow, Matt. And when you don't grow these days, you can damn well be sure you'll shrink."

"Maybe. But trying to rescue International Features is like trying to rescue the dinosaur from extinction. It would take an enormous investment of resources just to bring International Features up to the Associated Press standard. Why try when there are so many better uses for your money?"

"I have my reasons," Livy said. Trusted and loyal though Matt was, she had no intention of explaining that she wanted the wire service for Carey, as a kind of graduation present. Perhaps she could finally show him how much she cared and how she was thinking of his future.

When Livy presented her plans to Carey, she watched his face carefully. "You've been wanting a job with more responsibility," she said, "and I think it's time you had one. You'll start as my chief consultant for International Features—but I want you to know that I see you as editor in chief, in time. I want you to evaluate the current problems, to draw up a comprehensive plan for making IF competitive with Associated Press. . . . What's the matter, Carey? You don't look pleased."

"I'm wondering why you don't want me at the *Chronicle*, Livy," Carey said quietly, "or even in the management side of Walsh Communications. This job you're offering me . . . it sounds like I'd be taking over a white elephant—and riding it off to work in Siberia."

"It isn't like that at all!" Livy protested. "I thought you'd enjoy the challenge, Carey . . . the opportunity to shape and mold an important new division of Walsh Communications. Later, if you feel you've done all you can do with IF, we can talk about a move. I want you to be happy. I hope you know that."

Carey took the position that Livy offered and moved into an apartment in the Watergate complex. Six months later, Matt Frame died suddenly, of a massive coronary. Carey asked for Matt's job. "Before you tell me I'm too young," he said, "just remember that my father was even younger when he took over as publisher of the *Chronicle*."

"That's true. But he was forced to step in . . . and it would have been better if he could have waited. You can wait, Carey. You're doing such a good job at IF, it would be crazy to pull you out now."

He stared her down with those cool azure eyes. "When won't it be crazy, Mother?"

"Soon, Carey," she said. "All in good time."

Carey stared at her. "Whose good time, Mother," he said coldly, "yours or mine?"

But he left without waiting for an answer.

A year later, Livy heard from her mother that Carey had proposed to Sharon Cahill. She waited for her only son to share his happy news. It came in the mail—an engraved invitation to an engagement party at the Cahill home in Rye, New York. Livy's tears when she read it were more from bereavement than joy. She wasn't gaining a daughter, she had lost a son.

Alone in the house she had once shared with Ken, she struggled against seeking the consolation of alcohol. Twice she almost succumbed, and both times was saved by call-

ing Stevie at The Oasis, being given her reinforcement.
"Don't go backward now, Livy. . . ."

When she went to New York to meet her prospective
daughter-in-law for the first time, Livy was struck by
Sharon's resemblance to her own youthful self. She greeted
Sharon warmly, hoping somehow to reach Carey through
the woman he loved. "I've heard so much about you," she
said. "I hope we'll be good friends."

"I'd like that," Sharon answered shyly. "I've wanted to
meet you for such a long time, but—"

"It's all right," Livy cut in, sensing the girl's embarrassment. "Perhaps it will be easier after you and Carey are
married."

As the wedding day approached, Livy offered her son
the position of editor in chief of International Features,
along with a substantial raise in salary.

"Is that a wedding present, Livy?" he asked.

"I'm just keeping the promise I made you," she said
reproachfully. "But since you're getting married, I thought
you and Sharon could use the extra income."

"I don't see how I can take it," he said. "Being editor in
chief would be like being captain of the *Titanic*, Livy," he
said. "I think you should dump IF. Admit you made a mistake and get rid of it now, before it eats up any more Walsh
money."

"But sales are up twenty percent," Livy argued. "Let's
see what happens if we carry it a while longer."

"I know exactly what'll happen. That twenty percent
doesn't justify the money we spent to get it. In six months,
we'll be deeper in the red and sales will start going down.
Let me put some feelers out before the next annual report."

Reluctantly, Livy allowed herself to be persuaded,
knowing that she would once again be faced with the question of where to place Carey. More than ever, he would
want to be part of Walsh management, to share in the

power that had been hers alone. Yet whenever she thought of giving her son what he wanted, Livy felt the nagging tug of fear. Carey was so much like Ken, yet stronger. He was smart and ambitious; how long would it be before he would want her to step aside? She had nothing but her career . . . no husband, no lover, not even the affection of her son. She was too old to start over; Carey had his whole life ahead of him. What on earth would she do? It wasn't fair of him to be so impatient, not when she was more than willing to give him any number of good jobs that would provide valuable experience.

The day Carey found a group of investors who were willing to acquire IF, with an eye to selling off its assets, Livy bought a bottle of bourbon and put it in her desk drawer.

This time, though she thought of calling Stevie, she didn't pick up the phone.

She kept the bottle in her drawer, unopened, as a kind of talisman, touching the amber glass before telling her son he would be moving into the editor's chair at a home-decoration magazine that had been a thriving and profitable Walsh publication at which little had changed in the past ten years.

Curiously enough, Carey showed no sign of disappointment, but simply acknowledged with a smile that the job would not be difficult to fill. And for a time, tension between them seemed to ease. Sharon invited her mother-in-law for a Sunday dinner at their Watergate apartment, and though Carey excused himself after the meal, Livy felt that something positive had happened. A few weeks later the invitation was repeated, and this time Carey lingered, not saying much, but listening as the two women talked of Sharon's plans to begin looking for a house. "We're okay for now," Sharon said, "but Carey and I agreed . . . an apartment is no place to raise a family."

"Are you pregnant?" Livy asked.

"Not yet, but soon, I hope. We want lots of kids, maybe four or five—and dog and a garden. I guess that must sound pretty corny to a powerful woman like you."

"No," Livy said quietly, "it doesn't sound corny at all. I hope . . . I hope it all works out just the way you want it to." As she looked at her daughter-in-law, aglow now with hope and expectation, Livy felt suddenly old.

Ten months later, Kenneth James Walsh was born. It was as if that birth ended once and for all Carey's childhood—and any need he might have for his mother's goodwill. A month afterward, he resigned his position with Walsh Communications, and soon after that Livy learned—from an item in a rival newspaper—that she was in for the fight of her professional life. A takeover of Walsh Communications was being attempted by a group of investors led by her own son.

She took the bottle from her desk drawer and brought it home. And when it was empty, she sent the chauffeur out for two more.

On the morning of the third day, however, she resolved to fight. She called Stevie. "I need another miracle," she said. But Stevie had never promised miracles—that was somebody else's word—and she wouldn't guarantee one now.

In the midst of a battle to save all that she had been living for since her husband's death, Livy Walsh had to wonder if her allotted ration of second chances hadn't run out.

3

With her bag unpacked, Livy went to the dining room for lunch. It was comforting to be among the other Travelers—many more than the last time she had been here. In fact, the dining room was four times as big as it had been then. While still set up in cafeteria style, it was no longer a shed with rudimentary tables made out of plywood sheets, but a large mirrored room, beautifully furnished and carpeted. Whatever else happened, Livy felt she could take pride in the help she'd given to Stevie and The Oasis.

Livy picked up a tray, helped herself to a small salad from the buffet table, and looked around for a place to sit. It wouldn't surprise her to see more than one person she knew personally. Certainly, there were several she recognized—and who no doubt recognized her: a television star, the wife of a New York real-estate tycoon, a few women who'd made grist for the society pages of her paper and others over the years. Some gave her unabashed smiles of greeting, clearly ready to welcome her company.

But as Livy kept scanning—out of habit as a news gatherer perhaps, wanting to take the full census of Stevie's guests—her gaze suddenly riveted on a lone figure at a corner table. The face, striking even without makeup, was immediately recognizable. Livy's pulse quickened with excitement. No matter what else came out of her time at The Oasis, there would at least be a story—the kind that could shape events.

Quickly she crossed the room. "Hello, Anne," she said. "May I join you?"

Recognition—and then a trace of fear—passed across Anne Garretson's face. "Of course," she answered, trying to keep her voice steady.

Livy's mind was racing. She had been a big booster of Hal Garretson, using the *Chronicle*'s editorial page to further his quest for the presidential nomination. But now she felt betrayed. She had often seen Hal and Anne at Washington gatherings, and she had always believed both were blemish-free, cut from a mold different from that of so many of the other politicians. But Hal Garretson had a skeleton in his closet, after all—and she was sitting right here.

"I wondered where you'd gone after that Russian trip," Livy said casually.

Anne gave her a neutral smile. This wasn't supposed to happen, she thought, panic mounting with every breath. Livy Walsh was at the center of the media establishment. If she knew, was there any hope of keeping the secret until an announcement could be beneficially timed?

"What's your particular poison?" Livy asked bluntly.

"Livy," Anne began. "I don't think we should—"

"Ask such questions?" Livy cut in. "It's part of the therapy. There are no secrets here, Anne. Haven't you already found that out, working with Stevie?"

Anne's hands shook as she reached for a glass of water, spilling a few drops on the front of her blouse. Her eyes darted across the room as if seeking an escape, but there was none, no rescue from the cool, appraising scrutiny of the press. She wondered for a moment if she shouldn't try to turn the tables, concentrate on Livy's problem. But would that earn the understanding, the reprieve, she needed?

She turned back to Livy. "I . . . I've been using amphetamines," Anne said. "It's a problem I've had for a while, but now . . . it's behind me. When I leave here, I'll speak about it publicly. But not until then. So please, Livy, forget you saw me here. Don't do anything to damage Hal's career."

"I don't know, Anne," Livy responded drily. "Should we leave it to public servants to decide when to tell us what they please—spoon the truth out with so much sugar in 'it we can't get the real flavor?" Her tone hardened. "That's the kind of reasoning that gave us Watergate. My paper didn't cover up for Dick Nixon. . . . Why expect me to do it for Hal Garretson?"

"I'm not asking for a cover-up," Anne persisted. "I'm just asking you to wait until you have the *whole* story—with the ending. Please, Livy. I'll give you an exclusive interview when I get out of here. Hal and I will both talk to the *Chronicle*. . . ."

Livy picked at her salad through a short, thoughtful silence. Then she put her fork aside. "There's nothing personal in this, Anne. God knows I'm the last person in the world who could condemn you or anyone else for . . . this kind of weakness."

Anne's face began to relax. Then Livy went on. "But you've got to realize that, in your position, the consequences go beyond yourself and those around you. You've got to tell Hal that he can never be President."

Anne recoiled as if struck. "No!" The word exploded across the table. "Hal's the best man for the job, Livy," she argued, fists clenched at her sides, "and nobody deserves it more than he does. Your own paper has said he's the most able politician this country has seen in years. You've written about his leadership qualities."

"Yes," Livy acknowledged. "And his charisma—that all-important political asset. He's got it all, Anne. Hal Garretson may well be the best man for the job. But we're not just talking about Hal. The question is, are you the best 'running mate'? Let's face it, Anne: a president's wife is more important than a vice-president or even a cabinet member. What would happen if Hal was in the middle of a summit negotiation—or, God help us, trying to keep a cool head in the middle of a nuclear crisis—and his wife started to fall apart?"

"Stop it, Livy," Anne pleaded. "Let me explain how it started . . . how I know I can—"

"Answer the question," Livy insisted. "What happens if Hal has to nursemaid his wife when the country's fate is hanging in the balance?"

"I said stop it!" Anne screamed, at the same moment tossing the water in her glass into Livy's face.

Livy stood as she calmly blotted her face with a napkin. "And what would happen," she said, "if you lost control like that at a state dinner? You've just made my point, Anne. Your husband cannot, must not even have the chance to become our next president."

Anne started to lunge at Livy, her arms swinging around wildly, but Livy darted back. Two dining-room attendants rushed over and got between the two women. One of them put his hand on Anne's arm, as if to pull her away, but she broke free and ran for the exit.

Summoned by a silent alarm, Stevie appeared in time to catch Anne rushing out. "What's going on?" she asked.

Anne was sobbing uncontrollably, her face twisted with pain.

One of the attendants came running over to explain. "Mrs. Garretson attacked Mrs. Walsh. . . ."

Anne looked to Stevie as if to argue, but she could only shake her head.

"It's going to be all right, Anne," Stevie soothed. "Just breathe deeply and clear your mind. Can you get to your room on your own?"

Anne nodded. "Okay. I'll be in to see you in a few minutes. Whatever the problem is, you can handle it. I promise...." She touched Anne's face, trying to evoke a response, but the senator's wife seemed to be gripped by a formidable terror.

Anne walked away and Stevie went into the dining room, where Livy had resumed her place at a table while she went on mopping her blouse with a napkin.

Stevie sat down across from her. "You know Anne from Washington, of course...."

"I thought I knew her," Livy said sharply.

"But seeing her here changed your mind?"

"Not about her." Livy folded the napkin and looked earnestly at Stevie. "But I had to tell Anne a couple of facts of political life. In return for which she gave me a bath—and tried to land a right hook to the jaw. Not First Lady behavior, if you ask me."

Stevie cut her off tersely. "That's not what I'm asking. I want to know exactly what you said. What set her off, Livy? Tell it straight with no games.... We've known each other too long for that."

"Very well. I told her I didn't think the *Chronicle* could withhold news of her stay at The Oasis from the American public."

"Livy! You didn't! You know the rules.... Everything that happens here is confidential."

"Up to a point, Stevie. You can't set yourself up as being more important than a matter of national security."

"Dammit," Stevie exploded. "How would you have felt

if somebody blabbed when you came to The Oasis fifteen years ago?"

Livy shook her head. "It isn't the same, Stevie, and you know it. You know how much I respect you and The Oasis. For God's sake, the Walsh Foundation endowed two entire wings! But Anne Garretson isn't just anybody, and I don't think your rules apply here. If she were Imelda Marcos or any other leader's wife, I'd respect your rules. But they don't apply here. Hal Garretson wants to be president of this country, Stevie."

"And he can do it—with his wife. Anne Garretson won't be asking anyone to make their decision without full knowledge. But she deserves the chance to show just how much guts she really has. Let her lick this, Livy, and she'll be more than a match for any other woman who's ever been in the White House. She wants so desperately to heal herself, and she's been trying so hard—"

"Wanting and trying—even deserving—don't necessarily make miracles," Livy broke in. "You and I know that, don't we? We all have to face facts. And for Anne the facts are that she went to pieces when I challenged her, Stevie. Do you imagine for a single minute she won't be challenged over and over again when she leaves here?"

Stevie looked into the brown eyes of the woman who had been client, friend—and then patron of The Oasis. They were softer than one would imagine in a woman of such remarkable power, yet Stevie knew, better than anyone save Livy herself, the scars behind the facade. Knowing how much Livy had wanted her own miracle, Stevie now perceived something more behind Livy's crusading talk. "This isn't just about Hal Garretson or Anne, is it, Livy?"

"What else could it be?" Livy scoffed.

"Ken's death, maybe. You never allowed yourself to fall apart, did you? There was too much to be done. Even when you drank, you worked right through it—even though you paid a price, let your son slip away. But going to pieces completely, that was never allowed. And you can't allow to anyone else what you couldn't take for yourself."

Livy had gone rigid in her chair.

Feeling that she had struck home, Stevie made her final plea. "I need your promise, Livy, that you won't violate the rules and jeopardize Anne Garretson's treatment."

"I can't give it to you."

Stevie paused a moment, as if to gather strength. "You'll have to, Livy. Or else you can't stay."

Livy turned stricken eyes to Stevie.

"Don't decide now," Stevie added quickly as she stood up. "Think about it. I want to save you—both of you."

As Stevie walked away, she heard Livy calling loudly after her. "What gives you the right, Stevie? What gives you the right to decide who gets saved and who doesn't? What gives you the right to make all the rules?"

Stevie kept going. But once outside the dining room, she could no longer maintain her brisk, confident pace. She turned into the nearest empty room and leaned against a wall for support.

What, indeed? she asked herself—for the millionth time. What in her own hellish past had prepared her to believe she could save them all?

Book Three

1

New York, 1970

It was garbage-pickup day, and the sidewalk on East Seventh Street was lined with battered garbage pails, heaps of cardboard boxes, and leaking brown paper bags. In the summer months, the smell of rotting food could be overpowering; now at least the cold refrigerated the refuse from the neighborhood's kitchens, keeping flies and rodents at bay.

That was the good part of winter, Stevie thought as she emerged from the shabby walk-up tenement where she lived. The bad part was that her room on the fifth floor was like a freezer. The only thing the radiator seemed good for was to serve as a random alarm clock, waking her around dawn each morning when it began to clank noisily with the effort of steam to rise. For some reason, however, the steam never made it all the way up.

In the year she'd been in New York, Stevie still hadn't adjusted to the harsh realities that had confronted her since she'd arrived with only a few dollars, and even fewer job skills. Sometimes she would find herself thinking wistfully about the warmth of her room in the house on Shady Lane.

Yet whenever she felt herself slipping into anything like regret, she reminded herself that, if you were anything more than a household pet, there ought to be more to a home than shelter and food.

As she rounded St. Mark's Place, the atmosphere became slightly less dismal, thanks to the brightly colored displays of the head shops and the fragrance of fried sausage and fresh coffee from the neighborhood luncheonettes. A few more steps and she reached her destination, Grandma's Attic, a ramshackle store filled with military surplus, vintage furs, and antique clothes. Pushing the heavy door open, Stevie checked the enormous old church clock that hung over the mezzanine level. Nine o'clock, exactly. . . . Thank goodness. She had learned the hard way that people who hired inexperienced teenagers wouldn't put up with lateness or mistakes. Her present boss could be indulgent and kind, but she wasn't about to test his limits.

Patrick Menendez, Stevie's landlord as well as owner of Grandma's Attic, was at the front counter, poring over his account books. This morning he cut a dashing figure in his surplus Royal Air Force flight suit.

"Morning, Patrick," she called out.

"Hi, kid," he answered without looking up from his ledger.

She went over to him. "I really hate to bother you, but can I get a little more heat in my apartment? I've been freezing all week. . . ."

Patrick threw up his hands in a Latin gesture inherited from his father, while flashing the winning Irish smile from his mother's side. "Hey, Stevie, I'm doing the best I can. The building's old. The boiler drinks oil like water. A small landlord like me gets screwed every which way . . . taxes, rent control—"

"Give me a break," Stevie interrupted, rolling her eyes. "I work for you, remember? I know you're not exactly headed for the poorhouse." Patrick always complained about hard times, but he had more businesses going than she could keep track of, including a small bookmaking operation he ran out of Grandma's Attic.

"Why do you wanna live in that rat trap, anyway?" he asked, changing the subject. "A beautiful girl like you . . . you oughta get married, find some nice guy to take care of you."

"Yeah, right," Stevie hooted, "just as soon as you ask me. You know I'm saving myself for you." It was a running joke between them, a safe one, for Stevie knew Patrick was crazy about his live-in girlfriend, Eve.

"And I saved something for you," Patrick said, handing Stevie a brown paper bag. "Bought too much breakfast this morning. You finish it."

"Thanks," she said. Though he wasn't the greatest landlord, Patrick was a nice guy. She knew he'd bought the buttered roll and the cup of juice for her, the same way he bought "too much" fruit occasionally or an "extra" half-pound of cold cuts, managing to help Stevie without making her feel it was charity. Lunch was her big meal of the day. For the rest, she made do with odds and ends; it was the only way to stretch her meager paycheck so that it covered rent and necessities.

She went upstairs to the mezzanine, where she'd created a "department" out of Patrick's chaotically jumbled merchandise. Opening a barrel of clothing he'd picked up at an auction upstate, she began to sort through it. Some would go straight into the garbage; some would end up in the "Trash and Treasure" bin, to be sold "as is" for a dollar. The rest, the good stuff, would be bundled up and sent to the cleaner around the corner, who gave Patrick a bulk rate. When the clothing came back, Stevie would arrange it according to her own liking on the racks she'd marked "Vintage Victorian," "Roaring Twenties," "Fabulous Forties," and "Anything Goes." Since she'd come to Grandma's Attic, Stevie had developed a real flair for turning old clothes into fashion statements. It was her job, of course, but she had fun, too, taking a rumpled flapper dress, an old band uniform or tuxedo, and adding some personal touch here to create a head-turning outfit.

She didn't have much money for entertainment, but sometimes after work, she'd fix her hair and makeup, dress up in one of her creations, and walk over to Trude Heller's on West Ninth Street. There she'd join the noisy crowds spilling over onto the sidewalk, waiting for the chance to get inside and dance to the music of the Mashed Potato or the Twist. More often than not, a guy would try to pick her up, but Stevie never gave them more than passing conversation. Somehow what the Admiral had done to her had turned her off sex. She wasn't sure if it was psychological, or if she'd even been messed up physically by the operation. Maybe a guy would come along who'd get her interested again, but she wasn't holding her breath. Back at the naval base, Stevie had been a kind of reigning princess, picking her conquests and calling the shots. But in New York, she'd had a rude awakening. Here, in the mad scramble to have a good time, to prove how liberated and free they were, people used and discarded each other with a speed that made Stevie feel she was way out of her league. Lonely and vulnerable as she was, she found it hurt too much to play games she could lose, and so she'd become more careful and guarded. Besides, it took a lot of energy just to survive; being held and kissed and caressed had become another luxury she was learning to do without.

A shout of outrage rose suddenly from Patrick. "Jesus, Stevie, will you come downstairs and take a look! How's a man supposed to make a living with garbage like *this*?"

Stevie hurried down the short flight of stairs. Was it something she'd done, like sorting out the wrong clothes?

Patrick stood with a look of pained outrage on his face, pulling shirts and pants covered with olive-drab camouflage patterns out of a huge carton. "Look at this crap," he said, holding up a shirt with one long sleeve and one short one. "This is what they make for our fighting men! No wonder we can't win the damn war in Vietnam!" He flung the shirt atop the pile on the floor.

Stevie bent to pick it up. "How much did you pay for this stuff?" she asked, examining the shirt thoughtfully.

"Quarter apiece," Patrick admitted sheepishly. "But my supplier told me it was 'slightly irregular.' I figured that meant a snag in the weave, a coupla little holes . . . nothing our customers would care about. I didn't count on this garbage! I couldn't sell this to a—"

"Hold on," Stevie interrupted, holding the shirt against her body. "How about I just even up the sleeves with a scissor? Leave them unfinished, like cut-off jeans. Then we belt the shirt, either in the middle or on the hips, with one of those Army surplus webbing belts . . . and look, it makes a mini! If I put one of these on a mannequin, with khaki-colored tights, I'll bet you could get at least ten bucks for the outfit. What do you say? We'll call it some new kinda style—Viet Vogue. . . ."

Suddenly Patrick's eyes lit up as he calculated the potential profits on Stevie's newest design idea. "Kid, you're a genius! Get to work. If we make it a Christmas special, maybe we can ask twenty bucks, move the shipment before the end of the year. Listen," he added, "just to show you my appreciation, I'm gonna buy you a space heater tomorrow. No, tomorrow's Thanksgiving. But you'll have it by Friday, scout's honor."

"Thanks, Patrick, you're a prince. . . . Now do you see why I'm saving my love for you?"

* * *

It was after eight when Stevie closed up the shop. She'd barely made it halfway through Patrick's supply of irregular shirts, but she just had to stop. Her shoulders ached and her eyes were blurring with green and brown spots, the camouflage pattern etched into her brain. All she wanted to do was get home. If she kept the stove going with a couple of pots of water in it, she might even have a warm bath. . . .

As she climbed the outside stoop of her building, an old Polish woman who lived on the floor below her was also entering. The neighbor's arms were wrapped around a large shopping bag from which the legs and butt end of a large turkey protruded.

Thanksgiving. The word hadn't registered when Patrick had said it earlier. Then it had meant nothing but the inconvenience of having to wait an extra day to get a heater. But now, as she headed for her cold room, Stevie experienced a sudden childlike longing for warmth and security. As she mounted the stairs, assaulted by the aroma of someone else preparing food for the celebration the next day, she began to picture what it might be like in the house on Shady Lane. Irene was forced into sobriety on the holidays, she remembered. Perhaps there would be baking tonight, sweet fragrances wafting out of the kitchen. And tomorrow a few chosen officers and their families would come for turkey dinner—

No, it wasn't like that, she reminded herself as she felt her eyes misting. It was never happy and warm; it was awful. That's why you left!

Yet the yearning didn't go away. It only got sharper, like a knife pain, until she couldn't stand it any longer. Gathering up her money, she ran down to the nearest newsstand, got a handful of quarters, then went to a public phone and made a call to the number she couldn't forget. Listening to ringing on the other end, she tried to compose the words she'd say if someone answered.

"Hello?" It was Irene.

Her mother. Yet, filtered through a thousand painful memories, she could only hear it as the sound of a stranger. Stevie put the receiver down. Nothing Irene could say would ease the loneliness Stevie felt now. Nothing anyone did could make her a child again. Not even for a minute. Not even for Thanksgiving.

Patrick peered curiously through the window of Grandma's Attic at the black stretch limousine that had pulled up directly outside. Uptown types could sometimes be seen after dark around St. Mark's Place trying to score some dope, but their limousines rarely lingered on these streets in daylight. "Hey, Stevie," he called out, "get a load of this. . . . It looks like we're getting a visit from royalty!"

Stevie joined Patrick in watching the small entourage that emerged from the limousine and examined the storefront somewhat distastefully, as if it were an enemy beachhead that had to be stormed. There were three of them, led by a tall, striking woman with creamy white skin and a severe, deep-auburn chignon. Her carriage was regal, her clothes cut with a stunning simplicity—an emerald-green suit of raw silk was adorned only with a gold and ruby dragon pin. Flanking her were two mannequinlike young men with picture-perfect haircuts, wearing identical blue Italian suits.

As the party stepped inside the store, Patrick moved to greet them. "How may I help you?" He tossed a wink at Stevie as he aped the courtly bow of a Tiffany's floorwalker.

"Show us your antique clothes . . . whatever you have from the Forties," the woman said imperiously.

Still enjoying his joke, Patrick wafted a hand daintily

toward the ceiling. "Vintage clothes department upstairs. Miss Knight will look after you. . . ." He nodded to Stevie.

Dutifully, Stevie guided the group up the worn, dusty stairs. "Our Forties things are on those two racks," she explained. It struck her then that these unlikely customers might be seeking costumes for a party. "If you tell me what you're looking for, I might save you some time."

"Never mind," the woman said in a dismissive tone. "I'll know what I want if I see it." When Stevie lingered, she added, "I'll let you know if I need your help."

Stevie moved away and began going through the motions of straightening up some merchandise, all the while keeping an eye on the group as they started sifting through the racks. They didn't look like shoplifters, but these days you couldn't be sure. The woman, who was obviously the main shopper, lingered every so often over a dress or suit, examining the fabric, turning it inside out to check the cut and construction. Go figure, Stevie thought; with the top prices here not much more than twenty bucks, this uptown lady was putting the stuff under a microscope as if she were in Saks or Bergdorf Goodman's. Well, she certainly had an eye, Stevie decided, watching the woman put aside some of her personal favorites, including the floor-length Joan Crawford-style white jersey Stevie had dreamed of borrowing for New Year's Eve—if she had anyplace to go.

Suddenly she heard the clatter of heels on the stairs, then a heavy thud. "Oh, shit!" a voice shrilled. "Goddammit to hell!"

Stevie whirled to look down over the mezzanine rail, and saw a young woman who looked very much like an exclamation point sprawled on the stairs. Her vivid ginger hair stood out against alabaster skin further punctuated by startlingly black eyes and shiny coral lips still gaping in shock.

Quickly Stevie ran down the stairs and pulled the young

woman to her feet, brushing off her gorgeous gray lynx fur coat. "Gee, did you hurt yourself?" Stevie asked with genuine concern.

"I'll live," she said, climbing the rest of the stairs to the mezzanine. "But unless I'm too hung over to see straight, this place could do with a little more light."

"Tell me what you're looking for and I can—"

"I'm with them," the young woman said, pointing to the group at the racks. "Can't you tell? That's my mother, the Grand Duchess Anastasia. Don't tell me you can't see the resemblance. *Vogue* magazine says we look like sisters." There was a glint of mischief in the girl's dark eyes.

Now Stevie did see the resemblance. It was as if the older woman's features and coloring had been taken apart and reassembled by an artist with a sense of humor. Obviously the two were celebrities of some kind, but Stevie didn't have a clue about the identity of either woman, and she was embarrassed about her ignorance.

"I guess you don't read *Vogue*.... Well, good for you! I'm Philippa Mason," the ginger-and-white girl said, flashing Stevie a smile. "But everyone calls me Pip. And the Grand Duchess is known in the rag trade as Valentine. A made-up name, of course, but can you see a great designer being called Sadie?" The grimace of pain on Philippa Mason's face was so exaggerated that Stevie burst out laughing.

"And speaking of fashion," Pip rattled on, "where did you buy that marvelous outfit you're wearing? Is it a Rudi Gernreich?" Pip leaned over to examine the special camouflage mini Stevie had made for herself by removing the mismatched sleeves and adding a black turtleneck polo underneath.

"I didn't buy it," Stevie explained. "I just cut up some Army surplus shirts we had."

"Well, I'll be!" Pip laughed. "Don't let Valentine hear

you. She thinks if you can't afford her stuff, you might as well stay home and die of shame."

Stevie laughed along with Pip. She liked the way this ginger-and-white girl talked and smiled and looked. Though Pip was obviously rich, she didn't have a phony, put-together style. She looked as if she'd just . . . *happened*.

"What's your mother doing here?" Stevie asked curiously.

Haughtily, as if mimicking her mother's airs, Pip said, "It's a research trip, my dear . . . studying the designers of the past in order to achieve just the right balance of historic authenticity and originality in her mah-velous new Retro line." Her voice dropped. "To put it another way, Mum's scrambling around town buying old stuff to knock off and then sell for eight hundred bucks a pop."

Stevie laughed some more and wished that Pip wasn't just an uptown customer who'd soon be gone.

Pip seemed to catch Stevie's longing gaze. "Hey, want to grab a cappuccino or something? Valentine could be here forever, and my stomach is growling."

Stevie shook her head regretfully. "I can't. I have to work."

Philippa sighed. "Too bad. Though, if you'll forgive me for opening my big mouth, I don't understand why a girl as beautiful as you can't do something better than . . . this." Pip was silent a moment. "Hey, you must get time off for lunch?"

"I can take forty-five minutes at twelve-thirty."

"Okay. That'll give me time to wander the city and spend some of the Grand Duchess's money—my way." She started toward the stairs, then turned back. "Hey, you won't be insulted if I don't do my shopping here, will you?"

Stevie shook her head.

"Good. I'll be back at twelve-thirty." Philippa waved and hurried out, leaving Stevie feeling as if she'd just been brushed by a refreshing ocean breeze.

"Yecch!" Pip exclaimed as she bit into her greasy hamburger. "Don't tell me you actually *like* the food in this place."

For a moment, Stevie was at a loss for words. She had suggested the familiar corner coffee shop because it was cheap, and the owner occasionally threw in the beverage on her bill without charge. As much as she had reveled in Pip's company until now, if she was going to be laughed at for being poor, then it was hopeless to spend any more time together. "I don't like it or dislike it," Stevie declared. "I eat here because it's all I can afford. If it's not good enough for you, then I guess you shouldn't be here."

For a second, Pip's coral lips formed a startled O. Then she started to laugh.

Baffled, Stevie felt she'd totally misread Pip. She'd even begun to imagine they could be friends. But now she was being laughed at. Glaring at Pip, Stevie started to slide out of the booth.

Pip grabbed her wrist. "Hey, Stevie, don't get me wrong. I was laughing because . . . you just sounded so much like Valentine for a second—lecturing me on how spoiled rotten I am. But listen, she's right and you're right. I'm really sorry. . . ."

Stevie sat back, shaking her head. Whatever faults Pip might have, she could admit when she was wrong. What a golden virtue that seemed to Stevie after the years of dealing with the Admiral's unfailing self-righteousness.

"Of course," Pip continued, "it's her fault, you know. The Grand Duchess got to be a star before I was born, so I don't know anything about being poor. 'My daughter will have *everything*,'" Pip intoned in a deep voice. "That's what she said on the day I was born, and I guess I have had too much. . . ." She fixed Stevie with her enormous dark eyes. "That's my way of saying forgive me if I hurt your feelings."

"Sure," Stevie said. "I'm probably too quick on the trigger when it comes to certain things," she admitted with a candor that was new to her.

Pip took a bite of her hamburger, making an almost exaggerated show of enduring it for Stevie's sake. After a swallow of her Coke, she said, "Now I want to return the favor, Stevie. You've just given me a lesson in being poor, so suppose I show *you* how the other half lives. Let me take you to a party tonight, Stevie. It won't cost a thing, and I promise it will be fun."

Stevie was flattered by the invitation, but hesitant.

"What's the matter?" Pip asked, a frown creasing her creamy forehead. "It won't be one of those stiff uptown parties, if that's what worries you. It's at the Wherehouse." She waited for Stevie to react, and when that didn't happen, she added, "Hey, haven't you heard of the *Wherehouse*—Samson Love's place? He gave it the name because it's where he paints and makes his movies—and where it all happens. . . ."

Now it registered. Though Stevie didn't know much about art, she had certainly heard the name of the artist Samson Love. He was a trendsetter whose friends included movie stars, politicians, multimillionaire businessmen, even royalty.

"I'd like to go," Stevie said, "but . . . would I fit in?"

"Oh, don't worry," Pip said broadly. "You'll be right at home."

"Is the party . . . formal?"

"Nothing about Samson is formal in the strictest sense. He just makes everything up as he goes along, and everyone else tries to follow."

"Okay," Stevie said, "I'll go." She tried to remember if the Grand Duchess Valentine had bought all of Patrick's best things. After the sales Stevie had made today, he'd certainly let her borrow something special to wear.

"Just wait and see, Stevie. This will be a night to remember. And Samson will absolutely love you."

Pip's tone of pure conviction intrigued Stevie. "How do you know?"

"Because," Pip replied, "you're my friend. Aren't you?"

Stevie stared for a second at Pip. Friend. It was as if she were hearing the word for the first time. How assuring and solid it sounded, with a promise of something she'd never known before.

"Yes," Stevie said. "I am—I'm your friend."

2

Arm in arm, Stevie and Pip crossed Mercer Street on the frontier separating Soho from Little Italy and approached a looming onetime industrial loft building of several stories.

"Thar she blows, Stevie!" said Pip. "The Wherehouse—where it's at."

Stevie was a bit let down. For all Pip's talk about a fabulous party, the place they were going appeared rather unprepossessing on the outside, its drabness accentuated by many darkened windows, as though they had been covered by heavy drapes. The only hint of a party was the thumping beat of rock-and-roll music that leaked into the street, loud enough to be confused with distant thunder.

No sooner had the girls walked through the rusted iron doors at the street level, however, than Stevie's impression began to change. Lining the walls of the narrow lobby were some of Samson Love's well-known colorful paintings of Mao, and Marilyn, and Richard Nixon. And the floor had been spread with shiny, white, hard chips—making it look like an expensive driveway—in the middle of which stood a twenty-year-old Ford convertible. In the back seat of the convertible, formed out of what appeared to be thousands of plaster bandages stuck together, were

164

sculptures of a man and woman making love, the woman's legs sticking straight up in the air.

"Wow," Stevie said, impressed as much by a car parked inside a building as by the art.

"Great, huh?" said Pip. "Samson's been offered half a million for that—but he says he likes it too much to sell. It's called 'Peace.'" Pip laughed as if she'd made a joke.

Stevie looked at her blankly, which prompted Pip to explain. "Her legs, see . . . ?"

Now Stevie noticed that the woman's legs naturally formed a V—an echo of the popular peace symbol the antiwar protestors made with their fingers. Stevie chuckled a little too. She'd had very little exposure to art, but Samson Love's visual wit was enough to tell her he must have an amazing mind. She felt timid, suddenly, about being in his company.

But Pip was already pulling her into a large freight elevator. Pip closed the metal accordion gate and pushed the lowest of several huge multicolored buttons.

"He uses this whole building?" Stevie asked in amazement.

"Samson does a lot of different things," Pip answered vaguely. The elevator stopped. Pip pulled open the gate and motioned Stevie into a small hallway guarded by a large red metal door. Pip rapped her knuckles on the door loudly. "Sometimes it's *ages* before anyone answers. But don't worry, we'll get in sooner or later."

Stevie was less worried than enthralled. She'd met Pip only this morning, yet already she felt as if she'd been rescued from a meager and lonely existence.

Pip rapped again, even harder, and when no one came, she slid down to sit unselfconsciously on the grimy concrete floor, oblivious to the effect on her fox coat and expensive purple leather mini. Stevie sat too. Her own outfit was far less grand, and hastily improvised: an oversize black sweater belted with an imitation brass circlet, worn over black tights, topped by a Navy pea coat for warmth. "You look smashing," Pip said, as if she understood Stevie's need for reassurance. "I already promised that Samson would love you, so relax."

Again Stevie had to ask. "How can you be so sure?"

"Because you are what he likes. You're fresh and beautiful . . . and new. That's what he cares most about, Stevie, the new. New art, new thrills, and new faces."

Stevie couldn't think of herself as fresh or "new," yet she liked the idea that somebody famous would think so.

"Mind you," Pip said, "Samson doesn't take up with just anyone who's beautiful, though he likes lots of pretty people at his parties. No, it's that he can see things about you that no one else does, he *knows* things that even you don't know . . . and he brings those things out. Then he *has* to love you . . . because you've become one of his creations. Understand?"

Stevie shook her head doubtfully. "It sounds a little scary . . . kind of like witchcraft. I'm not sure I want my secrets known. And I'd hate having someone know more about me than *I* do."

Pip smiled, and in the dim light of the hallway there was a sadness in her expression that made her seem older. "It can be scary," she said quietly, "but it's exciting. Valentine says Samson's the twentieth century's answer to the Marquis de Sade. Though I think of him as Peter Pan—"

Suddenly there was the sound of a bolt being thrown on the big metal door.

"Well," Pip concluded, jumping up, "now you'll see for yourself." The red metal barrier was opened by a short, heavyset man with dark curly hair. His whimsical garb, a tie-dyed shirt and blue bell-bottom trousers, was slightly incongruous over his stevedore's tight, muscular build. A scar across the bridge of his nose gave him a faintly sinister air. Adding to the incongruity was the upper-class tone in which he spoke. "Good evening, Philippa." He flipped a finger at Stevie. "What's this? A new one for Samson's harem?"

Philippa scowled, as if to discourage such talk. "This is Stevie Knight, a very good friend of mine. Stevie, this is Paul Maxwell. Pay no attention to him . . . he's just jealous of Samson and has no manners whatever." She took Stevie by the hand and led her past the man.

"He's not very pretty," Stevie whispered.

"No," Pip whispered back, "but he's *very* rich, and that makes him interesting as far as Samson's concerned."

No sooner had they dropped their coats in a mound of others by the door than Stevie felt herself bombarded with bright colors and sounds. Hundreds of red and blue and yellow helium balloons were floating against a ceiling twenty feet overhead, complementing immense colorful paintings on the walls. Pinball machines clanged a counterpoint to the music of a hurdy-gurdy, and barkers called out invitations to carnival-type booths. Stevie clapped her hands like a gleeful child at the realization that an actual midway had been set up indoors. She had seen traveling carnivals that set up outside the Navy base, passed them on the way to town, but Irene had never taken her. This was like a childhood dream coming true—almost as if what Pip had said of Samson Love was already proving true: he knew her without ever knowing her, knew exactly what to provide. . . . Stevie breathed in the sweet smell of cotton candy merged with the salty, buttery aroma of popcorn. All around her, people were laughing and having fun, paying no attention to the movie cameras that moved among them. Stevie could scarcely believe her eyes.

"So," Pip said, "how do you like it?"

Stevie tried to hold her enthusiasm in check, afraid to be

dismissed as a small-town hick by her sophisticated friend. "It's really nice."

"Nice?" Pip's eyebrows arched. "Hey, Stevie, how are you going to enjoy a new experience if you pretend you've seen it all?"

Stevie broke into a grin. "Okay, it isn't nice . . . it's fucking spectacular!"

"That's better," Pip said. "Now let's get some drinks."

Stevie made a move toward a marble-topped soda fountain, where a young man in Gay Nineties straw hat, bow tie, and striped vest was dispensing milk shakes and sodas in ice-cream parlor glasses.

"Uh-uh," Pip said, "not tonight. Those beverages aren't as Archie Andrews as they look—and I don't want you wasting your first visit to the Wherehouse on another planet." She pulled Stevie to a small open bar, where bottles of liquor were displayed along with antique apothecary jars filled with brightly colored liquids. Pip filled a tumbler with ice and splashed a shot of vodka over it. "Here, stick with the old-fashioned stuff for now."

Stevie didn't care for liquor, but she wanted very much to fit in. She started sipping on the drink at once.

Pip led her around the room, introducing her to some people whose names meant nothing, though Stevie was sure they should have. The women were all beautiful, the men mostly handsome, and all were dressed fantastically. When she did meet a recognizable celebrity—one of the Rolling Stones—she was too tongue-tied to say anything but "hello."

At last, Pip cut her free. "Listen, you mix and mingle on your own for a while. I'll see if I can find Samson."

Stevie looked around at the groups of people, and instead of attempting to mingle, walked toward the row of carnival booths. When she had lived under the Admiral's shadow, being the center of attention at his parties was easy, a piece of cake. But in the big city, she had lost her nerve and felt the way she had in school, a solitary outsider, looking at but not able to share in the kind of good times she'd never known.

A barker in one of the booths held out a handful of baseballs. "How about you, young lady? Want to try your luck? Knock down the Kewpies and win a prize . . . ?"

Stevie smiled agreeably and accepted the balls. Taking careful aim with a baseball, she hurled it at a Kewpie doll. Down it went.

"Give the pretty lady a prize," said a voice behind her.

Stevie turned around. She'd seen only grainy newspaper pictures of him, yet she knew him at once. Nobody looked quite like Samson Love. His skin was the pale blue-white of oyster shells, his jet-black hair long and pulled back with a velvet ribbon. He wore a ruffled silk shirt open at the throat, close-fitting blue velvet trousers, and matching soft leather boots. His eyes were the palest silver gray and flecked with gold. He reminded Stevie of a wonderful romantic character in an old movie she'd seen on television once—a handsome, elegant man called Heathcliff. He smiled at Stevie as he offered her a furry stuffed panda, and suddenly he seemed much younger . . . like Little Boy Blue.

"Thank you," she murmured, accepting the panda—and wishing desperately that Pip were here to ease the shyness she felt.

"You're new," he said, appraising Stevie in a way that reminded her that "new" was the attribute he prized most. Taking her arm, he led her away from the carnival booth, the merrymakers parting before him. "Tell me your name."

"Stevie . . . Stevie Knight."

"Stevie," he repeated, studying her so closely she wished for an outfit as striking as Pip's. "And Knight. That's not too bad. But maybe I'll find something I like better," he added as if the matter of her name were completely up to him.

Curiously, she didn't object. She was flattered that Samson Love could take an interest in her.

"And how did you find us, Pretty Stevie?" he asked.

"I came with Pip . . . Philippa Mason."

"Ah, yes, Pip." He examined her again. "I can see how the two of you might be a match—our Pip . . . and someone like you."

Stevie didn't know what he meant, but she could almost believe the pale eyes flecked with gold *could* see everything.

"Are you having fun?"

"Yes . . . thank you."

"Having fun is important," he said. "It may be the only thing that really matters. . . ."

Stevie nodded, wanting to be agreeable.

"Tell me," he said, "are you a conventional person, or are you open to pleasure of all kinds?"

The question knocked Stevie off balance; her cheeks flamed as she groped for an answer. "I . . . I don't know."

"Well," he said, "that's better than being sure you're not." He stopped and tipped her chin with his forefinger. He looked to Stevie like a sorcerer, with his pointed eyebrows and his cat's eyes, his blacker-than-night hair. As their eyes held, she felt herself being beckoned into dark and mysterious places.

But a moment later the little boy was back. "Will you take a ride with me?"

"I'd love to," she agreed, "but what kind . . . ?" She looked around the Wherehouse, seeing no sign of a ride anywhere.

"Follow me!" Grabbing her hand, as Jack might grab Jill's, he ran with her toward the back of the loft. Opening a door to what looked like a closet, he switched on a light.

Stevie was speechless. It was a huge storeroom filled with toys . . . big, wonderful, expensive toys, like the kind she'd seen in an enormous toy store uptown on Fifth Avenue. Samson pushed aside an enormous stuffed giraffe, knocking it against a veritable menagerie of plush animals. "Here," he said, beckoning Stevie into the seat of a bright red fire engine, "get in."

Stevie climbed onto the toy and squeezed over, making room for Samson. He settled himself beside her and turned a key by the steering wheel. A tiny engine sputtered to life.

"It works!" Stevie exclaimed with delight.

"Of course it works. Hang on!" And, throwing the small vehicle into gear, Samson drove out of the storeroom, right into the party. "Ring the bell!" he shouted gleefully to Stevie. "Ring the bell so they'll clear the way. . . ."

Stevie clanged the fire bell, laughing as people scattered out of their path. Seeing Pip, Stevie waved, and got a thumbs-up sign in return. As they zigged and zagged the fire engine through the crowd Stevie turned to watch Samson, and suddenly he didn't seem so intimidating at all. Perhaps, in fact, they had a lot in common. As a grown-up, he'd bought himself a childhood because he'd had to do without as a child. Stevie clanged and clanged the bell, having the time of her life as Samson drove the little engine in winding figure eights, forcing his guests to laughingly holler and spill their drinks as he bore down on them.

Stevie was sorry when Samson braked the fire engine to a halt and called out, "Last stop . . . everyone out!" Of course, he had a thousand friends. He had to move on. . . .

But he surprised her by grabbing her hand the second she climbed out. "Come on . . . I'll give you the ten-cent tour."

Off and running again, he took her into a partitioned area. The first thing Stevie saw was a movie screen with Dustin Hoffman's face on it—a scene from *The Graduate*, she thought. But the sound was turned down, and instead there was the music of the Beatles' latest song, "Lucy in the Sky With Diamonds." Nearby, two soundless television sets were mounted in a bright red wall like paintings. News film was unrolling on one screen, images of flaming napalm consuming what looked like a small village. On another there were scenes of antiwar demonstrators being herded into police vans by nightstick-carrying officers wearing gas masks.

As Stevie gazed at the screens, Samson commented, "It's the end of Western civilization as we know it . . . if it hasn't already been dead for a hundred years. . . ."

"What do you mean, it's dead?" Stevie asked.

"Well, if it wasn't dead, Pretty Stevie," he said solemnly, "how in hell could someone like me exist?"

Stevie turned to regard him thoughtfully and saw a smile tugging at the corner of his mouth. "Hey, are you putting me on?"

The smile blossomed. "It's not impossible," the artist said, and gestured abruptly to something behind her. Turning, Stevie saw a man with a movie camera mounted on his shoulder; the whole conversation with Samson was being recorded on film!

Before she could react, Samson was tugging her away to another area. Here the walls were painted white, and hung with more of Samson's trademark paintings, his series of automobile parts—a Rolls-Royce grille, a Jaguar hood ornament, Cadillac fins. Above the paintings, in bright crayon colors, hung a sign that said "ART."

"What do you think?" Samson gestured to the wall.

"Is this a test or something?" Stevie asked, evading the question.

Samson laughed. "'Or something.' . . . But you see, now you've told me a very important truth about yourself."

"What?" she said, concerned at what she might have given away.

"That's for me to know and you to find out," he sing-songed. He swept up her hand and dashed to yet another corner of the vast loft space. Grabbing up an instant camera, he pointed it at Stevie and took two pictures. "I'll call these 'Before,'" he said, "but I think the 'After' will be ever so much more interesting."

Before Stevie could question his meaning, he'd pulled her on to a new situation—in front of a gumball vending machine filled with little Crackerjack prizes. "Got a nickel?"

Stevie shook her head, disappointed. But Samson simply opened the top and fished inside with his hand. "That's the fun of being in charge," he said. "I get to do anything I want." He pulled out a tiny yellow metal ring with a red stone. "Here," he said, slipping it on Stevie's pinky. "Call it a friendship ring, from me to you. Wear it always. Promise?"

"Promise," she said, and meant it.

"Now," he said with as much solemnity as if departing on an ocean voyage, "I must leave you."

"Can't I come too?" Stevie wanted more than anything to linger in Samson Love's enchanted hideaway, to be in his joyfully playful presence.

"Not tonight, Pretty Stevie," he said softly. "Adieu." He put his palm to his lips, then blew her a kiss. A moment later, he was gone. Exactly, Stevie imagined, as Peter Pan would fly off to Never-Never Land.

A hand touched Stevie's shoulder, and she jumped. It was Paul Maxwell, the man who'd let them into the Where-house.

"Having fun?" he asked.

Had Samson sent him to check up? Fun, Samson had

said, was the most important thing. . . . "Yes, thanks . . . the most ever."

"You seem very young. Do your parents know you're here?"

The question annoyed Stevie on every level, and she ignored it, turning to walk away.

Maxwell caught her by the arm. "If I were you, I'd leave right now and never come back," he said abruptly, as though she'd said something to make him angry.

"Well, you're not me," she snapped, "and furthermore, you don't know a damn thing about me!"

"Oh, but I will," he answered with a smugness that made Stevie want to slap him. "Stay in this playground, and I'll know everything about you. Just ask your friend Pip . . . if she really is your friend."

He let go of her then, and Stevie looked wildly around, feeling somewhat lost. Then Pip materialized. She could see Stevie was upset. "What's wrong?"

"That man—he's a creep," Stevie answered decisively.

"Paul's harmless. The worst thing he's ever done is squander his inheritance. His problem is that he wishes he were Samson, that's all. . . ."

"I don't care," Stevie cut in. "I just didn't want him to . . . to spoil it all."

Pip gave Stevie a quick hug. "Isn't Samson great? I told you he'd like you, and he did. You're invited back . . . officially!"

"Is that his real name?" Stevie asked tentatively, not knowing if it was all right to raise such a question.

"You must be joking." Pip laughed. "Samson's his own invention, from the ground up. His and his plastic surgeon's."

"Really?" Stevie was enthralled by the idea of a man manufacturing himself. If she could make herself over, she wondered, exactly what changes would she make?

Suddenly it occurred to her that Samson could tell her, if only she could stay his friend.

As he left the freight elevator on the top level of the Wherehouse, Samson Love opened a door heavily carved with mythical figures that looked as if it had been taken from a church. "Abandon Yourselves, Ye Who Enter Here," said words carved across the top.

Within, the walls were covered with quilted mylar, giving the appearance of a silvery mattress. The furnishings were few but carefully chosen—a twenty-foot U-shaped black sectional sofa, dozens of black and red cushions scattered alongside marble tables on highly polished hardwood floors. The lighting was low, the air was thick with smoke, and the atmosphere was heavy here, as if the thick black drapes that shrouded the floor-to-ceiling windows had never been opened, the place hermetically sealed against everything that prevailed outside these doors.

A twenty-thousand-dollar sound system provided the music to which a dozen or so couples danced, not so much with the beat as through it, in a stylized slow motion to rhythms heard only inside their heads. The couples were in various stages of undress, some completely naked. Samson gave them a perfunctory glance, no more. He'd seen it before, he'd seen it all before.

Out of the corner of his eye, he noticed one of his cameramen filming. At Samson's behest, his crew worked almost every night, rolling the cameras on every kind of happening that took place in the Wherehouse, not just those Samson personally orchestrated. Out of the millions of feet of film, he cut and shaped the movies—six, to date—that had at first been intended for his private collection but had since become part of his public body of art.

Samson moved in the direction of the camera. Through the semidark mist, he saw two young men, one white, the other black, naked except for their jock straps, reclining on a section of couch, oiling one another's bodies. The bodies were beautiful and well-exercised; the play of light, the gleam of oil, might provide some usable footage, he thought. He watched a while longer, as the white man began to kiss the other's body. The jock straps began to bulge, and the two men writhed together unselfconsciously, as if no one else were in the room. Samson's interest waned. Sex interested him only in its artistic permutations. Alas, he thought, most people didn't have enough imagination to make it physically compelling, let alone artistically worthwhile.

Moving in the direction of his private quarters, he paused to check the Wherehouse's Roman Bath, equipped with a whirlpool tub that could hold eight people, its walls covered with a primitive graffiti that looked like erotic cave drawings. It had been described in the press as "decadent," but nothing very remarkable was going on now; the tub was occupied by a single couple sharing an opium pipe, as the bubbling waters swirled around them.

Samson walked on through a door into his private quarters. The colors here were muted, the floors scattered with custom carpets, his favorite paintings woven into the design. His custom-made bed, which measured some ten feet by fifteen, was covered with a fluffy white fur throw. The atmosphere of the room resembled the innermost recesses of a cocoon.

Flopping down on the bed, he played with his Etch-a-Sketch, moving the controls, making funny cartoon pictures. Abruptly, he tossed the toy aside and rubbed his eyes like a small boy up past his bedtime. He *was* tired; but worse, he was bored. Opening a refrigerator concealed behind an enormous blowup of a Tarzan movie poster, he took a bottle of cream soda and poured it into a Flintstones mug. Then he reached for the World's Fair souvenir box that sat by his bed. Removing the lid, he ran his fingers through the rainbow assortment of pills and powders and syringes, and chose a large green tablet. He dropped it into the soda, stirred the solution with his finger, and drank. Then he pushed a button on a bedside panel, dimming the lights. He couldn't bear total darkness, any more than he could bear total quiet, even when he needed to sleep . . . these reminded him too much of death.

At last, he took off the evening's costume. Lying nude —in his birth state, as he thought of it—he settled himself comfortably against a nest of pillows. This had been a desperately dull evening, he thought idly—saved by that one bright moment with the pretty girl Pip had brought. He liked her, liked the fact that she was impressed with him without being completely taken in. His mind began to form a picture of what he could make of the raw material that was Pretty Stevie Knight. He detected, better than any psychiatrist or psychic, the most secret, private thing about Pretty Stevie Knight—a secret that, artistically speaking, was the single thread that wove itself into his best relationships. Before . . . and after. He toyed with the idea of what he could create with Pretty Stevie as his "canvas."

Comforted by the thought of such play to look forward to, he prepared for sleep. Pressing another button on the nearby panel, he brought a screen down from the ceiling and activated the projector. The reel he'd chosen for tonight began to unfold on the screen—a story Samson considered far more meaningful than the Bible as a parable of good and evil. Through half-closed eyes, waiting for the comfort of sleep, the artist watched Bugs Bunny bedevil Elmer Fudd.

3

Two days after the party, Patrick took a phone message for Stevie while she was on her lunch break from Grandma's Attic: a limousine would pick her up that evening at seven o'clock sharp.

"Was it Samson who called?" Stevie asked eagerly. She had told Patrick all about the party.

"No. Some flunkey."

"Can I borrow something to wear?" Stevie pleaded. "Samson is very particular about the way people look. . . ."

Patrick's nod came slowly, and Stevie turned eagerly to one of the racks. "Kid," Patrick said, trailing along. "This Love guy . . . I've heard things. . . ."

Stevie pulled out a red wool cape with black piping. "Sure, I know you're not deaf, Pat," Stevie said absently. "I've been jabbering about Samson for two days. He's fantas—"

"No, Stevie, I mean . . . well, you know there are people around here who are into the heavy drug scene. They talk about Love. I've heard he's really bad news. And I wouldn't want you to . . . get in over your head, you know?"

Stevie tried to ignore him. She didn't want anything to

spoil the pleasure of knowing Samson. "Hey," she said lightly, "you were the guy who told me to get married and settle down. Well, maybe Samson's my guy. . . ."

Suddenly Patrick vised his hand painfully on her arm and spun her around. His dark eyes drilled into hers. "Dammit, Stevie, listen to me. I *care* about you, get it? Shit, you're just a kid—" Seeing the expression of protest form on Stevie's face, he rushed on. "Sure, sure. You've been through a lot. But Stevie, you're good stuff. You've got guts and brains—use 'em and you can go anywhere. I was thinkin' even, well I might take you in as a partner someday. Fall in with a guy like Love, though, and I don't see it happening. Get sucked into that world—and you'll end up with your head spinning like you're in a mixmaster."

Touched by Patrick's affectionate concern, Stevie smiled. "Thanks, Patrick. But it's okay. I don't know what you've heard, but Samson's just like a big kid. He likes to play, that's all. It's all fun for him. People, his art. I'll bet tonight he takes me . . . to the zoo or a playground or to buy ice cream."

"You think so. . . ." Patrick said almost mockingly.

"I know it. And Patrick, I've been so down and lonely in this city, I want to have fun, too."

Patrick shook his head slowly in submission. "Okay, kid. But the minute it stops being fun, get out, huh?"

"Sure. Why wouldn't I?"

He paused, as if about to give her an answer. But then he started away, calling over his shoulder, "See those dyed alligator boots that just came in? They'll look great with the cape."

When Samson came that night, the limousine took them directly to Madison Square Garden where, for the next two hours, they cheered their heads off at a Knicks game. Afterward, Samson took Stevie down to the dressing room and introduced her to Red Holtzman as "my long-lost baby sister."

Every night for the rest of the week was almost as she'd predicted—fun, childish fun. Stevie felt as if she'd been given an "open sesame" to an enchanted kingdom, one that transported her far from her drab workday and the dinginess of East Seventh Street to new and different playgrounds every night.

On Tuesday, her horoscope was cast by Samson's personal astrologer, Charmaine. When Stevie's "stars" were pronounced compatible with Samson's, he solemnly declared Pretty Stevie Knight to be a Wherehouse Regular, then took her to his favorite ice-cream parlor to celebrate with banana splits. On Wednesday, they went to the opening night of a new musical starring Lauren Bacall, and to the cast party later at Sardi's. Though it was Samson, with his striking appearance and unmistakable plumage, that people strained to see when they were together, Stevie felt that she, too, was a tiny star of sorts, illuminated by his brilliant glow. The following morning, there was a photograph in the *Daily News* of Samson next to Bacall, with Stevie on his other side. The caption identified her only as Samson Love's "beautiful companion." Still, savoring even that thin taste of what fame must be like, Stevie felt transformed like Cinderella—yet with a wonderful difference: when midnight came for her it was only an intermission, not an ending.

Thursday night's amusement was an ice-hockey game—cheering and heckling at the top of their lungs. And on Friday, Samson conferred the very highest of honors; summoning Stevie to a private Chinese dinner at the Wherehouse, he announced that she would be his date for the gala opening night of his new show at the Castelli Gallery. Then he took her to his costume room. Standing Stevie before a wall-size mirror, he rifled through the floor-to-ceiling racks and shelves, rejecting one beautiful dress after another. Watching him, Stevie was astonished at the number of expensive garments he simply tossed aside.

"Where did all these things come from?" she asked.

"I'm a collector, Pretty Stevie," he said with pride. "If something's beautiful, I acquire it. Sometimes it's useful, and sometimes it's simply there to be looked at and admired. Ah . . . !" He held up a priceless gown made entirely of black maribou feathers. Without a moment's hesitation, he grabbed up a pair of shears and sliced the gown nearly in half, leaving only the tiniest of minis.

"There," he said with satisfaction, "now we need a wrap." From a long rack of furs, he chose a white ermine cape. "Dramatic, don't you think? Just the thing for an opening." And so it went, assembling an outfit that included black silk stockings, black suede shoes—he seemed to have everything in different sizes—and finally, a rope of pearls that hung down to her hips even after it had been tripled over. "That should do it," he said at last.

"And what are you going to wear?"

With his Cheshire-cat smile, Samson repeated one of his favorite homilies. "That's for me to know and you to find out."

"Oh, come on," she groused. "Do you always have to be so much in charge?"

His tone suddenly hardened. "Yes, I do, Pretty Stevie. That's the cardinal rule of the Wherehouse, and don't you ever forget it. First, last, and always, Samson is in charge."

It was so petulantly childish that Stevie almost laughed. But his voice warned that he was deadly serious, and so she gave him an obedient nod.

Having made his point, Samson smiled and patted Stevie's cheek. "Good girl. . . . I believe I will give you a preview of my costume, after all." He disappeared into the recesses of his vast dressing room.

As Stevie waited, she thought suddenly of the Admiral and how much he liked to give orders. But Samson was different. So what if he liked to boss people around? Samson was good to her; he'd done more for her than her parents ever had.

"Voilà!" Samson made his entrance, wearing an antique black tailcoat with a red cummerbund, a white pleated silk shirt fastened with diamond studs, and a black cape lined in red silk. With a grand flourish, he swept the cape over his face, his silver cat's eyes glittering with amusement.

Stevie giggled. "You look like Count Dracula!"

Samson dropped the cape, and for a moment, Stevie was afraid she'd said something wrong. "Hmm, Count Dracula," he mused, "also known as Vlad the Impaler . . . a prince of darkness, deadly but wise . . . a master of the erotic, yet profoundly lonely. I *like* it, Pretty Stevie, I like your notion very much." Snatching up Stevie's hand, he kissed it—and then bit her soundly on the wrist.

"Ouch!" she yowled, less hurt than amused. "Cut that out, or I'll put a stake through your heart!"

"Ah, but first you have to find it. And if you could, death might almost be artistically interesting, an authentic epiphany. Then if I die"—quickly he corrected himself—"*when* I die . . . of course I must die, just like everyone else . . . I'd like to be buried just as the pharaohs were, in a great pyramid above the ground, with all my toys and all my pleasures around me . . . and all my friends. Would you be buried with me, Pretty Stevie? Would you keep me company in the netherworld?"

Suddenly he seemed so utterly forlorn that Stevie ached to comfort him. "Of course," she said, stroking his hair. "I love you, Samson."

He glared at her. "No," he barked. "No . . . don't ever do that, Pretty Stevie."

Confused by his reaction, Stevie thought Samson must have misunderstood, perhaps imagined she was coming on to him. "I didn't mean it *that* way," she explained, "I just meant I love you . . . the way I love Pip."

He shook his head. "I know what you meant. . . . Don't love either of us if you can help it."

"But what's wrong with loving you and Pip?"

Samson shrugged, as if he'd tired of the conversation. "Let's just say it would be better artistically if you simply adored me and obeyed my every command."

Stevie fell silent. Sometimes it seemed that everyone at the Wherehouse spoke some private dialect, like children with made-up words and rituals. As much as she wanted to crack the code, she often felt that Samson—and even Pip —were talking to themselves, rather than to her.

"God, I'm depressed!" Samson wailed. "Why on earth did you ever start talking about love and death—such miserable, depressing things? All I wanted to do was dress up and have some fun, and now you've gone and ruined it all. I thought you were my friend."

Stevie listened in silence to Samson's ravings, astonished at the complete reversal of mood. A little while ago, they'd been trying on clothes and laughing, and now he was mournful and peevish—and blaming her!

"Well, don't just sit there like a lump," he said finally. "Either go home or make yourself useful!"

The words hurt, yet she swallowed them. All right, she thought, Samson was an artist; that made him different in ways that were difficult to comprehend. She, of all people, ought to be tolerant of being different. "What can I do?"

"Make a party," he said. "I want a party right now. Call Pip, tell her to round up some people. . . . She'll know what to do."

In less than an hour the Wherehouse was transformed. Stevie marveled at the number of people, even famous people, who would drop everything and answer Samson's summons.

Though people were dancing and drinking, apparently enjoying themselves, this party was different from the first Wherehouse party she'd attended, much less playful, darker and more intense. The mood of Samson's guests seemed to reflect his own feelings.

Within a very short time, the air was dense and smoky yellow in color. The first batch of "Dreamland Express" disappeared quickly from the punch bowl, as if the guests were impatient to abandon their inhibitions and fly to another planet.

"Is our little boy cranky?" Pip asked when she arrived.

"I don't know what he is," Stevie answered honestly. "All of a sudden he got so . . . angry, and I couldn't imagine what I said—"

"It wasn't you," Pip cut in. "That's just Samson in one of his Jekyll-and-Hyde moods."

The explanation wasn't completely reassuring. Stevie didn't like to think that, for no good reason, Samson could be her friend one minute, than act like a cruel stranger the next. She held her breath when she saw him prowling the loft restlessly. It came as a relief when, coming toward her, he favored her with one of his sweet smiles. "Would you like to dance, Pretty Stevie?"

She nodded and moved toward him, but his eyes had shifted to searching the corners of his private kingdom. "Ah, yes," he murmured, "I think Paul will do very nicely," and with a languid wave of his arm, he summoned Paul Maxwell. "I have high hopes for Paul," he said, "I think he has great potential . . . just as you do, Pretty Stevie."

Paul didn't seem to think it strange when Samson told

him to dance with Stevie, so she allowed herself to be led onto the floor as Samson moved aside to watch. Paul danced well; the longshoreman's body moved gracefully, and Stevie tried to match her movements to his.

"I've had my eye on you," Paul said, running his hand along her bare arm.

Stevie suppressed a shudder.

"Samson thinks we'd make an interesting couple," Paul went on. "I think so too."

Stevie started to say something rude, then held back. Why insult Paul Maxwell? Did it matter what he thought? She could put her own limits on what she would do to please Samson. She closed her eyes and tuned Paul's face out, bumping and swaying to the syncopated rhythms of the Wonders' newest song, snapping her fingers as Kanda Lyons wailed: "Say you love me, why you hurt me, uh-huh, uh-huh . . ."

When she opened her eyes, she saw that Pip had joined them, making a threesome, tossing her copper hair with abandon, her black eyes glistening with excitement. When the music segued into a slower dance tempo, she pulled Stevie away, flicking a "see you later" wave in Paul's direction.

"Come with me, Stevie. . . . Samson's sharing, and you've been summoned."

Stevie followed silently, feeling like a novice on her way to some mysterious pagan initiation rite. She didn't understand what Pip had said, but if it meant sharing some new experience with her friends, she couldn't refuse.

Samson's private quarters were quiet, soundproofed against the party noise and the music. He was wearing a nightshirt, and was cushioned against a nest of pillows. He patted the place on either side, indicating Pip and Stevie should join him. Without a word, he opened a large tin box decorated with scenes from the World's Fair logo and offered it to them. Pip helped herself to an Eskatrol and swallowed it with a glass of champagne from a silver cooler.

"What's your pleasure, Pretty Stevie?" he asked.

Stevie stared at the rainbow of drugs. She'd accepted the drinks, even sampled a couple of Pip's pep-up pills when she was tired, but this looked far more serious—tablets and powders and syringes. Stevie stared uncertainly at the assortment.

"Is this your first time?" Samson's tone had brightened. "Then this will be very special." Looking straight into her eyes, he asked quietly, "Do you trust me?"

Stevie nodded.

Samson shoved aside the box and, reaching behind the bed, produced a small metal tank, to which a hose and plastic mask were attached. Slowly, gently, he moved the mask to cover Stevie's face. "Breathe . . . nice and easy. That's right, Pretty Stevie, just keep breathing and wait for the magic."

As if from a distance, she heard a giggle and then a burst of laughter. It was her own voice, and that made her laugh even harder. There was nothing to be afraid of, nothing at all. She felt as if she were floating on air, as if she were lighter than air. She closed her eyes and felt herself soaring higher and higher.

"That's enough," Samson said all too soon, his voice sounding distant and faint. But Stevie didn't protest. She felt so mellow, and he was the magician who had made it happen. Now he was holding a shiny needle, thin and sharp, and he was smiling at her.

"Make a fist," he said. But Stevie couldn't. She was much too relaxed to tighten up, so he had to do it for her. She scarcely felt the jab of the needle.

"Nothing's happening," Stevie said after half a minute. But in the next instant, a golden light exploded in her head, a volcano erupted in her body, heating her blood to boiling, making her insides tingle.

"I envy my Pretty Stevie," Samson said, his voice muffled and far away. "The first time is so special, so unique . . . there's nothing quite like it, not ever again. Pip, show Stevie how much pleasure resides in her own body . . . show your friend how easy it is to fly. . . ."

She felt her clothes being removed—the sensation of her body being bared so incredibly wonderful . . . as if she were a flower ripening, emerging from a bud. Then there were hands, cool hands sliding over her skin, cool like water poured on her petals. God, was she a flower? Stevie opened her eyes to look down at herself, and saw Pip— naked too—bending over, hair hanging down and brushing lightly over her stomach. Samson, like a god, sat farther back, murmuring encouragement and approval. Then she felt Pip's tongue licking at her thighs, then flicking between her legs, drinking the honey from the heart of the flower. "Oh, yes," Stevie crooned, "yes . . ." as if granting permission for everything, forever, for everyone. Her flesh was molten, Pip's hands shaping and forming it into a thousand new and exquisite sensations. No one had ever felt this way before, no one had ever been like she was now, all heat and light and bright, bright colors.

"Oh, God . . . oh, God," her voice cried out in the distance as she began to pulse and throb on the waves of an orgasm that went on and on and on. . . .

Eyes flaring wide, she believed she might see the heart of the universe. But looking up into the darkness above her, there was Samson, floating above her and Pip—like the vampire Prince of Darkness hovering in midair.

4

Stevie trudged through the dirty snowbanks, her breath making white puffs in the winter air. Pip had offered to pick her up in a limousine, but although Stevie had the large bag to carry, tonight she relished the walk, a chance to take in the colored lights and holiday decorations that brightened the downtown streets with their message of brotherhood and love. How far she had come, Stevie thought, from that night a year ago when she'd been nothing but a friendless runaway.

As she approached the Wherehouse building, Stevie smiled at Samson's own special decoration—an enormous wreath over the street entrance with a large plastic finger pointing straight out of the middle, and a blinking neon sign beneath that proclaimed: "Peace On Earth—This Means You!"

The red metal door to Level One of the Wherehouse was wide open, and the sound of Christmas carols floated sweetly into the hallway. The scene that met Stevie's eyes was like every child's dream of a perfect Christmas. The entire loft had been decked with evergreen garlands. A majestic Douglas fir, at least twenty feet tall, stood in the center, adorned with red ribbons and thousands of twinkling white lights that looked like real candles. Elaborately wrapped gifts were heaped around the tree in merry profusion. Off to one side, Samson's electric train chugged along on its miniature track, and to the other, a holiday buffet had been set up, a feast of turkey and ham and game birds, salads and breads, cakes and pies, all stunningly arranged over a bright red linen cloth. The windows facing Mercer Street had been thrown open. Oblivious to the cold, the Wherehouse Regulars were lined up, singing carols to the accompaniment of a piano and violin, their voices so clear and lovely that Stevie's eyes welled with tears.

"Stevie!" Pip called in greeting, running over to give her a welcoming hug.

"Where's Samson?" Stevie asked.

"Dressing up to make an entrance, what else?" Pip laughed.

Stevie left her gifts near the tree and joined the singers at the window. As she took up the chorus of "We Wish You a Merry Christmas," she looked around at the select group that had been invited, feeling the warmth of their camaraderie. How lucky she was to be one of Samson's chosen. How different this was from the awful base parties over which Irene and the Admiral had presided.

Just as the carolers launched into "Santa Claus Is Coming to Town," Samson appeared, dressed as Kris Kringle himself and perched atop an old-fashioned sleigh drawn by two men in reindeer costume.

"Merry Christmas!" he sang out. "Merry Christmas, children. You've all been very, very good, so gather 'round and see what Santa's brought you!"

A thrill came over Stevie that she'd never felt as a child. For her, Christmas in the Admiral's house had meant one or two store-wrapped necessities masquerading as gifts, a new blouse, a few pairs of socks. But this . . . oh, *this* was Christmas. Stevie helped herself to a cup of steaming-hot punch and sat cross-legged on the floor near the tree, as Samson began pulling packages from his sack of gifts. "Well, right off the bat, here's one for our Pip," he said. "A little birdie told Santa it's just what you wanted."

Pip tore open the wrappings and squealed with delight when she found a gold Cloisonne pillbox exactly like the one Samson used—and which Pip had often admired aloud.

He went on calling out names—many the special nick-names he gave to all the Wherehouse Regulars. "A special gift for my old friend, Paul Maxwell. . . . And here's one for Baby Helen. Santa hopes it brings you good luck with your new album. . . . And this is for Robin Hood. . . ."

Stevie squirmed impatiently, then leaped to her feet when Samson called her name. "For Pretty Stevie," he said softly as he handed her a long, white rectangular box tied with a red satin ribbon. "Santa knows you had to wait a long time for this, and he's sorry. . . ."

Slowly, wanting to make every moment last, Stevie opened the box. And there, nestled in a bed of pink tissue, was the most beautiful doll Stevie had ever seen, the face made of delicate porcelain, with exquisitely fine features and soft blond hair. The dress was pink organza, trimmed with tiny handmade flowers and matching pink ribbons; the little shoes were handmade of fine, white kid and fastened with mother-of-pearl buttons.

Had she ever owned such a beautiful toy? All she could recall was a tiny rubber baby doll that had been "confis-cated" by the Admiral because she'd forgotten sometime to say "please" or "thank you"—she couldn't remember which.

She looked at Samson, her eyes full of wonder. "How did you know?" she said in an astonished whisper.

"I told you." He smiled. "I know all your secrets."

"Thank you," she said simply, but it carried the reverence of prayer.

When the treasures from Santa's sack were all distributed, Stevie picked up the presents she'd brought from under the tree, wishing they could be more. Shyly, she gave Samson the gift she'd found in a small Bleecker Street antique shop. She held her breath while he unwrapped it, and sighed with relief when he smiled. It was a miniature Rolls-Royce, a vintage model just like the one in his first important painting.

"It's perfect!" he exclaimed, "absolutely perfect!"

Turning to Pip, Stevie presented an antique scarf she'd found at Grandma's Attic—silk the exact color of Pip's hair, artfully embroidered in white with the letter *P*.

As always, Pip was generous to Stevie, in her appreciation and in her own gift—a pair of onyx earrings set in gold.

"Oh, Pip," Stevie said, "I'll never be able to thank you enough. Not just for the earrings . . . for everything. This is my best Christmas ever, and you—"

"Stop!" Pip commanded, putting her hands over her ears. "I *hate* all this cheap sentiment."

Stevie pretended to zip her lips.

Samson shed his white whiskers, popped the cork on the first bottle of champagne, and declared that dinner was served.

It was the early hours of the morning when the last bit of Christmas cake was consumed and the last holiday toast had been drunk. Stevie was watching *A Christmas Carol* on one of the many movie screens Samson had set up. Others were continuously showing such holiday classics as *Miracle on 34th Street* and *It's a Wonderful Life*. Stevie thought she might watch one or two of the others. She didn't want tonight ever to end.

Suddenly, in the darkness, someone poked her shoulder. She looked around and saw Samson, still wearing his Santa costume. "We have some naughty business, you and I," he whispered very low, signaling her to follow him on tiptoe.

She imagined he was taking her to his private quarters. Though it didn't happen every time, there had been several more trips upstairs, drugged hours during which Pip or other beautiful women Samson designated—the socialite daughter of one of New York's richest families, the wife of a television star—had made love to her while Samson watched. Stevie never questioned it anymore. She felt some hold on herself being weakened—it wasn't the kind of sex she would have preferred, though the sensations were pleasant—yet it was a small price to pay for the happiness Samson gave her. He was a magician, after all, able to provide the perfect Christmas; he was entitled to ask for his own return of pleasure.

However, when they were in the elevator, he pushed the button to take them down, not up. Stevie said nothing. She had gotten to know Samson well, and there were times, she knew, that he cherished his surprise and preferred not even to be asked to reveal it.

His new Mercedes limousine was waiting outside—bedecked for the season with its own strings of flashing Christmas lights. The chauffeur stepped up and held a lush coat of dark fur for Stevie. It fit perfectly. She gasped and looked at Samson.

"Is this—"

A finger to his lips cut her off, and they stepped into the car.

They drove through the silent streets, heading uptown. A light snow had begun to fall, as if Nature itself were cooperating with Samson to add perfection to his Christmas.

The car stopped finally in front of a building that was unknown to Stevie. The chauffeur popped the trunk open and Samson got out, motioning Stevie to follow. They went around to the back, where Samson donned his false whiskers again before lifting a big white sack from the trunk. There was a second sack, which Samson indicated Stevie should carry.

"Let's go," he said.

"What's this about?" Stevie asked. As long as she was going to carry this heavy bag, she didn't see any reason to rein in her curiosity.

"Business," Samson said, "Santa business. And you're my little helper."

As soon as they entered the big building, Stevie realized it was a hospital—which one she didn't know. Bellevue, or another of the big ones. The lights in the lobby were dim; a single security guard sat at the front desk, a cup of coffee off to one side as he read a newspaper. Only then— from a large clock on the wall—did Stevie realize it was four in the morning.

"Merry Christmas, Pete," Samson called out.

"Merry Christmas to you, Mr. Love. It's that time of the year again," he said with a chuckle, "and here you are, just like clockwork. Go right on up. The floor nurse will be expecting you."

They went up to the fifth floor and got off. The sign above the nurse's station said "Pediatrics." Without fuss or fanfare, Samson wished the floor nurse a merry Christmas and handed over his sack of gifts. Stevie automatically did the same. "The red paper is for the girls, the green is for the boys—and the white packages are unisex," he explained.

The nurse was starting to gush her thanks when Samson

grabbed Stevie's hand and made a hasty exit into the waiting elevator.

"That's such a sweet thing to do," Stevie said. "But why don't you deliver the presents yourself, when the kids are awake?"

"The fantasy of Santa Claus is much more interesting than Samson Love in a costume."

Stevie thought this over, and when they were back in the car, she said: "You left the hospital in such a rush, Samson. It's almost like you're . . . embarrassed to have anyone see you doing a good deed."

"It's not a good deed, Stevie. It's just my form of blackmail. If I'm a saint, maybe my luck will hold. . . ."

"Why can't you just say it's a nice thing to do?" she insisted. "Why not give yourself credit for it?"

Samson laughed, his false stomach shaking. "Oh, Pretty Stevie, that's priceless. I've been accused of many things, but modesty isn't one of them. I play Santa because it's fun. And remember: fun is—"

"The most important thing in the world," she chimed in. "But I still say you're a fake."

"Of course I'm a fake," he agreed. "And only I know how much. . . . Or would you like to see, too, Pretty Stevie? Can the fake show you something very real . . . ?" Without waiting for an answer, he tapped on the glass partition and gave the driver some instructions. And then he slumped back into his seat, his festive mood strangely dissipated.

The car sped through the Lincoln Tunnel, then traveled along Route 17 for almost an hour. It left the main highway, passed through a closed and shuttered main street, then drew up near a shabby gray frame house. The lights were all out, except for a string of multicolored bulbs that surrounded the front door, blinking on and off.

"There," he said, "is that real enough? My childhood home, if you can call it that. It's the place where I went to sleep at night and got up in the morning and wished I were dead. It looks innocent enough, doesn't it, Pretty Stevie? But if I were ever to paint a picture of hell, that's what it would look like. I could tell you stories," he said. "Yes, I could tell you stories. . . ."

Stevie took his hand, which was icy cold though the car was quite warm. It was as if she were revisiting her own childhood home, which looked innocent enough, too, yet for her, had been a prison, and often a kind of hell. "You don't have to tell me any stories," she said softly. "I understand, Samson, I really do."

"I knew you would. That's why I brought you. We're kindred spirits, Pretty Stevie. . . . That's why I've let you see what no one else has ever seen. I'll probably regret this tomorrow, and perhaps I'll even be angry with you, but sometimes it's lonely to have no past, and sometimes . . ."

Stevie tried to put her arm around him, but he shook it away. Yet of everything Samson had given her, she felt somehow most touched by this gift of his trust. She wanted to say something to ease the pain he tried so hard to hide.

"You don't need a past anymore, Samson. You have such a glorious present . . . and future. And what's out there, the pain it caused you, that's not reality anymore . . . that's ancient history. You're somebody different now, someone talented and successful and important. No one can hurt you anymore."

He touched her face in the darkness. "Ah, sweet Stevie," he said, "that's the biggest lie of all. Don't ever believe it . . . or you will be hurt over and over again."

He told the chauffeur to take them home, then he curled into a corner and dozed.

But Stevie couldn't sleep. She was thinking of what she

had said to Samson, and wondering if it could be true for her too. Was the pain of the past ancient history? Was she someone different now?

As they came back into the city, a pink dawn light was tinting the sky. The night was over. Her perfect Christmas already seemed to have happened long ago.

5

"How did you dare?" Samson raged at Stevie, waving a copy of the latest *Village Voice* in her face. "However did you dare say anything about me without my *permission*? I made you special, Pretty Stevie, and I can make you disappear if you think you can break my rules whenever you please!"

It was a Sunday afternoon, and Samson had called her to the Wherehouse, saying they were to have an intimate brunch—just the two of them and Pip. But she had barely come through the door when he had brought out the paper and begun to attack her.

Stevie was as terrified by his anger today as she had ever been by the Admiral's. Perhaps even more, because her father's she had been able to predict, to prepare for. Samson's rages seemed to come almost from nowhere. One minute they'd be the best of friends, and in the next he'd be a furiously threatening stranger.

And in another way this was worse. She'd been able to leave the Admiral, to run away. But she was inextricably bound to Samson. He had given her so much that she was afraid to lose.

In the past two months he had remade her life. She was

indeed his creation now, as much as one of his paintings or sculptures. It had started with the command, at his New Year's Day party, that she must give up her job. He could not have one of his Wherehouse Regulars, he said, being an "ordinary shopgirl."

"But what else can I do?" Stevie had said.

Whereupon, at his signal, one of the other partygoers had blown a fanfare on a trumpet, and Pip had marched in with two of Valentine's men in perfect Italian suits carrying a large trunk. The trunk was thrown open to reveal two dozen of her mother's most expensive fashion creations—stolen, Pip said, gloating, from Valentine's showroom while the designer was vacationing in Jamaica.

At once a helter-skelter photographic modeling session had begun, all orchestrated by Samson. For three hours, he had dressed Stevie in Valentine's clothes, made up her face with a succession of dramatic glittery eyeshadows and lipsticks, and posed her with other guests, in his fire engine, with his sculptures, and finally nude, on his bed—with a few of his large stuffed animals in somewhat suggestive positions. Stevie raced through it all unquestioningly, only half aware, but with eyes bright with thanks for the amphetamines that Samson doled out to her from his World's Fair box. At the same time, he also kept the movie cameras rolling.

In the succeeding days, Samson had cajoled his many contacts at the fashion magazines to look at the photographs, certain that they would be enthusiastically convinced to use Stevie as a model—which they were. Within two weeks, Samson had also arranged for his art film, "Stevie's Session," to begin showing at a small downtown theater. Literally overnight, she was a celebrity herself, as Samson had wanted. The film was still running, with lines around the block; and her first magazine cover shot had been rushed onto the stands.

But if he could make her overnight, then Stevie had no doubt that his claim was true: he could break her at will, turn the fairy-tale princess back into a toad. The Admiral had never been able to destroy her, or take away a dream. But Samson could.

"Listen, please," Stevie cried now, "I didn't know that guy was a reporter. I was looking at some clothes at a place in Soho, and he was there with his girlfriend, and he recognized me. We talked only ten minutes, and I didn't know what I said would get printed. I'm really sorry if any of it—"

"Sorry doesn't do it for me, Pretty Stevie," Samson declared coldly. "I don't forgive and I never forget."

"Oh, lighten up, Samson," Pip cut in, grabbing the offending paper from his hand and scanning the brief article that described Stevie as the artist's newest underground superstar. "Hell, there's nothing here to be mad at! All Stevie said was what you always say yourself—that you're responsible for her modeling career and you make all her artistic and creative decisions." Pip lifted the paper and read the final paragraph of the article out loud: "Pretty Stevie Knight, as Samson calls her, is as much his creation as Mr. Love himself. They both seem to have no past, at least not one this reporter can attest to with any degree of accuracy. It's all enough to make people ask whether Samson Love isn't a con man as much as an artist. He may have moved beyond pop art to invent a whole new genre—call it con art." Pip tossed the paper aside. "That's what really put the bug up your ass, isn't it? Those little potshots the reporter took at you."

Samson advanced on Pip, glowering, but she held her defiant pose. Stevie waited for the explosion that was bound to come. No one challenged Samson and got away with it.

But suddenly Samson burst out laughing. "Dear Pip," he

said, "always telling it like it is. Don't ever change, not even for me." He turned to Stevie. "And you, pretty one. Of course, I'll give you another chance. But the *next* time you feel like playing Miss Celebrity, call me first."

The crisis was over. As if it had never happened, Samson donned an apron and prepared brunch for them personally, blinis with *crème fraîche*, caviar, and smoked salmon, each capped by a different-colored pill like the cherry on a sundae —all washed down with Dom Perignon champagne.

Later, when Samson insisted on washing the dishes alone, Stevie took Pip aside and thanked her for coming to her rescue. "I was really shaking," she said. "I thought I might lose it all."

"Don't worry about it, Stevie. You can't. You've got something of your own now."

Stevie smiled, as if at a polite compliment. She couldn't believe that Samson couldn't break her as easily as she'd seen him shatter one of his plaster sculptures when it dissatisfied him. Then Stevie asked a question that had been growing in her mind at the same rate as Samson's influence over her had increased. "Pip . . . how come you're not afraid of Samson? I mean, when he's mad like this, everyone else backs off. But you never do."

Pip thought for a moment. "I guess I've never had a reason to be afraid of anyone—because I know my bogeymen are all in here." Pip tapped her head with one long tapered finger. "And they're so much worse, Stevie. I keep wishing they were as easy to stare down as Samson is."

The answer puzzled Stevie, since she had seen little to indicate Pip had any deep fears or insecurities—and she supposed that no one was closer to Pip. In any case, having to deal with private fears didn't seem so terrible to Stevie. Pip's probably had something to do with being ignored too much by her mother, and her father's having died when she was very young. Stevie's had sprung from the Admiral, and she had finally mastered them. But she wished she had some formula, as Pip said she did, for being unafraid of Samson.

In spite of Pip's defense, Samson didn't completely forgive Stevie's misstep. In the weeks that followed, he made a point of asserting his control over her at every opportunity. He gave her a five-page spread in his own *At* magazine, yet refused to allow Stevie to appear on a local talk show. He allowed her to accept a *Harper's Bazaar* cover job because he wanted a favor from the publisher, yet he refused permission for three other lucrative assignments, saying they offered the wrong kind of exposure. Stevie couldn't decide if he was punishing her or sensibly managing her career.

Then she was asked to appear—as herself—in a movie that was to be shot in New York. The part was small, the money modest, but the director was Calvin Knowles, the twenty-five-year-old whose first picture the year before had earned Luke James an Academy Award nomination. It was Knowles himself who telephoned Stevie.

"I like your face and your image," he said. "I think your underground persona would give authenticity to the downtown scenes in my picture."

When Stevie hesitated, Knowles added persuasively, "This could be a real showcase for you, a chance to break into feature films. Once you're started, Stevie, I think you could be a star."

"Can I think about it and let you know?" Stevie responded. "I . . . I'm just not sure I'll be free," she stalled, not wanting to say that the decision had to be Samson's.

"Okay, take a week, ten days. I'll have my secretary check with you. And if it'll help you make up your mind, we wouldn't need you for more than four or five days of shooting."

* * *

"It's an interesting idea," Samson said when Stevie brought the offer to him. "Pretty Stevie as herself. But Calvin Knowles? He's a commercial hack, Stevie, without any . . . vision. Do you really want to put yourself in the hands of someone like *that*?"

Stevie knew nothing about the nuances of directing—though it was obvious that Samson held himself up as a standard of genius. "I just thought the job might be fun," she answered cautiously, certain that it was best not to let Samson know how much she actually craved the opportunity with Knowles.

"Well, then," Samson said with a smile, "if you see the possibility for fun, I'll try to put my personal distaste for Mr. Knowles aside and consider whether any real harm can come of your working in his picture."

A week later, however, Samson brushed aside Stevie's request for an answer. And two weeks after that, Knowles's office informed her he couldn't wait any longer, and Stevie pleaded for a decision.

"I think not," Samson said. "I don't want Mr. Knowles undoing the results of my creativity and cluttering your mind with misinformation about acting."

"But Samson," Stevie complained, "it's only a small part, a few days' work. You said yourself there might not be any harm . . ."

"I've decided not to take the risk," he said. "Perhaps if you'd been a good girl, Pretty Stevie, I might have said yes, but as it is, you still owe me some penance, and I'm exacting it now."

Stevie could feel no anger, no emotion but mere dejection. Samson had created her. If he said she owed him penance, perhaps it was true.

But then he did another of his inexplicable turnabouts, and sent her spirits soaring. "In any case," he said brightly, "you won't have time for another project. Because I've just arranged financing for *my* new film—my first full-length extravaganza. And, of course, my Pretty Stevie, you will be my star."

She gazed at him gratefully.

"But of course, you deserve it," Samson said. "After all, the picture was practically your idea. . . ."

While Samson became totally immersed in complicated preproduction plans for his first epic, *Dracula's Dreams*, he paid little attention to Stevie's modeling offers. She was able for the first time to make her own decisions—and her career took off like a myriad of Fourth of July rockets. She had been on the covers of the American magazines, but now the calls came in from all over the world, and Pretty Stevie Knight burst brilliantly on the international modeling scene. One minute she was Samson Love's personal protégée, the next minute she was the darling of a world that craved variety as much as beauty. Where once she had been paid with Samson's approval and his favor, now her slender body, her heart-shaped face, and haunted knowing eyes commanded fees of up to a thousand dollars an hour. Where once her world was the island of Manhattan, suddenly she was being jetted to glamorous and exotic locations around the globe—to Paris and Rome, Hong Kong and Cairo, to Caribbean islands and atolls in the South Pacific.

Yet the brighter her star shone, the more Stevie earned, the less real any of it seemed—the fame, and particularly her sizable earnings, hundreds of thousands of dollars that passed through her hands as if it were play money.

Though Stevie had scant interest in homemaking and spent almost no time alone, she bought a spacious apartment on Central Park South with panoramic views of the city, and had it painted white. In one monumental shopping spree, she spent fifty thousand dollars on furnishings, all in white, accented with glass and chrome and stainless steel, creating a blank canvas—awaiting the imprint of a personality. Without Samson, she thought sometimes, she didn't know what to make of herself or her surroundings. No matter how many things she bought, and how much money she spent, the apartment remained a place without warmth or history, its opulence, bordering on excess, the only clue to the personality of its owner.

One day Stevie came home from a shoot atop the World Trade Center. It had been a breathless experience to be photographed from a helicopter, her hair whipping in the wind, a sheer chiffon negligee cascading around her body. Already in her mind's eye, she could see what the photographs would look like—ethereal, unreal, a woman perched on the tallest building in the country in her nightclothes. The world did seem to function a lot by Samson's dictum: paint a pretty enough picture and to hell with reality.

As Stevie stepped from her limousine, a doorman approached and deferentially picked up the crocodile cosmetic case that held the tools of her trade. "Miss Knight," the doorman said, "there's someone to see you. She arrived this morning, right after you left . . . and she's been sitting in the lobby ever since. Won't tell me who she is or why she's come."

A fan? Stevie wondered. Another of those sweet young girls who worshiped her success and came to see up close what the fantasies she represented looked like? She walked into the lobby, past the wall of mirrors and the doorman's station.

In an alcove beside the concierge's desk, sitting erect on the reproduction Louis XVI sofa, was Irene. Stevie stopped dead, speechless. With total clarity, she understood now why Samson locked out the past. There was no place for reality in his kind of fantasy life.

"Stephanie!" Irene said, leaping up, her faded features suddenly brighter. "Oh, Stephanie, it's been so long. . . ."

As she submitted to her mother's hugs, Stevie was flooded with a kaleidoscope of emotions, a confusion of memories. She had to force herself to lift her arms and return the embrace. But feeling how tiny and frail Irene had become, Stevie felt the old protective instincts return —the ingrained habit of mothering her own mother—and she wrapped her arms tighter around her shoulders.

Irene eased back at last, holding Stevie at arm's length. "Goodness, you've grown up so beautifully. It makes me so happy to see you."

"I'm happy to see you too," Stevie echoed. But there was truth in it, she realized. She linked her arm through her mother's.

"You found me through the magazines . . . ?" Stevie said as they rode the elevator up twenty-two floors to Stevie's apartment.

"Oh, I always knew where you were."

"How?"

"Your father has his connections—naval intelligence, you know," Irene went on.

So they had traced her . . . and yet left her alone. The Admiral had truly written her off. Stevie studied her mother. It seemed an act of courage that, even though she had delayed so long, she had finally made contact.

"I've been watching your career," Irene said. "I started a scrapbook." Shyly she added, "I thought about calling you, telling you how proud I was. But . . . the Admiral . . ." Irene nervously twisted the ever-present lace handkerchief.

"I know," Stevie said.

Her mother's face lit with gratitude for the gift of understanding.

Stevie turned the key in the lock, threw open the door to her apartment, and waited for a reaction. She wasn't disappointed. Irene gasped as she took in the twelve-foot white down-filled sectional, the glitter of glass and mirror, the sheen of white marble, the magnificent sweep of windows that framed the Park. "Oh, my . . . it's so beautiful, Stephanie. I've never seen anything like this."

Stevie took her mother from room to room, showing off the instant luxury with which she had surrounded herself. The canopied bed of stainless steel; the white mink throw carelessly draped over sheets of finest Egyptian cotton; the bathroom with its green onyx whirlpool bath; the adjoining dressing room crammed with dresses and shoes; the white lacquer bar stocked with vintage wines and champagne; the ivory-colored Chinese cabinetry that concealed a television screen that was rarely viewed and a sophisticated stereo system that was rarely heard; the sparkling white kitchen, used almost exclusively for making coffee—instant, at that.

Listening to Irene exclaim over this and that, Stevie felt at once triumphant and disappointed. Her possessions spoke for her. See how much I've accomplished without your help, see how wrong you were not to love me. Yet the moment of triumph couldn't balance the years of heartache.

"Where are your things?" Stevie asked.

"At the Sheraton Hotel."

"I'll send a car to pick them up. I want you to stay here," Stevie said decisively, determined to take control of the situation. New York was her city, not the Admiral's and not Irene's; here, things would be done her way. "Are you hungry?" she asked. "The doorman said you'd been waiting a long time."

"I didn't want to miss you," Irene admitted shyly. "But now that you mention it, a bite to eat would be nice."

"Good. Let me make a couple of calls. I'll take you out to lunch, and then . . . well, I'm sure we'll think of something to do." Stevie telephoned her car service. She asked for one of the largest stretch limousines to come to the house, and a second to go to the hotel for her mother's luggage. Next she phoned her favorite restaurant. "I have a special guest," she said after announcing her name, "so please don't keep me waiting."

Though her own senses had been dulled by months of excess, Stevie savored her mother's response to the chauffeured limousine. Like a parent offering a treat to a child, Stevie turned on the television set—and then distracted Irene from it with a comment on the sights passing by outside. Irene's eyes went several times to the built-in bar, Stevie noticed, to the amber liquid in a stand of crystal decanters. But she never asked for a drink, and Stevie didn't offer. Was it possible, Stevie wondered, that the problem was under control? Did that explain her mother's ability to break away?

At La Côte Basque, the maître d' gave her a cordial greeting. "Your table is ready as you requested, Miss Knight. So nice to see you again. And how is Mr. Love . . . ?"

Irene gawked at the celebrities they passed as they were led to a table, and kept turning to nudge Stevie. "Look, there's Henry Kissinger. . . . And isn't that . . . ?" It delighted rather than embarrassed Stevie, even the irony that her mother seemed totally unaware that her own daughter was attracting as much attention with her entrance as any other famous face in the room.

As Irene glanced through the magenta-covered menu, she gave a murmur of anxiety. "Everything's so expensive, Stephanie. . . ."

Stevie plucked the menu from her mother's hands. "Let me order," she said. "You just relax and enjoy yourself.

"The escargots to start," she told the waiter. "A green

salad for two . . . and then the veal with wild mushrooms. *Saignant*, please."

The sommelier appeared at the table, and Stevie started to wave him off. But Irene said, "Can't we have wine?"

The request was so plaintive that Stevie couldn't bring herself to object. She ordered a split of Cristal.

There was a silence after the wine steward left, as Irene looked here and there, completing her tally of celebrities. It went on so long, however, that Stevie began to suspect that her mother was avoiding conversation—in fact, avoiding a predictable subject. At last, Irene faced her again.

"Stephanie, dear," she began. "You know, your father might—"

Stevie's anger and resentment had been stoked by anticipation. "Don't speak about him to me," she said, seething.

Irene seemed taken aback by the heat of Stevie's response. "All right, Stephanie, don't get angry. Please don't get angry. But maybe later—"

"No. Don't mention him again. Ever."

Irene fell silent, so quickly and obediently that Stevie could only reflect it was her mother's training to take orders.

When the champagne arrived, the cork was popped discreetly, and the bubbly wine poured into slender flutes. Stevie raised her glass. For one awkward moment, she searched for a toast, then simply touched glasses with Irene and took a sip of wine.

She toyed with the food on the beautifully patterned French china, watching Irene as she ate slowly and carefully, using her silverware with practiced precision, like a good little soldier—or sailor—dabbing daintily at her mouth with the corner of her napkin.

As Stevie tried to match the woman beside her to the memories she had stored away in a corner of her mind, she wondered how Irene's life could have remained exactly the same while her own had been so dramatically altered. Why had she allowed the boundaries of her world to be dictated by the Admiral's iron will? Surely, somewhere within her was the capacity for joy, surprise, perhaps even love. . . . Yet there was no sign of it. In her blue dress trimmed with lace, her little beribboned hat, her mousy blond hair done in the tight little curls of a previous decade, Irene was a pathetic study in eternal sameness.

Stevie was struck by an idea. Being created by Samson had taught her something about the malleability of people. . . .

After indulging Irene's wish for dessert with three kinds of mousse—white, chocolate, and Grand Marnier—she called for the check and signed it with a flourish, overtipping as usual. Once outside, she instructed the driver to take them to Bergdorf Goodman's, where they went straight upstairs to the salon for designer dresses. Spotting her favorite saleswoman, Stevie introduced her mother and came right to the point. "We need a new look, Rose," she said. "Something different and exciting. A Norell dress . . . or maybe Scaasi. And a good suit, Valentino perhaps. What do you think?"

The saleswoman studied Irene dolefully. "Well, nothing to do but try," she said with typical New York frankness, and disappeared at once into the recesses of a back room where the finest originals were stored.

Irene submitted like a child to trying on the selection of beautiful clothes Rose picked out, pirouetting before the three-way mirror, her worn cheeks flushed with excitement as she asked Stevie's opinion. With her practiced eye, Stevie approved three pieces: a black gabardine suit, a green taffeta sheath for evening, a simple burgundy crepe that showed off Irene's petite, trim figure. "She'll wear the suit now," Stevie told Rose. "You can wrap the rest."

Irene gasped with shock as she watched Stevie sign the

charge slip without so much as a moment's hesitation. The bill came to almost two thousand dollars. "Stephanie," she protested, "I've never spent more than a hundred dollars for a dress in my life!"

"I know," Stevie said with a smile. "And we ain't finished yet." Leading her mother from one department to the next, she selected shoes, handbags, gloves, and assorted accessories, accumulating an ever-growing pile of packages that were sent outside to the waiting limousine.

When, at last, she left the store, Stevie ordered the driver to take them to Kenneth's Salon on East Fifty-fourth Street. It would have been a short walk, but Stevie was enjoying this new role more than she'd enjoyed any single aspect of her success. With all the fame and money and notoriety, there had been no family to applaud every step she took and to cheer her on. Now it was as if she were ten years old again, hungry for approval, waving a picture she'd drawn or a composition she'd written, begging someone to notice and care.

She touched her mother's hair with professional interest. "You could do with a blunt cut," she said. "And those curls, they're much too tight and . . ."

Irene's fingers flew to the hairdo that hadn't changed in years. "Oh, Stephanie, I don't know about that. . . . a strange hairdresser and—"

"Kenneth does Jackie Kennedy's hair," Stevie cut in. "Don't you think you can trust him to do yours?"

"But we don't have an appointment," Irene fretted. "If he's that important . . ."

"He owes me. I switched from Sassoon, and sent Kenneth thirty new models. Don't worry, he'll take the very best care of you."

It was as Stevie said. Kenneth Battelle welcomed them into his salon, never thinking to tell Stevie that his appointment book for the day was crammed. Irene was led straight to a cubicle, where Kenneth's chief colorist brightened her hair with subtle highlights and Kenneth himself replaced the pin curls of her youth with a stylish bob. At Stevie's instruction, Irene was also treated to an herbal facial and a complete new makeup.

When Irene emerged, she looked ten years younger—and Stevie had spent another $650.

As soon as the two women returned to the apartment, Stevie kicked off her shoes and stretched out on the couch, realizing suddenly how tired she was. She'd awakened at five-thirty, and was completely made up, dressed, and ready for work before seven, so the photographer could catch the early-morning light. But more than fatigue, Stevie was feeling a kind of anticlimax; now that the shopping and spending were over, she didn't know what else she could do for her mother.

"Oh, Stephanie." Irene sighed as she drifted toward the open bar. "This has been the very best time we've ever had together. If only . . ." she trailed off.

Stevie had long ago set aside her own catalogue of "if onlys." But she was tantalized by the manifestation of regret from her mother.

"If only what, Irene?"

". . . we could have done it before."

Stevie tensed. She was reluctant to let reality intrude, knowing it would be better if the visit could be limited to the kind of whirl they'd had this afternoon. Yet she couldn't help setting the record straight. "We couldn't have done this before, Mother—not what we did today. Because I was your child, and I couldn't take *you* nice places, and buy *you* nice things. But, Jesus, you could have done it for me . . . and you never did. Never took me anywhere." Stevie's voice rose to an accusing shout. "Dammit, Irene, I spent sixteen rotten years . . . just waiting for you to be a mother!"

Irene looked back with wounded eyes. Then without a word she turned to the bar—which was, in its way, the answer. Not just for herself, but to Stevie's charges.

Anger boiled up out of Stevie. "That's right!" she screamed. "Do what you always do . . . fix yourself a dainty little drink. What the hell—take the whole damn bottle!"

Staggering from the force of Stevie's sudden attack, Irene did exactly as Stevie said. Her hand closed around a bourbon bottle even as she protested. "But Stephanie, why are you so angry with me? Look how beautifully your life turned out . . . all the wonderful places you go, all the important people you meet."

"What turned out beautifully, Irene?" Stevie demanded, her lovely face tightened by pain as much as anger. "Christ, do you know what my wonderful life is like, what it really is? It's hotel rooms and studios, it's two days here and three days there, letting strangers with cameras love me—letting them take my picture until I could puke. And sometimes, Irene, they don't just want to love me with their camera. Sometimes they want to fuck me, too. And you know what? Usually, I let them, because I'm too damn lonely and too damn tired to say no. That's my goddamn great life, Irene. And there's more—"

"Stop it," Irene whimpered, covering her ears. "Stephanie, please . . ."

But Stevie went on. "I'll admit it could have been worse. In fact, when I got here after the Admiral was through with me, it was a helluva lot worse. But please don't tell me how great everything is . . . and don't think you can sweep everything under the rug the way you always do. Not when the plain, honest truth is that I didn't have a mother. You made me an orphan, Irene—you left me to the tender mercies of that son of a bitch you married!"

In her brand-new finery, Irene stood transfixed in space for a moment, like a butterfly pinned in midair by Stevie's anger. Then she crumpled to her knees, still holding the whiskey bottle as an infant hugs its teddy bear. "Forgive me, Stephanie." She sobbed softly. "Won't you please forgive me? I wanted to be a good mother. I tried . . ."

Stevie turned away and closed her eyes. Her anger spent, she felt as if she were choking in confusion. She couldn't bear the sight of Irene on her knees, yet neither could she give the kiss of forgiveness. She had always known that the whiskey was more important than she was. Yet why did it feel so bad now?

She didn't hear the door open and close; she didn't even know that Irene had risen to walk out, leaving all her gaily wrapped packages behind.

Maybe she'll be back, Stevie thought later that evening as she prepared for bed. After vomiting out the anger she'd harbored for so long, she felt better, lighter somehow. Yet she was worried. . . .

When Irene didn't return, Stevie decided she must have flown back to Virginia. Perhaps she'd ship the gifts that had been so much fun to buy but were now just a nagging reminder of the mother-daughter relationship that had never been.

Two days later, Stevie's telephone rang at a little before midnight. Worn out by a shoot, she had gone to sleep early. She picked up the receiver and murmured a hello.

"Where in tarnation is your mother?" the voice growled without preamble. "She was due back on the plane two hours ago. I sent my driver to the airport. He said she never made her flight. I've been checking with the airline. There was no cancellation. I checked her hotel, and she said her room hasn't been used, that her daughter called for her bags days ago. I want an explanation. Put her on the phone—on the double!"

"But she isn't here. . . ." Stevie answered weakly, unnerved by the sound of the Admiral's voice, by the sudden dark presence that loomed suddenly in her bedroom. "She left on Monday. I thought she went . . . back to Virginia. She's not at the hotel?"

"I told you she's not," he repeated, his voice rumbling with indignation. "Hell, you mean you didn't bother checking on her for two days? That's a lousy way to treat your mother after she made the trip to see you. Christ, Stevie, I've seen some of those pictures where you look so beautiful. But you're no better than you ever were, are you? I won't let you get away with this, though. You'd damn well better find your mother! Call me back ASAP. Do you read me loud and clear?"

"Loud and clear." Stevie hung up feeling as if she were ten years old again, her stomach tied up in knots with worry and anger and fear.

Retreating to the crazy hope that it was a lie, a torture dreamed up by the Admiral, she called the Sheraton Hotel herself. The clerk at the reception desk confirmed that Mrs. Knight hadn't checked out. "But she hasn't used her room, and there's a big bill running up. . . ."

Stevie didn't doubt it now. Something terrible had happened to Irene. She thought of calling the Admiral back, enlisting his help . . . but she couldn't bring herself to make the connection, to hear his voice and to feel his rage.

Instead she called the police and reported Irene missing. As she described her mother, detailing the clothes they'd bought together, the new hairdo and makeup, Stevie's remorse grew. She imagined a dozen calamities . . . a tearful Irene being hit by a car, Irene lying in a hospital, all alone . . .

One by one, she called the city hospitals, but there was no Irene Knight to be found.

Stevie canceled all her bookings for the next few days, ignoring the protests and threats that followed. She accepted no social engagements, so she could be near the telephone day and night. Terrified of hearing from the Admiral again, she answered every ring of the phone in a disguised voice, so she could pretend to be the housekeeper if he should call.

She checked with the police every few hours, begging them to make a greater effort to find her mother, refusing to be comforted by the assurances they gave. "No news is good news," said a Sergeant Paulsen. "She's not in any hospital, and she's not in the—Well, we have every reason to believe she's alive and well."

Two agonizing days passed before Sergeant Paulsen called with news of Irene. "Miss Knight? We have your mother here."

"Thank God! Is she . . . is she all right, Sergeant?"

There was a slight pause. "She's a little shaky right now, but I think she'll be okay in a day or so. Why don't you get right over here and pick her up."

"I'm on my way. Thank you, Sergeant . . . thank you."

Stevie didn't bother to call a limousine. A cab would be faster. She grabbed her purse and ran for the elevator.

When she reached the 12th Precinct station, she ran to the desk sergeant. "I'm looking for Sergeant Paulsen. He said my mother was here . . . Irene Knight. Where is she?"

The officer consulted a ledger, then pointed down a long corridor. Stevie whirled around—and came face-to-face with the Admiral, his face darker than thunder. "You've got some damn nerve, showing up here after all you've done! Turning your own mother into the street . . . not even letting me know if she was dead or alive!"

"But I've been looking for her since you called," she protested. "I found her—"

"You found nothing, you stupid tramp! It was *my* people who found Irene. After what you did to her, you've got a goddamn nerve showing your face here!"

"But what—"

"I told your mother to stay away, but she kept after me. You know the poor woman is delicate. She was in the hospital for a month last year. Do you give a damn? *No!* You break her heart again . . . She damn near killed herself, drinking for two days in some low-down bar—and then getting mugged by some lousy lowlife! We have you to thank for that, Stephanie . . . as if you hadn't already done enough!"

Stevie looked around at the cluster of policemen who were now listening intently to the Admiral's diatribe, but if she had hoped for an ally, there was none. The brotherhood of men in uniform held fast.

"Let me see her," she pleaded. "I just want to make sure she's all right. . . ."

"Hell I will!" he roared. "Just get the hell out of here. And stay away from us if you know what's good for you. If you ever bother either of us again, you'll wish you were dead. Hell, as far as I'm concerned, you *are* dead!"

Reeling from her father's assault, Stevie ran stumbling from the police station. In the street, she clapped her hands over her ears and howled, as though to drown out the cruel words still echoing in her brain. But she could hear them still, would hear them again and again, she knew, for as long as she lived.

6

It was midsummer when Samson's caravan of limousines and equipment vans left New York and headed north to Connecticut. The location he'd promised was an ornate stone castle adorned with gargoyles that sat high on a grassy hill, surrounded by a small moat. Built in the eighteenth century by a shipping czar, it had been boarded up for more than twenty years.

When Samson's scouts had found the place, it had a disconsolate, neglected, almost forbidding air. The swimming pool, added in the 1920s, was full of algae and moss. The once-magnificent grounds hadn't seen a gardener's touch in decades. Inside, however, under thick layers of dust, the splendor of a bygone era remained apparent in the two-story ballroom, the gold-leaf vaulted ceiling, Italian marble floors, broad staircases with carved mahogany banisters, and mysterious tower rooms.

It was the perfect site for Samson's first epic—*Dracula's Dreams*. All it needed to be made ready was the expenditure of a large production budget; and this, too, Samson had for the first time—money raised from rich members and friends of the Wherehouse Regulars. The main house was aired and cleaned, the furnishings refurbished by antique experts. The grounds were cleared and manicured. The pool was cleaned and repaired and filled with water, the pavilion around it repainted and wired for light.

A caterer was hired to provide meals for the company and a cleaning service engaged to clean up after them. And when everything had been readied according to Samson's instructions, the press was invited to a cocktail party on the sweeping front lawn for a briefing on "Samson Love's most ambitious project to date."

"What's the picture about, Samson?" every reporter wanted to know.

"It's a myth and an allegory," he said, standing before them, "a commentary on modern life, if you will. I can't say more, and if you've seen my previous work, you'll know why. A Samson Love picture is a dynamic, living organism. It can't be stuffed into a straitjacket of a script. It simply evolves."

"Is it true you're playing the title role yourself? And if so, what made you decide to face the camera as well as direct?"

"It's true," he said with a self-deprecating shrug, "but the title role is merely symbolic, and I'm attempting it as a growth experience, nothing more. The real stars are Pretty Stevie Knight, who plays Mina; my dear Pip, who plays Lucy; and Paul Maxwell, who plays Dr. Van Helsing."

A few more questions followed, and Samson answered them with a modesty that was, for him, unusual. The reporters lingered long enough to consume the canapés and liquor that had been set out. When they left, Samson declared the remainder of the evening free. "Enjoy your playtime, children," he said, "but get to bed early and take it easy on the pharmaceuticals tonight. I want everyone clearheaded and bright tomorrow morning." And with that, he retired alone to the tower room he'd chosen as his private retreat.

"I don't believe it," Stevie said to Pip. "Early to bed and early to rise? And 'easy on the pharmaceuticals'? Was that our Samson?"

"I do believe our Samson is a wee bit insecure on this one, Stevie. As long as he sticks to no-budget flicks, who can fault him if they're rough around the edges? Now that he's playing with some real money, he's got to deliver something more than just 'interesting'—or look damn foolish. And our Samson would rather die than look foolish. I just wonder where he got all the money.... I love his warped, twisted mind, but I wouldn't spend a penny of my trust fund on an *allegory*, not even for Samson."

Stevie giggled, feeling a little traitorous because she enjoyed the idea of Samson's insecurity.

Just then, Paul Maxwell came up behind her, slipping an arm around her waist. Stevie pulled away, resenting the proprietary touch. "I'm having a party in my room tonight. There's a case of Dom Perignon on ice and lots of the other goodies you like so much. Why don't you and Pip come by . . . about nine o'clock?"

Stevie shook her head. "I plan to be asleep by ten. Didn't you hear what Samson just said?"

"I heard. That's for everybody else, not me."

"You think you're better than everybody else?" Stevie asked sarcastically.

"Not better, just richer . . . and that amounts to the same thing where Samson's concerned. Don't forget, ladies . . . my room, nine o'clock."

"When hell freezes over," Stevie muttered as Paul walked away.

"How come you dislike him so much?" Pip asked.

"I don't know." Stevie thought for a moment. "Maybe it's because he tries to act like Samson when Samson's being a pain. But he hasn't got Samson's talent or his style or . . . his goodness."

"Silly girl . . . I told you that a long time ago. Paul's one of the most insecure people I know, and that's what makes him act like a pain. But he's harmless, and he certainly seems to like you. Maybe if you were a little more pleasant to him, he wouldn't come on so strong."

The following morning, everyone was awakened at six. Breakfast was served at six-thirty on the east veranda, and Samson himself supervised the service, reminding his cast to eat heartily "because we all need to be in peak condition today."

Pip and Stevie exchanged another giggle, but were quickly silenced by one of Samson's lethal dirty looks.

"Pay attention, boys and girls," he said. "You've all worked with me before, so you all know the routine. Give me your best, because I won't take less."

Pip whispered, "Next thing you know, he'll be telling us to get one for the Gipper."

Stevie bit her lip to keep from laughing. Samson certainly did seem earnest. With all his fame and success, could he be scared about doing what he'd done many times before?

She always thought acting in his pictures was more like play than real work. There were no lines to learn, no scenes to memorize. Only Samson knew what the movie was about, so only he knew what each day's setups would be. There were no rehearsals, only his instructions prior to shooting a scene. If he didn't like the results, he simply did it over and over until he was satisfied. At worst, the work was monotonous—though it didn't seem so because he kept the World's Fair box handy, and after a couple of hours everyone was pretty stoned—but it was never really hard.

When they'd finished breakfast, Stevie and Pip headed for the castle's ballroom. Paul Maxwell caught up with them, and Stevie had the feeling he'd been waiting. Remembering Pip's advice, she tried to be friendly and greeted him pleasantly.

"So you've seen the light, Pretty Stevie," he said, taking her arm. "I thought you would after Samson gave you the facts of life. . . ."

"What? What are you talking about?" She shook off his hand as if it were poisonous. "Look, Paul," she said, "we're all going to be together here for a while, so we might as well try to get along. Just don't get any ideas, because I'm not interested!"

As Paul stalked off in a temper, Stevie shook her head in wonderment. "Christ, doesn't he know how to take no for an answer? Why doesn't he bother somebody else? If he's as rich as everyone says, there must be someone who wouldn't think he's a jerk."

"Where's the fun in that, Stevie?" Pip laughed. "Some men want only the clubs that won't have them."

When the company had assembled in the ballroom, Samson called them to order. He took a sip of cream soda, cleared his throat, and began to speak. "I want you all to forget every Dracula film you've ever seen. Clear your minds of stale, horrific stereotypes and consider this: Dracula as the incarnation of every taboo, every dark human desire, every fear that fascinates. If he is a monster, and this is the central notion we will explore, he is an elegant monster, charismatic and seductive—powerful yet vulnerable, wise yet deeply lonely.

"Our first shot today will show the shipwreck, the scattered remains of the vessel that transported Dracula's coffin to his new home. We move to the countryside. . . . All is in full flower, rich and green, yet with music and lights there will be a suggestion of sadness, because these are colors and shadings that are forbidden to a prince of darkness. Then we'll introduce Jonathan Harker, perhaps show the pale, rather vapid nature of his relationship with Mina. . . . That's all for now."

The agenda sounded brief and simple enough, yet problems appeared with the first moments of shooting. The shipwreck looked fake, Samson complained, the colors of the hull too cheerful, the arrangement of the debris lacking in drama—and so on and so on. The set designer was ordered to work through the night if necessary, and the film crew packed their gear onto a Jeep. With Samson in constant attendance, they drove back and forth over the same few miles, in search of perfect combinations of summer foliage and open sky.

When the light had all but disappeared, the film crew was still working on the same outdoor scenes. "We'll try again tomorrow," Samson said tersely. "And it had better be right."

The next day it rained, and Samson was forced to choose between idleness and working on scenes that could be shot indoors. It wasn't an easy choice, for in spite of his languid airs, his nonchalance, Samson wasn't at all flexible about anything he considered important. He ordered the cast into the main house with a petulance that suggested the weather was everyone else's fault.

"We'll film Dracula's seduction of Lucy," he decided finally. After fiddling for what seemed like hours with Pip's nightgown and rearranging the furniture in what was to be her boudoir, Samson ordered her into bed and made the final adjustments on his own costume, a flowing white silk shirt, dark velvet trousers, and fitted handmade boots.

As he moved easily through the bedroom window, Samson was all he said Dracula should be—graceful, elegant, and romantic. As he approached the sleeping Lucy, there was a sexual tension in the room. Breathing became shallow as he bent over her exposed shoulders, her slender neck. And suddenly there was a giggle, suppressed at first, then escalating into a full-blown peal of laughter. "Oh God, Samson, you're tickling me with your shirt!" Pip cried out.

"Damn you!" he screamed, his handsome face twisted with rage, "damn you amateurs and philistines! You're trying to ruin me, all of you, you're trying to ruin me!" And with that, he fled to his tower room, locked the door, and refused to speak to anyone for the rest of the day.

In the days that followed, Stevie had to admit that Pip was right. Samson was nervous, and while it was hard to tell how that affected his creativity, it did make him moodier and more imperious with his company. He would tell them to be one thing one minute, change his mind the next—and then get angry if he didn't like the result.

To make matters worse, the summer-camp atmosphere gave way to a collective case of cabin fever. Accustomed to life in the city, the Wherehouse Regulars began to grumble about everything—the enforced waiting around, the lack of anything good to do at night. The nearest town was twenty miles away; its attractions were limited to one movie theater and four restaurants, all of which closed before ten o'clock. Stevie and Pip entertained one another, but even they began to feel that this picture wouldn't be finished for months. When the complaints and bickering reached mutinous proportions, Samson finally lifted his ban on drugs and asked instead for moderation.

Stevie couldn't help remembering the time she had stolen away and seduced Luke James, another lifetime ago. Strange, she thought, she'd felt so in charge, so in control, so sure of what she was doing. And now that she was something of an actress herself, she didn't feel in control of anything.

Inch by painful inch, the filming went on, and no one

could tell whether it was good, bad, or something in between. The lease on the castle was renewed, the contract with the caterers extended. Impatiently Samson drove his cast and crew, with anger, with threats, and, sometimes, with a force that seemed like desperation.

Alone in his tower room, working over the editing machine he allowed no one else to touch, Samson viewed the results of each day's filming. More secretive than ever, he shared his thoughts with no one, giving rise to the rumor that Samson Love was about to fall flat on his handsome face for the first time in his heretofore brilliant career.

He had saved the final scenes, in which Dracula is destroyed, until last, and as the time to shoot them drew closer, he became depressed, even distraught, as if he could not bear to contemplate the death of his own fictional creation. When the scenes could be postponed no longer, when it became clear that everyone was simply marking time and waiting for Samson to give the word, he withdrew to his tower room and stayed there. Concerned that he might not be eating or sleeping, Stevie and Pip risked his anger and tried to see him. They knocked on his door and called out. They tried the handle, but the heavy latch held the door shut. They knocked harder, fearful that something terrible had happened. Suddenly there was a loud crash, the sound of glass shattering against the door, and a muffled voice saying: "Go away, damn you, go away."

Yet the following morning, when the company assembled in the dining room for breakfast, there was Samson, looking fresh and rested, wearing his Dracula costume and obviously ready to work. He tapped a spoon against a glass to get their attention. "I have a bold new concept," he said with the first smile anyone had seen in weeks. "Dracula cannot be destroyed. . . . Everything he stands for is immortal. It's only small, frightened people that insist on his death . . . It is a false and artistically invalid climax to the story. Our Dracula will triumph. . . . In the end, he will seduce all those who attempt to destroy him!"

There was a buzz of conversation. Would this mean further delays, more reshooting?

"We will finish today," Samson continued, sounding more confident than he had in weeks. "The final scenes will be played in the pool pavilion. When Jonathan Harker and Van Helsing arrive with their stakes and crosses, there will be an eclipse of the sun . . . as if Nature herself intervenes to thwart their plans. Dracula arises from his coffin. It is in his power to destroy his enemies, yet instead he beguiles them with visions of their own hidden desires. The choice is theirs . . . will their so-called morality be strong enough to withstand the temptation? The struggle is real, but brief. Against the rich perfume of sensual pleasure, the abstract notion of virtue is no defense. The climax, boys and girls, will be a bacchanal that would shame the Romans. . . . Now, into your costumes and let's get to work!"

The pavilion was quickly lit with red fluorescents, bathing the pool and surrounding areas with a diabolical crimson glow that gave Stevie the creeps, even though she knew it was make-believe. Makeup was applied, costumes were fitted and checked with unusual efficiency and speed.

When the preliminary scenes were completed with only one take, the spirits of the company were higher than they had been for weeks. Soon the boredom and tension would be over; soon they would all be back in New York.

As the stage for the bacchanal was being set, the usual coffee-and-Danish wagon was taken away. In its place, Samson produced a rolling bar and a portable pharmacy: a selection of uppers and downers and amyl nitrate poppers; of hashish, cocaine, opium, and marijuana, not to mention the works for smoking, skinning, or snorting. Everything that had been withheld or rationed was now being offered with a bounteous hand.

"Indulge, boys and girls," Samson said gaily. "Help yourselves to anything and everything. Throw caution to the winds. . . . I want you to shed your inhibitions as you shed your costumes, to abandon yourselves to the delights of sensual pleasure."

Like children in a candy store, the cast fell greedily upon the powders and pills and alcoholic elixirs. Samson moved among them like a camp headmaster, murmuring words of encouragement as the potions took hold, directing his cameras to this pair of eyes or that body.

"Now, into the pool," he called out. "With or without costumes, whatever feels good. . . . Choose your partners and do it!" The cameras moved in closer as the couplings began, as naked and clothed bodies intertwined in various permutations of twos and threes or more, the sounds of sexual abandon mingling with laughter and splashing.

Dressed in only a filmy white dress, Stevie waited for her cue. She'd been told she would have to make love with Donny Glass, who played Jonathan Harker, and when she protested, Samson had explained how artistically necessary the scene would be. "Don't you see?" he'd argued, "Mina is Jonathan's own fiancée, yet in all their dull, boring courtship, he's scarcely touched her. And now Mina belongs to Dracula, who offers her to Jonathan . . . mockingly, enticingly. You understand, don't you?"

In the end, Stevie had agreed. She'd taken a drink and a Miltown, but she was still tense.

"You don't look right," Samson said, handing her a powerful concoction of vodka and Tuinal. "You aren't relaxed enough. We want a dreamy, otherworldly quality. Your muscles are tight and your eyes are too clear."

She drank the potion willingly, and soon the world around her swam out of focus. Her arms and legs turned to jelly, and she had to sit down and hold on to the chair, lest she fall. She lost track of time and place, and when Samson called "Places," she had no idea of what she was supposed to do. She allowed herself to be led to a bench in the center of the pavilion and propped up against a tree. "That's fine," Samson said. "Now all you have to do is wait . . . and go with the flow."

The lights were hot, and all Stevie wanted to do was slump over and go to sleep. She was dimly aware of Samson giving directions, of someone approaching. She looked up, vaguely expecting to see Donny Glass . . . but it was someone else. It was Paul Maxwell who took her hand, who pulled the nightdress from her shoulders, and pushed her back onto the bench. She tried to speak, but Paul's mouth covered her own, his body pinning her weakened limbs as he took her, roughly and with a savage kind of anger.

When she opened her eyes, she was in a strange bedroom. Paul's.

"That was worth it," he said with a satisfied smirk. "Expensive, but worth it."

"What are you talking about?" she asked, her head thick and fuzzy and devoid of recent memory.

"You . . . having you. It's worth all the money this movie is costing." When Stevie still didn't react, he said, "I agreed to put up the money for this flick after Samson said I could have all the traditional producer's perks . . . anything I wanted, casting couch privileges with anyone here. I wanted you."

Through the fog, Stevie registered what Paul was saying, and, mustering all her strength, she delivered a kick to Paul's groin. He roared with pain and then slapped her hard across the face. She staggered back, falling against the bed and cutting her cheek. Sobbing with pain and anger, she ran from the room and into the bathroom, locking the door behind her. Blood was streaming from the cut, running down her neck. She stepped into the shower and ran the cold water, standing there she didn't know how long, until her flesh was numb. Something ugly had happened, and while she despised Paul, it was Samson who had let it happen. This wasn't like doing things she'd never done, this wasn't like being open to new experiences that seemed strange and perhaps dirty when she wasn't high. Samson had sold her, like a pimp, and he had done it for money.

Finally she turned off the water and looked at her face. The cut had stopped bleeding; a thin pink line ran across her cheekbone. She threw on a robe and ran upstairs.

Without knocking, she invaded Samson's tower room. He was alone, bent over his editing machine and biting his nails.

"Damn you," she said, her voice trembling with anger. "Damn you, Samson. . . . I thought you were my friend!"

He looked startled, almost innocent. "What *have* you been drinking . . . or smoking or sniffing, Pretty Stevie? You're the picture of a bad trip. . . . And whatever happened to your lovely face? It's a good thing we've finished—"

"Damn your stupid picture, too," she cut in. "You sold me to Paul Maxwell. All that bullshit about art . . . it was just bullshit. How could you? You made me into a . . ."

"A whore?" he finished, his pointed eyebrows lifting in what looked like amusement. "Is that what your childish tantrum is all about?" he asked, as if she were the one at fault. "In truth, I decided it would be far more interesting to have the pious Dr. Van Helsing seduced by the lovely Mina. What's the harm in allowing Paul to think it was his idea? Especially if that little deception allowed us to make this film. Now we've done it," he said as calmly as if he'd been the one in bed with Paul, "and it was an interesting match . . . even better than I'd imagined. When you see the picture, you'll know I was right."

"You had no right," she insisted stubbornly. "You . . ."

"Be careful, Pretty Stevie," Samson cut in, his voice low and somehow more threatening, "you're walking on thin ice here. I've indulged you a bit because I can see how upset you are. Now calm down and just admit that we all do what we need to do. Go to your room and get some rest. Unless you'd like to leave. . . ."

Stevie retreated in confusion, the threat of excommunication struggling with the sense that something very wrong had happened to her—and that she was in over her head. Alone in her room, she replayed Samson's explanation against the ugly scene with Paul. Who was telling the truth and who was lying? And even if Samson was telling the truth, how far could she go to please him? She fell back into a drugged sleep without arriving at a single answer.

Yet that evening at dinner, Samson was so sweet, as if they'd never fought. "To my star, to my best and prettiest star," he said, toasting her with champagne. And later that night, she and Pip were invited to the tower room for a slumber party. Dressed in pajamas and robes, they ate chocolate marshmallow ice cream and played Monopoly until they couldn't keep their eyes open. By the time she fell asleep, it was hard for Stevie to know what was real and what wasn't.

Dracula's Dreams was scheduled to open on Halloween, at a private by-invitation-only gala at the Museum of Modern Art. Borrowing a trick from Truman Capote, Samson turned what might have been simply a glamorous opening into the media event of the fall season. He personally conducted a public-relations blitz, calling his pet columnists and letting them know just how select the guest list would be, how many rich and famous people had begged for the privilege of attending—and how disappointed those excluded would be. And soon it was exactly as Samson had said it would be. Not a day went by without mention in some column or other of film stars flying in from Hollywood, politicians from Washington, shipping magnates from Greece, and oil sheiks from the Persian Gulf. Invitations were coveted and bargained for, with favors and with money. It was rumored that the mayor of New York had offered to rename a street after Samson, if only he would invite a powerful party leader and his wife.

On the day of the party, Stevie had her hair done. She went through the motions of preparing her gown and her accessories, yet she felt no pleasurable anticipation, only an anxiety bordering on dread.

When Samson's limousine arrived to pick her up, she swallowed two Miltowns, needing their cushion of numbness before she could face the premiere ahead. Pip was waiting in the car, burbling with gossip and excitement, yet her friend's enthusiasm failed to ignite a similar reaction in Stevie.

As they turned onto Fifty-third Street, they passed a wall of people pushing and shoving against the line of mounted police that tried to restrain them. Flashbulbs began to go off even before Stevie and Pip got out. "Over here!" one photographer called out. "Give us a smile!" ordered another. Stevie responded, like the puppet she felt she'd become.

Inside, dressed in the antique evening clothes that had become his latest favorite costume, Samson was holding court with Paul beside him, charming and beguiling the celebrities who crowded around, eager to hear his anecdotes about the making of *Dracula's Dreams*. When he saw Pip and Stevie, he waved, inviting them to join the group.

Pip tugged at Stevie's arm, but she held back. "What's wrong with you?" Pip asked. "You've been acting awfully weird. Don't tell me you're still mad about that Paul business."

"Did Samson tell you about that?" Stevie felt curiously diminished by the possibility of Samson's confiding in Pip when she herself had said nothing.

"Of course he did," Pip replied with an edge in her voice. "Samson and I are friends too, you know . . . and I must say I agree with him on this one. Everybody sleeps with everybody else at the Wherehouse, on camera and off. I can't even *remember* the people I made it with during that orgy scene. I'll probably die of embarrassment if they turn out to be jerks, but I wouldn't think of blaming Samson. Friends don't judge each other, Stevie . . . that's for the rest of the world to do. That's why being a Wherehouse Regular is so great."

The words sounded convincing, yet Stevie wasn't persuaded. Sending Pip off to join Samson and Paul, she went into the auditorium and took the seat that had been reserved for her. Scanning the program, she noted the distinguished sponsors who had lent their names to this event. On the credits page was her own name in bold, black letters, along with a stunning photograph that Samson had labored over. She looked like a star, just as he'd promised. Yet she couldn't shake the feeling that her life was out of control.

Soon the auditorium began to fill up. With a rustle of silks and furs and programs, the guests settled themselves in their seats with an air of anticipation. When Samson appeared, flanked by Pip and Paul, there was a spontaneous burst of applause. When they sat down, the lights dimmed and the opening credits were revealed in a romantic montage of Samson Love drawings. There was an appreciative murmur.

Concerned as she'd been with her own thoughts, Stevie was surprised as the picture claimed her attention, drawing her into the story of a Byronic hero, misunderstood for centuries, seeking the solace of a soul mate for eternity. On camera, Samson was utterly beautiful, noble in his bearing as he fenced with his opponents, his speeches witty and ironic and contrasting sharply with the heavy pedanticism of the vampire hunters.

When her own character, Mina, appeared on screen, Stevie watched with a curious fascination. She had no memory of smiling in a particular way, no recollection of moving her body just so. Was she acting, she wondered, or simply acting as Samson's puppet, doing this or that in response to his directions? As the love scene between Dracula and Lucy began, Pip nudged Stevie. "Remember how mad Samson was when I wouldn't let him bite my neck?" she whispered.

"Hush!" commanded two voices in unison from behind them.

In the darkened room the sexual tension was felt, as it had been on the set. There was complete silence as Samson's Dracula courted and enchanted Mina, in a scene that was both chaste and palpably erotic.

"Lovely," a nearby voice whispered as the vampire embraced his chosen bride, and Stevie had to agree. Yet as Mina surrendered to the forces of darkness, Stevie couldn't help but wonder if there wasn't a parallel in her own life— and if, by embracing all that Samson offered, she hadn't given up her very soul.

The thought lingered, growing stronger as the bacchanal began. There were exclamations of surprise, reactions that were startled yet not disapproving, as the Wherehouse Regulars frolicked in and around the pool, at first like naughty children, then building to a climactic orgy of drugs and sex. At the center of it all was Samson's Dracula, his pale skin illuminated by the hellish glow of the red fluorescents, smiling as his adversary, Paul's Van Helsing, advanced to take the lure.

Stevie wanted to close her eyes, yet in spite of herself, she watched as Van Helsing's righteous demeanor gave way, as he dropped his cross and claimed his prize, losing himself in the pleasures of Mina's beautiful body. The classical score built to a crescendo, and suddenly the screen was blank.

There was a long moment of quiet, as if the audience didn't know quite what to make of what they'd seen, and then the applause began, growing louder and louder as Samson rose to acknowledge it.

As she listened to the chorus of bravos, exclamations of "Brilliant!" and "Daring!", it was clear that the picture would be yet another triumph for Samson.

He pulled his stars to their feet, inviting another wave of applause. Yet Stevie no longer felt like a star. In the company of her best friends, she felt like the lost souls in the picture, somehow cast adrift and not knowing where she could go.

7

Lee Harrison Stone tugged at the collar of his starched formal shirt. Then, remembering he was on display, he dropped his hands to his sides. A "prime eligible bachelor," the auctioneer had called him—and the word, reminiscent of a good cut of meat, forced a rueful smile from Lee. But if he played the part well, he ought not to look so nervously unwilling to be on the auction block.

"'Bidding for Bachelors' was one of our biggest moneymakers at last year's ball," Rosalind Fenwick had explained to Lee, "and all we want from you is to give some fortunate young woman—not necessarily a young woman, actually—a memorable evening." She was one of his mother's oldest friends—and chairwoman of the fund-raising ball at the Waldorf for the Metropolitan Foundling Hospital. "It's all tax-deductible, of course," she went on. "And such a good cause."

It *is* a good cause, Lee assured himself as he surveyed the beautifully gowned women who crowded around the bandstand for a better view of the twenty bachelors to be "sold." For that reason alone, he could forgive himself for buckling under Rosalind Fenwick's pressure. It was at once

Lee's strength and his weakness that he would do for philanthropic principle what he would forgo for love or money.

The auctioneer called the name of Lawrence Ivey III and went on to list the attributes that made him a prize worth bidding for—a degree from Harvard, a vice-presidency in the family brokerage firm, a Most Valuable Player trophy from last season's championship American polo team. The bidding began at $500 and moved along briskly until it peaked at $950. "Ladies," the auctioneer scolded, "that's such a paltry sum. Would you dig deeper if I were to inform you that Mr. Ivey is prepared to offer not just an ordinary date, but an entire weekend aboard his yacht, the *Azure Sea*?" The topping bids began to roll in.

When Lawrence Ivey III and his yacht were sold for $2100, Lee felt an unexpected twinge in the neighborhood of his ego. He'd taken Roz Fenwick at her word and showed up prepared to squire his purchaser to a good restaurant of her choosing, then to the theater. Had he been thoughtless . . . perhaps a bit vain? When he shaved in the morning, he was used to seeing a tall, athletic body, a strong face, lean and rugged, a square jaw ridged with a deep cleft and clear gray eyes. He was used to being called handsome, and to getting the kind of attention that went with that description. But he'd never been in this position before, looking to compel or inspire a woman to come up with a couple of thousand dollars for the pleasure of his company. He was nervous enough about being auctioned, but to be auctioned cheaply . . . that *would* be embarrassing. Maybe he should toss in a weekend at his country house upstate. No . . . he wasn't outgoing enough to pull off entertaining a stranger for a whole weekend.

As he half listened to the bidding on "Bachelor Number Two," Lee glimpsed his parents chatting with Roz Fenwick. They made a distinguished couple. Rebecca Stone looked splendid, elegant if not conventionally beautiful, in a vintage Norell gown and the diamond-and-emerald pendant that her mother's forebears had purportedly acquired from the Empress Josephine. Sherman Stone was slim and dapper in his Savile Row formalwear, his face still handsome, his silver hair striking against his year-round rich man's tan. By grace of Rebecca's flawless lineage and Sherman's easy charm, they were invited everywhere. Once, Lee had been proud of them—but that was when he still admired his father and believed it was connubial devotion that bound Sherman and Rebecca together.

When Lee discovered that Sherman was so much less than he'd imagined, when he'd learned the truth of Rebecca's seeming devotion, he vowed his own life would be different. He implemented that promise by rejecting everything his parents wanted for him—Ivy League schools, a career in banking, and a debutante wife. Lee had been the only member of his prep-school class who'd forfeited his draft deferment; he volunteered for military service in the Chaplain Corps. He tried halfheartedly to explain to his parents that he didn't support the war in Vietnam, but felt it was morally wrong to do nothing for the poor and disadvantaged who had no option but to serve or be branded—while the sons of rich men simply sat out the conflict in college or graduate school. His mother threatened a heart attack, and his father . . . well, his father condescendingly allowed that Lee had a lot to learn about life in the real world.

Lee felt he was still learning. But his way, not theirs.

"Our next bachelor, ladies and gentlemen, is Lee Harrison Stone." Lee snapped to attention, and the auctioneer launched into his pitch: "A self-made man by all accounts, founder and chairman of Stone Electronics—*Forbes* magazine calls him a marketing wizard and fearless entrepreneur—Lee stands at an inch over six feet and weighs in at one hundred seventy pounds. He sits on the board of the

Museum of Modern Art, enjoys tennis and photography. Now, which of you ladies would like to call him yours for an evening? Do I hear five hundred dollars for an opening bid? I have five hundred. Who'll make it six . . . ?"

Two women in the front row had a whispered conference and started giggling. Jesus, this was worse than he'd imagined. How on earth had he agreed to stand here in evening clothes and be stared at and appraised by sleek, yet obviously hungry, women?

"Nine hundred . . . twelve . . . fifteen . . ." The bids flew across the room so fast that Lee couldn't track where they were coming from. Sensing he had a hot property on the block, the auctioneer redoubled his efforts. "Ladies, ladies, are you trying to give this man a complex? Only twelve hundred dollars for a magnificent example of manhood, a genuine war hero who was decorated for bravery under fire? Lee . . . let's give the ladies more incentive to be generous. Can you dance?"

Lee managed to nod, not trusting himself to speak. Who the hell had told the committee about the medal? His mother . . . or father? Foolish braggadocio, he thought. Lee knew better than to think of himself as a hero. For him, there had simply been no question of running for cover when he'd spotted the kid from Delaware bleeding in an open field.

As the bidding moved along, Lee looked at the ceiling, the walls, and especially the exits—everywhere but at the women seeking to claim him. When he was "knocked down" finally for the evening's top price so far, $3200, it was the flurry of applause that broke through his embarrassed inattention. He stepped down from the bandstand—and saw that the woman coming toward him holding aloft a paper given out by the auctioneer was a knockout brunette whose height matched his own. Momentarily at a loss for words, Lee automatically accepted the ticket she pressed into his hand, attesting to her winning bid.

"You're mine," she said. "I'm Francesca Spaulding."

The name meant nothing to him, but her face and form struck him as vaguely familiar. Perhaps he'd danced with her at some deb cotillion a thousand years ago.

"Thanks for the vote of confidence," he said with a smile. "For thirty-two hundred bucks, I feel like I should throw in my letter sweater." She didn't smile back, but her face was gorgeous in repose. It amazed Lee that such a beautiful woman was not only available, but would buy a date. Charitable as she might be, there were other ways to give money.

She seemed to read his look. "Frankly," she said, "I needed a tax deduction. And my agent thought this charity thing would be good for my image. Wait and see, I'll get your price back a few times over in publicity."

Her charmless manner and preoccupation with business answered both Lee's questions. The publicity talk indicated it wasn't a deb cotillion where he'd seen her. But who was she? Whatever the answer, he had a powerful intuition that he wasn't going to enjoy the company of Francesca Spaulding one bit. A deal was a deal, however, and for the sake of charity it was his job to make sure she got her money's worth. "Which evening do you want to go out," he asked. "And is there anyplace in particular you'd like to go?"

"I'll let you know after my press agent arranges some coverage. Will there be any problem in scheduling on your end?"

"None at all," Lee answered, thinking the sooner Francesca Spaulding called, the sooner he could discharge his obligations to the Foundling Hospital. "Whenever you're ready, just call my private number." He handed over his business card, excused himself, and shook Francesca

Spaulding's hand briskly. This was, after all, business and not pleasure.

Lee Stone set out for his Saturday-night date with Francesca Spaulding in the company limousine. He usually drove an old Corvette, but somehow he couldn't see the statuesque Francesca comfortably folding herself and her finery into a bucket seat. A little research—nothing more, actually, than Lee asking his executive secretary if she knew the Spaulding name—had revealed that Francesca was the contract model for Aimee Myner, the cosmetics firm. What impressed Lee, mainly, was that Myner sold enough lipstick and nail polish to put them several notches above Stone Electronics in the Fortune 500.

Promptly at seven, his car stopped at the entrance of the tower of glass overlooking the East River where Francesca Spaulding lived. The chauffeur opened the door for Lee, and he went inside, where a doorman took his name and called upstairs.

He had expected, after being announced, to be invited up—at least to perform the gentlemanly tasks of fetching the lady from her door and helping her on with her coat. For $3200, he was ready to do no less.

But the doorman said, "Miss Spaulding will be down soon."

"Soon" turned out to be twenty minutes, during which Lee sat in the limousine, agitation rising to the point that he was on the brink of telling the driver to take him home. Charity had its limits. Just as Lee reached his, however, Francesca came sweeping out of her building—an exit that couldn't be missed as she swirled a chinchilla coat over a clinging, low-cut white silk creation with a floor-length pleated skirt.

Lee hopped out to receive her. In spite of his pique, he had to give her an approving glance. She, too, stopped to inspect his appearance—dark gray Savile Row suit, burgundy tie, handmade English shoes.

Before either could say a word, a flashbulb went off. Now Lee noticed the young man with several cameras hanging from his neck who had followed Francesca from the building.

"C'mon," Lee said, pulling Francesca quickly toward the car. "Let's duck the paparazzi. . . ."

She yanked her arm free. "But this is Buck Lansing," she said, "my *personal* photographer. I told you this was for publicity. Buck's going with us. . . ."

And, without waiting for Lee's consent, she and the photographer piled into the back of the car.

Lee paused on the sidewalk. He wasn't crazy about having his picture splashed all over town, not as Francesca Spaulding's new boyfriend. That certainly wasn't part of his agreement to go on a date. He weighed the option of sending them off in the limo and taking a taxi home. He could send the hospital his own check for $3200; suddenly that seemed cheap as a way of bailing himself out.

"Oh, c'mon." Francesca goaded him through the open door. "It's for a good cause, remember? Get in, Stone, and don't be such a silly old fuddy-duddy."

That did it. He'd been told by a number of women, mostly past lovers, that he had a tendency to take himself too seriously. He got into the back, not minding at all that the photographer ended up wedged between him and Francesca.

At Le Cirque, where he had booked dinner, Lee posed willingly for a dozen pictures and graciously changed the reservation to a table for three. In fact, he ended up enjoying Buck Lansing's company far more than Francesca's. The photographer didn't just do lightweight fashion work, but had spent time covering the Johnson White House and had been to Vietnam. They traded anecdotes while Francesca sat quietly, completely involved with her food.

It was only a few minutes past ten when they left Le Cirque. In the car, Lee asked dutifully, "So what now? Would you like to go dancing?"

Francesca smiled approvingly, as if Lee had finally caught on to the main purpose of this expensive evening. "Yes," she said. "But this time, *I'll* pick the place."

She leaned forward and spoke so low when the driver opened the glass partition that Lee couldn't hear her directions.

Lee regarded suspiciously the dark street where the car stopped before a factory-type building.

"What's this?"

"The Wherehouse," Francesca said.

As an art collector himself, Lee knew the name of Samson Love and had heard of his cliquish setup, half studio, half pleasure palace. But he had been no more curious about seeing it than he was interested in pop art. He preferred impressionism—and he preferred sanity.

But Buck was waiting with his camera, and obviously this was where the best publicity would come for Francesca and her sponsors. He trailed in behind her.

His worst suspicions were confirmed when they arrived upstairs. Lee was hit by a wall of sound as deafening as any artillery barrage he'd heard in 'Nam. And the air was so thick with marijuana smoke, one could get a contact high just by taking a few deep breaths.

Francesca evidently knew her way around, for when they removed their coats, she refused to part with her chinchilla until they located someone named Eddie. "Put these in the back storage room," she commanded the boy, signalling Lee to hand over some money. "I don't want any of Samson's playmates playing dress-up with *my* Fendi fur."

"Do you mean to say there's no respect for private property here?" Lee teased.

His answer was a dirty look that foreclosed any further attempts at banter. "Let's get started," she said to Lansing.

Though the Wherehouse was fairly crowded, and though Samson Love was nowhere in sight, he materialized as soon as Buck began snapping pictures of Francesca and Lee, almost as if he'd been alerted to their presence by a personal radar system. The shoot was apparently all prearranged, because he kissed Francesca and hugged Buck.

Francesca started by flattering the artist. "I love that shade of periwinkle on you," she said, indicating Samson's ruffled silk shirt. "And you're an absolute angel to let us do this."

"Angel my ass. Didn't that sleazy company you work for promise to buy two of my paintings for their corporate headquarters? And I'll want my pound of flesh from you, too, Frankie. Got a part you'll have to play in my next film."

"Not if I have to bare my tits, Sammy. I have an image to uphold."

Samson laughed. "You don't have any tits, Frankie. We all know you're really a man in drag. In fact, the part is a man. . . ."

"All right, then," Francesca said agreeably. "Now, can we shoot?"

Samson gave his blessing, they kissed, and away he went.

To say this wasn't his world was an understatement for Lee. But he did his part, posing for a succession of photographs, until Francesca drifted away from him and began talking with others in the room. Again, it crossed his mind to leave, but sheer breeding made him linger to bring her home. If she wanted to cut and run from him, all right, but he would leave as he arrived—a gentleman.

Lee headed for the bar in search of a drink to nurse, though Samson's reputation for drug orgies made him wonder if it was safe to eat or drink anything here. He looked with disgust at the huge bowl of colored pills, sitting on the bar like candy. Lee didn't think of himself as a prude. Hell, he'd tried a lot of things once, and that was enough for a man who didn't plan to waste his life hanging around places like this, playing pharmaceutical roulette with his brain. He found an unopened bottle of vodka, broke the seal, and poured himself a stiff one.

With time to kill and nothing better to do, he started watching the dancers, some jumping and twisting and turning frenetically to the music, others moving like zombies, halfway between consciousness and sleep. Almost at once, Lee noticed the girl. She was beautiful in spite of the white makeup, the dyed black hair falling over her face. She looked like a fairy princess caught in an evil enchantment, her eyes closed, a childlike smile on her face. Her slender body was draped, almost like a scarf, over a stocky man whose face was almost hidden from view; she seemed oblivious to the fact that he was feeling her up right there on the dance floor.

Then the man pushed her toward the mammoth black couch and dropped her, like a rag doll, onto the upholstery. She made a soft sound. Was it a protest, Lee wondered, or simply part of a drug-induced dream?

A moment later, Samson appeared and poked the girl as one might prod a sleeping pet, waking it up to play. She opened her eyes, and when Samson whispered in her ear, she responded with the same sleepy smile Lee had seen before. Samson summoned one of his ubiquitous cameras, and without so much as a moment's hesitation, he pulled the girl's blouse off, revealing her creamy white breasts.

A small group gathered round as Samson tweaked her nipples with a proprietary air and began, with colored felt-tip pens, to draw pictures—little cartoon figures—on her chest, her arms, and her bosom. The camera moved in for a close-up, and when he was finished, Samson signed his name across the girl's navel with a flourish. He bowed slightly and acknowledged the applause of his fans, then turned to the stocky man Lee had seen before and made an expansive gesture with his hand, as if to say "She's all yours." The man slung the girl, who still seemed barely conscious, over his shoulder and headed toward the back of the loft.

"Did you enjoy Samson's little 'happening'?" Francesca's voice startled Lee, made him feel as if he'd been caught watching a peep show on Forty-second Street.

"No. It was sickening. . . ."

"But you watched, didn't you?" Francesca gloated.

Lee was struck dumb. Perhaps he couldn't deny some streak of corruption within himself—something from his father's side. In a moment of unbearable loneliness and isolation, he'd once visited a Saigon bordello. He'd witnessed decadence that masqueraded as eroticism, fantastic scenes far more bizarre than what he'd seen here. But they left him feeling sadder and lonelier, and he'd never gone back. He felt now as he did then, angry and repelled. He'd had the urge to punch both Samson and his buddy in the face, to drag the girl out of this place, to rescue her from whatever evil spell made her a Wherehouse captive as he might liberate a war prisoner from the enemy.

"I think you liked it more than you're willing to admit," Francesca persisted. "Men always enjoy Samson's follies. He gets people to do things for his cameras they wouldn't do for Cecil B. deMille, not for any money. And you don't find that the least bit titillating?"

"No," Lee repeated. "That poor girl Samson was mauling is so wrecked she doesn't know what the hell she's doing."

"That 'poor girl,'" Francesca said with an edge, "is

Pretty Stevie Knight. Samson's also done a lot for her. Don't tell me you've never heard of his underground superstar?"

"His underground is a sewer," Lee said. "I don't go there."

"But you *are* here, Stone," Francesca purred smugly. "Maybe you're just a hypocrite—and that's worse than the rest of us, who know what we like and don't mind getting it. I think we can declare our date officially over. You're not my kind of man."

Lee held his tongue—though it would have been easy to supply a retort—and Francesca whirled and disappeared into the crowd.

So he was free to go. But he was held for a second, thinking of the girl he had seen misused and then taken away. The image of Stevie Knight, drugged and lost, wouldn't let go. Something about the heart-shaped face, something spoke to him of innocence forgotten but not lost. Rescuing her—now, there was a good cause. . . .

But then he reproved himself. Stay out of it, Stone. If she wants to be Samson Love's drug geisha, it's none of your business. He looked around for the boy who had taken his coat. Not seeing him, Lee walked toward the back of the Wherehouse. He tried the first door he came to; it revealed an enormous bathroom decorated with graffiti, all of it sexual. Inside, two naked young women sat in a bubbling whirlpool bath, smoking marijuana, their heads thrown back against the rim of the tub in an air of contented abandon. Lee ignored their giggling invitation to party and closed the door.

The next one he tried proved to be the storage room. It was the size of a small ballroom and was filled with racks of clothing and furs, shelves of boxes and hats and shoes. Francesca was right about one thing, he thought—Samson and his playmates certainly seemed to enjoy dressing-up games.

In the dim light from the outside, Lee poked around until he found his coat. He turned to leave, then stopped, his attention caught by a soft rustling noise, like that of an animal burrowing somewhere. He scanned the floor, but all he could see was a heap of garbage in the corner. He moved closer, and suddenly he saw that it was the girl— Stevie Knight—naked except for her stockings and shoes, her hazel eyes open and vacant. For a horrible moment, he was afraid she might be dead. He touched her hand. It was icy cold. He bent his head toward her face to see if she was breathing. Her eyes opened for a moment, rolled alarmingly, then drooped shut. Lee draped his coat around her and started to rub her hands.

She made a sound, almost like a baby's whimper. Lee looked again at her face. The heavy makeup was streaked, a false lash hanging off one eye; she seemed no more than a kid who'd fixed herself up with her mother's cosmetics. Where the hell were her parents? he wondered angrily. Didn't anyone care that she spent her nights with drug addicts and degenerates—that at this rate, she'd be dead in a couple of years?

Lee stood rooted to the spot, fighting a battle that common sense would lose. Pretty Stevie Knight was a total stranger, yet she drew him like a magnet.

With a heavy sigh, he pulled her to her feet—she was painfully light—and, after wrapping her in his coat, carried her out of the Wherehouse. No one tried to stop him; they didn't even seem to notice.

"Just drive," he told the chauffeur after he'd settled the girl comfortably in his waiting limousine. For he had no plan, no idea of what he would do with this stranger he had rescued. As the car pulled away from Mercer Street, Lee adjusted the coat around her and turned up the collar to keep her warm. She half opened her eyes and twined her arms around his neck, drawing him closer. For one unguarded moment, Lee responded to the touch of soft hands, the sweetness of her perfume—and then he pulled back with a jerk, angry with his own weakness, angry with this child beside him for . . . for her irresistibility.

"If you don't wanna fool around, then why are we here?" she asked, her words slurred, her expression puzzled and childlike.

Lee's anger dissipated into remorse. "I didn't bring you with me to take advantage of you," he said gently, immediately feeling clumsy and foolish for expressing himself in such an old-fashioned way. "You were pretty much out of it," he fumbled along. "I thought . . . I thought you could use a good strong cup of coffee."

"Coffee?" she repeated. "Sure . . . why not?" A second later, she fell back to sleep.

Now what? Lee asked himself, contemplating the unconscious girl. She was in no condition to go anywhere public, and he had no idea of where she lived—or with whom, for that matter. What she needed was a chance to clean herself up, clean the drugs out of her system, and face some hard decisions from a new perspective.

Suddenly he smiled. Okay, Stone, he said to himself, you elected yourself knight in shining armor . . . now do it right. He gave his driver a new set of instructions and settled back into his seat for the long ride ahead.

Lee's country house was a six-room cabin located some fifty miles from New York, in a small community that had enjoyed a brief moment of fashionable chic after World War II and then fallen into gradual decline. Property had turned cheap, and Lee had acquired, for a mere pittance, a solid home along with thirty mountainside acres overlooking a six-mile lake. He had added a small caretaker's cottage and a garage to house the Jeep that provided ready transportation in all kinds of weather.

Though Lee's brownstone on Central Park West was far more luxurious, he thought of the log cabin as home, for here he was safe from intrusions by the Beautiful People and free to enjoy his solitude, hiking the Appalachian Trail with little likelihood of interruption, other than from a passing raccoon or a stray deer.

It was three in the morning when the company limousine pulled into the long, winding driveway that was hidden from the road by towering pines and ancient oak trees. Lee dismissed his driver and carried Stevie, who had scarcely stirred, up the small flight of stone stairs. Fumbling for his key, he opened the door. Once inside, he punched the buttons on the electronic control panel that would turn on the heat and light the main rooms.

He carried Stevie into a guest room paneled in old, weathered pine and placed her gently on the bed. He thought about putting her into a pair of pajamas but couldn't bring himself to handle her naked flesh—not after he'd seen her used like a body without a soul or a will of her own. So he simply removed her shoes and stockings and tucked her under the warm down quilt, still wearing his overcoat.

Almost as an afterthought, he went into the adjoining bathroom, dampened a washcloth, and brought it back to wipe the makeup off her skin. The face underneath had a startling vulnerability, a freshness that contrasted starkly with what he'd witnessed. Almost unconsciously, he touched her face with his fingers, a tender good-night gesture, just before he turned out the lights and went to his own room.

Lying in his massive oak bed, surrounded by the simple early-American furnishings he'd gathered at country auctions, Lee felt tired but not ready for sleep. He was keenly aware of another presence in his home, a disturbing, disconcerting presence. He had practically kidnapped the girl; heaven knew she wasn't in any shape to consent. Maybe she'd wake up and cry rape or mayhem. Maybe she was as crazy as the rest of Samson's Wherehouse crew. Maybe he should have just left her there—but he didn't really believe that. Looking the other way was a cop-out, and Lee Stone didn't believe in looking the other way when he saw something wrong.

In many ways, Lee had felt like an anachronism, his values obsolete, or at the very least, out of fashion with his own generation. He was patriotic, though he saw the need for change. He'd marched for civil rights, but he refused to dishonor his flag or burn his draft card. He had little patience with self-indulgent whining and believed a man was responsible for shaping his own destiny once he'd reached the age of reason.

Lee had grown up with privilege, though not enormous wealth. He had gone to Andover, because that had been his father's prep school—and that was the last time he'd retraced any of his father's footsteps.

Sherman Stone was a charmer, there was no doubt about that, and as a young boy Lee had been captivated by his hearty laughter and his easy way with people. Yet even then, he'd instinctively recognized something different in his mother, something he later came to see as breeding and true class.

As he got older, Lee realized it was Rebecca's quiet strength that sustained their small family, while his father dabbled in first one business venture and then the next, achieving an occasional small success and all-too-frequent failure—trading heavily on his wife's pedigree and social connections as he searched for a shortcut to fortune.

His parents rarely quarreled, for Rebecca Harrison considered marital bickering a lower-class prerogative. But once, when he was twelve years old, Lee heard her voice raised in anger. It was after she learned that Sherman had sought to capitalize yet another enterprise with a loan from her brother. Sherman had coaxed and cajoled, and then he'd hurled an angry accusation at his wife, charging her with willful sabotage, with holding him back from the success he deserved.

She had responded with a cold disdain Lee had never heard. "Can you honestly assure me that you would honor your obligation to my brother, regardless of the outcome? I think not.... So perhaps you should search your conscience, as I constantly search mine. Perhaps then you'll find who and what it is that prevents the success you crave so much. The Harrison family has had its share of pirates and buccaneers, but I'm proud to say that none of them masqueraded as honest businessmen. Show some integrity, Sherman, and you'll have my support as well as my family connections. Show me weakness of character, and the best I can offer is neutrality, providing you stay away from my family."

Lee understood then that there was something wrong with Sherman's way of doing things, though it wasn't until a few years later that he would begin mentally drafting the indictment that would separate him emotionally from his father.

He'd come home from prep school for the Christmas holiday. He and his roommate, Rob Petersen, had gone to an afternoon movie—it was *Cat Ballou*, he still remembered as if it were yesterday—and then traveled downtown to Manero's for steaks and baked potatoes. There he spotted a familiar face at a corner table. It was Sherman, deep in conversation with a young woman. Maybe it's a business meeting, Lee had told himself first, wanting to disbelieve his eyes. Yet this wasn't the kind of restaurant Sherman normally frequented, and when Lee saw him lean over and whisper in the girl's ear, touch her hand in a manner that was more than simply friendly, he knew his father was messing around. Feeling sick to his stomach, he got up, fists clenched rigidly at his side, and walked over to Sherman's table. "Hello, Dad," he said.

Sherman blanched visibly. His eyes shifted for a long, revealing moment before his usual easy manner returned. "Hi, Lee," he said. "What are you doing here?"

"Having a late lunch with Rob. What are you doing here?"

"Also having a late lunch," Sherman explained with a chuckle. "I don't think you know Marilyn Weller. . . . Marilyn, this is my son, Lee. Marilyn's in our accounting department, and she was nice enough to work right through lunch on some papers I needed. The least I could do was buy her a decent meal when she was finished, right?" Sherman's eyes still refused to meet his son's as he added, "Would you and Rob like to join us?"

"No. No, thanks."

"Well, then," Sherman said affably, as if he had nothing to hide, "I'll be seeing you at home this evening."

Lee returned to his table, feeling as if his world had been shaken by an earthquake and left standing, with great yawning cracks in what had once been bedrock. He picked at the food he no longer wanted and cut off Rob's questions and guesses on what was wrong. It might have helped to unburden himself, to vent his anger, but Lee felt he couldn't expose his tarnished family pride to an outsider, not even to a friend.

Later, when the boys called for the check, the waiter announced that it had been paid by Mr. Stone. The gesture heightened Lee's anger, for he saw in it a clumsy attempt to buy his silence.

For the rest of the day, his honesty struggled with his love for his mother. Should he hurt Rebecca or should he deceive her? Lee was still torn when, at dinner, Sherman preempted the decision. Exuding candor and confidence, Sherman mentioned ever so casually that he'd bumped into Lee at a restaurant, and that he himself had been lunching with "someone from accounting." If Rebecca suspected anything, there was nothing in her well-bred smile to suggest it.

From that day forward, Lee divorced himself from his father and aligned himself with Rebecca's brand of honor and integrity. He refused to apply to Dartmouth, Sherman's alma mater, and announced instead his intentions to seek admission at New York University. He ignored Sherman's scorn of the college, his insistence that there were no valuable connections to be made there, his dire threat that Lee would be sabotaging his own future.

Better that than a future like yours, Lee thought. And better to stay close to home, where he could look after his mother and keep an eye on his father. Once Lee had pronounced Sherman a weakling and a cheat, it was easy to gather supporting evidence: An overheard conversation with his accountant, the panic over an audit, a whispered flirtation with one of Rebecca's friends, an angry visit from a business colleague, accusations of malfeasance, threats of criminal charges—the last withdrawn only after Rebecca covered the loss by liquidating a portion of her slender stock portfolio.

"Why don't you leave him?" Lee asked his mother once when he'd found her shedding quiet tears in the privacy of her bedroom.

"Harrisons don't get divorced," she answered. "I promised 'for better and for worse.' That wasn't just a pledge to your father, it was a commitment to myself . . . and I intend to keep it. Life wouldn't have much meaning for me if I couldn't trust myself. There wouldn't be any point in giving my word if I knew it was worthless."

Lee mulled over Rebecca's words for a long time; they seemed to make sense when little in life did, and especially when he felt out of step with people his own age.

After two years of college, he enlisted in the Army and was sent to Fort Hamilton in Brooklyn for training in the Chaplain Corps. He began his tour of duty as an idealist in search of affirmation. But the purest part of his idealism had died in Vietnam. He had left the war more of a realist, ready to use the system as part of finding a way to involve himself with good causes.

And tonight, Lee thought as he traveled north, he had a cause that, oddly, touched his heart deeper than any he'd ever known before.

8

Lee slept lightly, getting up every hour or so to look in on his guest. Prudently, he'd left his telephone book on the nightstand, opened to the number of a doctor in the nearby village. But Stevie's breathing seemed regular and her pulse even.

At eight A.M., he rose, went to the kitchen, and opened the refrigerator, which had been crammed full of fruit and vegetables, farm fresh eggs, and butter. Lee grinned and made a mental note to compliment his young caretaker, Tim Fallon, for being on the job. In the seven months since Lee had taken Fallon out of a juvenile home and provided him with a job and a place to stay, the boy had never given him reason for regret.

After squeezing some fresh orange juice into a pitcher, Lee took down a brightly polished copper pan from the overhead rack and started frying bacon. He enjoyed puttering around his spacious yet cozy kitchen, but he rarely entertained here; it was a place for solitary pursuits. Not for a long time had he brought a woman to his bachelor's retreat. The society belles who filled his mailbox with bids to parties and coming-out balls were suspect in his eyes, for they belonged to the world of Sherman and Rebecca

Stone. His mother often chided him for being "wedded to his work," a criticism he couldn't deny. For now, perhaps, it was necessary; how else could he have parlayed his grandfather Harrison's modest bequest into a dynamic, thriving business? He'd settle down one day, he promised Rebecca, when the time and the woman were right.

Breaking four eggs into a bowl, he began whipping them lightly with a wire whisk. It wasn't until he caught himself humming "Strangers in the Night" that he realized he was enjoying the prospect of tending the young woman who occupied his guest room. Slow down, Stone, he warned himself then. Remember, this is a good deed, nothing more.

Still, when he prepared the white wicker tray, he stepped outside the door to pluck a few sprigs of early forsythia and put them in a small vase. Just to make the breakfast more appealing, of course. Then he went to the guest room and drew open the old-fashioned wooden blinds.

In the morning sunlight that streamed through the windows, the sleeping girl was angelically beautiful. It was hard to believe he had seen her so degraded just the night before. He shook her shoulder gently, then a little harder. She yawned and stretched and opened her eyes.

"Good morning," he said quietly, not wanting her to feel frightened or disoriented. "I'm Lee Stone. You're in my house. I don't know how much you remember, but you . . . were really out of it last night. You said okay to a cup of coffee," he added with a reassuring grin, "so here it is . . . with all the trimmings."

Stevie sat up, rubbed her eyes, looked at the breakfast tray and then at the ruggedly handsome man who offered it. Had they slept together? she wondered. Was that why he was looking at her with such tender concern? She noticed now that she was wearing nothing but a man's overcoat. Jesus, she thought, things had gotten real bad if she was blacking out and having sex with total strangers. To her mind, that was a few steps down from sleeping with the people at the Wherehouse; there, even if she barely knew them, everyone was . . . a kind of family. Stevie reached deeper into her memory of the previous night at the Wherehouse. She'd done some Quaaludes and booze, she remembered. Paul had kept filling her glass. But how did she get here? Glancing to the window, she saw the flowered vines that trailed around the outside sills, the expanse of trees beyond, and the backdrop of water shimmering like a field of diamonds under the morning sun. Christ—shanghaied to the goddamn wilderness, no less!

Stalling for time, she picked up the mug of steaming coffee and took a sip, eyeing the man over the rim. He was very attractive, she thought. If she'd let him fuck her, she certainly could have done a lot worse.

"You make a good cup of coffee, Mr. Stone."

"That's not all I do well," he said—and for just an instant Stevie thought he was being suggestive . . . until he pushed the tray nearer. "Try my omelet."

She looked at the eggs and touched the fork. But then she asked suddenly, "Are you a friend of Samson's?" It occurred to her that she could have been set up with this man, the way she'd once been set up with Paul.

But Lee's reply was unequivocal. "Not on your life," he said with an expression of open distaste. "And if you ask me, Samson Love is no friend of yours either."

"I didn't ask you," Steve said stiffly. It was one thing for her to be upset with Samson; it was quite another to let a stranger speak against him.

Lee didn't want to get into an argument. He pointed to the eggs again. "C'mon, have some breakfast. . . . If you liked my coffee, you'll love the eggs." When Stevie continued to view him with suspicion, Lee speared a morsel of omelet with the fork and brought it to her mouth.

Stevie parted her pouting lips and ate the eggs without comment. Then she accepted another forkful.

Lee couldn't help smiling at her petulance.

At last, as if grudgingly, she took the fork into her own hand. "Okay," she said, "they're good."

As she chewed the bacon, a dull throbbing pain invaded her head. She leaned back against the pillows and rubbed her temples.

"What's wrong?" Lee asked. "Are you feeling sick?"

"Headache," she whispered. "A bad one."

He went into the bathroom and returned with two aspirin and a glass of water. "Here," he said, "take these. If you have a hangover, maybe you shouldn't eat any more until later. When you're feeling better, you might want a bath or a shower. You'll find soap and towels in the bathroom and some clean clothes in the closet. I'll look in on you later."

What's this guy's game? Stevie wondered as Lee left the room. He seemed to be well fixed for money, and he was certainly great-looking. Was he one of those uptown types who got his kicks from hanging out with the Wherehouse freaks? He had treated her in a funny kind of old-fashioned way, but she still didn't know whether that meant he wasn't after her body—or if he'd already had her.

She closed her eyes and rested awhile, letting the aspirin do its work. In an hour, she got up and ran some water in the big, claw-footed bathtub. Checking inside a wooden cupboard, she found a stack of fluffy bath towels and an assortment of perfumed soaps and bath salts. One thing was certain, she thought. The guy must be married—his wife away, probably. It had to be a woman who kept the bathroom so nicely stocked.

After a long, luxurious soak in the warm soapy water, she dried herself and looked in the closet where she'd been told there were clothes. Scanning the shelves and hangers, it struck her that there was no female clothing, after all.

Oddly, that pleased her—though why she should give a damn she didn't know.

She put on a blue pullover, a pair of too-large jeans, which she tightened around her waist with a leather belt, and a pair of moccasins that almost fit after she'd slipped into two pairs of wool socks. Looking at herself in the oak-framed mirror, Stevie ruefully decided she looked like a twelve-year-old kid—a far cry from the sultry cover girl.

When she didn't find Lee anywhere in the house, she stepped outside. The air was cool and bracing, lightly scented with a hint of spring. Behind her was the rushing sound of a waterfall; beyond a lawn, the sapphire lake; above her, a dazzlingly clear blue sky. A beautiful place, Stevie admitted, almost magical, yet different from the kind of magic that Samson made with pills and powders and sleight of hand. Hearing a sound from around the corner of the house, she followed it and found her host cutting a yew hedge with an old-fashioned hand clipper. He stopped working when he saw her. "Feeling better?"

"A lot, thanks."

"You're lucky you got away with just a hangover," he said sternly. "One of these days you might not be so lucky."

She rolled her eyes. "Give me a break. Maybe I overdid a little last night, but I don't need a lecture. I'm okay now."

"Oh, yeah?" He put his hands on his hips and studied her. "If you'd come with me, I'd show you just how *not* okay you are."

"Come where?"

Instead of answering, he moved abruptly to grab Stevie's hand and then started pulling her toward a trail that led into the dense forest behind the house. She might have resisted, but the piney smell and cool air in the woods was invigorating. "C'mon, follow me," Lee said as soon as they were on the trail, "up to the waterfall. It's only a mile . . . a piece of cake. Ready, set, go!"

He broke into a slow, steady run. Stevie watched for a second. There was the faintest echo of the Admiral's know-it-all attitude in this guy's smug challenge. Well, she'd show him a thing or two. She charged after him, infuriated at the way he was making such a show of pacing himself, of holding back for her sake. Marshaling all her energy, she sprinted forward and passed him with a triumphant laugh. Ignoring the tree branches that slapped at her face, Stevie pumped her legs faster, pushing her limits as if her life depended on it. Yes, she'd outrun them all—the Admiral, and Samson, and this smug SOB.

But as the incline grew steeper, she tired quickly, and the muscles in her thighs began to cramp. When Lee passed her effortlessly with a jaunty wave, she pushed harder, until the crisp mountain air felt like a hundred sharp knives slicing her lungs. And finally, when Lee disappeared from sight, she fell to her knees on the cold, damp ground, panting with exhaustion.

A few moments later, he ran back into sight. "That's pathetic," he called across a gap of ten yards. "I thought you'd give me a run for my money, but you're so messed up, I could beat you blindfolded and on crutches!"

"Oh, yeah?" she shot back. "That's because I have no interest in running any stupid race. And furthermore, these shoes don't fit, and these clothes are falling off and . . ."

"Sure," he said with a taunting grin that made her want to slap his face, "and I'm the Queen of Romania. Listen, Stevie, I'll make you a bet. I'll take you into the village and buy you new sneakers and clothes that fit. If you can finish the mile, I'll eat my words. . . . Hell, I'll even eat my sneakers!"

Stevie's eyes shone at the prospect of such sweet revenge.

"How about it?" Lee asked, holding out his hand. "Do we have a bet . . . or are you too chicken?"

"You're on," she said, accepting the handshake.

As they walked down the hill and toward the garage, they came upon a young man clearing the dead branches that choked the path. "Hi, Mr. Stone," he called out. "Bad storm a couple of days ago. . . . Sorry I didn't finish cleaning up before you got here."

"That's okay, Tim. Take your time. You're doing a great job, and if you need some help with the outside work, let me know." Lee introduced Stevie to Tim Fallon, who eyed his employer's guest with more than a little curiosity.

As they walked on, Stevie said, "That kid who works for you was staring at me like I came from Mars. I guess I don't look like the ladies you usually bring up here?"

Lee laughed. "Tim's not used to seeing *anyone* but me up here. Though that wouldn't be his only reason to stare." A thought occurred to Lee, which he tried to frame tactfully. "But be nice around Tim. I mean, you're obviously attractive, Stevie, and if you come on to Tim at all, he—"

Stevie erupted. "What do you think might happen? That I'll do a striptease for him, get on my back and let him—"

"Stevie, I didn't mean—"

"Oh yes, you did. And why? Is that what I did for *you*? How the hell did I get here, Mr. Stone? What the hell did you want with me, anyway . . . ?"

He paused. "I wanted to help you," he said sincerely. "That's one answer. The other is . . . no, Stevie, we didn't sleep together."

Confused and chagrined, Stevie turned and walked ahead. Lee caught up and explained quietly the circumstances that had brought him to Samson's, how he'd found her in the cloakroom when he was leaving, and his inability to abandon her in that condition. "But, listen, if you don't want to stay here . . . I understand. Is there anyone I should call to pick you up? Your parents . . . ?"

She faced him. "I have no parents."

"Then . . . do you want me to drive you to a bus?"

"No."

Lee spread his hands, not sure of what she meant. Maybe she wanted to leave but expected him to drive her to the city.

She didn't know herself until this second, until she was suddenly sure that everything he said was true: he was a good guy who just wanted to help. "I'll be damned if I'll leave here," Stevie said brassily, "until I see you eat those sneakers."

Lee laughed, and pointed her to a rusty Jeep in the garage.

They went shopping in the village, which consisted of half a dozen shops and a gas station. At the general store, where they purchased sneakers and clothing for Stevie, she found herself the subject of some open gawking by the young salesgirl—no doubt a reader of the fashion magazines who'd recognized her. But at the bakery, where Lee picked out an assortment of fresh breads, the gray-haired man behind the counter also stared at her curiously. And a clutch of other customers, who greeted Lee warmly, gave Stevie the kind of wary once-over she hadn't gotten since she was a nobody being escorted around town by Samson.

"Why am I getting the eagle eye every place we go?" she asked as they emerged from the candy shop after buying the New York papers.

"Maybe my good neighbors are wondering if you're the right kind of girl for me," he teased—and immediately felt foolish. He wasn't supposed to be flirting with Stevie, he was supposed to be saving her from bad companions and bad guys. Yet Lee was beginning to feel that, in spite of

Stevie's unpolished manners and dangerous habits, he might be the one in need of rescue.

"Well, you can tell your good neighbors not to worry, Mr. Stone," she said with a patronizing smile. "You're not my type."

"Oh? And exactly what is your type, Miss Knight?" Lee demanded, cut by her airy dismissal. "Someone who feeds you booze and drugs instead of bacon and eggs?"

"My type," Stevie said, unbowed despite his direct hit, "is someone who likes me the way I am."

"Well, I do like the way you are . . . right this minute," he said, to his own surprise. "But the way you were last night . . . I hated that."

He got into the Jeep and over-revved the engine. She jumped in beside him.

"Then why didn't you leave me?" she asked.

"Because I was pretty sure that *wasn't* the real you," he said, backing away from the curb a little too fast.

They were on the road out of town before she spoke again. "But what if it is?" she said, a tremor of fear in her voice. "Suppose what you saw last night is the real me . . . ?"

Lee swung the Jeep to a halt by the side of the road and studied Stevie's face, which seemed infinitely more beautiful without any makeup. Looking into green eyes that were clear and alert and full of promise, he said quietly, "It wasn't. I know in my heart it wasn't. Last night was a mistake, Stevie, a bad one. And maybe you've made other mistakes, hundreds of them. But mistakes can be fixed." He weighted every word with a conviction based on experience. Hadn't he built a life and a career out of good intentions and perseverance?

Stevie sat back without argument, and Lee steered the car back onto the road. She said nothing the rest of the way to his house. His smug certainty unsettled her—his confidence was even a little frightening somehow—but she was relieved that he could dismiss whatever he'd witnessed last night as a mere mistake.

They didn't run the race again that afternoon. To be fair, Lee said, she needed to "train" first. Instead, he packed a picnic basket with sandwiches and fruit and a Thermos of coffee, and, after getting her bundled up in a heavy wool sweater and oilskin slicker, he took her down to a lakeside dock where a small but graceful wooden sloop named *Bella* was tied up.

Stevie had seen many boats back in Newport News, but few as elegant as the *Bella*, with her mahogany hull, teak deck, and burnished brass fittings. Lee helped her aboard and into a life jacket, undid the lines, and cast off. "I'm counting on you to crew for me," he said. "It isn't hard if you'll just follow directions. Can you do that, Stevie . . . take orders?" he asked with a mischievous twinkle.

The shadow of the Admiral reared up like a demon. For a second, her temper was uncontrollable. "No, I'm much better at giving them," she snapped. And, to show that she knew a thing or two about handling boats, she hauled out her supply of Navy talk as she jumped over the gunwale into the cockpit. "I'll take the tiller. You just cast off, raise the sails, handle the jib, and stow the gab."

Lee reared back with exaggerated bemusement. "Aye-aye, Captain," he said.

They tacked out nicely into the middle of the lake, with Stevie's expert handling of the helm and the sheets earning a series of admiring—and puzzled—glances from Lee.

"Where did you learn to sail?" he asked at last.

"That's private," she said in a way that clearly put the subject off limits. She didn't want to think about it—those times the Admiral had thrown her in a boat and told her she'd learn . . . or she wouldn't eat. Yet she didn't want to kill conversation completely.

"Who's the boat named for?" she asked Lee. She imagined it might be an old girlfriend.

"Bella is the Italian word for beautiful," Lee said. "I fell in love with her at first sight, and we've been together ever since." He'd found the boat on Cape Cod several years ago, he explained, buried in a marine junkyard with her hull half rotted out and her brasswork black. Getting her back into condition had taken all his weekends for nearly two years.

"But *Bella* was worth it. . . . she's a true classic. Just look at this pegged decking. . . ."

Lee's obvious love of things maritime was a worrying echo of the Admiral, but Stevie listened attentively, taken more by the animation on Lee's face than the story he told. Bundled up as she was against the cold, she enjoyed the bracing breeze that tousled her hair. And the sound of his voice was different—he didn't seem so arrogant now.

She lost all track of time as he took over the helm and they went on tacking lazily across the lake. She realized it was about to get dark only when Lee turned on the *Bella*'s deck lights. The colors of the sky changed suddenly as the sun turned a deep red-orange and dipped behind the mountains, shading the countryside with a palette of pink and blue and lavender. The approach of night brought a feeling of intimacy aboard the *Bella*, reminding Stevie of what she had almost forgotten—the circumstances of her meeting with Lee. To have come from that . . . to this seemed—*was*—too good to be true.

"We really didn't . . . do anything together last night?" she blurted dubiously at the moment when he was maneuvering the boat into the dock.

He looked as if he'd just been punched in the gut. "Stevie," he said, shooting a burning glance at her, "when I make love to a woman, I want her *with* me, with me in every way . . . not off in some private dream of her own— not to mention a private nightmare. If you were too far gone to know whether or not I was even there, I'd never want you." Having been distracted from the rudder, he let the *Bella*'s bow bump hard against the dock. He turned from her angrily to attend to tying up.

Stevie's embarrassment gave way to shame, and in her humiliation she struck out at Lee. "Well, if I'm so far gone, then you'd better take me home. Right now, before you waste another minute of your precious time!"

He turned from cleating a line, and for a moment the words wouldn't come. He didn't want her to go. That was the last thing in the world he wanted. "Look, I'm sorry I ruffled your feathers. I'll take you home if you insist . . . but I wish you'd stay out the weekend."

"Why?"

Good question, Stone, he said to himself. Was it only concern for Stevie's welfare? And would she buy that when he wasn't so sure anymore himself?

"Well . . . there's that race to train for. . . ."

They exchanged the briefest of smiles before Stevie said, "Okay. I'll stay."

9

The first rays of sun were just breaking over the lake when Stevie opened her eyes. She lay for a minute letting memories of the night surface, such lovely memories, floating through her mind like colored bubbles on a breeze.

They had prepared a simple dinner together. Steak, salad, fruit, and cheese—her "training menu," he called it. There had been little talk, and yet as each minute passed she felt she was getting to know him better. Once or twice, eating at the pine table in his dining room, she'd been tempted to reveal a bit more about herself, but only tempted. If he liked her as she was now—was ready to overlook what he had seen at the Wherehouse—then why call attention to anything before now? With Lee, she felt, she must have no past. After dinner, they had sat before a fire in the living room, and he had answered her questions about his business. Then he had pulled out a banjo—which he played terribly, though he could sing a fair folk song. And when she gently rebuffed his own efforts at gathering biography, they had said good night and gone to their separate rooms.

Lee Stone was a revelation to her—a strong man, of whom she didn't have to be afraid. Feeling safe in a way she hadn't for years—perhaps never had—Stevie pulled the down comforter over her head and snuggled deeper into the bed.

And then she smiled and bolted up, seized by a notion that seemed infinitely preferable to sleep.

She washed and dressed as quickly and quietly as she could, then drank a glass of orange juice from the pitcher in the refrigerator. Tiptoeing out of the house, she made her way to the same mountain trail that had defeated her so ignobly.

She took a few deep breaths and started to run. In her new clothes and sneakers, Stevie was better equipped, but the going was still rough. Lee was right, she admitted to herself, she was out of shape and she moved like an old woman. But at least away from his watchful eye, she could stop and start without embarrassment. And so she huffed and puffed all the way to the waterfall and back.

The house was still quiet as Stevie slipped off her clothes and went back to bed. She pretended to be tired and sleepy when Lee woke her with another breakfast tray. This time, she needed no coaxing to eat.

"That's better," he said approvingly. "Do you see what a difference a little clean living makes?"

"Absolutely," she solemnly agreed. "And don't forget the good company." Yet though she was poking fun at Lee, Stevie had noticed how little she missed the pills and powders she sampled so freely when she was around Samson and Pip.

Later, as she cleared away the breakfast dishes, she passed Lee's room. The door was open, and she heard him talking on the telephone. "Stone here," he said. "I'll be out of the office tomorrow. In fact, I'll be gone for a few days ... I don't know how many.... No, you can't reach me.... I'll check in tomorrow."

Stevie hadn't meant to eavesdrop, but she was flattered

by the realization that Lee was rearranging his life just to be with her. She thought again of Samson and Pip; if she didn't get in touch soon, they would think it strange. Yet she felt reluctant to call, to let her other life intrude on her time with Lee. Later, she'd leave a brief message with Pip's service, telling her not to worry. As for Samson, let him wonder where she was and with whom. Maybe he'd be sorry he had treated her so carelessly.

As Stevie stacked the dishes in the dishwasher, Lee came into the kitchen and ruffled her hair. "Ready for another run?" Lee teased.

"Any time," she answered breezily.

As they ran along the mountain trail, or rather, as Lee ran and Stevie struggled to keep up, there was an affectionate undertone to his teasing. And when she faltered, he praised her for making the effort. "You deserve a reward," he said, "not to mention an A for improvement. Have you ever been to a country auction . . . ?"

Stevie shook her head.

"Like to go?"

"You came from an auction, didn't you? There must be something good about it. . . ."

Lee smiled. "That one was different—just for money. This is a little like a treasure hunt," Lee said. "All kinds of junk, but you never know what you'll find. There's a place near here that has one every weekend. Sound like fun?"

Stevie nodded enthusiastically—and then thought of Samson saying fun was the most important thing in the world. Of course, a country auction would not be *his* idea of fun. But, Stevie decided, Samson hadn't been right, either, about what was important.

The auction was held in an old shed several miles outside of the town. It was obviously a popular local attraction. Dozens of cars were pulled up in a grass field alongside, some of them luxury sedans that, Lee told her, belonged to other weekenders from the city. Dressed in the wool shirt and jeans that had become her basic costume, Stevie had thought she might be out of place among women from the city. But here, she soon noticed, everybody dressed down.

The sale was already in progress when they entered the shed. A clutter of bedsteads, pictures with ripped canvases, Victorian marble washstands, and other bric-a-brac was being sold off by an auctioneer who looked to be about eighty years old.

As they took a place, standing on the fringes of the crowd, Lee got a few nods of recognition from the local people and Stevie got a few more of the wary looks. Unthinkingly, in a reflex reach for protection, she put her arm through Lee's and felt him respond with a slight squeeze.

Watching the ancient items being sold off, Stevie saw a few that appealed to her. But she had no money to buy . . . and, anyway, none of it would fit in the decor of her apartment. When Lee finally bid, she admired his choice, an old butter churn, its wood gleaming from years of use and handling.

"That's beautiful," she said. "What are you going to do with it?" Most people, she knew, turned them into lamps.

He looked at her wide-eyed. "What else would I do? I'm going to try to make butter. . . ."

Unable to participate, Stevie's attention had begun to wander when she became aware of Lee bidding again. Turning to the front of the room, she saw one of the auction helpers holding up a black velvet box containing an old silver-backed dressing ensemble of brush, comb, and mirror. It surprised her when the bidding went over two hundred dollars and Lee continued to chase it; then she recalled the considerate way he had stocked his guest bathroom. He bought it at last for four hundred dollars, and shortly after told Stevie he was ready to call it a day.

When they returned to the house, Lee spent a while deciding where in the living room the churn might look best "until he got around to making butter." Moving it here and there, he kept asking Stevie if she liked how it looked. Just when she was thinking he was being a little too fussy, it came through that his repeated question was a special form of sharing—almost as if asking was a way of saying he wanted her to go on being comfortable with everything in his home.

"There, near the mantel," she dared at last. "I like that best."

"I think you're right," he said, and put the churn down. Then he picked up the velvet box. But he didn't carry it to the guest room; he brought it to her.

"And this is for you, Stevie. It's my way of saying that I . . . I want you to take good care of yourself."

She reached out slowly, as though reaching for a mirage. It wasn't the gift that touched her so deeply, not the gift at all, but the thought alone.

"Thank you," she said, mustering only a whisper.

She sat on the sofa and opened the box, then lifted out the articles. The silver of the brush and comb were engraved with scrolled initials, she saw, and when she turned over the mirror she found it was etched with a message: "To our dearest Charlotte, on her Sweet Sixteenth."

She fought against the tears; she didn't want Lee to see her collapse, didn't want the questions that were bound to result. But then the past won, and she broke down.

Lee sat beside her. "Hey . . . was it something I said?"

"No, you didn't say anything. It's just that my sixteenth wasn't so sweet, and now . . . I wish I could go back. . . ."

He put his arm around her shoulder, and she nestled against him. "I understand," he said. "Sometimes things happen and you can never go back and do it over, no matter how much you want to."

Strange, she thought, Samson's assurance had been so different. He had made her believe that childhood could be lived again—yet, after trying to recapture that childhood with him, she felt so much older than she had before.

"What about you?" she asked Lee. "Are there things like that in your life?"

"The usual," he said with a deprecating smile, "nothing that entitles me to any sympathy. I figure at some point you have to put all the ghosts and demons of the past to rest . . . quit blaming them for everything that goes wrong and take your own shot, do your best."

"Just like that?" she asked.

He shrugged. "What's the alternative, Stevie?"

She had no ready answer, and while she envied his matter-of-factness about the past, she resented it, too, because she couldn't share it.

They sat together until the room grew dark. Then he got up and made the dinner, alone this time—spaghetti carbonara washed down with Poland Spring water, another training menu.

As they cleared and washed the dishes together, Stevie began to anticipate the evening to come. Surely, he felt it too—the closeness, the stirring of desire.

But tonight there was no fireside chat or foolish strumming on the banjo. Tonight, he apologized for having some work to do and beat a hasty retreat. "Wouldn't hurt you, either," he said, "to keep country hours. . . ."

She nodded. What hurt was that he'd obviously decided to go so far and no further.

The following morning, Stevie got up early once again and began her slow, hard run up the mountain. Don't stop, she told herself, don't stop. Just one more minute, and after that another. You can do it, you can do it . . . And somehow, miraculously, she did! Winded and exhausted, she found enough breath for a triumphant Indian whoop that bounced off the walls of rock and came back at her. She couldn't believe how good she felt over such a small, stupid thing. Wait till Lee woke up, she thought, wait till he saw her. At this rate, she might even beat him in a week or so—though how did she even know she'd be around in a week or so? This was crazy. She jogged back to the house and looked in Lee's bedroom, but he wasn't there.

She waited on the porch, but there was no sight of him. When Lee returned, it was obvious he'd been searching for Stevie and was frantic with worry. "Thank God you're okay!" he said with obvious relief, his voice trembling, holding her so close she could hardly breathe. "I couldn't imagine where you'd be. . . . I thought maybe you'd left."

"I was running," she admitted in a small voice. "Up to the mountain. . . . I wanted to surprise you."

They looked at each other. His gray eyes melted. Something had happened, something magical. She felt breathless and dizzy and wonderfully happy all at once. Lee's face told her he was feeling it too. He kissed her gently at first, and then with a growing passion. He picked her up and carried her to his big oak bed, laid her down tenderly. He touched her as if she were precious, every bit of her, tenderly, lovingly, murmuring sweet words against her throat, her breasts. It was as if she'd never been with a man before, and she hadn't, not like this, not with such tenderness and warmth. She felt as if she were melting into Lee.

She lay in his arms feeling more complete and more at peace than she'd ever felt in her life. It seemed he had taken everything that was missing and made her a gift of it, erased everything ugly that had ever happened and made her new again.

"I've never brought anyone else here before," he said before they went to sleep.

"Good," she said. "Then I won't have to scratch anyone's eyes out."

The next three days were like a dream. Lee was lover and friend and parent, pampering Stevie as she'd never been pampered before. They hiked in the woods, they went to the movies and ate popcorn, they sat up late. And best of all, in the quiet early morning, Lee said, "I love you." Stevie knew there were people who threw the word around. But from Lee the word meant something real. It was as if she'd wandered and wandered and finally come home.

"Do we have to go back?" she said. "Why can't we stay here another few days—or weeks?"

"Don't worry," he said, caressing her cheek. "I'll love you in the city too, Stevie. What we have isn't just for here."

When Stevie let herself into her apartment, she couldn't help noticing how sterile it felt, more like a department-store model than a home. There were a dozen messages on her answering machine, all from Pip, and one more urgent than the next.

"Where the hell have you been?" she demanded when Stevie called her. "I've been worried sick—and Samson is *furious*."

"I left a message with your service," Stevie said. "I'm sorry you were worried, but I was away . . . with a man. You know how it is. . . ." She trailed off, allowing Pip's imagination free rein. Somehow she couldn't say any more about Lee Stone or her time with him; it was . . . sacred.

"Tell all, you sly thing," Pip insisted. "Who's the lucky guy? And how is it I've never met him? Have you been hiding a secret lover all this time?"

"No, I haven't been hiding him. We met last week. He . . . he invited me to his country house and I went. You know me, I'll try anything once." She laughed. "Is Samson really that mad?" she asked then, torn between her feelings for Lee and her loyalty to her friends. "What did he say . . . ? About me, I mean?"

"Oh . . . the usual Samson tantrum-stuff. He'll get over it. He'd better. After all, he may *think* you can't go to the bathroom unless he says okay, but you're a big girl, Stevie, and you have every right to spend a few days with a guy without getting a green light from him. Now, when are we going to meet this hunk of yours? Tonight, I hope?"

"I . . . I can't," she stammered, feeling like a traitorous hypocrite. How could she tell Pip what Lee thought about the Wherehouse and everything connected with it?

"I understand . . . new love. It's all very exclusive. Call me when the fires ebb. We'll all get wrecked and have a blast."

Pip's understanding only made Stevie feel worse. How long could she make excuses to her friends? And how could she make Lee understand that her friends weren't a threat, either to Stevie or to the feelings she and Lee shared? Maybe she could arrange something neutral. Maybe they could all go out together, and then Lee could see that the Wherehouse wasn't just about drugs and sex.

For the next two weeks, Lee saw Stevie almost every night. Dinners at good restaurants, or movies together, and making love afterward, staying with him through the night at his apartment. He hinted a few times that he wanted to see her place, but she was ashamed of it, its absence of personality—its part in her past.

While she loved being with Lee, she felt that it wasn't the same as when they had been in the country. It had been so simple there. And he had been with her every minute. Now, when he was working during the day, she felt shaky, isolated. Her days had no real purpose, and she began to feel as though she was just marking time. How could she sustain the feeling she had for Lee? Or should she bother trying . . . ?

She thought about calling one of the editors who'd used her in a fashion layout, but she was afraid that Samson would hear of it. So she fell back into the habit of sleeping late, then roaming the city shopping for the kind of clothes she could wear on her dates with Lee. She lunched occasionally with Pip, gaining weight, she noticed ruefully, now that her interest in food had revived. Marking time until she could be with Lee.

One evening, as she was waiting for him to arrive, she received an apologetic phone call. "I have to go to Washington," he said, "in less than an hour. It's an emergency. . . . I'll be away for a week, maybe ten days."

Stevie was seized by panic. "Take me with you," she said. "I won't be in your way, and at least we can be together at night."

"I can't, Stevie," he said with obvious regret. "There's nothing I'd like better than a trip with you, but this can't be it. My government contract is in real trouble, and I'll be in meetings 'round the clock until I can straighten out these problems. I'll make it up to you when I get back. That's a promise. Take care of yourself. I mean really take care of yourself. . . ."

"I always take care of myself," she said, thinking already of the empty days ahead.

"You know what I mean. Promise me, Stevie. . . . I'm not hanging up until you do."

"Okay, I promise."

She tried to keep that promise, but with Lee away, it seemed that his magic had gone with him. All she had were his daily phone calls, and they just weren't enough when she felt lonely and bored and frightened. How could he go away and expect her to be all alone? And how could he expect her to give up her friends?

Finally, after eight days, she called Pip.

"So soon?" Pip teased. "I guess passion isn't what it used to be. Don't tell me I'm finally going to meet the mysterious Lee."

"He's away on business," Stevie said. "But when he gets back, we'll do something, I promise. But tonight, I thought . . ."

"You want to be with your oldest and dearest friends, of course."

10

Stevie dressed with special care, in the leather outfit Samson had chosen from one of his favorite designers. She made up her face the way he liked it and put on the two pairs of false eyelashes that had become her trademark. And all the while, she felt the way she had the first time she'd gone to the Wherehouse with Pip—nervous and scared and desperate to fit in. Automatically she reached for the bottle of reds in the medicine cabinet. There were just two left. She'd never intended to take any again after that weekend with Lee. . . .

A picture of him rose in her thoughts, a memory of running with him through the cool, pine-scented woods . . . and then of being in his arms. She felt a rush of guilt at abandoning the new hopes he had given her. . . .

Hell, he was the one who had gone away, abandoned her. Left her to fend for herself when he, more than anyone, knew how much she depended on him. She swallowed the pills; she'd have to be up tonight, at her best.

By the time she met Pip, she was feeling a lot better, a lot more in control. When they reached the Wherehouse, they were laughing and joking together, the way they always did. Stevie couldn't remember why she'd been so worried.

The party tonight was a small one, only for Regulars. Samson was reclining on the black couch; beside him was a young girl with blond hair and green eyes. He was studying her palm intently as he spoke: "The life line is rather short . . . that means you're one of the fortunate few who never has to worry about getting old and ugly. The love line, on the other hand, is very strong, which is even better. . . ."

Pip and Stevie went over, and Stevie sat down on Samson's left. "Hi," she said warmly.

He paused a second, then, without even looking at her, went on with his reading: "It means for as long as you live, you'll have men wanting you, dying for you. Now the career line—"

"Cut the shit, Samson," Pip said sharply.

He looked up now, and smiled at Pip. "You don't like my interpretation? Perhaps you'd care to read this adorable palm." He lifted the blonde's hand in Pip's direction.

"What I don't like is your giving Stevie the cold shoulder," she said.

"Oh dear, you're right," he said silkily. "Where *are* my manners? Stevie, Pip, I'd like you both to meet Baby Jean. She's not only the prettiest thing I've seen in years, she's extremely talented. I can make her a star, don't you think? She'll be perfect for my next picture. And all the magazines want her for their new cover girl. . . ."

Stevie felt as though she'd dropped twenty floors in an elevator. She stared at Baby Jean for a long moment, taking in the blond hair, the bright, sparkling eyes; it was like looking into a mirror that showed her own past. Trembling with hurt, Stevie got up without a word and moved away, walking first, then running, until she had slammed out through the metal door.

In the concrete hallway, she leaned her head against the wall and began to cry. She couldn't believe Samson would be so cruel. Yes, she'd been angry with him, but weren't they supposed to be a family of friends?

Pip ran after her. "Don't cry, baby," she pleaded, holding Stevie and trying to comfort her. "Samson can't let anyone be close to him for too long. . . . That's how he is. He's a kind of cripple, Stevie. That name of his—Samson Love—it's another of his arty jokes—"the epitome of strength and love." But he can't love anyone, Stevie . . . because that would make him vulnerable like everyone else, and he just can't allow that to happen. When he really likes someone, the best he can do is give you a special, wonderful time—ten minutes in the spotlight, he calls it. He'll make all your wishes come true . . . and then he pushes you away, turns the spotlight on someone else. But it was going to happen anyway, Stevie. It always does. Your ten minutes was over even before you went away with your new boyfriend. So don't let it break your heart. It's not the end of the world. . . ."

"That's easy for you to say." Stevie sobbed. "It didn't happen to you."

"But it did," Pip replied softly. "My ten minutes in the spotlight came a year before yours. Samson took me everywhere. We were like brother and sister . . . and with me, Stevie, he even went further. He slept with me, Stevie. He didn't just watch, he made love to me a few times, until I thought . . ." She broke off and looked away. "Christ, it doesn't matter what I thought. Because then he just cut me off. I'd walk in here, and he'd look right through me; I'd try to talk to him, and he'd do that number he just did on you. I should've cut loose, too, but I couldn't. You know what this place means to people like us—it's home . . . family. So I couldn't leave, even if it hurt like crazy when I saw him do it again and again. That's when I forgave him.

And I think he actually likes me more than ever now ... because I don't expect him to be a real friend. ..."

Stevie was staring at Pip. "You mean, you knew when you said he'd like me ... you knew this would happen, too ... ?"

Pip shrugged. "It's the way he is. But Stevie, wasn't the ride worth the fall ... ?"

Was it? Could she forgive Samson? Nothing made any sense if the people you cared about abandoned you, no matter what you did.

"Come on, Stevie," Pip urged, "come on back inside. Show Samson you're strong enough to get right past his crap. He'll respect you for it—and that's more than he's done so far."

It was a thread of hope that Stevie needed to grasp. Otherwise, she thought, she would be alone again, without family. To the Admiral she was dead. To Lee she was someone disposable. She might not even keep Pip as a friend if she didn't stay near Samson.

"Okay," she declared to Pip. "So the prescription for this heartache is to stay with Samson even if you have to dance in the shadow outside the spotlight. Well, let's go for it. I may even get him to swing his goddamn spotlight back my way. ..."

She blotted her eyes with a handkerchief so as not to disturb the lashes, and marched back through the metal door and straight to the bar. Reaching into the big jellybean jar filled with multicolored pills, she grabbed a Dexedrine. Then she ordered a beer to wash it down. "Here we go," she muttered to Pip, who'd followed in her wake. "I'll show Samson I don't need his carnival in order to ride a merry-go-round."

She looked at the multicolored lights flashing over the area used for a dance floor and grabbed the first unattached man she saw. It was Paul Maxwell. Perfect, she thought.

Who better to send Samson a message that she could be a good sport, any place, any time?

Paul didn't need any persuasion to fall into movement with Stevie. Throwing her head back the way Pip did, Stevie began moving with wild abandon.

She never slowed down. Nothing, nobody could touch Stevie when she was high, and she wanted to be high forever, on top of the world—on top of the *stars!*—free and beautiful and immune to pain. She drank the champagne that Paul kept feeding her and inhaled the cocaine he shared so generously. And when he led her to the big black couch in a darkened alcove and removed her clothes, she simply felt glad he still wanted her. She needed so badly to be wanted by *someone*.

Two hours later, sitting beside Paul in his Mercedes sports car, the cocaine high dulled by the swirl of cool air around her head, Stevie felt the first pang of remorse. Why had she ever let Paul touch her when it was Lee she loved? What was it that made her do such crazy things?

Paul stopped the car in front of Stevie's building and draped his arm around her shoulders. "Why don't you come home with me tonight?" he asked, trying to draw her closer. "Wouldn't you rather spend the night with me than in a cold, lonely bed?"

"No, I wouldn't," she said, pulling away, anxious now to leave Paul and the memory of what she'd done with him.

"I don't like being jerked around, Stevie," he said angrily, "and I don't like this hot-and-cold act of yours."

"It's not an act," she said wearily. "I'm just tired, and I want to get some sleep." She got out of the car, stumbled against the curb, and nearly fell. Paul made no attempt to help. Without looking back, Stevie righted herself and hurried into the lobby.

The first thing she did when she entered her apartment was check the answering machine. No message from Lee. Now her remorse gave way to anxiety tinged with anger. He promised, she thought, he promised to call every day. . . .

There was a loud knock on the door. Dammit, she thought, if Paul thought he could follow her in and force himself on her . . . "I told you I was tired!" she shouted, yanking open the unlatched door.

Lee stood on the other side, a different Lee from the one who had left her with assurances of love. "So am I," he said in a quiet, strained voice.

"How did you get up here?" she asked, stalling for time to collect herself. "The doorman didn't—"

"I slipped him ten bucks," he said grimly. "I came home early to surprise you. I was waiting outside for three hours . . . and just walked around the corner for a cup of coffee before coming back. Stupid of me, huh? All I had to do was drive to the Wherehouse. Isn't that where you were coming from? I saw your boyfriend drop you off—"

"He isn't my boyfriend!" Stevie countered. "I can explain, Lee, just let me explain. . . ." She reached for him, but he grabbed her arm, marched her to the bathroom, and forced her to look in the mirror. Her eyes were bleary, her pupils dilated, her makeup smeared. Stevie's face told the story of her evening better than any words could.

"Explain this," he said with disgust. "Explain that guy's hands all over you, Stevie. Explain how you could barely stand up when you left him."

"It's all your fault!" she shouted. Desperate to escape his accusing words, to erase the pitying look in his eyes, she ran into the bedroom.

He pursued her. "My fault? Okay, explain it. This ought to be good. . . . I'm waiting to hear."

"I begged you not to leave me alone, but you did anyway. I needed someone with me," she went on, her voice growing soft and childlike.

"Someone?" he echoed pointedly.

"You!" she cried. "I needed you! I can't help it, Lee—I'm not ready to be alone. Maybe someday, but not yet. And you left me. If you didn't want me to see my friends, you should have taken me with you."

Lee's eyes narrowed. "Stevie, I want to be your lover, not your nursemaid. Are you saying that if I'm not watching you twenty-four hours a day, seven days a week, you'll start poisoning yourself and sleeping with whoever gives you the poison?"

"No!" she screamed, her body shaking, "it isn't like that. Can't you understand, Lee? I've had so little I could trust . . . I have to learn that, Lee. Give me a chance." She groped for the words that would explain how wonderful she felt in his arms, how lonely and frightened she got when he went away, how empty her days seemed when he wasn't there. "I love you," she said finally, reaching for him. "I love you. . . ."

He caught her hands at the wrists, holding her away. "For me, Stevie? For myself? Or am I just a crutch— someone, some*thing* to hang on to when there's nobody else around? That's the way it looks to me now, and I can't take you on those terms."

She pulled her hands free and turned away in despair. Why was he twisting everything around? Why couldn't he just put his arms around her and hold her, tell her he understood, and that he wanted to protect her forever . . . ?

From behind, she heard him at her shoulder, his voice very gentle. "Don't you get it, Stevie? You won't be able to love me until you love yourself—until you don't trash yourself. Love is a prize, Stevie, a treasure—and it doesn't come cheap." He took her by the shoulders and turned her around to face him. "And I'm a man, Stevie, not a crutch. I want you to love me the way a woman loves a man. God knows how much I want that, but . . ."

Stevie had stopped listening. As she watched Lee's lips move, heard the tone of his voice and saw the look on his face, she knew she had lost him. He had promised her love, but he had lied, like everyone else, and now he was trying to make that her fault.

". . . maybe you need the kind of help I can't give," he went on. "It hurts like hell to see you like this, but I care about you. I suppose I was wrong to think you were strong enough to just walk away from that Wherehouse crowd and everything they stood for. And if that's so, let me help you get some treatment . . . whatever it costs, Stevie . . ."

The offer touched a raw nerve, reminding her of the Admiral's approach—the godlike assumption of his own perfection while everyone else needed to be trained and given treatment under his orders, the way he'd arranged "treatment" to have her baby killed.

"I don't need any goddamn treatment!" she lashed out, shrieking. "And I don't need your charity or your help. If you think I'm such a helpless loser, then get out and find yourself some uptown bitch who's as perfect as you are!"

Lee stood rooted to the spot, staring at Stevie, as if waiting for her to take back what she'd said. She stared back and said nothing. She'd played this same eyeball-to-eyeball game with the Admiral, and intended never to give in again.

At last he spun around and left without a word, closing the door quietly behind him. But the soft click of the latch detonated in Stevie's ears with the force of a bomb. It was a sound more ominous to her than a door slammed in the heat of anger; in his peaceful acceptance of departure, there was a finality more devastating than an angry rage that at least suggested some possibility of second thoughts, reparations, some later effort to make up. No, Lee had given up on her, had judged and condemned her at last in the space of a single heartbeat.

She wanted to cry, to pound the bed and soak her pillow with tears. But tears wouldn't come. All she could manage to find was a pathetic whimper of pain. As if thinking it might give her the energy to set free the full cry of misery, she went to one of her drawers and rummaged in the back —sure there must be some loose pills. She found one, blue-green; she couldn't remember what it was called. She took it without water, heedless of the bitter taste, then slid onto the bed. In a while, her body began to throb and her mind seemed to go mercifully blank. What was love? She tried to remember. Who was Lee . . . ?

11

"I hate Thanksgiving in New York," Pip declared with a broad gesture that took in the penthouse apartment and all it represented. "I hate the Macy's parade, and cranberry sauce, and the stupid fucking Pilgrims, and I hate Norman Rockwell."

Stevie wasn't sure whether to second her friend's feelings or argue against them. It had been a year since her first lonely Thanksgiving in New York. Wasn't this one better? Instead of being alone, she had Pip. And so many wonderful things had happened to her in the space of twelve months.

Yet in some ways it seemed as bad as last year. . . . Worse.

Pip lit another cigarette and began to pace. "I should have gone with Valentine to Palm Beach. You could've come too, Stevie. . . . At least we would have had some sun, even if it is deader than a cemetery there."

"Your mother wouldn't want me there," Stevie said. She had noticed, in spite of Pip's assurances to the contrary, that Valentine had grown less cordial when they talked on the phone or met at the apartment.

Pip stopped in front of one of the windows and stood

brooding before a view of the city's jagged skyline. "The damn truth is, Stevie, she didn't really want me, either. Not unless it was completely on her terms. If she liked me, wouldn't she take me the way I am?"

"Sure," Stevie said. "Who wouldn't love you the way you are?"

And me . . . ? Stevie was lost for a second in thoughts of Lee.

Pip scooped up the tumbler of vodka she'd left on the windowsill. "You too, lovable Stevie. Here's to us!" She hoisted the glass and swallowed the contents. Then she stared out the window again. "Why do they call the turkey a bird?" she asked idly. "It can't fly. We're not birds, are we . . . ?"

They were both in a strange mood—reflective, bored, restless, not sure of what to do with themselves. It had been this way since Samson had frozen them out. There had been no official excommunication, no message given. They had simply gone to the Wherehouse and found it all but deserted, the Regulars away "on location," they were told, shooting Samson's new movie. With a couple of phone calls, Pip had learned that the location was, in fact, a town house that Samson owned on East Seventy-first Street, near Central Park. He had bought it years ago, but had never lived in it. On the top floor, he had a skylit studio where he retreated to work when he needed to get away from the madness of the Wherehouse. The rest of the house was used for storage. As Samson had often said himself, he was an incurable collector; he was always buying—furniture, clothes, art, jewelry, coins, antique toys, old refrigerators—and he kept much of it in the uptown house, heaped to the ceiling.

A couple of days before, Stevie and Pip had mustered the nerve to go to the house, intending to ask Samson to forgive them, to take them back. But the front door had been answered by a muscular young man with a Bronx accent dressed as a butler who had told them no one, but *no one*, was being allowed in or out of the house while Samson was at work on the movie. Pip, always defiant, had persuaded the young man to take in a message that she and Stevie were eager to be part of the "fun." After waiting ten minutes, the young man—not a butler, Pip had guessed, but a stud playing a part in the film—had returned and handed them two limp balloons. They were, said the butler before firmly closing the door, the whole of Samson's answer.

Stevie had been mystified. But Pip had always possessed better insight into Samson's cruel wit. "That's for our fun," she explained. "We're supposed to take them . . . and blow."

Since then they had been at loose ends, desperately trying to keep each other amused.

Pip refilled her tumbler of vodka from the antique French sideboard that served as a bar and took another long drink. "So what if Samson's gone uptown," she said with a broad shrug. "He'll come back to us, wait and see. He'll miss the action and the freaks . . . and he'll miss us."

"Do you really think so?" Stevie asked, wanting to believe Pip's prediction, needing to believe at least one loss would be temporary and that Samson would soon reclaim them.

But the flame of optimism in Pip's dark eyes flickered out. "I don't know, Stevie. This time, I think . . ." She trailed off, and resumed walking aimlessly back and forth. Her relentless pacing across the Aubusson carpet began to stretch Stevie's nerves to the breaking point.

"Hey," Stevie said, "we're forgetting our Thanksgiving dinner. That stuff the caterer brought smells great. We'll eat, then go to a movie or a show. Come on, Pip, we don't have to be down. We still have each other. . . ."

Pip looked at her friend with an expression of tenderness. "You're right, kiddo . . . what else do we need? Let's give thanks. . . . We'll give thanks 'til it hurts." She put a four-year-old Peter, Paul, and Mary album on the record player and went about laying the antique refectory table with Valentine's best Belgian-lace tablecloth, her Spode china, Cristoffle silver, and Waterford crystal.

"There," she said. "I'll bet those tacky Pilgrims never dreamed of anything like this. Now, let's get to the feast."

They went into the spacious old-fashioned kitchen, where Valentine's favorite caterer had delivered a picture-perfect roast turkey with candied yams, a mixed salad, and a still-warm pumpkin pie. "Yum. This looks wonderful," Stevie said as she carried one of the platters and a chilled bottle of champagne into the dining room. She wasn't particularly hungry, and in spite of her attempt to cheer up Pip, she'd been struggling with her own feelings of emptiness ever since she had awakened that morning. She shook her head, as if to throw off the jumbled images of "home," of her parents and Samson, of Lee, who had let her believe for a little while that his love would make her whole. No point in dwelling on might-have-beens; better to fake a little cheer until the real thing came along.

Pip popped the cork on the champagne, appraised the table, which was now laden with food, and asked, "What's wrong with this picture?"

Stevie played along. "I give up."

"Wait and see," Pip said, running off to her room. She returned quickly and dropped a handful of assorted pills in front of each place setting. "There," she said. "Now we have turkey with *all* the trimmings."

"Great," Stevie enthused, welcoming the euphoria she knew would come soon. "Shall we dig in?"

They sat down.

But Pip hesitated. "Wait a second. First we have to give thanks." She folded her hands and bowed her head.

Stevie was astounded. She had never seen a religious side to her friend.

But then Pip began to intone her special prayer. "I thank my mother for giving me everything, so who needs to work? And I thank her for leaving me alone so I can do what the hell I like. And I thank the guy who invented the Pill, so I can fuck anyone, anytime I want, and not have to worry about getting knocked up." She looked at Stevie. "Did I leave anyone out?"

"Yeah," Stevie said, raising her glass, "you left out Pip Mason. Thanks for being my friend—so who needs Samson or anyone else?"

Pip's beautiful face twisted with pain; two bright tears appeared in her big dark eyes. Then she caught herself. "Hey," she said sharply. "You're breaking the rules. Cheap sentiment is *out*!"

"Okay, okay," Stevie agreed. "Then here's to good times." She closed her eyes, picked a pill at random, and washed it down with champagne. "Your turn."

But Pip was gazing absently at her plate.

"Hey," Stevie said, "don't be a turkey. I want to fly together."

Pip looked up, and a spark came back into her eyes. "Oh, I'll keep up. In fact, let's make it fun—the way Samson would." She made a row of all the pills by her plate. "I challenge you to a game of 'Who's Still Standing.' The loser cleans up—after she wakes up." Pip swallowed down a pill.

Stevie took up the challenge, drinking down a second pill.

Between bites of Thanksgiving dinner, they matched each other's pill-popping two, three, four times.

Then Stevie noticed tears running down Pip's cheeks. "What is it . . . ?"

"Everything, Stevie. It's everything. The good times are all over and never coming back."

Stevie had never seen this before; Pip was always up, bubbling, ready to climb over any obstacle. "Hey, Samson wasn't God. There'll be other—"

"It isn't just Samson, Stevie. It's everything. The Sixties, Woodstock, love . . . it's over."

"Hold on, baby," Stevie said, sensing a kind of emergency in the crash of Pip's mood. "You must have taken too many downers. Try a couple of reds. Get yourself up. We're supposed to be having a good time, remember?"

"Yeah . . . you're right. It must be the downers." Pip picked two amphetamines out of the mound by her plate, leaned back in her chair, and closed her eyes. A few moments later, she rose unsteadily from her chair. "'Scuse me, Stevie. I have to go."

Stevie wasn't quite sure what Pip meant until she saw her heading toward one of the apartment's several bathrooms.

"Want me to help you?" Stevie asked, noticing that Pip could hardly walk.

Pip gave Stevie a funny look. "No, I'll do this on my own. But thanks for asking." She wobbled over to Stevie's chair and kissed her cheek. "I love you, Stevie," she said. "The only one . . ."

Stevie swallowed two more pills. She was feeling fuzzy now, not exactly happy, but not sad, either.

It seemed a long while before she realized that Pip had not returned. But perception of time couldn't be trusted in her condition. Perhaps it was thirty seconds, perhaps thirty minutes. Stevie waited a while longer.

At last she pushed herself up and went to the closed door

of the nearest bathroom. She knocked. "Pip?" she called out, "Pip, you in there? You feeling okay?"

No answer. Stevie tried the knob, and the door opened. The bathroom was empty.

There were three more bathrooms in the apartment, and Stevie went to every one. They were all empty. With rising alarm, she started to run through the bedrooms . . .

The shriek of sirens penetrated from the street below. Then, in Pip's bedroom, Stevie saw that a door to the penthouse terrace was standing open. She tripped and fell in her haste to reach it. Her heart was pounding furiously as she hung over the railing and looked straight down . . . fifteen stories. A crowd of people milled around like ants near a tiny police car and an ambulance. Then Stevie saw the square of white cloth spread on the ground. From the distance it looked like a handkerchief—but Stevie knew it wasn't. A cry of anguish tore her throat, and then she crumpled to the floor.

It was worse than a nightmare. It was all too horribly real . . . sitting amidst the rubble of their Thanksgiving feast—the barely touched food, the partially consumed drugs—feeling dazed and sick to her very soul, struggling to answer the police's questions when all she wanted was to swallow a handful of pills and sleep for a long, long time, maybe forever.

The questions came at her over and over, the same ones, as if the police believed she was lying, when the truth was that she could scarcely think and couldn't bear to remember the last moments she'd spent with Pip. Though their voices were insistent, the officers weren't unkind. Yet she could hear contempt mingle with pity in their questions, see the disgust overriding compassion in their eyes. She desperately wanted them to go away.

Had Pip been despondent? they wanted to know. A little,

Stevie answered, but she was changeable in her moods; it was hard to know exactly what Pip Mason was feeling at any particular time.

What kind of pills, and how many, had Pip consumed? they asked. Stevie didn't know; she wasn't sure. She tried to explain the game they'd been playing, and when she saw the officers shake their heads, she said no, it wasn't like that, Pip had been unsteady, but not out of her mind. She wasn't what they were thinking, some drug-crazed, spoiled rich kid who'd flown out the window. "She doesn't . . . didn't like acid," Stevie explained. "It was just uppers and downers. She said she was going to the bathroom . . . that's all. Maybe she was feeling a little sick. Maybe she went outside to get some air. It was an accident. . . . Oh, God, it had to be an accident." Stevie began to sob uncontrollably, her slender body shaking with a crying that produced no tears. She felt a strong hand on her shoulder, but there was no comfort in it.

Someone handed her a glass of water. She drank a little, coughing and hiccuping so hard she could scarcely catch her breath. When she steadied herself, the questioning began again. The officers wrote down everything she said, yet she felt they believed her account to be worthless. They took her address and said she might be questioned again.

When they offered to drive her home, Stevie shook her head. She couldn't bear to be home alone, not now. But where could she go? All she could think of was Samson. He'd been at the heart of her friendship with Pip, and though he had turned his back on them he was the one person who would know how much Pip meant to her.

"I'm not leaving," she screamed when the girl who answered the door said Samson was in the middle of his Thanksgiving dinner. Forcing her way in, she stood in the marble foyer and cried his name louder than she'd ever called for anything. "Samson! *Samson* . . . !"

He came down the stairs a moment later, dressed in a costume of blue ruffled shirt and blue velvet breeches— Little Boy Blue all over again.

He smiled and held out his hand, as if welcoming her in on a simple social call. "Pretty Stevie . . . what a nice surprise," he said. Then, as if her terrible shriek hadn't already alerted him, he glanced into her distraught face. "But tell me what's wrong?" he asked quietly.

She tried to speak, but the words wouldn't come and she simply threw herself into Samson's arms. He held her and stroked her hair; the tender gesture made Stevie ache for all that had been lost to her. He led her into the living room, which was piled high with boxes and crates, sat her down on the sofa, and touched her cheek gently. "What's wrong?" he repeated. "Are you in some kind of trouble, Pretty Stevie?"

"It's Pip," she blurted out. "Oh, God, Samson, Pip's dead, she's dead. . . ." She buried her face in his chest and began to murmur the details until she was overtaken by sobs, flooding his silk shirt with salty tears. He sighed but said nothing, and through the sound of her own weeping, Stevie could hear the swinging pendulum of the grandfather clock that stood at the entrance to the room.

Finally, Stevie pulled away and looked into his eyes, a silent entreaty of her own. She needed a reaction from him. He didn't seem shocked or surprised or even sad. "She's dead, Samson," Stevie repeated. "This isn't make-believe."

Samson gave her a thin smile. "Oh no, Pretty Stevie, I know that. Only what came before was make-believe. Death is the realest thing there is. But Pip was ready for it."

"Ready?" Stevie shied away, Samson's callousness affecting her with almost the force of a physical blow. "Samson, she was so young, and so full of—"

"And her ten minutes in the spotlight was over. She was a has-been, Stevie, and she knew it."

Stevie shook her head, amazed at Samson's cold, cruel reason and unwilling to accept it. Though she saw now that others of Samson's coterie had come partway down the stairs to watch and listen. All this was nothing but a performance for them.

"Why don't you go home and try to get some rest," Samson said. "You look—"

"No!" she cried, hating Samson, yet still needing him, wishing that all the painful realities could be made unreal again, wishing she could see the tragedy of Pip as nothing more than an episode in a staged drama. "Oh, please, Samson, could I stay with you for a little while? Please don't send me away now. . . ."

He hesitated, but only for a moment. "All right," he agreed with a sigh. "I'll give you something to help you sleep. When you feel more rested . . ." He left the thought unfinished as he searched the pillbox he always carried and produced two Nembutals.

Stevie took them obediently and retreated to an upstairs room. She fell on the bed fully clothed and waited for sleep. But the downers weren't enough to erase those last moments with Pip, to keep her brain from playing them over and over. Had Pip suddenly decided life was unbearable? Stevie knew what it was like to feel beaten and lost, to feel it was just too much trouble to go on, but she couldn't imagine actually taking that final step from which there was no turning back.

Staring up at the blank ceiling, Stevie had a horrible vision of Pip falling through space—seeing Death waiting below, with great shrouded arms ready to embrace her—being so afraid and so terribly lonely. She cried out, feeling

Pip's pain as if it were her own, and then she was embraced herself by a consuming darkness.

She returned slowly to consciousness with a throbbing headache. Her eyes seemed to be glued shut, and it was with great effort that she forced them open. With vision came memory—and an inescapable anguish.

She dragged herself into the bathroom. The face in the mirror was frightening, the skin pasty and colorless, the eyes dull and vacant. She ran some cold water and splashed it on her face. The effort exhausted her, and though she felt she should do something, she didn't know what. Samson would know, she thought, Samson always knew. . . .

The house was quiet and still as Stevie searched for him, making her way past the cartons and shopping bags that held years' worth of voracious collecting. She found him on the top floor, in the spacious skylit studio he'd made from three smaller rooms. He was bent over a drafting table, completely absorbed in what he was doing, and when he saw Stevie, he frowned, as if he'd forgotten or no longer cared that she was here.

"I'm busy working," he said, and when Stevie didn't move, he added, "Take it out of here, Pretty Stevie. I can't change what happened to Pip, and I can't help you anymore. Black clouds are contagious, and if you want to hang on to yours, take it to the Campbell Funeral Home. They're having a service for Pip this afternoon. Quite a gala affair, I gather. The Grand Duchess is even interrupting her holiday in Palm Beach to attend."

"A service?" she repeated, grasping at the chance to be somehow with Pip, to express her love. "Come with me, Samson . . . please? Just that, and I won't ask—"

"No!" he cut in sharply. "Save your breath, Pretty Stevie. I don't do funerals or wakes." He fished out his faithful pillbox again. "If you need a friend to get you through, here are a few."

Stevie picked out a couple of uppers. "But didn't you care about her, Samson . . . even a little bit?"

Samson turned his back, and for a moment she thought he was dismissing her again. But then he faced her once more, wearing the ironic smile she'd come to know so well. "Yes," he said softly, "I did care for our Pip. And that's why I wouldn't dream of partaking in some dreary ritual. Our Pip was born again last night right here, Pretty Stevie. I haven't finished, but I'll break the rules this once and let you see it now. Behold our Pip . . . the way I'll remember her." Samson moved away, allowing Stevie to glimpse the work on his drafting table. It was a montage of photographs over which Samson had drawn some colored outlines that somehow made each of the images even more vivid—Pip laughing, her head thrown back in careless abandon; Pip clowning, her tongue stuck out at Samson's camera; Pip dressed up for Halloween, so alive that Stevie could scarcely bear to look. She ran all the way down the stairs and out of Samson's house.

Stevie sat in the back of the crowded chapel, nervously twisting her handkerchief and tugging at the black dress that seemed far too short for such a solemn occasion. She tried to concentrate as a man she didn't recognize eulogized the only friend Stevie ever had. But he seemed to be describing a Pip she didn't know. A girl who had graduated from the Brearly School with honors at age sixteen. A young woman whose debutante ball had been the talk of New York. A skilled horsewoman who had won blue ribbons for jumping and dressage.

Was that really our Pip? Stevie asked herself. And why did she leave those parts of herself behind?

More, Stevie thought, I want to know more about her.

But the speaker had no more to tell of Pip's life and talked instead of her death, of "a bright, shining light tragically extinguished before its time." A wail of anguish drowned out his closing remarks and cut through Stevie like a knife. It was Valentine, heavily shrouded in black. "My baby," she screamed, "my baby's gone forever." Friends reached out to comfort her, but Valentine's sorrow would not be contained. "Oh, God," she lamented, "she was so young, so beautiful . . . she had everything to live for. . . . Why didn't you take me instead?"

Why? Stevie repeated to herself. She closed her eyes for a moment and tried to feel Pip's presence here, amidst those who had cared for her. But no answers came. She heard only the rustle of clothing, the muted murmur of consoling words as the mourners began to file out slowly.

She opened her eyes and saw Valentine rise from her pew, supported on the arms of two friends. She stumbled like an old woman, broken and without hope. As she approached the doors of the chapel, Stevie put out a hand. "I'm sorry," she whispered. "I . . ."

Valentine turned pain-glazed eyes in her direction. When recognition came, she recoiled, giving Stevie a look redolent with hatred. "Are you satisfied with your work? Murderer! My baby was an angel . . . a beautiful angel, until you and your kind stole her away. Now you've killed her! You've killed my Pip!"

Her friends bore Valentine outside, leaving Stevie reeling from the force of her attack. She slumped back into her pew, Valentine's words imprinted forever on her brain. She wanted to tell herself that Pip's mother was wrong, that she would never have done anything to harm her only friend, not when she loved her so. But the seed of guilt Stevie herself had planted now bloomed with the accusation. She could have done something to save Pip . . . she *should* have done something. Why did she go along with that stupid game? Why didn't she see or hear that something was wrong? And why, oh why, did she let Pip walk away from her?

Somehow she found her way out of the dimly lit chapel and into the street. She stumbled along, not knowing where she was going, feeling half dead herself. She couldn't think, and she didn't want to feel when feeling brought such terrible loneliness and pain.

She wandered aimlessly, not noticing the cold that reddened her face and chilled her fingers. The uppers had all but worn off, and Stevie was dreading the moment when there would be nothing between her and complete awareness. She had pills and liquor in her apartment, but she couldn't go there now, not to be more alone than she'd ever been before.

Stevie remembered Lee's strong arms, his honest gray eyes, his tender touch. Would he think of saving her now, give her love and comfort when she was so desperately needy? Or would he turn away in anger and disgust? She couldn't bear that, not now.

Then she thought of Paul Maxwell. He wouldn't turn away; he'd always wanted her, and though there was no love between them, he was better than being alone. If he couldn't offer comfort, he had plenty of what it took to reach forgetfulness.

The purple dusk of evening was falling across the East River when Paul Maxwell returned to his house on Beekman Place.

Stevie sat watching the light die. Paul had been out when she arrived, but the Oriental housekeeper knew her by sight and had admitted her to wait.

"What's this?" Paul said, advancing into the living room, which was hung with some of the largest and most valuable of Samson's paintings. "Brought me an early Christmas present, Stevie?"

When she continued to stare at him vacantly, he softened. "I heard about Pip, Stevie. . . . I'm sorry. I know how close the two of you were."

His words made her feel more kindly toward Paul than she had toward Samson, more sure of her choice. "I need a place to stay," she said.

"For how long?"

"I said," she replied, "to *stay*."

A thin smile oozed across his face. "Well, well," he crooned. "So it's like that now, is it?" He thought for a moment, considering the possibilities as Stevie held her breath. Then he summoned the houseboy. "Miss Knight will be staying with us for a while, Hashi. Check the room next to mine and make sure she has everything she needs?" He turned to Stevie. "Did you bring anything with you?"

She shook her head.

"Never mind . . . we'll send for it all tomorrow. You can move right in, make yourself at home. What would you like for dinner? Hashi can make you a tray if you're tired. . . ."

"I'm not hungry, Paul. I can't eat. But I . . . I need . . ."

He nodded. "Yes, I can see that. Follow me."

Over the next few weeks, Paul became Stevie's protector and provider. He supplied everything she wanted—food and clothing and shelter, and most important of all, the drugs that freed her of thought and responsibility.

In the stately house on Beekman Place, no one required Stevie to do anything, not to wash a dish or pick up after herself—or even to consume the delicious meals that were set before her. She was allowed to sleep, day or night, swaddled in silk sheets and cushioned against grief by the abundance of Paul's basement storage room. In return, all he took was the occasional use of her body, either in bed or at the downtown parties and orgies he liked to attend, in Soho and the Village. In those places, where memories of Stevie's celebrity lingered, Paul enjoyed showing her off as his personal pet.

At first, he seemed pleased to own her, even if ownership came through default. He bought her gifts—jewelry and furs to adorn the closetful of designer clothes he'd purchased. Yet as Stevie's dependency on him grew, as her spirit dulled and all but disappeared into the chemical fog that shrouded her every waking hour, Paul became resentful and cruel, as if she had somehow defrauded him and delivered merely the empty shell of the prize he'd once desired.

He began to taunt her with savagely cutting remarks about her ravaged beauty, with reports of fascinating people he'd met and enjoyed at Samson's parties, taking pleasure in reminding her that he, thanks to his wealth and social standing, was still welcome there, while she would be only tolerated, if he deigned to take her. If he was looking for a show of anger, a flash of fire, he was always disappointed, for Stevie endured his provocations as long as he provided her with drugs. The more secure he became about her dependence, the more he played with making her suffer. He had handcuffs, and sometimes manacled her in the shower, and made her sleep naked, standing up. He whipped her with a belt, and demeaned her with animalistic sexual demands.

On the morning of New Year's Eve, he delivered an ultimatum. "Enough is enough," he said. "Whatever your problem is, you'd better shape up or find another place to stay. I have seventy people coming in tonight, and I want them to have a good time. I don't want you walking around like a zombie or taking one of those crying jags. Now, if you can make yourself look decent, if you can help my guests have a good time, you can join the party. If not, stay in your room—and start packing."

The threat struck Stevie with terror. She would do whatever Paul wanted, anything to keep him from throwing her out.

She tried hard to make herself beautiful again. She forced herself out of the house and into a nearby beauty salon, using a hundred-dollar bill to bribe the owner into squeezing her into his full afternoon. Her hair was hastily cut and styled, her nails manicured, her dull skin revived with an organic facial.

When she returned to the house, she was careful to avoid running into Paul. She took only one upper though her body cried out for more, and asked the housekeeper for a Thermos of coffee. With shaking hands, she coated the dark circles under her eyes with heavy makeup and applied color to her cheeks and lips. As a final touch, she added the two sets of lashes that were once her trademark. She studied her handiwork in the mirror. She didn't look beautiful—but neither did she look like the zombie Paul had accused her of turning into. She slipped into a red Givenchy gown and offered herself for his inspection.

"Better," he said with measured approval, "much better. Just make sure you don't get too stoned or too drunk."

That part was harder, for as Paul's guests arrived, Stevie felt her panic mounting. She had nothing to say to anyone, yet she knew Paul expected her to be up and on—to perform, the way she used to at the Wherehouse. She started with a glass of champagne and surreptitiously swallowed a couple of reds. Willing the combination to work, she smiled brightly and began to flirt with a man who'd come without a date. Soon he was joined by another, and Stevie redoubled her efforts, searching their faces for the admiration she'd once evoked in every man's eyes.

As the house became crowded with people, however,

her anxiety grew. The air seemed too thin to breathe, the noise too loud to tolerate. Feeling giddy and faint, she excused herself and ran out through a rear door to a garden overlooking the river. Shivering against the icy winter wind, she wondered whether it wasn't time to join Pip.

"What the hell do you think you're doing?" Paul demanded, appearing behind her. He grabbed her arm and spun her around. "Are you drunk already? I warned you, Stevie. . . ."

"No," she protested, "I'm not drunk. I just needed some air. It's so stuffy inside."

"That's too damn bad," he said, "because we're about to show a Pretty Stevie Knight film festival, and we can't start without you. Now, move."

She obeyed, following Paul to the second-floor screening room. "Here's our star," he announced genially as he cut the lights. "Our first attraction is Stevie's last film— *Dracula's Dreams*—produced by yours truly. Enjoy it."

Stevie sat in the darkness and watched the flickering images on the screen. It all seemed so long ago, a different life and a different time, just as Samson had said. When she saw Pip's face, she choked back a cry and closed her eyes. Now she heard only voices, the voices of her past, talking and laughing. Suddenly she felt a hand on her thigh. She froze, but it didn't go away. Her eyes flew open. It was the man she'd been talking to earlier, and he was smiling with secret anticipation. "I've seen this picture before," he whispered. "Let's find someplace private where I can get to know the real Stevie Knight."

She wanted to say no, to push the hand away, but she was afraid to make a scene, afraid of what Paul might do if she offended his friend. She had nowhere else to go, nowhere in this world. She allowed herself to be led out of the screening room and into a darkened bedroom. She closed her eyes as she was pushed onto the bed, kept them shut as hands pushed up her dress, tore at her underclothes.

"Wake up," her companion urged. "This isn't much fun if you don't play along." Her arms went through remembered motions, draping themselves around his neck. Her legs parted, allowing him entry, then wrapping around his back. He thrust a few times, waiting for a response, and when there was none, he began pumping to his own rhythm. He finished quickly, grunting as he pulled out of her.

"Is this a private party, or can anyone join?" a new voice cut through the darkness.

"She's all yours," the voice beside her answered with a laugh.

Stevie heard the rustle of clothes, the closing of a zipper —then felt another body pressing on hers, warm breath on her face. Hands squeezed her breasts. Lips captured her own, insinuating the taste of alcohol into her mouth. The coupling repeated itself—and before it was done there were others, collecting around her, a crawling profusion of hands on her body, while some men used her mouth and others thrust inside her. It went on and on, and she didn't care.

When they were gone, she lay on the bed for a long time, imprisoned in her own inertia. Finally she got up and began straightening her clothes. She turned on the light and shuddered with disgust when she saw herself in the mirror. The expensive dress was torn; her face was smeared with makeup, her eyes dead. Pretty Stevie Knight wasn't pretty anymore. Worse than that, she'd become a dirty joke. How did it happen? she asked the mirror. Why did all the men in her life turn into the Admiral? a voice inside her asked. They looked different, they sounded different for a time, so why did it always turn out the same? The mirror answered:

Because you are worthless, Stevie, and you deserve to be treated that way. But what about Lee? the tiny voice of hope argued. He wanted only to help me, and he didn't ask for anything in return. Surely he was different? Ah, but he didn't want the real Stevie Knight, the mirror replied. He wanted someone decent and good, someone you don't know how to be.

No, no, Stevie screamed silently, pounding the mirror with her fists, oblivious to the flying glass that slashed her hands and arms. No, no, no, no . . .

She tried to move, but she couldn't. Her arms were bound to her body, which was stiff and cramped. She couldn't see much, but the smell told her she wasn't in Paul's apartment. It was a stale, human odor permeated with disinfectant. Her throat burned, her mouth was cottony, and she desperately craved a drink of water. She heard a hum of voices and activity, but it seemed to be coming from a far distance. With a great effort, she tried once again to free her arms, but succeeded only in bumping her head against what felt like a pillowless cot.

She was cold, her every muscle ached, she was thirsty, but most of all she was frightened. Suddenly she inhaled the fragrance of lavender, glimpsed an older woman's face, blond hair—and relief flooded over her. At last, she thought, at long last. "Mama," she moaned, "oh, thank God, Mama, you took me home." Stevie clutched at her white dress. "Oh, thank you, Mama. I'll never be bad again. I'll even do what *he* says. . . ." Stevie pointed to the Admiral, standing across the room, turned out in his dress whites.

The woman laid her hands over Stevie's and gently but firmly unhinged them from her dress. "I'm not your mama, child."

And Stevie realized then that the man in a white jacket and pants wasn't the Admiral.

"But if you think I am," the woman went on with a laugh, "you've certainly come to the right place." As if to answer the question forming in Stevie's eyes, she added, "Welcome to Bellevue."

Book Four

Unsettled as she already was by the confrontation between Anne Garretson and Livy, Stevie was completely thrown off balance by a simple telephone call. The voice on the wire belonged to Lee Stone. He greeted her warmly, a shade too heartily, she thought, and then reproached herself for making assumptions. Perhaps she was nothing more to him than an old love, pleasantly remembered.

"It's been a long time," he said. "Too long. I've wanted to get in touch, but . . . well, you know how it is."

"Yes," she said, "I know." It was easier to leave what had been painful alone, easier by far than trying to resurrect the broken promises of a love that had once seemed so right. "You sound so close," she said, striving for lightness.

"I am," he said. "I'm in Santa Fe . . . at Los Milagros."

Against her will, Stevie pictured the romantic old hotel she had once visited, alone, the warm, cozy room with a fireplace—a perfect hideaway for lovers. "What are you doing in New Mexico?" she asked, forcing herself into reality.

"I came to see you," he answered as promptly as a

heartbeat. "I know this is short notice, but I was hoping . . . Stevie, is it okay if I drive out tomorrow morning?"

"Yes, it's okay. I'll look forward to seeing you again," she said, the formal words belied by her racing pulse, the flush that warmed her cheek.

The day seemed to drag on endlessly, her excitement mounting with each passing hour. She rested little that night, and her attempts to sleep were punctuated by fantasies of Lee that lingered like an unfinished melody.

Unrested and confused as she was, Stevie felt almost light-headed as she waited for Lee to arrive. She tried to conduct her morning group session as usual, only realizing how distracted she was when one of the women snapped, "If we're boring you so much, Stevie, why don't you just go back to sleep?"

"I'm sorry," she said hastily. "I . . . I just have a lot on my mind." Stop it, she told herself, stop acting like a lovesick teenager. Lee is history, and your life is here.

But when he finally arrived, when he put his arms around her and held her close for an all-too-brief moment, common sense flew out the window, and Stevie found herself laughing and talking in a nervous rush, as if she could somehow fill in the years they had been apart. Taking Lee by the hand, she gave him a tour of The Oasis, proudly showing off her accomplishments, as if to prove once and for all that she was not the same woman he had judged and rejected.

"Enough!" he said with a laugh after it seemed they'd walked for hours. "I've seen enough. If you're trying to get even with me, you've succeeded."

"Get even?" she repeated, a puzzled look on her face. And then she remembered . . . the early-morning run in the mountains, with Lee in the lead, Stevie huffing and puffing as she tried to keep up. . . . God, it seemed like a lifetime ago, yet she could still recall every detail.

"Never mind," he said, disappointed that Stevie had obviously forgotten their time as lovers. "Can I buy you some lunch? At this point, I'll take any excuse to kick back and relax."

"Lunch is on the house. I'll call the kitchen and have something sent to my quarters."

She felt a pang of self-consciousness as Lee walked through her bedroom—the scene of her nocturnal fantasies about him—and out onto her patio garden. She felt it again when Gus Timmons, a senior member of the kitchen staff, delivered lunch. With elaborate care, he set the outdoor table with a linen cloth and napkins and then produced an artistic display of chicken breasts and wild mushrooms on sparkling white china plates. With the ceremonial touches of a wine steward, he poured sparkling water into two crystal glasses, then added twists of lime. "Do you need anything else?" he asked Stevie with a broad grin, a mischievous twinkle in his eye.

"No thanks, Gus . . . that's all."

"He thinks we're an item," Lee observed in a pleased tone of voice after Gus had left.

"We're just one big family here," she feinted. "Everyone looks out for everyone else."

"I can see that. Stevie, you can't imagine how proud I am of everything you've done."

"I didn't do it alone," she cut in. "Nobody like me can do it alone, Lee. . . ."

"That's why I'm here. Stevie. . . . I wanted to ask—"

"No! Please don't say anything else," she begged, fighting the remembrance of desire. "It just isn't possible for us . . ."

Lee flushed, and for a moment she thought he was angry. "I'm sorry, Stevie. . . . I should have explained when I called. The reason I'm here . . . it's about a woman. She needs your help. I hoped . . ."

"I see," she said, struggling to recover. "Are you married?" she asked, trying to mask her embarrassment.

"No." He gave no amplification, no details of the relationship. "She . . . she's a celebrity, Stevie. She's worried that being at The Oasis could damage her career."

"She doesn't have to worry. Everything that happens here is confidential."

Lee shook his head, his clear gray eyes pleading for understanding. "This isn't about your principles, Stevie. . . . She's involved with the news . . . She thinks *everything* is fair game."

"But I don't," she said quietly. "Tell your . . . friend she can trust me." Well, that's settled, Stevie thought. The choice isn't mine to make after all.

As Lee drove away from The Oasis, all he could think about was Stevie, more beautiful now than when he'd fallen in love with her, her face strongly defined with character and strength, aglow with the warmth. He had known it would be hard to see her again; he hadn't realized how painful the reminder of what he'd lost would be.

He had told himself it was only help for his lover he was seeking, yet it hurt like hell to know Stevie was beyond reach.

You blew it, Stone, he thought. You didn't even get to tell her how much you've changed since you let her go. Yet knowing all she'd been through, how could he clutter her happiness with his own problems? How could he explain the relationship he was in when he could scarcely understand it himself? She had blown into his life like a tropical storm, shaking him loose of all his moorings, drawing him into her path . . .

He'd been at a Washington reception for a Japanese trade delegation, expecting nothing more than to reinforce his business relationships when she had breezed through the door, swept the room with her eyes, and headed straight for him. "Are you someone I should know?" she asked, not bothering to introduce herself, confident apparently that everyone would know who she was.

Taken by her directness, Lee had laughed. "Why don't you find that out for yourself?" he said. She had proceeded to do just that. She'd been so vital and alive, so bright and sparkling—so much in control that she was able to magnetize a roomful of people with her restless energy.

She had bedded Lee with the same kind of determination she brought to her career, and for a time, he believed that life had given him a second chance. She broke into his loneliness, challenging him to keep up with her racing mind, her driving ambition—and her raw sexuality.

At first their lovemaking had been like nothing he'd ever experienced, wild and abandoned, more exciting than any adolescent fantasy because she was so vividly real. There was no time for complacency or even for the kind of easy comfort that comes with familiarity; she wouldn't allow it. She was always pushing the boundaries of their relationship in her headlong rush toward . . . what? Lee still couldn't answer that one.

The first time she asked him to hurt her in bed, he thought she was joking, that she wanted the kind of playful tussle that ended up with two people making love. And then she had shown him the leather handcuffs, the riding crop . . .

No way, he said, no way would he hit a woman.

"You don't understand," she said, showing an anger that was real, not playful. "If you want to make me happy, you'll play my game. . . ."

Against his every instinct, and because he wanted to make her happy, Lee tried. But he just couldn't bring himself to really hurt her, to meet the challenge in her glittering eyes.

And when she saw that he would not play, she mocked him for his reticence—and then, in the next moment, started making love with an intensity he couldn't fathom.

She bedeviled him with inconsistencies. Loving evenings alternated with broken dates. Wild, fantastic explanations or none at all. Once, when they were supposed to go away for the weekend, she simply disappeared; he learned from her secretary that she'd flown to Israel for an interview with the Prime Minister. There were no apologies when she returned, only astonishment that there had been a previous claim on her time.

It was the memory of Stevie, the remembrance of how he had broken their relationship, that made Lee try harder to understand the strange behaviors. And when he felt as if she were two different women, he tried to love them both.

Yet as her career moved forward with dazzling speed, her moods grew stranger and blacker. On camera and in public, the woman he'd admired and loved was always on display, but when they were alone, the other one, the one who was driven by needs that seemed alien to Lee, began to surface with disturbing regularity. When he suggested that she see a doctor, she lashed out with a fury that left him breathless.

Would he have left her then? he wondered. He'd never know, because when she told Lee she was pregnant with his baby, the bond between them was forged.

Yet she rejected marriage; she even rejected living together. "I have to be free," she told him with a throaty laugh. "I have to go with the winds. But I'll come back to you, Lee darling. Don't I always?"

Strangely enough, the bond between them seemed to grow stronger when she miscarried. She'd been in Cannes, interviewing Hollywood's hottest and most controversial couple, a pair of tempestuous stars who delighted the press with their public brawls and torrid reconciliations. She had asked Lee to come along, to make the trip a vacation, but he'd been unable to fly to France with her—and promised instead to join her in a few days. By the time he arrived, she was in a small clinic in the south. Looking as wan and weak as a child herself, she told him brokenly how she had slipped and fallen in her hotel bathroom, how there had been no one to help her . . . how it had been too late to save the baby.

Determined to save the relationship, Lee had gone to visit The Oasis. Yet how could he tell Stevie why he needed her help? He had no right, none whatever; he'd forfeited any claim to her understanding a long time ago, and now . . . now life had shown him how arrogant and wrong he had been.

2

Alone in the stillness of her office, Stevie stood staring off through a window at the desert landscape, a palette of golds and reds, studded by the broken spiny forms of cactus. In the contemplation of timeless nature, she searched for some serenity.

With a deep sigh, she turned away from the window and reached for the wire basket that was overflowing with mail. Work was the cure for her heartache; bury the concerns about herself by helping others. It had never failed.

Placing the basket in the center of her desk, Stevie sat down and grabbed up a handful of envelopes. Almost at once, her eye was caught by an official-looking seal embossed on the flap of cream-colored vellum. Quickly tearing the envelope open, she read the engraved card within:

The President of the United States
takes great pleasure in announcing the award of
The Medal of Freedom
to Ms. Stephanie Knight,
for her tireless compassion and heroic work
on behalf of—

With mounting excitement, Stevie raced to the end of the announcement, to the words that summoned her to the White House two weeks hence to receive her award from the President himself at a dinner where only four other Americans would be similarly honored—all of the others older, more distinguished, and already more celebrated.

How could she have doubted herself? Stevie asked. She was traveling the right road, and even if it meant times of loneliness and longing, she was making a difference in the lives of others—a difference that was recognized even in the highest sanctums of power.

Clutching the announcement in one hand, she charged out of her office, eager to share the news with the members of her staff who were on weekend duty. But as Stevie turned through the door, she collided forcibly with a woman coming along the corridor, a stunning redhead with topaz eyes and flawless skin.

"Oh, God," Stevie said. "I'm sorry."

"That's all right," the woman said in the full, deep-throated voice that was part of her appeal. "I've had grenades thrown at me. This wasn't much worse."

The voice struck a chord of recognition in Stevie, and when she paused to examine the woman's face, that also seemed familiar. But she couldn't put a name to it.

Hastily, Stevie stooped to retrieve the scattered contents of the woman's handbag. By force of habit, she took an inventory of the items as they went back into the bag. Two things surprised her: the only addictive stimulant was a pack of unfiltered cigarettes; there was also a smallish, but not insignificant, switchblade knife. Stevie hesitated a second before dropping it in with the other items.

"Here," she said as she snapped the bag shut and handed it over. Stevie's eyes rested once more on the woman's face, trying to place it. A face glimpsed in a newspaper, perhaps.

"You're Stevie Knight, aren't you?" the woman asked. Again the voice registered with Stevie, a husky throatiness with the suggestion of late nights, whiskey, and cigarettes.

Stevie nodded.

The redhead eyed her critically for a second. "I was just coming to see you."

No appointment had been made. Furthermore, someone at the reception desk should have met all visitors. Stevie formed her own impression of this woman as the type who rammed straight through all barriers.

"Listen," Stevie said, "all visitors are supposed to sign in at—"

"I'm not a visitor," the woman announced. "I've come to check in . . . to be one of your, whatchamacallits, Journeyers." She spoke in a slightly snide tone, almost as though working deliberately to alienate Stevie.

"Travelers," Stevie corrected calmly. "If you need help, we should talk and arrange for you to get it. But I can't spend time with you now, and you can't just . . . 'check in.' That isn't how The Oasis works. The usual admission procedure—"

"I know all that. I've done stories about it," the redhead cut Stevie off impatiently. "Don't you know who I am?"

Suddenly it came to Stevie. She had seen the face on television, would have identified it sooner if she watched television more often. Deni Vickers was the highest-paid anchorwoman in the history of American broadcasting, a star in her field, famous for her on-the-spot reportage in hazardous situations that tried the courage of even the most seasoned male correspondents. Deni had traveled the alleyways of Beirut to interview terrorists, and gone into a Bronx slum to negotiate the freedom of a woman and several children being held hostage by an insane lover with dynamite strapped to his body. And, just last week, smack in the middle of a story on a band of Afghani freedom fighters sent by satellite from the mountains outside Kabul, Deni Vickers had abruptly stopped reporting to drift into a fantastical account of a childhood trip into the mountains of Tibet. The station had cut to a commercial, and when it was over, the male co-anchor was sitting in Deni's chair, picking up the story where she had dropped it.

Deni saw the light of recognition come into Stevie's eyes. She didn't wait for a verbal acknowledgment before she rushed on. "Listen, Stevie, I'm . . . on the ropes. I need to show my network that I'm not cracking up—or, if there was any chance I might, that I've done something about it. I can't wait six or eight weeks. By then, they won't need me. There'll be some new face filling in . . . showing the execs how dispensable I am. . . ." She tried to say it with a light twist, but Stevie could tell she was truly terrified of being drummed out, replaced.

Even while she started to shake her head at the impossibility of finding an empty bed, Stevie observed Deni's fingernails, bitten to the quick and strangely incongruous with her impeccable onscreen image, the rigid set of her shoulders, the tightness around the mouth. She watched Deni light a cigarette with trembling fingers, draw on it with a nervous hunger that reminded Stevie of the way Pip used to smoke—and knew without a doubt that this was a woman on the edge.

Trailed by Deni, Stevie stepped back into her outer office and checked the chart showing the dates when each Traveler was scheduled to leave against the chart that listed prospective arrivals. The Oasis was filled to capacity; it was unthinkable to postpone anyone who had been given a commitment. "It can't be done, Ms. Vickers. But if you want help badly enough, you'll hang on."

Deni was silent a moment. "My problem isn't like other people's, Stevie. It isn't just a matter of trying to throttle down some craving for booze or pills or coke. I can't just hang on." She advanced on Stevie, as if she meant to give her next words the same emphasis they would get on camera from a close-up.

"If you send me away, Stevie," Deni said simply, "I'll die."

The particular choice of words reached deep into Stevie. The Admiral had sent her away, ordered her out of his house. Hadn't that been a major step in her long slide down?

"I won't send you away, Deni," she said. "Let's find a place for you somewhere. We can do the admission interview after you've had a chance to settle in."

3

As Deni followed Stevie down a long corridor, she felt a dizzying sense of relief. It's going to be all right now, she told herself. Everything's going to be all right. She wasn't crazy and she wasn't ill. She was simply very tired, and now she would get the rest she needed.

Deni felt as if she'd been treading water all her life, and when she was tired, when her ratings wobbled even a little, the terror of going under grew so big that it swallowed up all possibility of pleasure in the glamorous, exciting life she'd made for herself.

She took chances—wild, crazy chances, because that was the way to grab another headline, to make the network bosses smile and say, "Atta girl, Deni, way to go"—and she'd be safe just a little longer. Of her nerve under fire, it was said that Deni Vickers had big, brass ones, and she liked that compliment better than any other. It was the kind of accolade her father would have bestowed on someone he admired; long after Jack Vickers's death, it was his standards that dominated Deni's life.

Settling into the cheerful but spartan room was easy; Deni dumped the contents of her cosmetic bag on the bathroom shelf and hung in the closet the carry-on bag that had circled the globe.

From her handbag, she took a small silver frame and placed it on the white birch dresser. In the frame was a photograph of "Black Jack Vickers," dapper and still rakishly handsome at fifty-eight, laughingly "crowning" his two-year-old daughter with his yachtsman's cap. Even now, twenty years after his death, he seemed so compellingly vibrant and alive. Was it any wonder, then, that almost every man who had courted and loved Deni seemed pale and dull by comparison? The stories he had told her about himself over the years—the stories they had made together—were as real and exciting to her as anything she'd ever reported.

By anyone's standards, Jack Vickers had lived life to the hilt. A bootlegger during Prohibition, he had wined and dined New York gangsters and socialites at his East Side speakeasy with the same unfailing charm. And when Prohibition ended, Jack converted his bootlegging business into a liquor-distribution business and his speakeasy into the "Black Jack Club," acquiring legitimacy and a nickname all in one easy stroke.

Women adored Jack; young and old, rich and poor, they pursued the handsome, dashing bachelor, each hoping that she would be the one to entice him, with the blandishments of either beauty or wealth, to the altar.

Among those who nearly succeeded was Brenda Frazier, the stunning and irrepressible debutante whose madcap antics were almost as highly publicized as Jack's. When the two met, it was like fire meeting fire; their romance blazed for three riotous months and sparked rumors of an imminent engagement. Then, abruptly, it was over.

Jack Vickers jilted the beautiful Brenda, it was said, after they had a knock-down-drag-out fight at his club that ended with her hurling a bottle of champagne at him and storming out in a rage. That was okay with Jack; he liked a show of spirit by his women. He might even have apologized, for he knew that women needed to have their way once in a while. But before any of that could happen, Brenda turned up at the Black Jack Club with a new man, laughing and carrying on as if she'd already forgotten her lover and was enthralled with someone new.

Naturally, all eyes were on Jack; it was his move, and he made it like the consummate actor he was. He sent a magnum of vintage champagne over to Brenda's table with a jaunty wave and a "no hard feelings" smile. He did it with the air of a gentleman salving the hurt feelings of a discarded lady, and that was what everyone believed, no matter what Brenda said. They might have believed differently if they'd seen what happened much later that night, after the club closed, when Jack went over to Hoboken and picked a fight with the biggest guy in the waterfront bar.

He fought savagely, letting out all the fury he'd held in check, and when he was finished, his unfortunate opponent had a fractured jaw and three broken ribs. Jack peeled three hundred-dollar bills from the roll he always carried, dropped them on the chest of the fallen man, and walked away with a dashing cut under the eye and his manhood intact.

Where other men might have sowed a few wild oats to assuage disappointment, Black Jack Vickers mounted a campaign of seductions that would have put Don Juan himself to shame. It was only as he neared the half-century mark that Jack began courting Susan Bellefort with anything resembling honorable intentions. Susan was beautiful and young; her family was distinguished and old. She was enthralled with Jack's rakish charm; but her family was appalled by his reputation.

Susan was warned to give him up—or else. She refused, choosing to forfeit the bulk of her inheritance, with the exception of an irrevocable trust fund, to marry Black Jack Vickers in a splashy, defiant wedding of just the sort her family would most scorn. The two hundred guests ranged from famous to notorious: movie people, artists, gangsters —definitely "not our sort, dear."

Having made such a costly bargain, Susan Bellefort Vickers tried valiantly to get her money's worth. As headstrong in her way as Jack was in his, she set out to prove her parents wrong by making her marriage work. Jack, in turn, proved Susan wrong by continuing to bed all the desirable women who were attracted by his dangerous reputation.

In desperation, Susan played her trump card: she became pregnant. And for a time, the prospect of fatherhood at age fifty-six kept Jack closer to home. Soon little Denise was born, the name a tribute to Jack's father, Dennis. It wasn't long after that Jack grew restless again. Susan began to manifest a variety of symptoms—fainting spells, memory lapses, periods of disorientation when she imagined she was a girl again. In the years that followed, Susan shuttled back and forth between an expensive sanitarium and the Vickerses' Fifth Avenue apartment. Left to the care of nurses and housekeepers, to the wildly fluctuating attentions of her adored father, Deni's emotional diet ranged between benign neglect and lavish abundance.

Alarmed by reports of their daughter's disintegration, Susan's family finally forgave her act of rebellion and stepped in with a battery of specialists. One blamed her condition on the hormonal changes connected with pregnancy and childbirth, another on the stresses of an unhappy marriage. Jack blamed it on the Bellefort bloodlines. "Too damn much inbreeding," he said to his in-laws when they proposed a divorce. "Go ahead and take her back! She's no damn good to me!" he roared as little Deni listened from behind a door.

With bated breath and a knot in her stomach, she heard her own name mentioned, talk she didn't quite grasp about "custody." "If she were a boy, I'd kill you all before I let you take her!" Jack growled at his soon-to-be ex-in-laws.

Deni understood, feeling as diminished by her father's words as she had been seduced by his extravagances. She grew to adolescence in her mother's childhood home, under the shadow of a madness that was discussed only in hushed whispers and careful euphemisms. "Your mother's very tired today" could mean anything, Deni learned, a crying jag, utter silence, or worse—the hallucinations that had Susan talking to the figments of her own tortured imagination. In this grim setting, Deni became a silent rebel, released only by her visits with Jack, when she became an eager supplicant, hungry for affection and approval.

She learned to smoke and drink and ride. She learned to hunt by her father's side—duck in Idaho, bear and deer in Maine—and to judge horseflesh on the thoroughbred stud farms of Kentucky and Ireland. Imitating Jack's swaggering brand of courage, she was always ready to take a dare or a challenge.

Jack paid Deni the ultimate compliment when she was sixteen. He had taken her on shooting safari in Kenya—"none of that pansy stuff with cameras," he said—and she had been first to bag a rhino. "If I couldn't have a son," he crowed around the campfire that night, "thank heaven I had a daughter like you."

Though prep-school boys were drawn by Deni's beauty and vivacity and fearless air, she couldn't muster a reciprocal interest. Though she wasn't given to deep introspection, she didn't have to think too much about the reason: no boys her age could measure up to the formidable Black Jack Vickers. She always preferred to go out to dinner with her father and his friends, and felt no brake on flirting outrageously with men three times her age, challenging them to drinking contests and arm-wrestling duels, which she won as often as not.

A week before her seventeenth birthday, Jack gave Deni a Jaguar convertible, capable of speeds of up to 160 miles per hour. "Push it to the limit," he said when they took their first test drive together on a deserted Long Island road. "Atta girl!" he said, laughing when she floored the accelerator without a moment's hesitation. "That's my girl, my Deni! Don't ever be afraid to push life to the limit. Anything less is for cowards. . . ."

He's right, Deni thought as she hurtled past meadows and farmlands at dizzying speed, exhilarated beyond description by the raw wind that stung her face, the rampant beating of her own runaway heart.

And after she had passed this latest test, proving once again that she could take any risk and survive, Jack gave his daughter another birthday gift—a month of cruising around the Greek Islands aboard his sailing yacht, the *Hi-Jacker*.

Roaming the open seas with her father, alone except for Nicos, a young Greek, as additional crew, Deni felt happier than she'd ever been. More than anything, she wished they could go on forever, from ocean to ocean, seeing the world and all its wonders together. Under the Aegean sun that bronzed her body and painted her copper-red hair with golden highlights, she looked like a young pagan goddess.

It was only natural that Nicos would find Deni irresistible, that he would test the waters of some careful flirtation, if only to fill the long hours at sea. Deni flirted back, more out of habit than anything else, for while she could admire the boy's hard, muscular body, she had no real interest in him. He simply fell too far below the level of her ideal. Jack Vickers seemed to encourage the flirtation, however, taking pride in Deni's captivating beauty and finding amusement in the way she bewitched the unsophisticated young crewman. But one afternoon, after he had started drinking even earlier than usual, the sight of Deni and Nicos laughing together as they worked sent Jack into a dark, ugly depression.

Later that evening, after the boat had been moored in a secluded cove, Deni tried to lift her father's spirits by challenging him to a drinking contest with his favorite malt whiskey. Yet the alcohol served only to make Jack maudlin; he seemed preoccupied with his own accumulation of birthdays, rather than with Deni's. "I don't like it," he growled. "Old age stinks, Deni, and don't let anyone tell you different."

"You aren't old," she protested, meaning every word. "You just get better every year . . . like good red wine."

"Sure." He laughed. "And if you believe that, I have a bridge I can sell you when we get back."

"But it's true, Daddy," Deni insisted, "you're better than any man I know. . . ."

"Better than that young Greek stud?" he teased with a gleam in his eye.

"Him? He's nothing compared to you."

"Ah, Deni," he sighed, "if that were only so. . . ." Jack reached out to stroke his daughter's bare shoulder. The gesture seemed warm and loving, but a moment later, Jack was drawing her closer, so close she could feel his warm breath against her lips. His breathing grew ragged, his hand moved along the curves of her body.

She thought of crying out, pushing him away. But another part of her was ruled by curiosity. What would it be like with him? Not her father; she didn't think of him that way. He was Jack Vickers—the most exciting man she had ever known.

He leaned closer into her, aroused by her lack of resis-

tance, and slid his hand down inside her hiphuggers, probing. . . .

"Daddy," she whispered then, a small protest formed
spontaneously.

But he mistook her breathless exclamation for a final
invitation, and probed deeper, beginning to remove his
own clothes.

She couldn't stop him then. It was a sacrifice she had to
make for his sake, she told herself, rather than deliver a
rejection that would wound his ego. She couldn't bring
herself to do anything that would diminish him, plant some
doubt that he was any less than the best. For he was . . . and
she wanted him.

"Forgive me, Deni," he said when they were done, lying
on the deck and staring at the sky. "I love you too
much. . . ."

But there was nothing to forgive, she thought. She
wanted to hold him again, keep him with her, have him
inside.

But he pulled himself up and went off along the deck.
The last words he ever said to her were his plea for forgiveness. The following morning his bunk was empty, and he
was nowhere to be found. Though they were anchored
hundreds of yards offshore, the dinghy was still in place,
secured to the outrigger. Frantically, she and Nicos
searched the boat for anything, for a sign of an accident—
even, finally, for a note.

But there was nothing left of him—nothing but the
memory of that last night.

The sympathy of the Greek authorities almost broke
Deni. She didn't deserve it, and she felt like twenty kinds
of a hypocrite accepting kindness when she deserved punishment and blame. Binding herself to eternal silence, Deni

vowed never to tell her story and never to tarnish the name of Jack Vickers.

When Deni flew back to the United States, she was met by a legion of her father's friends, all moved by a single purpose—to immortalize Black Jack Vickers with the biggest send-off New York had ever seen.

There was no funeral—his body had never been recovered—and besides, dead or alive, Jack would have had no use for snuffling and gnashing of teeth. There was instead a celebration, bigger and brassier than even his wedding had been, held at the Black Jack Club. It started at seven in the evening with some three hundred people—Jack's favorite mix of show business, politics, and organized crime; they were all the same, he used to say, boasting he had the scars to prove it.

Louder than an Irish wake, bawdier than a French cabaret, the party grew in volume throughout the night and went on into the next day, until the club was littered with grown men passed out at their tables.

But Deni was still standing. If she had ever needed proof that there would never be another man like Jack Vickers, she had it now, in the colorful tributes paid, the songs that were sung to celebrate his life. If once she had been the mascot of Black Jack's personal club, she was now its most important member, the person who could help his friends keep him alive. What could they do for Deni? they asked, these men of power and influence. What did she need? Name it, and it would be hers.

Deni had no needs, no thoughts or plans beyond her consuming grief. "I want to be like him" was all she could say. They understood, all her honorary uncles, for hadn't many of them had the same wish at one time or another? Time would heal, they promised, and for now they would simply be there, ready to help Jack's little girl in any way they could. They swept her off to their country homes for weekends, treated her as one of their own. They spoke to her of college and the future. No, she said, college would be dull.

Yet idleness didn't suit Deni either, and when she graduated from high school, she thought for a time she might become an actress. "Uncle" Ted Fielding, a producer of Broadway musicals, made a single telephone call—and Deni was accepted into the Actors Studio, Lee Strasberg's "atelier," where the likes of Brando and Monroe and Newman and Steiger were then participating.

She studied acting for about six months, long enough to learn that she adored the spotlight . . . and detested the soul-searching and rigorous preparation, the weeks of routine drudgery that laid the groundwork for even the tiniest part. No, Chekhov and Ibsen and Tennessee Williams were not for Deni Vickers; she wanted excitement and glamour, and she wanted it now.

Deni turned to "Uncle" Harry Stroud, vice-president in charge of programming for the second-largest television network. No problem. With her stunning looks and considerable charm, Deni was a natural for television, the instant medium. Uncle Harry found her a job as a weathergirl, with two whole minutes to show her stuff in a noon spot. Knowing nothing whatever about the science of meteorology, she did know how to captivate people, how to look good and flirt and beguile. She even knew instinctively to cover her mistakes with a throaty laugh and a "Whoops! I did it again!"—a phrase that became a kind of trademark slogan. Appearing in a different costume every evening, Deni made the most of her first opportunity, and soon her face was more widely recognized than those of the more serious members of the news team.

For her first bit of success, Deni repaid Uncle Harry

with a weekend in bed he'd never forget. It didn't actually start out that way; it certainly wasn't his idea. Harry had invited Deni for a weekend at his country house in Bucks County, just a chance for her to get away from the grind of the city, let her heart do a little mending after the loss of her father. It was late in March, but warm; spring was in the air—a time for renewal.

But there could be no renewal for Deni. She ached to be able to see her father again, to undo whatever had caused his loss. Knowing that was impossible, however, she took what seemed the closest route. Though Harry Stroud was sixty-eight years old, he had been a friend of Black Jack's. Though Harry Stroud's infidelities to his wife had long been confined to after-hours trysts with call girls and willing secretaries, Deni saw in him an opportunity to fill a vacuum in her life—or perhaps to re-create the moment she was trying to relive and comprehend, a moment of passion with a man old enough to be her father. Late at night, after Harry's wife had preceded him to bed, Deni offered herself to her father's friend. It was an offer that Harry was too weak to deny. And when he discovered some of the kinks that Deni seemed to enjoy, he was happy to continue their relationship beyond the weekend.

"Why do you like to be tied up?" he asked her flatly after one of their afternoon "meetings" in a hotel not far from his offices.

"Do you have to know why?" Deni responded. "Isn't it enough that it gives *both* of us a kick?"

She would be asked many versions of this question in years to come, and supply many versions of the answer. For, in bed, Deni was ready to go to the limits of abasement. She would invite men to do things with her and to her that some had only imagined in their wildest and sickest fantasies—and that some could never have imagined at all. Sometimes it involved not only degradation but pain.

Why? the men would ask, some of them caught in an odd grip of emotions between love for her—and revulsion. She was beautiful and talented and bright; why did she need to do this to herself?

But if she never actually supplied them with answers, she did try to grapple with the reasons herself. The exact equation never came clear . . . but, of course, it had something to do with Black Jack. With sex, she had killed him; so it was fitting justice that she should punish herself with sex.

Her tenure as weathergirl lasted only a few months. She grew bored soon with costumes and cuteness, convinced she was destined for greater things. The greatest tribute that could be paid to her drive and her abilities was that they remained recognized, even by many who knew how little self-respect she evinced in the bedroom.

When the sports reporter on the local evening news was taken ill with botulism after eating a tainted seafood salad at a press conference for the latest Heisman Trophy winner, Deni was on the phone to Uncle Harry in a flash. If she could do weather, how much better could Jack Vickers's daughter do sports? And when she sensed a tiny bit of hesitation, she added her closing argument: it was only for a few days, a week at most, until the regular man was back at his desk. Surely a pinch-hitting assignment by a beautiful woman would be an interesting novelty, one that could generate a bit of excitement, a little publicity? And if she made any mistakes, well, most of the viewers would be men, wouldn't they? There shouldn't be any doubt about her appeal to men. . . .

Uncle Harry and Deni struck a bargain—they would indulge each other's whims.

Deni made no mistakes, she made sure of that. What's more, she ensured that her temporary spot would be seen in the best possible light. In a chameleonlike turnabout, she put aside her fluffy-redhead persona and turned up at the studio in a man-tailored suit that served only to accent her curvaceous body. The cameraman—whom she had thoughtfully seduced—zoomed in for a flattering close-up; the anchorman, his cooperation ensured with an unforgettable quickie in the men's room, introduced Deni in the most glowing terms. "Aw, shucks, Tom," she said, "just think of me as one of the boys." And then she went on to prove it, by delivering a letter-perfect three-minute commentary on the Knicks' stunning victory over the Celtics, the spate of injuries suffered by the Giants' defensive line, and trade rumors surrounding a popular Yankee pitcher.

Not content to rest on the laurels of a single evening's success or even to simply demonstrate an appearance of competence, Deni searched out an opportunity for more recognition—in the person of Daniel Xavier Collins, Black Jack's oldest friend and the dean of New York bookmakers. "Dandy Dan," they called him, for he looked more like a banker than a bookie.

Deni found him at his "office"—a corner table at the Black Jack Club. He rose from his chair to greet her with a courtly bow. "I saw you on the television last night, Denise . . . and I must say you looked lovely. You've done Jack proud, my dear . . . you've done all of us proud." In fact, Dandy Dan had also begun to pick up a few rumors about Deni that weren't exactly reason to applaud. But he was a practical man who didn't try to judge what he couldn't understand; furthermore, although the bedroom was not an arena in which he had gone very far outside the conventional limits, he was not above breaking the rules in his own sphere.

"Dandy," Deni said, "that spot they've got me in is only temporary. A couple of days more and they'll send me back to weather. Unless . . ."

"Unless what, my dear?"

"Unless I can show them I'm better than that. Dandy, you know *everything* about sports . . ."

"Not everything, Denise," he demurred modestly. "But what is it you're after?"

"I need a scoop, something nobody else has. Can you help me?"

"Do you mean something on that rumored trade you mentioned last night?"

"I was talking about something . . . a bit more impressive. Something that could put me on the map, and win me a lot of faithful viewers overnight."

Dandy Dan looked into the topaz eyes of his unofficial goddaughter and noted they glittered with excitement. "I take your meaning, my dear," he said after a moment, "and it's something of a tall order."

"Black Jack always told me I shouldn't ask for less. A short order, he used to say, is something you can get in any 'greasy spoon' over the counter."

Dandy Dan laughed with her at the memory. "Denise, my dear . . . it occurs to me I may have just what you need."

Later that day, as millions of New Yorkers were about to sit down to dinner, Deni Vickers came on the air, following the news and before the weather. After she read the scores and gave highlights of games played the previous evening, she leaned into the camera, wet her lips and said; "Now, for all you fans who lost money by betting the Giants in their game with the Packers two days ago, let me offer a word of consolation—and advice. Next time you decide to back the home team, you might want to huddle with a certain Giants tight end who, according to an unimpeachable source, wagered a bundle *against* his own team! I wonder what the NFL will have to say about this. . . ."

Deni's scoop triggered a decent-size scandal, leading to

the expulsion of three players from the league. It also gave her a taste of what it was like to make news—and the certainty that she would never go back to thinner, duller fare.

Uncle Harry Stroud was so delighted with Deni's coup that he offered a regular sportscaster's spot on the late-night news, an unheard-of position for a woman. But Deni had her eye on an even more exclusive men's club—that of broadcast journalism. And for that, even Deni knew she would have to pay some dues.

She spent the next five years working at network-affiliated stations in Cleveland and Dallas and Boston. For the first time in her life, she started reading newspapers—the *Christian Science Monitor*, the *New York Times* and the *Washington Chronicle*—and she took crash courses in half a dozen languages, not for fluency, but for just enough vocabulary to seem knowledgeable and self-assured in any milieu.

By day, Deni Vickers was a model of deportment, as she fed her ambitions and her need for acclaim. But by night, she fed her darker need—a hunger to engage in acts that would have made most women cringe with disgust. There were always men ready to service her, whether she met them through work, through the many interviews she did to gather news, or found them after hours—anonymous strangers she met in bars, at theaters, sometimes even on the street. Of course, there were those who retreated when they found out what would be asked of them, and there were always a few who wanted to find her help, or preach to her, or try to redeem her with love. But she could not be diverted from her appetite for rough sex, one that seemed to keep growing. She would accept beatings and whippings—as long as the bruises could be restricted to parts of her body that didn't appear on camera. She would allow men to penetrate every opening of her body, inflict every kind of punishment . . . and she called it pleasure, because it helped somehow to relieve her guilt.

In her career, she went from success to success, returning to New York in a white heat of publicity as the first major female anchor. It was said of Deni Vickers that she never waited for stories to break—she simply went out and made them happen.

She had her detractors. There were those who complained that her brand of journalism was both cynical and irresponsible. There were those who found her interview with the deposed Shah of Iran not only ghoulish but dangerous—as she badgered the dying monarch to reveal secret negotiations with the secretary of state at the very moment that American lives were being threatened by the revolutionaries who held the Embassy in Teheran. Yet surveys showed that more than half of all the television sets of America were on when the interview aired—and Deni Vickers once again thumbed her nose at her critics. Sour grapes, she said, and as long as she kept producing ratings, the network was inclined to agree.

There were many, too—among them the Surgeon General of the United States—who damned her coverage of a disease that had decimated villages in Africa and was now afflicting the gay population of several American cities, and for her suggestion that America was in danger of a plague of unprecedented proportions. But Deni didn't care what the Surgeon General said—and neither, apparently, did her network bosses, who met her growing demands for more money, more power, and more perks every time she came to the bargaining table.

There had always been money, but now she lived like a queen. Her duplex apartment on Fifth Avenue was every bit as ostentatious as money could make it. As she did in her work, Deni scorned understatement, even good taste, in favor of flash—just as Jack Vickers had done. Her neighbors were corporate CEOs, movie stars, high-ranking diplomats and exiled nobility, domestic and foreign millionaires . . . and Deni could hold her own with the best of them.

There wasn't a door in the world that her name couldn't open. Her Rolodex of private numbers would have fetched a king's ransom on the open market. Heads of state took her calls—even when they were "too busy" to talk to other heads of state.

Her life was more exciting than any fantasy. Yet as her star rose ever higher, Deni's personal life kept growing darker, spinning more out of control with each success.

And then she had met the man who made her think that, as far as she had descended into depravity, it was still possible she might be redeemed.

Ever on the prowl, she'd dropped in that night at a boring Washington party . . . for five minutes, no more, just to check out the scene. He had been there, unattached, a wealthy businessman who seemed to know enough of the right people, if not all of them. He wasn't Black Jack Vickers; no one could be. But he had the good looks she admired, and if Jack was kind of a black knight, then Deni's man was the white version.

She won him easily, too easily. If he had known how much Deni loved a challenge, he might have put up a greater fight, but he was taken with her—and Deni did enjoy the victory. Especially after she learned that there had once been a special woman in his life—and no one else since.

And then Deni did something that surprised her. She stayed with him, even after he refused to play the bedtime games that gave her satisfaction. Was it because he seemed a kind of safe harbor, a man she could trust? Was it because she recognized something in him that might save her? Or did she simply need a friend in a world that now seemed to be made up of fans or enemies? She tried to have an ordinary kind of romance, the kind she saw in the movies, in the streets of cities on warm summer nights. But a part of herself wouldn't allow it.

She kept this ordinary romance alive—compartmentalized it as one part of her life. But she would also sneak away from her lover, change her clothes and makeup and cover her distinctive red hair, then prowl the roughest bars in the city, looking for the kind of men who would satisfy her compulsion. Late one night, she picked up a sailor from a Panamanian freighter and coaxed him into smuggling her onto his ship. He tried to take her to his bunk, but Deni wanted something else. They went down into the hold, where he tied her up, naked and spread-eagled on a hard, filthy mat, and beat her sexual organs with a knotted rope until she was whimpering with pain. Then he summoned those of his shipmates who were still aboard, and they all took turns, using her more brutally than they'd use a waterfront whore. And when they were finished, they relieved themselves on her body and threw her onto the pier like a dirty piece of rubbish.

She had to stay away from her lover until the worst of her bruises healed. But still he noticed. She told him she'd been mugged by a gang of drug addicts on her way home —and she saw the guilt in his face for not having been there to protect her.

In a vain attempt to quit the bars and dives she frequented, Deni pushed her man hard, hoping to provoke him into an act of savagery that would bind her to him as all his whispered love words and tenderness never could. But anger and disillusionment only made him pull away, challenging her ability to draw him in again.

Once, after she'd disappeared for weeks without word, she thought she'd almost lost him for good. And then she learned that her body had betrayed her again—but in a different way: she was pregnant. She had no idea who the father was—it might have been her lover . . . or any of the faceless pickups who satisfied her sexual addiction. But whoever had planted the seed in her body, the thought of a child filled Deni with loathing, disgust . . . and a cold, nameless fear.

She told her lover it was his, watched his face light up with tenderness. He proposed at once. Of course, that's what white knights always did—made an honest woman of any maiden they knocked up. Not like Jack Vickers, who bragged he'd spawned enough bastards to start his own army.

She'd gotten rid of the thing, as she thought of it, in a discreet clinic far away from home. She had refused anesthesia, biting down on her lip until it bled as they scraped the growth out of her. "Take everything out," she screamed finally. "It's all rotten. Take it and get rid of it. . . ."

Thinking she was delirious with pain, the doctor soothed Deni, explaining in a gentle voice that there were better ways to guard against pregnancy, especially for a beautiful young woman who would surely want a family one day.

She told her lover she had fallen when she was alone, that there had been no one to help her until it was too late. He bought the story hook, line, and sinker.

Too bad, she thought. If they'd both been men, they might have been the best of friends. Hell, there was a lot they could do together—drink and fish, hunt and ride. Too bad. As it was, everything he wanted from her had nothing to do with what she wanted for herself.

And yet there was a tiny part of her, a small voice rarely heard and scarcely heeded, a voice that said: He'll save you if you let him.

While the other voice mocked: Save you from what?

Deni Vickers isn't afraid of anything. Deni Vickers knows how to push everything to the limits.

She had to go on believing that; to settle for less would be to betray the memory of Jack Vickers, and she would never do that.

In the days after Deni's first arrival at The Oasis, Stevie was drawn to her, not only because when Deni was at her best she was especially bright, forceful, and humorous, but because it was clear that, without special attention and effort, Stevie could probably not succeed in cracking through Deni's well-built defenses to help rebuild her inner confidence and self-respect. There was a story Deni had told in one of the group sessions that exemplified her problem for Stevie. Black Jack (the name by which she almost always referred to her father) had taken her mountain climbing in Nepal. Not one of the harder peaks, Deni said, laughing— not Everest or K-2—but of course, she had been only fifteen then, and this was her first climb. Even so, the challenge Black Jack chose for her was plenty tough enough. She had been constantly terrified of falling, but, roped to her father and a couple of Sherpa guides, she had made it all the way to the summit.

And that, Stevie knew, was exactly the way Deni had made it through life: she had scrambled to the top, scared out of her wits every single step of the way that, with one slip, she would plummet straight to the bottom.

As unalike as the two women were, the depth of Deni's need aroused in Stevie the keenest memories of her own youthful misery. But, as much as Stevie wanted to help, Deni was extraordinarily resistant. It was more than a matter of having strong defenses—a cast-iron shell constructed over the whole of her life. Unlike the other Travelers, who had to be cut loose from some stimulus *outside* themselves in order to be salvaged, Deni had to be separated from an essential inner core of her own personality, that part of her determined to show no weakness, almost eager to endure any suffering and still come smiling through. Deni's addiction was not to any substance that caused pain, but to the pain itself.

And so the more Stevie leaned on Deni to participate in the routine of The Oasis, the more Deni resisted—and welcomed Stevie's disapproval. She seemed almost eager to goad Stevie to anger, to invite reproof in front of the other Travelers. Stevie thought she understood what Deni was doing, yet she had difficulty overcoming her own human emotions. Deni warped all the balances in a way that affected the dynamic of the community as a whole, and Stevie found it harder and harder to excuse.

Sometimes, as she wondered why Deni should seek help and then be so resistant to accepting it, Stevie's frustration shaded over into suspicion. Deni was a newswoman, after all, a correspondent who went to the front to gather first impressions. Perhaps it wasn't help she'd really come seeking, but a story about The Oasis, an exposé. Indeed, even if self-betterment was her goal, if she retreated from it, she might have little compunction about using some reportage as a consolation prize.

Late one night, after Deni had spent her first week at The Oasis, Stevie received a visitor in her living quarters. Though her privacy was respected, it was understood that her door was always open to any Traveler with an extreme need for comfort or advice. The visitor on this night was Lorna Kashen. Lorna and her husband, Rory, were both singers and, as a duo, had been star attractions in Las Vegas and other places on the high-class club circuit for two decades. Then, last year, after one closing night at The Sands, Rory had told Lorna he was leaving her for a twenty-two-year-old showgirl. Afraid to try making it as a single act, Lorna had gone into "retirement"—which meant living with a succession of men young enough to be her sons, and teaching each one how to shoot her up with vitamin B cocktails laced with heroin. She was here to break the habit, and get up the guts to go on a solo tour that had been booked for next autumn.

What Lorna wanted to tell Stevie was that, while out for a walk on one of the nature trails, she had noticed Deni sitting on some rocks talking into a tiny portable tape recorder. The implication was clear: there was a possibility that Deni was using the tape to dictate notes for a story.

After Lorna left, Stevie worried over what she'd heard. Of course, if a recorder had been spotted in the usual spot check of luggage when Deni arrived, it would have been confiscated. Had Deni kept it deliberately hidden? Or had it merely slipped through, mistaken for the kind of portable cassette player used to listen to music—which would have been acceptable? But even if she was using it, that didn't prove her intention was to report her observations. Perhaps she was keeping a kind of diary, recording aural notes for the sake of studying her own reactions, trying to understand herself better.

Stevie was jarred from her concerns by the ringing of her bedside phone. She was still distracted when she answered it.

"Hello, Stevie."

There was a pause. It was a voice she could neither forget nor believe. Was it possible she would not mistake it after all these years . . . ? She dared an answer:

"Hello, Lee. It's very nice to hear from you." She tried to stay in the safe territory of understatement. . . . But did he detect the quaver of excitement?

There was a silence, as if he was uncertain of how to continue. "Stevie," he said at last, "the reason I called . . . I'm trying to locate someone . . . a friend of mine. I thought she might be with you . . . I mean, in your care."

Stevie felt herself deflate. His words were enough to fill in the gap in his own story. Whoever the woman was, Lee was obviously involved with her, concerned about her, enough of a confidant to know her secret weaknesses. It didn't surprise Stevie, either, that it was someone who would need help. Lee had always been a do-gooder in the best sense.

"Who is it?" Stevie asked, trying to keep her tone level and professional.

"Deni Vickers."

Now Stevie *was* stunned. Of all the women . . . But now much of what Deni had told of her recent life made sense. There was a man she was involved with, she had said, but he was too good for her. He had tried to help her, and the more he tried, the more she seemed driven to cheat on him, to degrade herself with other men, and yet pretend she was faithful—to soil the very best she'd ever had with perfidy and lies.

So the nameless man of whom Deni had spoken was Lee. The revelation muddled Stevie's feelings about him. Should she think less of him for being involved with someone so deeply troubled?

How could she? He had loved her, too, once. And perhaps she still . . .

No, it could end now, could be locked away. "Yes," Stevie said, her tone firmer. "Deni has been here for a week."

"Thank God she's somewhere she can be helped. I'd hoped she might head for you. She talked about it. . . ."

Stevie forced out the question. "And when she mentioned coming here, did you tell her you knew me?"

He hesitated a moment. "How could I, Stevie? If you know Deni now—know how weak the threads are that hold her together—you should understand. It might have kept her from seeking your help. I didn't want to do anything that might set her back."

"I do understand," Stevie said. "It won't be mentioned by me."

"Stevie. There isn't a better hope in the world of helping Deni than having her there with you. And if she can just get straightened out—"

She could guess what he was going to say. If Deni could only escape from that destructive part of herself, she would be a fabulous and fulfilled woman, someone he might happily stay with. She didn't want to hear it.

"I know," she said. "I'll do everything I can, Lee, don't worry. Don't say any more."

One more brief silence. "All right, Stevie. God bless. . . ." The line went dead.

Lee . . . with Deni Vickers. For a long while after the phone call, Stevie sat thinking. Had Lee truly loved Deni, or was she another of his Good Causes? Had he known everything about her, and still chosen to remain with her? Perhaps . . . though it hurt Stevie to think so, since he had given up so much more easily on her. The questions nagged at her through a long, sleepless night.

4

A slender fingernail of desert sun was just clawing its way over a mountain ridge to the east when Stevie climbed out of bed and put on her bathing suit.

She was feeling more agitated—more vulnerable—than she had in years. The fitful patches of sleep she'd managed during the night had all been marked by jumbled images of past and present, Lee and Pip, herself and Deni, Livy and her mother, the Admiral and Samson—all interchangeably flitting in and out of tortured scenes that were half dream . . . and half memory. She could almost remember what it was like to feel so haunted and pained that it was worth seeking the brief, artificial happiness in some pill or powder.

Her answer to an occasional spell of discontent or self-doubt was generally to plunge into work or, as a cure for more serious distress, to meditate. But this morning she needed something more to drive the demons out of her, to lose herself in sheer physical exertion.

She went to the pool, plunged into the bracingly cool water, and started doing laps. It would be almost two hours before the Travelers began to rise and the usual routine of The Oasis went into gear. Time after time, Stevie swam the

345

length of the pool, losing herself in the simple rhythm of an act endlessly repeated, letting her body will itself to ignore and supersede the preoccupations of the mind. Rigorous exercise was a remedy she had used a lot once, before she had taken total command of herself—a remedy that Lee had taught her. . . .

"Do you think that could help me too?"

The voice that called to Stevie took a moment to penetrate awareness. She kept swimming to the shallow end of the pool, then stood and looked around. With her eyes clouded by water, she could see only a murky silhouette of the woman who stood at the far end of the pool, the sun rising behind her. She appeared to be wearing a flowing gown—a peignoir, probably. Someone who'd risen from bed to spend the night pacing.

"Remember when I came here the first time, Stevie?" the woman said. "There were nights I couldn't sleep. . . . I'd walk around outside, and often you'd be out here at dawn, swimming back and forth. You told me it helped clear your head . . . and you tried to teach me to swim, too."

Smiling, Stevie remembered. Now she knew. "I haven't forgotten, Livy."

"You kept saying I'd be a hell of a lot better off if I could learn to swim like a fish instead of drink like one." Livy's gentle laugh rose into the soft morning air. "You kept trying, even though every time I'd sink like a stone."

"You were a good student where it really counted," Stevie said affectionately.

Livy walked toward her along the edge of the pool. "Was I, Stevie? I didn't learn well enough to stop making the same mistakes."

Stevie pulled herself up the pool ladder and grabbed the towel she'd left on a chaise. "Maybe not," she said, starting to dry off. "You certainly didn't hang on to the most important lesson of all." She stopped rubbing her hair and gave Livy a direct look. "Never to ask perfection—from yourself or anyone else. To know we all cope with mistakes and weaknesses. To forgive yourself, Livy. And," Stevie added with emphasis, "to forgive others."

Stevie hoped her pointed reference to Anne would give Livy an opening to say that she had changed her mind, that Anne would not be exposed—not yet. Wasn't this what Livy had been wrestling with all night?

But Livy didn't pick up the cue. She sat down in one of the pool chairs. "Last night," she said, "I had a very early supper. There were only four or five others in the dining room when I went in. I suppose, in fact, I planned it that way—I didn't want to tangle with Anne again. But I did see someone else I've had a few run-ins with over the years. She and I are in the same business, Stevie, but we don't usually see eye-to-eye on how things should be done." She leaned forward. "Deni Vickers. She's a great newsperson in some respects. But you ought to realize she's absolutely unscrupulous. And I don't think she should—"

Stevie broke in. "Livy, we're back to the rules. I don't engage in this kind of one-on-one backbiting about any Traveler. In a group, okay, we can all lay into each other. But not like this."

"Wait a second, Stevie. This isn't really about Deni. It's about you and me. It's about the fact that you want me—no, you've *ordered* me—to protect Anne Garretson or leave . . . and yet you've exposed her to an even greater danger."

Stevie sat down on a chaise next to Livy, taking a moment to compose her reply, to filter out any hint of the part that Deni Vickers played in her own life. "I think Deni will respect confidentiality," she said, needing to believe that was so. "She came here because she's desperate for help. I don't think she's ready to risk losing that help—even if you are."

Livy studied Stevie a moment, as though she had detected a trace of strain in her voice—the effort Stevie had in keeping a placid facade while discussing Deni. Then she said, "That doesn't mean you're home free. Stevie... Senator Hal Garretson is the most attractive prospect we've had for president in a long time. He's got all the pundits and party big-shots—and even a few foreign leaders—ready to give him a boost. It would be a major scoop to give out the news that would bring him down. I don't think that Deni Vickers will be able to resist."

"Because you can't?"

"No, it's because I know the value of the news. What you ought to consider is that if I break the story, do it first, I'll report it responsibly—and do everything I can to tell Anne's side fairly. I'll tell the truth. If Deni does it, she'll paint it the way it gets the biggest audience; she'll make it as sensational as possible. And Anne could be hurt even worse."

"So what's your pitch?" Stevie asked sharply. "You want me to give you the okay, tell you to go ahead and break the story—and the sooner the better. Well, I can't give you that permission, Livy. Your business may be to tell the truth, mine is to give Anne—everyone who comes here—the best chance for recovery. We're on opposite sides of this one, Livy. If you cross me, I'm finished with you."

"And if Deni breaks the story?"

"The same." And then, as if she needed to prove to herself that she could treat Deni like any other Traveler and give her the benefit of any doubt, Stevie added: "But Deni hasn't given me any reason to think she will."

"Maybe that's because she and I are different," Livy came back. "I tell the truth." She stood up, preparing to go.

Stevie rose with her. "Livy . . . maybe you've made too much of telling the truth."

Livy spun to face her. Disappointment and accusation marked her expression, but whatever obvious defense of the truth she might have made, it didn't come forth before Stevie continued:

"The truth is that, from the day Ken died, you've needed to throw yourself into work, to take over for him, to do everything you could to forget he wasn't there to do the same things himself. And the truth is you've been fighting such a life-and-death battle to hold on to the power you deservedly won that you've been ready to sacrifice your son to do it. That's a truth you haven't minded telling . . . and Carey was the first one to hear it. So he's fighting you now, Livy, because he wants more—and maybe he's entitled to get it."

The hard look of resistance left Livy's expression. She turned away for a moment to look at the sunrise. "This is a beautiful place, Stevie," she said at last, "and you do beautiful things for people. But there are problems you can't fix. I'm stone cold sober now, and it still feels as if my life is about to blow up around me." She looked at Stevie again. "If I let Carey steamroller me out of the *Chronicle*, I'll lose what's left of my own future. I can't see Olivia Walsh spending the rest of her life in a rocking chair, can you?"

Stevie smiled. "No, I sure can't. But you have a grandson now, Livy, and I can't see you spending the rest of your life without the joy of watching him grow. You already missed watching your son. . . ."

For another moment Livy kept her composure, nodding at Stevie as though simply approving a headline. But her eyes began to fill, and her features softened. "Oh Jesus, Stevie," she said, "I don't know what to do."

Stevie caught her in an embrace—the kind of support she would have liked to give her own mother.

"Livy, it doesn't have to be a choice between Carey's happiness or yours. You set it up that way, held on to your territory so fiercely that Carey had to declare war on you to get what he wants and needs. But he's not just *your* son, he's Ken's—even if Ken couldn't finish raising him. I'm sure Carey wants to do the things his father would have passed on to him. And you've kept all the power for yourself."

"There isn't any choice. Either you run things, or you step aside." Livy eased away from Stevie. "And then what's left for me?"

"Livy, just because you've never learned how to share power doesn't mean Carey is the same. Talk to him . . . like a mother and not an employer. Hear him out, find out what he needs. Maybe, just maybe he doesn't want it all . . ."

Livy nodded slowly and smiled. "Maybe I will. Thanks, Stevie. And listen . . . if I'm going to start facing some new truths—and being a little more careful how I tell them—maybe I can rethink what I do about Anne. . . ."

Stevie's face lit up. "Then you'll hold the story for now?"

"I will . . . as long as Deni Vickers does the same."

"Good enough," Stevie said. "I'll make sure she does."

They embraced again. Then Stevie held Livy at arm's length. "You know, we still have an hour before breakfast. How about another swimming lesson? There really is nothing like it for—"

Livy broke free, laughing. "No, thanks! You taught me enough for one day."

Watching Livy walk away, Stevie wished it could be as easy to set herself on the right path as it was to help others. Her need to clear the air with Deni had become only more imperative, yet Stevie wasn't sure she could handle the confrontation. She couldn't imagine facing a woman who had been so involved with Lee—who had needed and used him in exactly the way she had herself—and keeping up her professional front.

She went back to her quarters and phoned the kitchen on the intercom to ask someone to bring breakfast to her office. Usually she ate in the dining room among the Travelers, but having coffee alone would give her a chance to get some correspondence out of the way.

It was only after she had been sitting in the office for nearly an hour—the coffee finished, the correspondence still untouched—that she realized her purpose was actually to avoid seeing Deni Vickers. It was senseless, of course. How could she hope to go on functioning if there was any single one of the Travelers she couldn't face?

Still she lingered another half hour—managing at least to write a gracious acceptance letter to the White House honors. She was just sealing the envelope when there was a sharp knock on the door. Even before Stevie could respond, Jeanne Felber, one of the staff social workers, entered the room.

"Sorry for barging in," she said urgently, "but you're needed up front, Stevie."

"What's the problem?" Stevie asked. Rarely did anyone summon her this way unless it was an emergency of one kind or another.

"Kanda Lyons has just arrived," Jeanne replied.

"Oh." Stevie didn't need to ask any more questions. Everything about Kanda Lyons—her career and her personal life—had become a series of emergencies and disasters. Her decision to come to The Oasis was, in fact, the direct result of her most recent arrest and conviction on charges of theft, assault, and drug possession. Judge William Hardesty of the Superior Court of Los Angeles had not been convinced by Kanda's story that she hadn't intended to take the fifteen-carat emerald necklace from Cartier's on Rodeo Drive or her claim that the two ounces of cocaine found in her purse by a store detective didn't belong to her. Nor had he believed she had acted in self-defense when she attacked the security guard who arrested her. Use her three months' probation to get straight, or she would go to jail for hard time—that had been the judicial ruling. And now it was up to Stevie to mete out the sentence.

Leaving her office, Stevie took a shortcut to the entrance past the gym, where a game of volleyball was in progress. *Mens Sana in Corpore Sano*, the motto over the door, sounded pompous, but Stevie knew it was true, as she had learned when, too young to believe in her own mortality, she had all but destroyed her body—and very nearly her soul. Now she was a firm believer in the golden thread that linked mind and body; she had seen over and over again that when physical health was threatened, it altered the mind, and vice versa. So while she guided her Travelers' struggle emotionally through the ravages of addiction, she also helped them heal the bodies that had been punished and sickened.

As she walked, Stevie thought of what she knew about Kanda Lyons, and could only shake her head at the sad chronicle of waste that had brought Kanda here. Kanda Lyons had made a dozen platinum record albums, and had won an Academy Award in the one and only movie in which she'd starred. Now the brilliant career was in ruins, destroyed by a cocaine habit Kanda never bothered to hide, millions of dollars had been stolen or dissipated, and she was locked in an ongoing battle with the IRS, which had placed liens against all her remaining assets. Stevie was all the more personally saddened because she could remember how much the music of the Wonders—the group from which Kanda had sprung—had been a part of her own youth, how much the voice of Kanda Lyons alone had been background music to Stevie's youth. By reflex, Stevie started humming their big hit from the late Sixties, "Look What Love Has Done to Me."

As she went past the fountain in the tiled lanai and approached the gracefully arched entrance to The Oasis, Stevie was shocked out of the music by the sound of voices raised in an angry shouting match. She took in the situation. Two local taxicabs were parked in the driveway. Charlie Matthews, a taxi driver who often drove Stevie personally, was berating Stevie's personal assistant, Pam Delaney, who was trying to calm him down. It had to be a significant problem to raise Charlie's temper, Stevie thought. He was a laconic man with such a pleasant disposition that she had often told him—more than half seriously—that, if ever he was interested in doing therapy with her clients, she wouldn't mind giving him a job at The Oasis. To which he always answered: "Miz Knight, it's hard enough sometimes just having your customers in my cab. Why would I want to spend all day with 'em?"

Stevie advanced along the driveway. "What's going on, Charlie?" she asked. "It's too nice a day to get your blood pressure in an uproar."

"Morning, Miz Knight," he said, lowering his voice. "What's going on is that Dave Huggins and me picked up one of your . . . your people at the airport. She says she needs two cars, one for her and one for her bags. We say fine. Dave was real gentle with her stuff, and I took special care of the lady myself, same like we do with all your people. Now the lady's here"—the driver gestured toward the second cab in the drive—"and she doesn't want to pay the fares!"

"It's a misunderstanding, Charlie," Stevie said soothingly. "I'll get it straightened out right now. You know how much I appreciate all that special care you give . . . so just be patient, and I'll make sure you get paid."

A moment later, the door of the second taxi opened. A tall, very slender, almost emaciated black woman wearing a dark-green Chanel suit stepped out, long legs encased in sheer stockings and matching suede pumps. A mane of wildly tossed black hair framed a thin, almost gaunt child's face caked with heavy makeup. The eyes were covered with enormous sunglasses, but the face was as recognizable as the voice that went with it.

As Kanda glided along the flagstone path toward Stevie, her bearing was regal, but the closer she came the more the illusion wore thin. Stevie could see that the classic designer suit was spotted, the silk blouse underneath smudged at the collar—and she felt a sudden surge of compassion she knew she had to hide, at least for now.

"Welcome, Kanda," she said, extending her hand. "I'm Stevie Knight. What seems to be the problem?"

"I don't have a problem," Kanda said haughtily. "It's these taxi drivers who have the problem. They were rude and insolent at the airport, and as if that weren't bad enough, that man over there called me a nigger!" She pointed to Charlie Matthews, who had moved in closer to hear the conversation.

"Never happened, Miz Knight!" Charlie protested, his anger mixed with bewilderment. "I swear to God. You know me, Miz Knight . . . anytime somebody at your place needs a taxi, they call Charlie Matthews. Never a complaint, though I could tell you a thing or two about some of the people I bring here. . . . But I figure, live and let live. I don't insult my customers, Miz Knight, and I don't know why this lady is saying I did."

Stevie had no doubt she was hearing the truth. And with some Travelers, she might have risked calling them on the lie. But instinct told her that she had to do everything possible to avoid taking a position that Kanda could interpret as forming an alliance against her.

Stevie turned to Pam. "Pay Charlie and Dave out of petty cash. Miss Lyons and I will settle later."

As Pam led the two men inside, it seemed that Kanda might challenge Stevie's decision, but she simply shrugged and said, "So you're the warden of this establishment. . . ."

Good, Stevie thought, now it was all upfront, the arrest that had brought Kanda here. "We have no warden at The Oasis," she replied. "That's the other place you're thinking of . . . the one you'll end up in if you don't make good use of what we have to offer. But you know that, I'm sure."

Now the big sunglasses came off, and Stevie could see that the huge dark eyes were red and swollen, whether from crying or heavy drug use, she couldn't tell. She could feel herself being weighed and measured.

"Well, then," Kanda said, striking a pose with her spidery hand angled onto her almost pointed hip, "if you have no warden, what is the program at this establishment?" Her manner seemed to suggest that Stevie was little more than a hotel clerk.

"First we'll get you settled," Stevie said pleasantly. "Then you'll get a list of the house rules. We—"

"I was told I had to be here for six weeks," Kanda cut in sharply. "I assume your . . . guests *do* get some time off for . . . for good behavior?"

"That's still the other place you're thinking of," Stevie said cheerfully. "Here it's six weeks for everybody. We didn't pick the number out of a hat. . . . It just seems to work best."

"And what if I should decide to leave here sooner?" Kanda pressed. "Will you inform the authorities?"

"I told you . . . I'm not your keeper or your jailer. Or an informer, for that matter. You can leave anytime you want. Take the same cab back to the airport, if you like. Just don't expect to walk in here again. The next time I make room, it'll be for someone who wants it."

Stevie held her breath. She wanted to help Kanda Lyons, maybe more than she'd ever wanted to help anyone, but dammit all, Kanda had to do her part, too—and not just walk through The Oasis like a prisoner serving time.

Kanda's frail shoulders seemed to slump for a moment, as she stubbed the ground with the toe of her expensive pumps. Then she straightened up. "Okay, Miss Stevie, I get the picture. I'm dispensable, since you've made a deal with the court to take me in *gratis*. I imagine you'd be much more anxious to have me stay if I could afford to pay up front for this . . . this treatment of yours."

One day at a time, Stevie reminded herself as she answered in an even tone, "You can call me Stevie. And you're dead wrong about the money part. When your manager phoned and said you needed help, that was good enough for me. Dammit, that would be good enough for anybody who loves your talent and your music the way I do! Why you'd want to flush it all away . . . and all for the sake of some lousy white powder . . ."

The singer gave an odd smile. "All for the lousy *white* powder," she mused, but said nothing else. She stood beside the Louis Vuitton cosmetic case that had accompanied her, as if waiting for a bellman to appear and take it. She hadn't done anything for herself in years, not with an army of retainers, people she hardly knew who'd been on her payroll for no other reason than to pick up after her or satisfy her craving for an ice-cream cone or a line of cocaine.

Stevie picked up the bag easily. "Let me help you," she said clearly, so there could be no mistaking her meaning. "But as for most of this other stuff," she said, indicating the mountain of matched Vuitton luggage, "it won't fit into the space you're allotted. The Oasis may not be jail, but it isn't the Plaza Athénée either. Pick out whatever will fit in three dresser drawers and half a closet. The rest goes into storage until you leave."

Stevie thought she caught a trace of a smile, but a second later realized she was mistaken. The expression on Kanda's face was a grimace of pain, as if she were holding herself together with a supreme effort of will. Stevie could guess how humiliating it must be for a brilliant star like Kanda to be here as the recipient of charity, and she wanted to reach out and comfort her. Right now, though, she knew that might do more harm than good. So she walked ahead, holding doors and making easy small talk as she showed Kanda the public areas—the gym, the tiny gift shop, and the dining room that was her pride and joy.

"Who's your decorator?" Kanda asked, taking in the mix of comfort and Southwest native. "Mary Poppins or Billy the Kid?"

"Funny," Stevie said, not disapprovingly. Okay, she thought, take a couple of free shots, Ms. Lyons, if that makes it easier for you.

They reached the door of Room 210 in the west wing of the sprawling Spanish-style building. Stevie knocked on the door, then turned the knob. "Your roommate's name is Carla Willis. I think she's in a group session right now, so let's take advantage of the privacy to get you settled. The first part of the drill is to check your bag. Will you open it . . . or shall I?"

Kanda stiffened, her dark eyes clouding with anger and suspicion. "If this isn't a prison," she said stiffly, "then what gives you the right to paw through my things?"

"House rules. And incidentally, we've got dozens. Anyone who stays, follows them."

Kanda shrugged, as if to give warning that she couldn't be expected to toe the line. Stevie faced the singer squarely. "Listen, I won't swear I know what you're going through, but there's a good chance I do. And I can't promise that being here will change your life. But I think we can save it. What I *can* promise is that if you don't do something to change course, and damn soon, you'll either be dead or so messed up you won't know the difference between dead and alive."

As Stevie was speaking, Kanda was nodding her head in that mocking way that children use against teachers. "If I'm not making sense," Stevie said, "ask yourself why a woman who earned enough money in one year to run a small country would shoplift a fifty-thousand-dollar rock right under the nose of two store detectives, a surveillance camera, and a dozen customers? Pretty stupid, right? The folks who don't want to be caught, Kanda, go in through the vault wall."

Kanda almost smiled this time. "So tell me why I did that, Miss Knight. You sure do have all the answers."

"No," Stevie said, shaking her head. "It's you who have all the answers. . . . But maybe, just maybe you wanted to be caught. Maybe the Kanda Lyons who was smart enough to make herself a star finally figured out a way to turn her life back around—to head in the right direction."

Now Kanda did flash a patronizing smile. "Is that from a book on psychology . . . or do you just make it up as you go along?"

"I made it up once, but now I know it by heart. So let me give you the first part of the drill, just so there's no mistake. First, we go through your luggage. Any kind of drug, prescription or otherwise . . . it goes. Ditto for any kind of alcohol, and that includes cologne and perfume."

Kanda began to perspire visibly as Stevie worked her way through the cosmetic case. From the top tray, she removed a bottle of aspirin, a tin of over-the-counter painkiller, and two bottles of Opium perfume. She continued her search and found a suede jewel case. It held no pearls or rubies. It did hold Kanda's particular brand of temptation—at least three ounces of cocaine. Strange, Stevie thought, no matter how broke an addict was, somehow she always found a way to get the drugs. She pocketed the bag of white powder without comment.

Kanda was trembling now, her struggle for self-control obvious. "Bitch," she muttered between clenched teeth.

Stevie didn't take the epithet personally; she never did. In the early days, she had assigned staff members to do this part of the job—"search and seize" they called it—but somehow she felt that was a cop-out, letting others take the anger and frustration, even the hatred that some Travelers felt when all their crutches were taken away. She picked up a paperback that was protruding from Kanda's handbag. "I'll have to take this too," she said.

"Oh? This establishment bans books, Miss Knight? I thought I was still in America. . . ." Kanda's voice was ragged and harsh.

"We ban books and newspapers only for the first two weeks," Stevie explained. "I know that's rough, but the fewer distractions you have, the better the treatment goes. The social worker assigned to your case—Miranda Fields —will be by in a few minutes. You've missed breakfast, but lunch is served at twelve . . . in the main dining room." Stevie turned to leave.

"Just a moment, Miss Knight," Kanda called out imperiously. "I'm not sure I care to have lunch in your dining room. Are there any decent restaurants nearby?"

"There's a good French restaurant . . . and a Spanish one, too. But everything outside the grounds is off-limits for the first four weeks."

"Then you'd better direct me to the nearest telephone," Kanda said coldly. "I need to discuss this situation with my manager."

"Sorry," Stevie said evenly, "but there are no calls in or out for the first week."

Kanda's face was rigid with tension. "It appears," she said, "that I would have been better off in prison. At least the inmates there are allowed a few privileges."

"If you believe that, then you've still got the option. What the court told me is that you stay here—or you go to prison. Which will it be?"

Without waiting for an answer, Stevie left the room.

When the door closed behind her, Kanda's frail body crumpled onto the narrow bed, like a broken puppet. She looked at the tiny pile of belongings that Stevie had stacked neatly on the single bed—and felt a soul-shaking frisson of dread. It all seemed so little, after there had been so much. She'd earned millions, and now she had but a single twenty-dollar bill in her purse—so little she hadn't been able to pay for the two taxis from the airport and had been forced to invent an excuse.

For so many years she had defined herself by possessions and luxuries, by the number of people who ran to do her bidding. She could buy them, not only with money, but with her celebrity. When she'd had her first platinum record, she was surprised by the number of people—even white people—who were willing to serve Kanda Lyons, just because she was the new queen of rock and roll.

Surrounded by luxury and adulation, Kanda could almost believe she was as good as or better than anyone, that she'd left behind forever the little black girl who'd prayed to die and be reborn with white skin.

Now in this place that was worse than a jail, stripped of the entourage and the drugs that had been as much a part of her day as breathing, Kanda knew that something had ended for her, something that had started a long time ago, when she was even skinnier than now—and even blacker, she thought bitterly.

Had she been better off? she wondered. What was the use of dreams that came true if you ended up with nothing anyway? Had Mama been right to think that no matter what she did, Kanda would still be her father's daughter, worthless and bad?

Frightened and tired and desperately in need of something to steady her nerves, Kanda began to cry, a little girl's heartache racking her frail body, almost as if it would break apart. And then suddenly she stopped. Footsteps outside, getting closer. The instinct that had made her a street fighter, the pride that had made her so angry she couldn't be anything else but a star, made her choke back the sobs—and wait.

There was a knock on the door. A petite woman with a young face and salt-and-pepper curls came in. She introduced herself as Miranda Fields and, without preliminaries, picked up where Stevie had left off. "Your first stop is the doctor's office," she said. "We want to make sure that everything's as okay as it can be."

Kanda had nothing to say. Her encounter with Stevie had made it clear she'd have her work cut out for her here. And in spite of her bravado, Kanda didn't want to trade this place in for a real jail. No way. She would beat these people at their own game, for she was sure it was a game, just like everything else in life.

So I'll follow the bitch, she said to herself as she went out of the room and down a long corridor. As they were walking, Kanda caught sight of Somebody Famous... Jennifer Kane, the star of *Police Beat*. In spite of her own celebrity, Kanda still reacted like a fan in the presence of anyone else's fame. Funny, she thought, the Kane woman had always seemed so squeaky-clean white, like a teacher or librarian.

"Wouldn't imagine someone like Jennifer Kane would end up here," Kanda mused half aloud.

The social worker bitch smiled, all puffed up and proud like Kanda had just given her a medal. "She's at The Oasis because it's the best," she said, stopping in front of a white door marked HOWARD SLOAN, CHIEF OF MEDICAL SERVICES. She walked Kanda into a spacious, airy office with a panoramic view of the surrounding red hills, introduced her to an old guy wearing a white coat and a goofy smile, and said she'd wait outside.

"Your last album was great," Dr. Sloan said. "I bought it for my grandson, but I changed my mind and kept it myself. The way you did 'My Man' . . . boy, it gave me goose bumps."

Kanda nodded, and not knowing what the right move would be, kept her mouth shut. They probably kept track of everything you said in this place, and she didn't want to add any more hard time to her six-week sentence.

Dr. Sloan went on to check her weight, her heart, and blood pressure. He didn't frown, as her last doctor had, and he didn't make any of those scary doctor noises as he examined her eyes, her throat, and her nose. When he was finished, he looked her straight in the eye and asked, "When did you do your last line?"

She was surprised, not so much by the question but by the easy way he asked it, as though he knew all about her. She pretended she had to think hard because it had been so long. "Last week sometime."

He gave her that goofy smile and said softly, "Know how you can always tell when an addict is lying?"

"How?" she asked, not really wanting to hear any stupid joke.

"When you see his lips moving."

Kanda didn't laugh. Her stomach was turning, and her head throbbing.

"Feeling pretty bad right now?" he asked sympathetically.

As if on cue, she jumped off the table and ran to the bathroom. She retched for a long time, and though she couldn't remember when she'd last eaten, her stomach wouldn't quit. She wished she was dead. If getting straight was going to be this bad, she might as well be dead, because she couldn't see much point in feeling nothing but misery.

When she returned to the old doctor's examining room, he handed her a towel and a glass of club soda. "This happen often?" he asked.

"Sometimes," she answered cautiously, meaning *Only when my supply is cut off*.

Sloan nodded sympathetically. "I know how it is. . . . I'm a drunk. I just haven't had a drink in fifteen years."

She cocked an eyebrow and thought what a funny way they had of talking here. But she didn't care. All she cared about was feeling better, and right now, she almost would have killed somebody to make that happen.

The doctor handed her some pills. "These will help you with the detox," he explained. "It takes a lot longer for drugs than with alcohol, but your system will clean itself out in about ten days. Meanwhile, these pills will help with the side effects. Anything else I can do, I'm here. So is Stevie. We have a full staff here—ministers, social workers—so you never have to feel like you're alone. Anything I can do right now?"

Even in her misery, Kanda couldn't resist the opening. "Not unless you can find me something a lot higher grade than this," she said with a wicked grin.

Sloan winced, almost as if she'd struck him. "Try some other high-grade stuff, Kanda," he said earnestly. "Try life. . . ."

Kanda downed the pills hungrily and left the office. What did an old drunk know about her? She *had* tried life, and all life had done was betray her. Two worthless husbands who'd cleaned her out and left her with two kids who were even darker than she was. Even the talent that had been her ticket out of the ghetto couldn't be trusted; it had let her down when she needed it most, making her a has-been in a world that cared nothing for yesterday's stars. Her only friend was the white powder. It always gave relief, and you could always count on it.

The social worker bitch was waiting for her. "Let me show you the main room," she said.

Leave me alone, Kanda wanted to say, but she caught herself quickly. Be cool, girl, she told herself, be cool and play the game.

The main room looked like one of those big lounges in the resort hotels she'd played. There was a lot of glass and a picture-postcard view, like maybe there should have been a golf course outside.

A bunch of people were sitting around, some writing in notebooks or talking in small groups. No one seemed crazy or weird, and the way they looked in her direction, Kanda could tell they recognized her and were pretending she was just like everyone else. She was used to that, and she didn't know what bugged her more, the phony cool, or the way some people pushed their way into her face, demanding autographs and conversation, just as if they owned a piece of her.

"Let's sit over here," said Miranda, leading Kanda toward a sunny corner that was slightly private. She produced a sheaf of papers from her battered notebook and began to read out a schedule. "We're up at six here. You make your bed—"

"I don't make beds," she said stiffly, feeling fractionally more in control now that the pill, whatever it was, had started to take. "That's maids' work."

"Everyone makes her own bed here. Next comes breakfast, then a walk, then . . ." and here the Fields woman hesitated for just a moment, showing an insecurity that Kanda relished. ". . . then we do a therapeutic chore."

"What's that—in English?" Kanda challenged, sensing that the social worker wasn't as much in control as she pretended to be.

"It's a small job . . . setting up the tables in the cafeteria, filing in one of the administrative offices, or . . ."

"I understand you people gave Penny Farlow the toilet-scrubbing detail," Kanda said, grinning slyly as she repeated a bit of gossip she'd heard about a famous Broadway musical star.

Miranda Fields shook her salt-and-pepper curls vigorously. "There's no such thing here," she said emphatically. "At The Oasis, we've found that a menial chore is therapeutic. It's a reality connector that assists recovery."

"Really?" Kanda laughed bitterly. "I wish someone had told my mother that. She did menial chores all her life . . . and then she dropped dead when she was forty-two. Poof, doing menial chores ended her connection to reality real quick."

"I'm sorry," Miranda said softly, her face getting that funny scrunched-up sympathy-for-the-underprivileged look Kanda remembered so well. And then she moved back to something she understood—the schedule. "Morning lecture's at nine. At ten, you and four others meet in my office for group. Lunch is next, followed by an afternoon lecture, then group again.

"Finally, we have exercise in the pool or gymnasium, dinner at five-thirty; evening lecture, then reading and writing assignments, then bed. Any questions?" She smiled brightly like one of those do-good Bible-school teachers Mama used to bring home for Sunday dinner.

When Kanda failed to respond, Miranda glanced at a folder she was carrying. "If you have no questions for me, then I'll ask one: Why are you here?"

"The judge said . . ."

"Why are you here?" Miranda repeated, as though she was deaf or something.

"I'm trying to tell you," Kanda said with exaggerated politeness. "It was either here or jail."

"That isn't an answer to my question," Miranda persisted, looking Kanda straight in the eye.

"I'm sorry you don't like my answer," she said in the same polite tone. "What would you like me to say?"

"How long have you had a drug problem?"

Kanda stiffened with resentment. "I don't have a problem with drugs," she said haughtily. "It's people that give me problems."

The social worker nodded knowingly, and for a moment Kanda wanted to slap her smug, white face. "I see you were arrested twice for possession. Once on charges of neglecting your two daughters, who were later remanded to the custody of your sister, Charlene. Most recently, a shoplifting arrest at Cartier's on Rodeo Drive. . . . The report said you left the store with a valuable emerald pendant, that you became abusive when the store detective asked you to return it, and that you later assaulted the man with your high-heeled shoe, causing an injury that required three stitches."

"If you know all of that, why are we having this quiz?" Kanda asked, trying to keep control of the conversation.

"Are you a drug addict?"

"If you know everything about me, you—"

"It's not me we're talking about," Miranda interrupted. "If you can't admit you have a problem, you can't begin to solve it."

Kanda rose, striking a brash, curiously youthful pose. With her long skinny legs and her short skirt, she looked for a moment like a twelve-year-old dressed in her mother's clothes, about to stick her tongue out at the teacher. "May I be excused now?" she asked politely.

"This isn't a jail," Miranda replied with a heavy sigh that told Kanda she was winning. "We have rules and schedules, but it's your choice to follow them or leave." Without further comment, she handed Kanda a copy of the house rules.

As Kanda walked through the main room, she was aware that all eyes were on her, and she tried to sustain that sassy swagger her fans used to love. When all else failed, she could still muster her pride, and maybe, just maybe, that would get her through this high-class reform school. Now all she had to do was get back to her room without falling apart.

Once she was there, however, the tears came again. This time when she threw herself on the bed, she buried her face in the pillow and screamed into it with rage and frustration. But the cause wasn't The Oasis, she realized suddenly. She was crying exactly as she had when she'd been a kid in her mama's house, and screaming at the things that had roused her fury then—the filth, the need for Mama to work so hard, her father's desertion, and not having enough nice things.

For the first time in years, she was back inside the skin of that little girl she had pitied and hated so much, that goddamn little black nobody with no clothes and no money and no papa . . . with nothing at all but the music in her heart to call her own.

5

As her voice soared higher and higher, reaching for the last sweet notes of "How Great Thou Art," Kanda felt God's presence lift her far above the run-down storefront that housed the congregation of the Divine Lamb. She didn't believe everything the minister said on Sunday, but in the "hallelujahs" of the choir, in the company of voices raised joyfully in song, Kanda felt the power of God, the power of hope. She could believe in the promise of a better life and dream beyond the cold-water Chicago flat she shared with Mama and her baby sister, Charlene.

"Turn to page two fifty-two, brothers and sisters," said the choirmaster, Franklin Eldridge, "and let us sing 'Amazing Grace.'" Kanda didn't need the songbook; she knew the words to all her favorite hymns by heart. As the organ sounded the introduction, she hit the opening notes hard, and soon she was snapping her fingers and singing to a blues beat that was caught up by her friend, Lonette Jones, and then passed on to the other singers, who praised the glory of God in a smoky, hard-driving hymn of the streets.

"Make a joyful noise unto the Lord!" shouted Brother Eldridge, who never minded a little improvisation, as long as the music was fervent and the voices strong. Of all the ranking members of the congregation, Kanda liked him best, for he'd allowed her to join the choir last year, when she was only eleven, a year short of the required age.

The rehearsal was over all too soon, and Kanda lingered, though she knew she should go home and start supper. She wasn't ready to put her singing aside, not when that was the best part of her day, and not when all that waited at home were the usual chores and the usual bleakness of a latchkey childhood. She waved to Lonette, who was making polite conversation with some of the adult members of the choir. Lonette was only fourteen, yet to Kanda, she seemed mature and sophisticated. It was she who'd told Kanda her voice was too good to waste in a church choir, and it was she who'd come up with the idea of forming a singing group.

"Wanna come to my house?" Lonette asked after she'd put away her hymnal and gathered up her schoolbooks. "My cousin Maline's gonna be there, we can practice that new arrangement Lee did for us."

"Do you think he'll be awake yet? Do you think he'd play for us?" Kanda asked eagerly. Lonette's brother, Lee, played piano at the Tophat Club on Chicago's State Street, and sometimes if he wasn't too tired, he'd accompany the Wonders as they practiced their growing repertoire of songs.

"Maybe if *you* ask him real nice," Lonette teased, knowing that Kanda wasn't interested in boys. All Kanda cared about was making music and talking about how it would be when the Wonders got the chance to play for money.

"No way," Kanda replied firmly. "I'm not about to mess with your brother, Lonette, and if he doesn't want to play his miserable piano, then we'll just sing without him."

Hand in hand, the girls ran to Lonette's house, and though it wasn't much grander than her own, Kanda would have been happy to spend all her waking hours there. According to Mama, the only good music was gospel music, but Kanda couldn't agree, not when her voice was her only talent, her only hope of escaping the poverty she'd been born to. And so she kept her dream a secret. It wasn't like lying, she told herself; she'd tell Mama one day, when the Wonders were ready, when the dream had a chance of becoming reality.

As they let themselves into Lonette's frame house, they heard the sound of Lee's old upright piano—and a strong, husky voice belting out "My Boyfriend's Back."

Rushing into the living room, Kanda saw Maline, having a good old time flirting with Lee as she sang, her shiny processed hair falling over her face, her well-developed sixteen-year-old body swaying provocatively.

"Hey," Kanda said indignantly, "that's *my* solo you're doing, Maline! Why don't you practice your own part?"

"Hey yourself," Maline responded with a throaty laugh. "Maybe it oughta be my solo, seeing as how I sing it better."

"Oh, yeah? And I say *I* sing it better!" Kanda argued, stung by Maline's brass. She had mistrusted—and envied —Maline Powers from the first time they'd met. She could sing and she was beautiful, with pale golden skin, dramatically chiseled exotic features, and slightly slanted almond-colored eyes.

"What do you say, Lee?" Maline asked. "Don't you think the solo sounds better when I do it? After all, who's gonna believe skinny little Kandy Kane even *has* a boyfriend?" She smiled seductively, inviting Lee to take her side.

Lee grinned at Maline, shaking his head. "Uh-uh," he said, "I'm not gettin' in the middle of any catfight here. If you girls think you're gonna be professionals, you better learn how to work together . . . and that means *somebody* better be happy singing backup."

Hands on hips, Kanda declared, "Well, it isn't gonna be me who sings backup, I'll tell you that!"

Ever the peacemaker, Lonette stepped in. "Lee's right," she said. "We're never gonna amount to anything if we don't get some teamwork going. I say Kanda and Maline take turns with the solos for now. After all, there's no sense arguing when we haven't even got an act ready. What do you say, Maline?"

Maline smiled agreeably at the suggestion, which was half a victory for her, but Kanda was silently angry. She wanted to push the argument, but she was afraid she'd lose it, and then she'd have no choice but to quit the group. Her pleasure suddenly soured by the bitter taste of defeat, she resigned herself to sharing an imaginary spotlight with Maline. But only for now, she promised herself, only until I can take it away.

It was well after dark when Kanda tore herself away from Lonette's house and hurried home, feeling like a guilty sinner for neglecting her chores.

She ran up the four flights of stairs and rapped on old Mrs. Baker's door. She heard the slow, dragging steps that told of Mrs. Baker's arthritis, and as the door opened, she inhaled the sweet aroma of sugar-water candy the old woman made for Kanda and Charlene.

"Slow down, child," Mrs. Baker scolded. "Slow down and catch your breath. Here," she said, offering a piece of the sticky candy, "have a little sweet and put a smile on your pretty face."

Kanda took the candy and rejected the compliment. She knew old Mrs. Baker was just being nice, just as she knew she wasn't pretty.

"I'm here for Charlene," Kanda said, but her sister was

planted in front of Mrs. Baker's black-and-white television set, watching the cartoons that were her favorite entertainment.

Hearing her name mentioned, Charlene began to plead. "Do I have to go home? I finished my homework, so can I stay a little while longer? Please, Mrs. Baker, please?"

"It's okay, child," Mrs. Baker said to Kanda. "Charlene can keep me company while you get supper ready for your mama. I'll send her home in a little while."

As Kanda turned to go, she felt a stab of resentment. Charlene was eight years old, but she still acted like a big baby. She didn't help out around the house, yet Mama seemed to like her best, always praising her gentle nature and quiet ways, letting her do anything she wanted. Hell, Kanda thought, Charlene wasn't quiet, she was just plain dumb, and it wasn't fair that she had things so easy. Mama said it was because she was younger, but Kanda thought there was another reason: Charlene was delicate and light-skinned like their mother, while Kanda, according to the pictures she'd seen, was the image of her absent father, tall and gangly and black as ebony.

Taking the key that hung around her neck on a ribbon, she went across the hall and opened the door to the three rooms she called home. The place was spotless, Mama made sure of that, no matter how tired she was from cleaning other people's houses all day.

Kanda went into the kitchen and opened the old GE refrigerator that made funny noises all night long. She took out a head of broccoli—Mama insisted on something green—and the chopped meat that would be their supper. She washed and cut the broccoli, and put some water on the stove to boil. She shaped the meat into three hamburgers, and was just starting to fry them when Mama came through the door.

Kanda felt a surge of pride when she saw her mother,

thinking how different she looked from the other neighborhood women, and how no one could guess that she spent the day mopping and scrubbing and ironing. With her high cheekbones, her fine features, her hair pulled back tight, she looked more like an African princess than a cleaning woman. She carried herself straight and tall, no matter how tired she was; her clothes, like her home, were neat and well tended.

"Hi, honey," she said, gathering Kanda close for a hug and kiss. Kanda wrinkled her nose against the smell of ammonia and lemon oil, pulling away from this reminder of her mother's occupation. "Charlene's still next door," she announced. "I told her to come home, but she wouldn't."

Martha smiled and shook her head wearily, too tired to referee or take sides. She sat down at the kitchen table and began to empty her shopping bag. Kanda hated it when Mama brought stuff home from the places she worked, but she watched as her mother pulled out an old picture and wiped the glass with one of her cleaning rags. The picture was of a pretty blond girl riding a white horse against a background of rocky mountains. The frame was cracked and shabby, but Martha Lyons handled it reverently. "It's a Winslow Homer," she explained to Kanda. "He was a fine American artist."

"It looks like a piece of junk to me," said Kanda, who had never seen a mountain or a white horse. She knew her mother wanted her to appreciate what she called "the finer things," but she thought those things were a waste of time when you lived on Fifth Street. Maybe someday, when she was rich, she'd buy some pictures of her own, but they sure wouldn't be in any broken old frames.

Mama shook her head again as she reached into the bag and pulled out a powder-blue party dress that looked almost new. "I thought this would look pretty on you, honey. All it needs is a tuck or two around the waist. . . ."

"Why don't you save it for Charlene?" Kanda said, hating the idea of charity more than she hated doing without.

Mama put the dress down and took Kanda's hand. "Kanda, honey, there's no shame in accepting something that's given to you. I've tried to teach you the difference between dignity and pride. Dignity is a private thing . . . it comes from inside you, and no one can take it away, no matter how poor you are. But pride is a weakness and a sin . . . it eats away your soul. I'm afraid when I see it in you. It reminds me . . ." Her voice trailed off, but Kanda knew what Mama left unfinished. She was like her father, in another bad way. She pulled her hand away and went back to the stove.

A moment later, Charlene burst into the apartment, showering Mama with hugs and kisses and making her laugh the way Kanda never could. She exclaimed over Mama's pretty picture and the party dress, screaming with delight when she learned it would be hers.

Kanda set the table, cut the bread, and laid out the simple supper. But it was Charlene who entertained Mama with silly stories about what she did in school and how she'd been picked to be a Pilgrim in the Thanksgiving play.

"That's wonderful," Mama said. "What about you, Kanda? How was choir practice today?"

"Same as usual," Kanda replied tersely, feeling more like an outsider because Mama made the effort to include her.

When the meal was over, Kanda cleared the table and washed the dishes, while Charlene brushed her teeth and got into her pajamas. Then came the usual evening ritual, as Mama tucked her into the big double bed she shared with Kanda.

"Tell me about the house now," Charlene said, giving

Mama the cue for the story she'd heard a hundred times before.

"When Albert . . . your daddy finds a job in Detroit," Mama began, "he's going to send for us. Then we'll pack our things and get on a train. And when we get to Detroit, Daddy will be waiting there, in a fine house in a good neighborhood. . . ."

"We'll have a yard, won't we, Mama?" Charlene filled in, "and a swing and a jungle gym, right?"

"And a swing and a jungle gym," Mama repeated. "Perhaps a rosebush or two. . . ."

Kanda listened to Mama's story in silence. Once she had eagerly asked questions, the way Charlene did now, but after four years, she didn't believe the story anymore. It was just a fairy tale, and Daddy was never coming back. There would never be a house with a yard, at least not from him.

After Charlene fell asleep, Kanda turned on the bedside lamp, reached under the bed, and pulled out the big cardboard box that was filled with fairy tales she could believe in—movie magazines and pictures of recording stars who had once been poor and were now rich and celebrated . . . Dionne Warwick, Barbra Streisand, Lena Horne. She read and reread the stories that told of their success, then examined her reflection in the mirror that hung over the dresser. Remembering Maline's cruel taunts, she wondered if she could ever be a star, looking the way she did. She knew she could sing, better than Maline, no matter what anyone said, but what about her nappy hair, her little girl's face, and her boy's figure? Would the day ever come when she could look in the mirror and see a reflection that would make her happy?

It was on Thanksgiving Day that the stories about Daddy and the new house stopped. Mama got up early to start the turkey and the chestnut dressing. Then she put on her Sunday dress and announced they would have a guest for dinner. A good friend, she said; his name was Calvin Johnson and he drove the bus she rode to work every day.

Kanda didn't like the idea of a stranger, especially a man, at a holiday dinner. But Charlene got all excited, asking questions about what he looked like and where he lived. When he arrived, shortly after one o'clock, with a bunch of flowers for Mama and a box of candy for the girls, Kanda began to wonder if her mother had been keeping secrets too. After all Mama's talk about sin, did she have a boyfriend?

Mama introduced him shyly, as if pleading for approval. He was a nice-looking man, quiet and kind of shy himself. He told the girls he was a widower and that he had a grown daughter who lived in Florida. Kanda didn't like the sound of that, and when he complimented Mama's cooking and said he couldn't remember when he'd tasted anything so delicious, her suspicions about her mother and Calvin Johnson grew. Charlene might be taken in, but Kanda had no use for any man coming in and messing up their lives. If their own father had abandoned them, why would Calvin Johnson be any better?

Two weeks later, Mama told Kanda that Calvin would be moving in. "It isn't natural for a woman to be alone, honey. Calvin's a good man, and he wants to take care of us."

"But you aren't alone!" Kanda protested. "You have me and Charlene. We don't need anyone to take care of us! We're doing just fine. Besides," she said, summoning up her strongest argument, "you can't live with Calvin. . . . You're married to my father!"

Mama sighed. "I wish you'd try to understand, honey," she said. "I've done my best to raise you alone, but I've been so lonely for such a long time. I think God will forgive me for loving Calvin. Can't you do the same . . . for my sake?"

Kanda had no answer to that, but she watched and waited, sure that she was right and Mama was wrong. For a while it was true that Calvin's quiet presence made their lives easier, maybe, Kanda grudgingly admitted, even happier. Mama didn't seem so tired after work, and on the weekend, Calvin took them to the movies and then to dinner at Howard Johnson's. On Sunday, they went to church together, almost like a real family, and when Christmas came, they had a tree and presents, brand-new dresses bought from Marshall Fields, a doll for Charlene, and a pair of patent-leather pumps for Kanda.

Then, as suddenly as he had arrived, Calvin went away, the second week of spring. Mama said he'd gone to visit his daughter in Florida, but she started crying at night when she thought the girls were asleep. Kanda got up once and tried to comfort her, and though she didn't much care if Calvin ever came back, she swore aloud that she'd kill him for hurting Mama's feelings. But Mama just hushed her up, saying that that kind of talk wasn't Christian, and that relationships between men and women didn't always work out, even between two good people.

Kanda listened. Mama's fine way of speaking always made her explanations sound good. But she still didn't understand why her mother needed a man if he was going to end up leaving and she was going to end up crying her heart out.

She understood even less when Mama brought home Bill Timmons, who wasn't as nice as Calvin Johnson, who drank heavily, and who cursed when he was angry. With all her good manners and talk of dignity, how could Mama close her eyes to these things? When Kanda asked that question, Mama looked so sad and unhappy that she was sorry she'd opened her mouth.

And so she kept quiet, resenting Mama's weakness, even more so since Charlene didn't seem to care who lived with them as long as she got a treat and a little pocket money now and then. Kanda spent as little time at home as she could get away with, throwing herself heart and soul into her music. The Wonders acquired a new member, Sondra Leeds, who was even dumber than Charlene but had a resonant alto voice that added richness and variety to the rock-and-roll arrangements that Lee provided. Best of all, Sondra was happy to sing backup.

A month after Kanda's thirteenth birthday, she came home from a session at Lonette's house, ready to make supper as usual, and found her mother in bed, moaning with pain and flushed with a high fever. "What's wrong, Mama?" she asked, trying not to show how frightened she was.

"It's nothing, honey," Martha said weakly. "I wasn't feeling well, so Mrs. Connor told me to take the afternoon off. The flu's going around again . . . I'm sure that's all it is. If you'll just make me a cup of tea . . . get me a couple of aspirins, I'll be fine."

Kanda had never seen her mother so sick. She called Mrs. Baker, made the tea, and sat by Mama's bed, watching anxiously as she tried to drink it.

"It's that flu, all right," Mrs. Baker said at first. "Just give your mama lots of liquid and lots of rest." But when the pain and the fever got worse instead of better, when Mama began to tremble and shake, Mrs. Baker took Kanda aside and said, "Maybe you'd best take Martha to the emergency room over at the hospital, child. I'll call a taxi for you . . . and I'll look after Charlene till you get back."

The word "hospital" struck terror into Kanda's heart; it conjured up images of death and dying. But she tried to push these away as she dressed her mother and helped her down the stairs and into the waiting taxi.

"County General Emergency room," she told the driver,

clutching the ten-dollar bill Mrs. Baker had given her. When they reached the hospital, she settled Mama on a bench in the waiting room. "My mother's real sick," she told the nurse at the reception desk.

The nurse glanced over at Martha Lyons and nodded. "Everyone here is sick, dear. You'll just have to wait your turn."

"I said she's *real* sick!" Kanda shouted, pounding the desk. "My mother needs a doctor right now, and if anything happens to her, I'll kill you, do you hear me?"

"What's going on?" asked a passing intern.

Kanda grabbed his arm. "Please," she begged, "please look at my mother right now. She's got something bad, I know it, and if you don't do something quick . . ."

The intern looked at Kanda's frightened face and put his hand on her shoulder. "Okay," he said kindly, "let's have a look." He helped Mama into an examining room, but said "No" when Kanda tried to go with them. Watching her mother walk so slowly, doubled over in pain, she felt completely helpless—and lonelier than she'd ever been in her life.

What if Mama died? What if she was so sick the doctor couldn't do anything? What would become of her and Charlene? How would they live and who would take care of them? Except for poor old Mrs. Baker, there was no one who cared about them, no one at all. And in that moment, Kanda realized there was no one in the world she could really count on, no one except herself. The thought was painful, but it gave her a curious kind of peace, as she settled herself on the bench and waited.

It was hours later when the doctor came back and told Kanda that he'd admitted her mother. "She has a bleeding ulcer," he explained. "But that isn't as bad as it sounds. We'll be doing a little operation, and she'll be as good as

new. I'm going to let you see for yourself that she's fine
. . . but just for a minute, and then you have to go home."

Kanda followed the doctor into the ward, where Mama lay
still and quiet against the white sheets, trying to force a smile
for Kanda. "Just for a minute," the doctor reminded her,
drawing the curtain so they could have some privacy from the
seven other patients in the room. "Please get better," Kanda
pleaded softly. "Please come home soon, Mama."

"Don't worry, honey," Martha soothed, stroking her
daughter's hair. "It's going to take a little time, but I promise I'll come home. I wouldn't leave my little girls . . . you
know I wouldn't do that."

But Kanda wasn't reassured. Seeing how weak Mama
looked now, remembering how sick she was a short time
ago, she didn't want to leave. But a nurse poked her head
inside the curtain and chased her away.

"I'll take care of everything," Kanda promised as she
was leaving. "Don't you worry about anything, Mama. . . .
You just get better."

Kanda kept her promise—and more. Every day that
Mama was in the hospital, she prayed hard, swearing to be
as good as she knew how, if God would only bring her
mother home. And just so God would know she was sincere, Kanda gave up singing with the Wonders for as long
as Mama was sick. Every day after school, she went directly home and cleaned and scrubbed and made sure there
was a hot supper. She didn't fight with Charlene, no matter
how much of a pest she was, and tried to be nice to Bill,
even though he was drinking a lot and bringing his rowdy
friends over to mess up the apartment. And every evening,
she went to the hospital and sat with Mama until visiting
hours were over.

One day, Bill came home early, waving a package
wrapped in silver paper and red ribbon. "It's for you,

Kandy Kane," he said, using the nickname she hated. Inside the box was a necklace set with green-colored glass stones. "That's for doing such a good job while your mama's so sick."

She started to say "No, thank you," to suggest that the necklace would make a nice present for Mama, but he put the box in her hand and covered it with his own, so tightly that she struggled to get free.

"It's getting pretty lonesome around this place," he said, still holding on to her hand. "A man can't wait around forever. . . . Maybe I'll just have to find me a new place to stay."

Kanda was glad for a minute and then she felt guilty, remembering how bad Mama felt when Calvin moved away.

"You gonna miss me if I go, Kandy Kane?" he teased, mistaking the look of concern on her face.

"Maybe it's time someone started bein' nice to me," he said, half coaxing, half threatening. And when she still didn't answer, he picked her up and carried her skinny body to the big bed in Mama's room. She knew what was going to happen; she'd heard about such things from the girls in the neighborhood. Yet she never imagined it would happen to her, not after she'd been so good and done everything she was supposed to do.

She cried out when Bill tore the flimsy cotton dress from her body, but he covered her screams with his big, sweaty hand and growled, "None of that, hear? Else I'll tell your mama how you drove old Bill away."

Kanda stopped screaming. There was no one to protect her from the rough, hurting hands that pinched and bruised her young flesh, no one to stop the terrible pain of Bill's assault as he rammed himself inside her, cursing when he found resistance, grunting and groaning as he pushed harder and deeper till Kanda felt she was being torn in two. She stared at the cracks in the ceiling and swore she'd never forgive God for this awful betrayal.

When Bill was finished, he gave Kanda a knowing smile, as if they were now partners in a secret. "You remember what I told you, now . . . best not say nothin' to your mama, hear? Break her heart, maybe even kill her, seeing how sick she is. . . ."

The smile and the words made Kanda realize that she'd never be safe again, not as long as Mama wanted Bill in her house. The loneliness she'd felt the day Mama got sick took hold of Kanda, and now it seemed like the only real truth.

That night, she took Charlene to old Mrs. Baker's and asked if they could stay there until Mama came home. The old woman agreed and asked no questions, as if she already knew all the awful things that could happen if you were poor and black and female.

Once, she ran into Bill in the hallway, but he just smiled and waved, as though he knew what she was up to and was confident he'd get what he wanted anyway.

When Mama came home, Kanda had no choice but to return to the apartment. She tried desperately to stay out of Bill's way, but he kept finding ways to get her alone, to use her body and ensure her silence with threats—until she bought a switchblade from one of the boys on the street. The next time Bill came after her, she pretended to acquiesce, and when he was finished, she cut him on the face. "You touch me again, I'll kill you," she said, and he must have believed the hatred in her eyes. A few days later, he was gone.

Kanda gave up the choir, because she could no longer bear to sing the "hallelujahs." She started skipping school to make more time for her singing, badgering Lee to listen, to tell her when she sounded good and when she didn't, ignoring the distress in her mother's eyes when she saw the report card detailing the unexcused absences and the failing grades.

Together with Lonette and Sondra, she begged Lee to help the Wonders get a start. "You must know somebody who can get us a job, Lee," Kanda pleaded. "Just help us this one time, and we won't bother you again. Please . . . ?"

"Now, why don't I believe that?" Lee teased. But in the end he agreed to arrange an audition with Barnett Hawkins, an agent who booked some of the acts that played the Tophat Club. Barnett booked them for a single weekend, for twenty dollars a night, with the understanding that there would be more work if the club's customers liked the Wonders.

No sooner was the arrangement made than Kanda took on Maline. "I'm singing lead," she said. "And if you don't like it, I'm walking—and you can kiss this job good-bye." Hands on hips, she waited for Maline's answer. There was no way Kanda was walking out now, but she wasn't about to share the solo spot with anybody, least of all Maline. And if she had to get tough and mean to get her way, so what?

"That's a dirty trick, Kanda Lyons," Maline replied. "That's a real dirty trick to play on your friends."

"It's no trick," Kanda said, knowing she had won. "I'm doing my friends a favor. . . . You just wait and see."

Kanda undid her braids and processed her hair into a big, shiny bouffant. She boosted a watch and a string of pearls from Marshall Fields and turned these over to Barnett, in payment for her first professional costume—an aquamarine satin sheath trimmed with matching sequins and chiffon.

Mama raised hell the first time she saw her little girl with the bosom of her dress stuffed with tissue paper, her face masked with pancake makeup, bright red lipstick, and false eyelashes. But Kanda stood fast. Stung by what seemed like Mama's hypocrisy, Kanda said she'd rather look like a painted tramp than to live like trash.

Though she couldn't read a note of music, Kanda sang of lost innocence, of heartache and pain, with a voice that was clear and pure, with feelings that were real and true, and the audience seemed to know it. That was the biggest payoff for Kanda, more than the twenty dollars in cash the Wonders received—the spotlight and the applause, the whistles and cheers that came back to her over the harsh stage lights.

The Wonders played the Tophat Club for fifteen weeks, with Barnett at practically every performance, clapping and cheering, especially for Maline. And when the show was over, he'd drive the other girls home in his Oldsmobile convertible and then take Maline to a fancy restaurant for a late supper. Kanda wasn't jealous; hell, she told Maline if Barnett was really stuck on her, he'd get them some better-paying jobs.

The Wonders moved from the Tophat to the Elite and then to Chez Paris. To Maline and Lonette and Sondra, this was success, but to Kanda it was just a beginning. It was Kanda who came in early each night, who talked to the musicians and tried to explain that the music they made had to be somehow different, fresh and original, and it was Kanda who pushed the girls into trying difficult arrangements, so the Wonders wouldn't sound like imitations of Motown groups like the Ronettes or Martha and the Vandellas.

And when the Wonders finally had an act that blended the pulsing sounds of the street with the gospel beat of the Divine Lamb choir, Kanda pumped the other girls up until they were ready to demand that Barnett get them a spot on the Apollo Theater's Amateur Night bill and advance them bus fare to New York.

The appearance earned the Wonders no money, but it did bring them the attention of Frankie Sedutto, who owned a small record company, and a couple of important disc jockeys and a talented songwriter who'd recently defected from the Motown label. Sedutto offered the girls a three-year contract, on the condition that they get rid of Barnett and put their careers in his hands.

Kanda agreed in a minute. But Maline was in love with Barnett, and as she argued his case, her almond-colored eyes pleaded for understanding. "Barnett got us started," she pleaded. "It isn't fair to dump him now, after all he's done for us. . . ."

"What's he ever done for *us*?" Kanda demanded. "Maybe you're getting a little something extra, Maline, but the Wonders get nothing but two-bit clubs, because that's all Barnett can ever do."

The other two girls listened, like spectators at a tennis match, as arguments bounced back and forth, as anger mounted and passions flared.

"I'm going," Kanda said finally. "It's me the man wants anyway," she bluffed, "and if you all want to stay around here, singing for nickels and dimes, I'll just tell Mr. Sedutto to hook me up with some girls who want to make real money. . . ."

A vote was taken. Against Kanda's ambition, Maline's love for Barnett fell short. Bitterly Maline surrendered, tears streaming down her face. "I hope you get what's coming to you," she said, sobbing, her beautiful features contorted with pain, "I hope you feel what I'm feeling now. Just you wait, Kanda Lyons . . . someday you're gonna love a man, and I hope he does you dirt!"

"Sticks and stones . . ." Kanda laughed, feeling strong and powerful. *She* was the voice of the Wonders, so what did Maline's curses matter, now that Kanda's dreams were about to come true?

The Wonders' first single for Sedutto's Unicorn label, "Living on Hope," just grazed the charts; it was enough to affirm their talent and saleability. Frankie beefed up his investment in the group, bought them flashier costumes, and booked them as the opening act for Johnny Mathis's twenty-city tour.

Their debut album, *Blues From the Street,* made the Wonders a starring act; the single "Look What Love Has Done to Me" stayed on the charts for fifteen weeks. Suddenly the girls had more money than they'd ever imagined, and as Kanda spent her way through one check after another, she felt as if she were living the kind of story she used to read at night, as if her own personal fairy tale had finally got started and would soon get better and better.

Though she'd been sending money to her mother regularly, Kanda hadn't been back to Chicago at all. It was guilt, as much as triumph, that took her back for her first real visit. Mama wasn't going out to clean anymore, but the three-room apartment on Fifth Street was much the same, except for a fresh coat of paint and a few new pieces of furniture. Kanda didn't have to ask where her money went, not after she looked in Charlene's room and saw the closetful of new clothes, the color television, and the stereo.

"Why don't you buy yourself some new clothes, Mama?" Kanda asked, pressing a handful of bills into her mother's hand. "A nice fur coat for the winter," she suggested.

Martha smiled and touched her daughter's face gently. "I already have everything I need," she said. "It's you I worry about, honey. . . ."

"I'm just fine," Kanda cut in, holding back her anger. After all she'd accomplished, was Mama still seeing her father in everything Kanda did? She'd show her once and for all how different they were.

Before she left the city, she put a deposit on a white brick house on Lake Shore Drive. It was surrounded by shrubs and trees, and in the back was a bank of rosebushes and an old-fashioned swing. "Here," she said as she handed her mother the deed, "here's what *he* was supposed to give you, so now you don't need no trashy men around . . . and now you know I'm not like him!"

And then she set out to bury the fatherless little black girl who knew too much of life and not enough about love.

She took an apartment in New York, so she'd have some privacy away from the hotel rooms she shared with the other girls. Though she had a lingering affection for Lonette, she felt set apart from the others. She began to notice how badly they talked, and, judging them, she judged herself. Secretly she took speech lessons, thinking how strange it was to be paying someone to teach her what Mama had taught herself, what she had wanted to teach her girls.

She began to notice the kind of clothes that rich New York women wore, to compare them with the cheap, flashy garments the Wonders wore, offstage as well as on. And most important of all, Kanda realized that she was the only one who cared about the music, and not just the money it brought them. During one recording session, they pouted like children when Kanda insisted they do "Heartache's My Name" over and over until they got it right. And when she tried to show them what was wrong, they just couldn't seem to hear.

"I'm tired," Maline grumbled, "and I'm hungry. . . . And if the queen still isn't satisfied, I say too damn bad!"

"Know what your problem is?" Kanda responded. "You get satisfied too damn easy. If we listened to you, we'd still be singing for twenty bucks a night!"

Maline shot Kanda a look redolent with hatred, as if to say she still remembered what success had cost her.

"Let's not fight," said Lonette, who was still the peacemaker, the bridge between Maline and Kanda. "We're all tired and we're all hungry. But studio time costs money, so let's try the number again, and let's make it a wrap."

Though Kanda had her way, there was no more pleasure in beating Maline. The arguments wore her down, and she was tired of pushing and prodding.

In her loneliness, she took a lover, a studio musician. He

was good-looking and, more important, he was white. And when she was finished with him, she took up with a white stockbroker, who sent her flowers and showered her with gifts. Remembering the horror of Bill Timmons, she knew she would never let a black man touch her, not ever again. Remembering how Mama's men had always left her, Kanda vowed that she would be the one to leave.

Though she never discussed her affairs with the other girls, it wasn't a secret she could keep, and when the *Daily News* printed a picture of Kanda with the stockbroker, Maline cut it out and brought it to rehearsal. "Ain't you heard that black is beautiful?" she taunted. "Looks to me like you're trying awfully hard to be white. . . . What's the matter, Kandy Kane, think you're better than the rest of us? Is that what you think?"

Kanda slapped her face and walked out of the studio. I'm not going back, she told herself, I'm not ever going to work with that bitch again.

But when her anger cooled, her professionalism took over. It was crazy to break with the Wonders now; to walk away from her Unicorn contract could wreck her career. But soon . . . one day soon, she'd show Maline—hell, she'd show the world—just how much better than the rest of them she was.

She visited the showroom of designer Jean-Claude Sourir and asked him to make her look like a star. By the time he finished designing a wardrobe that was all costly slink and glitter, Kanda had a new offstage look and a new husband, a white husband who was part of what she'd been reaching for—the fairy-tale world she'd read about in magazines, where people were beautiful and rich and happy.

Jean-Claude was an experienced and skillful lover, and when she told him how she'd been hurt as a child, he was so sympathetic and so sensitive that she almost cried with gratitude. "But you're still a virgin," he murmured, promising to show her how good it could be between a man and a woman. He gave her what he called *la douce poudre blanche,* to make her forget, just as old Mrs. Baker used to soothe her with sugar candy. But Jean-Claude's powder did more than soothe her fears and insecurities; it made her feel beautiful and wonderful, as if she owned the world, as if everything in it were hers for the taking.

After a few nights in Jean-Claude's bed, Kanda was so hooked on his brand of loving, so intoxicated by the idea of being loved by an elegant white man, a successful one —unlike those chumps and losers the other girls tied themselves to—she would have walked through flames to keep him. She wouldn't have trusted a love that asked nothing, and so she was almost relieved when it turned out that all Jean-Claude needed was a loan to help him expand his business . . . and a short time later, another loan, to help protect his original investment.

The Wonders made two platinum albums in succession, the royalty checks got bigger and bigger, and Kanda learned the truth she had always suspected: that you could buy anything with money—people, friendship, gratification of every whim, and, of course, the white powder that gave relief from every pain.

When she learned that Jean-Claude was cheating, she was furious. Forgetting the speech lessons she'd bought and paid for, she screamed and shouted like the child of the streets she was, calling her husband names and threatening to kill him.

Jean-Claude endured her tantrum, and then he apologized, abjectly and sincerely. The affair meant nothing; surely as a woman of the world, she could understand that a man sometimes yielded to temptation? He loved Kanda, only Kanda, and to show just how deeply he cared, he opened his arms and took her to bed, smoothing the path to love with tender words and a line of purest cocaine.

The next day, he sent an enormous bouquet of birds of paradise. Tucked amidst the flowers was a delicate platinum pin engraved with a message of reconciliation: "To my own exotic bloom, my own true love. J.C.S." Kanda put the pin in her jewel box and hired a private detective to follow her husband. She was angry with Jean-Claude—not beyond forgiveness, but she wasn't about to let any man make a fool of her.

The first detective's report was ambiguous; Jean-Claude seemed to know a lot of women, but it was impossible to say if he was faithful or not. "That's not good enough," Kanda said, throwing the report down. "I'm paying you good money to get me some answers. . . . Don't come back here till you do that."

Two months later, the detective brought Kanda an envelope of photographs. She looked at them, one by one, and started to laugh, bitterly, hysterically. She thought she was ready for the worst, but she'd never imagined this. Jean-Claude was having an affair with his newest model—a black woman! And suddenly the prize she thought she'd captured was cheapened beyond redemption, her marriage reduced to a bad joke.

Her pride savaged, Kanda thought only of revenge. She could file for divorce, but that would be too easy. She wanted to hurt Jean-Claude, the way he'd hurt her.

She bought her revenge the way she bought everything else—with hard cash. For $1000, two men were hired to beat Jean-Claude as he left the apartment of his mistress.

Kanda sat in her bedroom, next to the phone, and waited for the call that would tell her Jean-Claude had been punished. That call never came. Luck, in the form of the New York police, had rescued Jean-Claude. The men were arrested; a plea bargain led the police directly to Kanda. And suddenly she was in the middle of a scandal that threatened not only her career but her very freedom. The newspapers milked the story for all it was worth, painting Kanda Lyons as a pathologically jealous wife, a woman scorned—or the foolish victim of her own naïveté. For weeks, Kanda lived in limbo, as her lawyers bargained with Jean-Claude's, trying to buy his forgiveness—at least as far as the police were concerned. His price, Kanda learned, would be more than a few flowers and an engraved trinket. The package—the divorce and the dropping of charges against her—cost a small fortune and illusions Kanda didn't know she had.

Out of the notoriety came a remedy for Kanda's bruised pride, the offer of a movie role that would add another dimension to her career. It was a part that would give her the chance to wear dozens of beautiful gowns and sing onscreen. During the first week of shooting, she learned she was three months pregnant. She lost the part she wanted—and had the baby she might have wanted once. A little girl with dark, melting eyes and mahogany skin. A bitter disappointment, a final betrayal by Jean-Claude, who hadn't been white enough to give her a cream-colored child. She named the baby Alberta, after her father; that was Kanda's way of accepting the joke life had played—making her rich and famous, and then dealing her the same hand it had dealt Mama, a worthless husband and a baby to raise on her own.

To redeem her tarnished image, she gave photo interviews, dressing her baby in fine Irish linen, showing off her motherhood like a badge of honor. "My career comes second now," she said. "Being a single mother, I'll just have to work that much harder to make sure Alberta has all the love and attention she needs. I know what it's like to grow up without a father, and I intend to protect my little girl from knowing that kind of pain."

Yet a few months later, when the Wonders were offered a million dollars for a week's engagement in Las Vegas, Kanda hired a nurse for Alberta and took the first plane out of New York. She said she needed the money, but in truth she needed the work more, to take her away from the baby that reminded her of the worst mistake she'd made.

The engagement was a success, but her reunion with the girls only showed Kanda that she was right to want to leave the group. Maline was bitchier than ever, smirking triumphantly as she showed off her new boyfriend, a handsome black actor who was being proclaimed as the next Sidney Poitier. Lonette's sympathy was just as bad, for it made Kanda feel she was a failure, in spite of all the money she'd earned.

Before the week was up, Kanda hired a Hollywood agent who had sent his card backstage. "I want to make some changes," she said, "and I want you to get me a movie. I don't care about the money . . . just make sure I'm the star."

The picture was a long time in coming, and so she went on making records for Frankie Sedutto, using ever-larger amounts of *la douce poudre blanche*—the only one of Jean-Claude's gifts that hadn't let her down—building her resentment against the Wonders, who, she was now convinced, were riding the gravy train on her talent, eclipsing the fame that should be hers alone.

When she was finally offered another movie role, it was so dreary, so unglamorous, so painfully evocative of the miserable life she'd left behind, that she almost fired the agent. It was the story of a crippled black girl, abandoned by her parents and left to the mercies of one bad foster home after another. Enduring poverty, rejection, and abuse, the girl creates a private world of music and song, growing up to be a famous gospel singer, celebrated the world over.

"Take the part," the agent urged. "You're already loaded with glamour. Be something else. Everybody will say you're brilliant. Trust me," he said, "the time is right for Kanda Lyons to show the world she has acting talent and soul."

In the end, Kanda made the picture to avoid going on tour with the Wonders, to signal her intentions of leaving them behind, just as she'd left every other reminder of Chicago behind. The movie won worldwide recognition and two Academy Awards, including one for Kanda.

After she accepted the award, wearing a flame-colored gown and maribou wrap and enough diamonds to outshine the Queen of England, she went back to her new house in Malibu to celebrate alone. No one called to offer congratulations. Not Mama, who was in the hospital again, or Charlene, who was on her honeymoon. Certainly not the Wonders, who had started bad-mouthing her in the press, painting Kanda Lyons as an ingrate and a user. Hell, Kanda didn't care. She'd fought and struggled for everything she had, and if people wanted to believe differently, then let them. She filled her heart-shaped bathtub with champagne and treated herself to eight hundred dollars' worth of cocaine.

When she met Winston Hammond III, Kanda wasn't looking for romance, only for a capable adviser who could straighten out her tangled and messy finances. She was making more money than she ever dreamed possible, yet she always seemed to be in trouble. After an audit that cost her tens of thousands in accountants' fees, the IRS demanded a million dollars in back taxes.

Not knowing how such a thing was possible, she went to see Hammond, financial adviser to many of Hollywood's biggest stars. "This is shocking," he said after he'd reviewed Kanda's records. But the way he said it, he didn't seem to be blaming Kanda, only the people who worked for her. "Shocking," he repeated. "A woman in your position, an artist, you shouldn't have to concern yourself with money matters. You should be protected by someone who can maximize your earnings and ensure a comfortable— no, luxurious—retirement."

It was a relief to Kanda that Hammond didn't ask her to explain the thick stacks of receipts that reflected how she spent her money. She couldn't explain how she went on spending binges, buying things she didn't want, giving them away, how she purchased houses the way other people bought clothes and then spent hardly any time in them. She liked the sound of Win's upper-class speech and manners, and when he promised "security without pain," she was intrigued by his confidence.

She put her financial affairs into his highly recommended hands. When he invited Kanda to dinner, she was first surprised and then flattered. Win Hammond was white, his blood was blue, his personal wealth considerable. He was eighteen years older than Kanda, and he seemed to know everyone and everything that mattered. Like a loving father, he instructed and advised with patience and care; he made Kanda hope that with him at her side, nothing bad could happen.

They were married six months later, and Kanda felt she had come home at last. Win kept his promises, one by one. He appealed the IRS's judgment, and miraculously he had her tax bill reduced by half. He formed a new record company, with himself as chief executive officer and Kanda as principal stockholder and premier artist. He screened every offer that she received and made certain she appeared in all the finest hotels and concert halls in America and Europe, earning more than any headliner except Wayne Newton and Frank Sinatra.

She had another baby girl, and though this child, too, was dark-skinned, Kanda didn't mind quite so much. She was at the pinnacle of her career, and her personal life was smooth and well ordered.

Kanda was in London when Win was arrested and charged with conspiracy and fraud. She got the news, not from him, but from the headlines in the *Los Angeles Times*. She flew home to be by his side, but by the time she arrived, he had fled the country, taking with him not only the wealth of many investors, but also most of Kanda's liquid assets.

The shock of this betrayal, the loss of so much, was like an avalanche that buried Kanda. She shut herself in the Malibu house for weeks, eating little, sleeping less, existing on drugs and despair. After she missed two recording dates and an opening night at Caesar's Palace in Vegas, stories began to appear, likening Kanda to Billie Holiday and Judy Garland, stars who had shone brightly and then burned out.

When Kanda saw these pieces, she was more afraid than angry, fearful that everything she'd worked for was about to disappear in a downward spiral over which she had no control. When her mother died, she was so coked out that Charlene had to make a dozen calls before Kanda could comprehend what she was saying.

At the funeral, she had to endure Charlene's bitter scoldings and a barrage of photographers and reporters who tortured her with questions and insinuations for which she had no answers.

Like vultures smelling blood, the IRS came after Kanda again. And though she felt too sick to work, she was forced to go on tour, because that was the only way she knew to stave off ruin. The tour was a disaster, and for the first time in her life, Kanda Lyons heard boos and hisses —from audiences who didn't know why her once-powerful voice wavered and cracked, didn't care why she couldn't remember the lyrics to songs she had made famous.

Feeling whipped and defeated, she slunk home to Malibu, where she was arrested on charges of child neglect and endangering the welfare of minors. It turned out that her housekeeper and nurses had quit, taking Kanda's fur coats in lieu of back pay. They had handed her two girls over to neighbors, who were appalled by their thin, waiflike appearance, and who had called the child-welfare authorities.

Of all the ugly stories that plagued Kanda, this was to be the worst. By the social workers who investigated the case, she was branded an indifferent and neglectful parent, a habitual drug user who showed no interest in her girls and who had abdicated their care to strangers. The hearing, though it was supposed to be private, turned into a media circus, with Charlene trashing her own sister and pleading for custody of the children, whom she promised to love as her own. "Unfit!" screamed the headline in the *Daily News*, showing a picture of Kanda's haggard face after the judge took her children away.

The judgment was repeated when she went to her manager and desperately pleaded for work. "No one wants to take a chance on you," he said bluntly, "not for any money. You've got to clean up your act, Kanda, and you'd better do it quick. Get off the drugs, show people you can still deliver, and I'll get you more bookings than you can handle. But until then . . ."

"Fuck you!" she said, and stalked out.

She could scarcely remember the weeks that followed, only that there had been a lot of parties she couldn't pay for in the Malibu house. She had only the dimmest recollection of driving to Beverly Hills one morning, of wandering through the stores on Rodeo Drive, of seeing the pretty green necklace—and the fight outside the store.

6

There were times when Stevie ran her group sessions like a seasoned conductor, plucking resonant memories from the intricate labyrinth of forgetfulness, eliciting chords of emotion buried under layers of repression. But today wasn't one of those times. With her own emotions and memories in disarray, Stevie found herself surrounded by disharmony and discord.

The first sour note was struck by a small gesture... Deni lighting a cigarette, inhaling deeply, and releasing a puff of yellowish smoke in Livy's direction. Livy responded with an exaggerated hacking cough—and then an attack on Stevie for allowing smoking in group. "After all the fuss you make about health and fitness," she scolded, "I simply don't understand how you can allow *certain people*" (and here she cast a withering glance at Deni) "to poison the air we all have to breathe!"

"One thing at a time," Stevie said lightly, hoping to defuse Livy's dislike of Deni, thinking it was bad enough she had her own confused feelings to deal with. "I can't expect anyone to give up every temptation at once. And besides," she added with a smile, "unless I'm mistaken, there was a time when you had the nicotine habit yourself."

But Livy wouldn't let go. "You're not mistaken," she said primly, "but I've given up that filthy habit, and I don't see why *other people* can't do the same."

"Maybe other people don't aspire to sainthood," Deni said mockingly. "Personally, I can't think of anyone duller or more insufferable than a reformed smoker . . . unless it's a reformed drunk."

"Is that what you think, Miss Vickers?" Livy said, her fair complexion flushing dangerously. "Let me tell you—"

"Cut it out!" Stevie broke in. "If you *ladies* want to bicker, do it outside of group and on your own time!"

"That's fine with me," Deni said agreeably, pursing her lips in a sensual *O* and then blowing a smoke ring in the air.

It was at that moment that Kanda Lyons sauntered in, just as if she were making an entrance on a Vegas stage.

"You're late!" Stevie snapped, pointing to the wall clock, "and this isn't the first time."

"Awfully sorry," Kanda replied in an affected upper-class accent. "I guess I just lost track of the time."

"Sorry doesn't cut it," Stevie said. "Why don't you tell us why we should have one rule for everybody else and another just for you?"

"She's new," Anne Garretson interjected. "Kanda isn't used to the kind of hours we keep here. It takes time to get used to—"

"Kanda ran out of time," Stevie cut in. "That's why she's here."

"Are we gonna take turns picking on people," Francie Evers complained, "or are we gonna get something useful done this morning?"

Stevie agreed that Francie had a point, yet sticking to it was another matter entirely. Each time she tried to use one of her tried-and-true techniques for keeping the truth-telling on track, she found herself detoured by the alliances and enmities that had sprung up among key members of the group.

When, for example, she tried to get Anne to open up about her marriage, to reveal how she really felt about being overshadowed by Hal's driving ambition, Anne cast a fearful eye at both Livy and Deni . . . and then responded with defensive platitudes. "We have a good marriage," she said. "Hal loves me and I love him. The way things have been . . . it's just temporary, until his future is decided. He's promised we'll have some time together, as soon as—"

"I'm not asking about Hal or the future," Stevie pressed, "I'm asking how you feel about the kind of marriage you have right now."

"For Chrissake, leave her alone," Kanda jumped in. "What are you . . . some kind of district attorney? You asked her a question and she answered."

"But she didn't answer," Stevie explained, more patiently than usual. This was the first time Kanda had contributed anything to the group, and even if she did so only to repay Anne's support, Stevie still didn't want to discourage her from speaking. "Anne has a lot more to say about her marriage and her relationship with her husband. I'm just helping her to face that fact, so she can deal with it."

"Maybe it hurts too much to face facts," Kanda said in a low voice.

"Maybe there's trouble in Paradise," Deni chimed in with a knowing smile. "Maybe Anne's just not ready to admit that because she doesn't know how to deal with it."

Stevie felt a sudden throb of anger. Though Deni had said exactly what she herself was thinking, Stevie resented her insight; it was as if Deni had somehow usurped something else that should have been Stevie's. "If Anne's not ready to tell the truth, how about you? Why don't you take a turn in the hotseat?" Stevie said, trying to keep the edge from her voice. "We've talked round and round your relationship with your father, but it seems to me there's a lot you haven't said."

"I don't know what you mean," Deni said. "I've already confessed my . . . sexual preferences. The rest of my life's an open book. In fact," she drawled, "if you pick up enough back issues of *People* magazine, you can find out anything you want to know about me . . . even what size bra I wear."

Livy snorted derisively. "Come on Deni, what do you take us for . . . a bunch of teenage fans? You must really think—"

Stevie stepped in to head off another personal confrontation. "Answer one question for me, Deni. If you could say just one sentence to your father right now, what would it be? Quick, answer me right now!"

"I'm sorry," Deni blurted out, then slumped into her seat, as if those two words had exhausted her.

"Good . . . now what are you sorry about?"

Deni was silent. She had already said too much, revealed too much. She had sworn a solemn oath to take the secret of that dark night in Greece to her grave, and she'd be damned if she'd allow Stevie Knight to trick it out of her. She lit another cigarette, drawing heavily on it. "The usual things," she said carelessly, "not being good enough, not saying enough . . ."

"I don't believe you."

Deni shrugged, refusing to be baited. "You're the boss," she said with a throaty laugh.

"No," Stevie said, "I'm just the guide around here. Answer me this, Deni, if you have no unfinished business with your father, then why is it you can't seem to have a normal relationship with any man? Why is it you have to dirty every good thing that happens to you? Why is it . . . ?" Stevie went on and on, unable to stop herself. In the curious stares of the other women, she saw that she was going too far and too fast, but when she tried to rein herself in, one final question forced itself out: "Why, Deni, when you have a man who loves you, are you so determined to destroy the best relationship you could possibly have?"

Though she had remained calm, almost smug throughout Stevie's harangue, Deni now leaned forward and licked her lips, in the same unconscious gesture she used when she was about to skewer some hapless celebrity on her own version of the hotseat. "You know, Stevie," she said, "I just might give you some of those answers . . . if you give me a couple first."

Stevie failed to see the trap. "Okay," she said. "Shoot."

"Well," Deni said slowly and with exaggerated politeness, "I know you'll forgive me if I'm mistaken, but it looks to me like you don't practice what you preach, Stevie. If you think I'm in such bad shape because I can't make it with a man, how come you're alone? How is it that you're such an expert on marriages and relationships when you're all alone? Unless you count being married to this place . . ." she continued with a smile.

Stevie felt as if she'd been slapped. "We're not here to talk about my life, Deni," she parried weakly.

"Why not?" Deni pressed, leaning forward. "We're supposed to say what we think. You're not just a work machine, are you, Stevie? Or are you?"

"That's enough," Livy cut in, her personal dislike for Deni coming to the fore. "This isn't one of your cheap interviews, this is my friend you're talking to. If you knew Stevie the way I do, you wouldn't ask such a question. She has enough love in her heart for the whole world."

Deni threw up her hands with a triumphant laugh. "My point exactly. People who love the whole world find it a helluva lot easier than loving one person."

Stevie sat in her chair wanting nothing more than to run

and hide. It had been a long time since she'd personally experienced what she dished out every day, but now she knew all too well what the hotseat felt like. They were all waiting for her to speak, to utter the plain truth on which she set such high store. Yet how could she when right now she didn't know what that was? Memories of Ben's reproaches flooded her consciousness, overlaid with memories of Lee. And superimposed on it all, the long, dark shadow of the Admiral.

"Cat got your tongue?" Deni teased. "You never let anyone else get away with the silent act."

"I know," Stevie admitted quietly, feeling shamed by her inadequacy. "I just don't know what to say."

"Copout!" Francie said with disgust. "You're doing a crummy copout!"

Yes, Stevie thought, that's exactly what I'm doing. Yet she felt as if she had no other choice. How could she begin to explain why she was alone without invoking Lee's name, without admitting she desperately wanted him . . . or revealing why she couldn't have him?

Book Five

1

Could anything be worse than this? Being trussed up like an animal, being fed against her will, hearing nothing but sounds of confusion and despair hour after hour, Stevie came to hate the drugs with which she was repeatedly sedated. Strange, she thought during a moment of clarity; where once she had traded her body for those trips to forgetfulness, now she wanted nothing more than the chance to think, to figure out how in heaven's name she could free herself.

I was wrong, she said to herself as she listened to a disembodied voice mournfully chanting the alphabet against a counterpoint of manic laughter. I thought my life was as bad as it could get, but this is worse, so much worse. Paul had degraded and used her, and she had let him, as long as he kept her supplied with the drugs and liquor that kept her from facing the one person she couldn't escape—Stevie Knight. Now she yearned for all the everyday things she had thrown away or taken for granted—the freedom to move around, to choose what she ate or when she woke up, to think clearly, and, most important, to manage her own life. Prison might have been better, she thought; at least in jail you could still use your mind freely. But here they tried to take that freedom away, along with the sharp objects, shoelaces, and anything else that might spell escape, if only in a body bag. How did this happen to me? she asked herself. How did the pretty make-believe world of Pretty Stevie Knight turn into a nightmare from which there was no awakening?

"Can you remember how you hurt yourself?" asked the young psychiatrist who had been assigned to her case—just one of more than sixty in his caseload. "Can you tell me what was in your mind when you put your arms through the mirror?"

"Can you tell me how the hell to get out of here?" Stevie demanded, feeling like a prisoner of war. "I don't need a shrink. All I need is *out*."

"Stevie," the doctor appealed wearily, his voice chalky with fatigue. "You're only hurting yourself with your hostility. We want to help you get better."

"I'm not crazy," she cut in. "I don't belong in this place."

"Nobody's calling you crazy," he said gently. "But what you did—cutting yourself up, attacking the people who tried to stop you—that wasn't your usual party behavior, was it?"

Stevie smirked. "My usual behavior, as you put it, was pretty wild, so if you're going to judge by that . . ."

The psychiatrist stared at Stevie, silently inviting her to continue. But what else was there to say? How could she convince this stranger that she wasn't trying to kill herself when she herself could scarcely remember—let alone explain—what she had done?

"Then help me understand, Stevie," the psychiatrist said after accepting Stevie's sullen refusal to speak. "Help me to know that you aren't going to hurt yourself again—or anyone else."

Stevie got the message. Her ticket out depended on proving she could be good, falling into line and doing exactly as she was told. Well, she thought bitterly, she could do that all right; her years with the Admiral had prepared her well.

"Okay, Doc," she said with a sigh, "I was drinking and doing pills. That was stupid, I know, but I was feeling down. It was New Year's Eve. . . ."

The young doctor nodded encouragingly, and Stevie went on with her narrative, watching his tired face, constantly checking for signals that she was on the right road, the road that led through the double-locked doors and back out into the world of the living . . . where she could do what she pleased.

The light that filtered through the grime-encrusted windows was always gray—dark or light, depending on the time and weather, but gray nevertheless. Stevie wrote that down in the little notebook she'd earned after ten days of good behavior. She had no conscious purpose for it, other than to remind herself that she was sane in this forgotten place where sanity was much more relative than on the outside—and reflected by such standards as a clean face, hair that was combed, and the ability to string a few lucid sentences together.

She was living now in Ward B, "The GAP," as it was called by the inmates—their abbreviation for the *G*eneral *A*dult *P*sychiatric unit. In this section, as opposed to the "Max" ward, security was more relaxed and such freedoms as using a pencil (though, of course, under supervision) were allowed.

Stevie, however, was not about to relax her guard. She had seen with her own eyes that it didn't pay to believe even for a minute that a misstep of any kind was without consequences. "They punish here," she wrote in a letter to Samson after seeing an inmate shot full of Thorazine simply for raising a fuss over a box of candy that had been stolen. "They punish people whose only crime is being sick and afraid." She wrote Samson often, never imagining that he read any of her frequent letters, but needing someone to connect with on the outside nevertheless.

Having listened to the way the staff talked about patients as if they weren't present, as if they had no names or identities, were merely symptoms like "schizophrenic" or "manic-depressive"—or locations, like "Bed Number 10" —she wrote: "They like to pretend we aren't people anymore. It makes their job easier, but it isn't right."

Even knowing these things, however, Stevie found it hard to remain detached from the life around her. As determined as she was to get out, she took pity on those who had no hope of leaving and those who had lost the ability to take care of themselves. Without even realizing she had done so, Stevie adopted the woman whose bed was next to hers. Her name was Kate, and the nurses described her as "catatonic"—that was all Stevie knew. Though there were streaks of gray in Kate's dark hair, her face was as smooth and unlined as a teenager's. Left on her own, she would spend the entire day in bed, her vacant blue eyes staring into space. When Stevie ran a comb through her thick tangled hair and wiped her pale face with a damp cloth, Kate didn't protest. Nor did she resist when Stevie helped her out of bed and walked her around the ward, her thin legs shuffling uncertainly in the paper slippers, as if they had forgotten what to do.

What terrible experience had damaged her so? Stevie wondered. What had taken away her will to speak or even to move her own body? There must have been a person once behind those empty blue eyes, but where had she gone? Stevie noticed that the psychiatrist didn't even bother talking to Kate when he made his rounds, but simply took her vital signs and scribbled a few notations on his clipboard.

Once, when the doctor was about to leave, Stevie asked impulsively, "What happened to her? Why is she like this . . . ?" She knew she was stepping out of line, but she was plagued by the question.

The psychiatrist shrugged dismissively. It was, after all, inappropriate to discuss one patient with another. But as he turned away, he glanced at his case file and stopped. "You know, Stevie," he said, "Kate came in almost the same time you did. She was in a coma . . . full of so many chemicals, we couldn't even get an accurate breakdown. We didn't expect her to live, but she did. Unfortunately," he added softly with a gentle wave in Kate's direction, "this seems to be all we can hope for by way of recovery."

"No," Stevie argued, "that can't be true. There must be *something* you can do. . . ."

"It's all been done, Stevie. When you damage the machinery up here," he said, tapping his head, "sometimes it will fix itself, but sometimes . . . sometimes the breakdown is irreversible." Seeing the sadness in Stevie's face, he added, "The only reason I've told you this is so you'll know how lucky you are. You got a second chance, kid. Use it, because you can't count on another."

A second chance, Stevie thought after the doctor left. Even in her most fervent longing for hope, she hadn't imagined Bellevue as a second chance. And yet . . . she was alive, her mind intact. Unlike Kate, she had a future away from this place, even if she had no idea of what it would hold. For the first time in many months, she thought of herself as fortunate—at least in comparison to Kate.

Knowing that this other woman would probably never

again experience life's simplest pleasures and freedoms made Stevie even more protective.

"Hey!" she shouted at the aide who shoved Kate out of her bed after she'd wet it. "Don't be so rough, dammit! You have no right to treat her that way just because she had an accident!"

The attendant replied by throwing the dirty linens at Stevie and reporting her for causing a scene.

Stevie's intervention earned her a dose of Stelazine, to which she submitted quietly, rather than risk being returned to the violent ward. For hours, she felt like a zombie. Her limbs were like rubber, her mouth was dry, her eyes grainy, but worse than that, she couldn't focus, and it took every bit of concentration she could muster to put one leg in front of the other or to get a bit of food into her mouth without spilling it all over herself.

But Stevie wasn't sorry she'd tried to help Kate, even if the result was a black mark on her behavior record. She wrote in her notebook: "There's something very wrong here. I don't know what it is, but it can't be right when people who are supposed to be helping you use their power to hurt."

Visiting hours brought the same tired parade of relatives wearing expressions of false cheer or dutiful resignation, and bearing writing paper and clothes, books and magazines. Rarely did Stevie hear any kind of real conversation around her. It was as if the people on the outside had accepted as gospel that those on the inside were alien creatures, frightening and somehow even disgusting.

She told herself that she couldn't expect any of the old Wherehouse crowd to come to this awful place to see her; they had all been reared on Samson's dictum that only fun was worth pursuing. But to soothe the hurt of being neglected, she told herself she didn't want to be seen like this anyway.

One Saturday morning, as Stevie walked Kate around the day room, she thought she saw a flicker in Kate's eyes, a slight turn of the head toward the television set. "Do you want to watch the cartoons?" Stevie asked.

There was no response. Stevie repeated her question as she led Kate to an empty chair in front of the set. "It's Bullwinkle and Rocky," she said. "Do you hear me, Kate . . . ? Do you remember anything?"

Kate didn't answer, but her eyes were on the screen, and so Stevie stepped back, behind the double row of chairs to see if the cartoon might somehow evoke a forgotten memory. Suddenly Kate stood up and walked toward the screen, one hand outstretched. There was an angry cry of protest; a moment later, she was knocked to the ground by a heavyset woman screaming curses and throwing savage punches. Stevie ran to Kate's rescue, threw her body between the two women and pushed against the attacker with all her might. A shrill whistle sounded, and two attendants joined the fray, but before they could break it up, Stevie saw the glint of a metal nail file and felt a hot, searing pain down the side of her face.

"No more television for you, Pat," an attendant said roughly as she wrenched the forbidden file from the heavyset woman's hand and dragged her away.

Stevie began to laugh at the absurdity of it all, even as her eyes filled with her own blood. Gentler hands pressed a towel to her face, and strong arms carried her from the room.

"It's a damn shame," the young resident said as he sutured Stevie's cheek.

Anesthesia dulled the pain, but she could feel every tug

and pull, and as she began to count, she realized that the stitches ran almost the entire length of her face, from her eyebrow down to her chin.

"Lucky she didn't lose an eye," a nurse murmured.

Lucky, Stevie thought dully. Maybe if I'm lucky, they won't make this a reason to keep me here forever.

The injury put Stevie in the hospital ward, where she could be carefully monitored for traces of infection. "Healing nicely," the resident said each time he checked her dressing and applied antibiotic ointment. But he avoided meeting her eyes when he made these optimistic pronouncements.

And when the dressings were removed, Stevie understood why. I look like Frankenstein, she thought. I look like someone who could scare little children on Halloween. She had always taken her beauty for granted, yet now that it was so badly damaged, she felt a terrible sense of loss. It was as if Pretty Stevie Knight had been obliterated, leaving someone different and yet unformed behind.

The man at Stevie's bedside looked as if he'd just stepped off a yacht. He had a ruddy outdoorsy complexion, though it was winter. His thick silver hair was cut unfashionably short, yet the style suited his strong, well-defined features, setting off the high cheekbones, the aquiline nose, and startlingly beautiful dark eyes. He was wearing a blue cashmere blazer and well-tailored gray trousers—and looked utterly out of place.

"So how the hell did you end up here, Stevie Knight?" he asked in a richly expressive baritone voice.

"Who wants to know?"

"Benjamin Hawkins, M.D., at your service."

"You don't look like the rest of them."

He laughed. "That's because I'm not. I'm a plastic surgeon, Stevie. I've come to see what I can do with that lovely face of yours—"

"You look expensive," she cut in, not knowing what she could or couldn't afford anymore.

"I am," he laughed again, "but for you, it won't cost a cent."

"Charity?" she asked with an edge to her voice.

"Nope. I do volunteer work one day a week. I think of it as playing Robin Hood. You wouldn't deprive me of that fun, would you, Stevie? I know how important your face is to you."

"How do you know?" she asked. "Don't tell me you read fashion magazines."

"I don't read them," he smiled, "but I saw your beautiful face on at least a half-dozen covers. It's my business to remember beautiful faces, Stevie. Especially when my patients point them out and ask for your nose or your cheekbones. . . ."

"Really? My nose . . . and my cheekbones?"

"Really." With his fingertips he touched the ugly raised scar that ran down the side of her face. "I can make you beautiful again," he said.

Though Stevie had known more than her share of boasters and braggarts, somehow she believed that Ben Hawkins was the genuine article, a man who could deliver on his promises. She could see that he was waiting for her to speak.

"What's wrong?" he asked. "Do you have some questions, Stevie? I can explain the surgery, if you like. . . ."

"No," she said. "I think I'd rather not know."

"What is it then?" he pressed gently. "Are you afraid?"

She nodded an admission of weakness, drawn in by Ben's easy confidence. "I've always been afraid of doctors and hospitals. I've never had any reason to change my mind."

"I can't say I blame you," Ben interjected. "And I'm sorry you've had such bad experiences."

Stevie noticed that Ben didn't dismiss her feelings or the inherent criticism of his profession, and she liked him for that.

"But," he added, "if you can manage your fear for a while, I'll do everything in my power to help you. I'm good at what I do, Stevie . . . very good. I think you'll be glad you took a chance."

She decided to trust him.

A few days later, at seven in the morning, she was taken by private ambulance to Ben's clinic on Park Avenue. And as she was being moved, she caught a glimpse of blue sky, felt the winter sun on her face. How precious those moments felt, how fresh and new. Why had she never noticed before how healing a breath of crisp, cool air could be, how uplifting a gentle touch of sun?

The clinic was like nothing Stevie had ever seen, more like a luxury hotel than a hospital. The reception area was thickly carpeted in burgundy wool and beautifully furnished in an eclectic mix of period reproductions and genuine antiques. The walls were a soft pink shade and hung with paintings of serene English landscapes. Ben's staff— his receptionists and nurses—were attractive and well-groomed, as if to underscore the theme of serenity and loveliness. Stevie couldn't help but notice how different it felt to be in such surroundings, and she wondered if the poor, tortured souls in Bellevue might somehow feel more hopeful, or at least less defeated, if they were moved to a place like this.

Mindful of Stevie's anxieties, Ben waved aside the nurse, saying, "I'll prepare this patient myself, Miss Appleby." He handed Stevie a pink cotton gown, showed her to a small, well-appointed dressing room, and waited until she changed. "Now," he said, "here's what's going to happen, Stevie. In a few minutes, you'll be put to sleep. I'll be watching very carefully to make sure you're comfortable. I'll need two hours or so to repair the damage to that lovely face . . . and then you'll have a nice, long rest in one of my private rooms. Does that sound all right to you?"

Stevie nodded. Ben squeezed her shoulders. "Good. Then let's get started."

Ten minutes later, Stevie was lying on a narrow table, surrounded by gowned and masked figures, waiting for the surgery to begin. When Ben appeared, he winked at Stevie, as if they were sharing some private joke, and suddenly the cool, sterile room felt warmer. However, when a nurse began to fasten the restraints that bound her arms to the table, Stevie cried out.

"It's for your own good, dear," the nurse said soothingly. "We don't want you to hurt yourself while Dr. Hawkins is working."

"It's all right, Miss Appleby," Ben intervened, removing the cushioned canvas bands. To Stevie he said, "I understand how you feel, but it is necessary. After all," he joked, "we don't want you taking a wild swing at me just when I'm about to do my best work. Suppose we wait until you're asleep. . . . Will that be all right, Stevie?"

Stevie agreed, trusting Ben more with every passing moment. She knew that he was an important surgeon, yet he treated her feelings with the same kind of respect accorded to him. As the anesthetist inserted a needle into her arm, she looked into Ben's dark eyes, and as the sleep-inducing drugs dripped into her veins, she was sure he was smiling at her through the mask. The last thing she heard was his rich, gentle voice saying, "It's going to be all right, Stevie. I promise I'll take very good care of you. . . ."

When Stevie opened her eyes, she was in a lovely room decorated in shades of peach. A trio of flower paintings hung on one wall; on the other, a double window framed a leafless maple tree.

"I see you're back with us," said a nurse at Stevie's bedside. "You must be someone very special. . . . Dr. Hawkins said you weren't to be left alone for a minute." Stevie tried to speak, but her face, encased in heavy dressings, felt stiff and numb. "Don't try to talk just yet," the nurse suggested. "Rest as much as you can, and you'll be back to normal in a little while."

Normal, Stevie thought as she closed her eyes again. What would normal be for someone like me?

The next time she woke, there was a large colorful bouquet of flowers on her bedside table. "I was right, wasn't I?" the nurse said with a glance at the flowers. "You're someone *very* special. Dr. Hawkins sent these in a few minutes ago." She offered a glass of water with a flexible straw. "I'll bet you're ready for some of this. . . ." Gently she propped Stevie's head against her arm and helped her to drink. "Easy now . . . not too much," she warned. "It's best to take everything slowly after this type of surgery. Are you in any pain?"

Gingerly Stevie moved her head from side to side.

"Good. Dr. Hawkins will be in to see you as soon as he finishes his last procedure."

Carefully and with the nurse's help, Stevie sat up in bed. As she looked at the lovely bouquet, she noticed a card perched rakishly atop a shasta daisy. On it was a hand-drawn smiley face. Stevie felt her own face relaxing into an answering smile. She *did* feel like someone very special. How could she help it when someone like Ben thought she was worth caring about?

When he came in to see her, Ben had exchanged his surgical uniform for slacks and a sweater. He sat down on Stevie's bed and squeezed her hand in greeting. "It went smooth as silk," he announced jauntily. "You'll have to wear your hair around your face for a while. In six months, though—maybe less—the scar will be almost invisible. But," he grinned conspiratorially, "that isn't what I told the folks at Bellevue. For them," his voice sank in a burlesque of grave sobriety, "I talked of . . . complications."

"But why? You said it went—"

"I thought you wouldn't mind if I kept you here for a few more days . . . under close observation."

"That's great!" Thrilled by the prospect of more precious freedom, Stevie tried to declare her appreciation loudly. But her jaw was held together too tightly by the bandages. Her exclamation emerged as little more than a mumble. "Thank you so much, Dr. Hawkins. . . ."

He nodded, and then plucked a flower from the bouquet, which he handed to Stevie. "Suppose you just call me Ben. My 'doctor' work is over, and I'd like to . . . to be plain Ben, if that's all right with you."

Stevie nodded. "But couldn't you get in trouble if the hospital finds out I didn't have complications?"

Ben smiled. "Hey, if there's any question about it, I can always *make* complications. Meanwhile, I'll take the chance. I have a feeling you're better off here than back at the GAP, don't you agree?"

Settling back into her nest of pillows, Stevie agreed completely.

She spent the next few days rediscovering luxuries she had once taken for granted—the comfort of a good bed, the privacy of a sparkling bathroom filled with such amenities as French soap and thick, fluffy towels, and the taste of real food.

Best of all, there was Ben, who managed in spite of his busy practice to brighten her recuperation with brief but frequent visits. Even when he only had a moment to spare between patients, he'd knock on her door and give her a wave and a smile before he rushed off.

In the evening, he'd deliver Stevie's dinner himself—special dishes of chicken or fish tender enough to chew without effort, and sent in from fine neighboring restaurants. He would sit with her while she ate, occasionally sharing her meal or reading aloud from the collection of leather-bound books in his office, passages from Twain or Thurber that would make her smile or giggle behind the swaddling of white gauze and cotton. And then he'd applaud, as if she'd done something remarkable.

"Atta girl, Stevie. A good laugh is nature's best medicine, even in my line of work," he said once. "You'd be surprised at the number of people who never grow into the beautiful faces I give them because they don't know how to laugh—and don't care to learn. That's why I love doing the volunteer work. When I can take a kid who's been badly burned, who's scared his whole life is over, and help him to laugh again, then I know I've done something worthwhile . . . and that he and nature will finish the job of healing."

"You don't sound like any doctor I ever met," she commented.

Now it was Ben's turn to laugh. "There are a few like me around. But a lot of my esteemed colleagues take themselves so damn seriously that they lose touch with the very people they're supposed to help. You know what the problem is, Stevie? The minute a young doctor finishes his training, he—or she—becomes part of the priesthood of medicine. That's the reward for all those years of study, all those forty-eight-hour shifts without sleep, all that scut work for less than minimum wage. Suddenly you're a doctor and you're supposed to know all the answers, Stevie. Hell, your patients insist on it, they want you to be a god. After a while some of us can't resist playing the part."

"What about you, Ben?" she asked. "Do you know all the answers?"

"Hell, no. . . . The longer I practice medicine, the longer my list of questions gets. I guess you could say I've always been a heretic at heart."

Stevie smiled. She didn't really know why, but it just made her feel good to be with Ben.

"Hey, I'm serious," he said. "If you saw my library, you'd know what I mean. I've been collecting heresies for more than twenty years . . . books on herbal cures and acupuncture and faith healing, right along with the latest bulletins from the American Medical Association."

Stevie loved listening to Ben talk, especially about helping people in trouble. He never used words she couldn't understand, never acted as if he were smarter and wiser, though she was sure he was. And when it was time for him to leave, she was always sorry. Where did he go after he said good night? she wondered.

She had noticed the curious glances from Ben's staff, even a hint of jealousy among the nurses. She had learned —from some shameless eavesdropping—that he was a widower. And though she told herself it was none of her business, Stevie couldn't help but wonder if he had more than a professional interest in any of the lovely women who assisted him in his work. Or if, perhaps, there was someone else, someone special who waited to welcome him after he finished tucking Stevie in for the night.

"I'm going to remove your bandages again," Ben said five days after the surgery, "and this time, they're going to stay off. I'll give you a mirror . . . and I don't want you to be disappointed . . . because it'll be another four or five weeks before it looks the way it should. Right now, what you see won't be pretty . . . not unless you have a thing for puffy faces with purple and yellow blotches, like you went a few rounds with Muhammad Ali. . . ."

"I can take it," Stevie said. "I've already gone a few with guys who were even meaner. . . ."

Hearing something in her voice, Ben paused in his explanation and sat down on Stevie's bed. "Do you want to tell me about it?" he asked. "I'm a good listener, Stevie."

Stevie believed and trusted Ben, yet habit made it difficult to reveal what she had hidden and repressed for so long. "It's a long story." She sighed. "You don't have the time to hear it. . . ."

"I'll make all the time you need," he said, picking up Stevie's bedside phone and instructing the receptionist to hold all his calls. He waited expectantly, but without a hint of impatience in his handsome face. "C'mon, give me an earful about little Stevie Knight," he prompted. "Was she a happy child?"

"No." The single word spoke volumes of anger and bitterness.

Ben nodded thoughtfully. "Bad times at home? Tell me about your parents, Stevie. . . . Please, don't hold back. It only hurts more when you keep all that pain bottled up inside."

Stevie stared out the window, looking beyond the trees and buildings and into her own past. She began to speak, slowly, haltingly. But after she'd put the first small rent in the veil of silence she herself had spun, the words came more quickly, gathering momentum as she described her childhood, her fear and hatred of the Admiral, her disappointment and shame in Irene. Without meeting Ben's eyes, she told of her promiscuity, her seduction of Luke James, her pregnancy, and the baby that had been taken out of her.

Ben took her hand then in a silent gesture of encouragement. Stevie spoke of her early struggle in New York, of finding Pip and Samson, of making them into the family she had never known and the Wherehouse into her first real home. She touched lightly on the success that had meant so little, and then, sparing herself nothing, moved quickly into the downward spiral of drugs and degradation that had ended in Bellevue. Finally, she met Ben's beautiful eyes and searched them for a hint of revulsion or disgust. There was none; nor was there a trace of pity. There was only the warmth and compassion Stevie had seen whenever Ben spoke about people in trouble.

"Do you know what I think?" he said softly. "I think you're a remarkable woman, Stevie Knight. I think you've made mistakes, bad ones, but I also think—I know—you have the courage to learn and grow. To make all your experiences count for something."

She shook her head doubtfully. "All I've ever done is mess up. I've already had chances, friends, an exciting career. And I threw it all away. My best friend killed herself, and I didn't do a thing to—"

"You couldn't," Ben cut in crisply. "You're not God, Stevie. You were in no position to help your friend. . . . You couldn't even help yourself. First be responsible for what happens to you. Then you can begin to help the people you care about."

But I've been taking care of myself for years, Stevie was on the brink of telling him. Then she realized how foolish that claim would be. She said nothing as her thoughts came back to the present. It was time to go back to Bellevue, she felt, to leave the nurserylike sweetness of Ben's clinic and the care he had given so unstintingly, and return to reality. It was time to grow up.

As if he knew what she was thinking, he said, "The ambulance will be here this afternoon. I'll come to see you every day, but you have to do your part too. You're a survivor, Stevie Knight, but I want you to do better than that.

It isn't enough just to survive. I want you to start living again."

"In Bellevue?" she said tartly. "That's a tall order, Ben."

"Even in Bellevue. Look, Stevie, I don't pretend to know it all, but I've seen human beings perform miracles. When I was a surgical resident, one of the attending physicians brought in an old man for tests and exploratory surgery. He was a German shoemaker, an immigrant who could hardly speak English. It turned out the patient had a stomach full of cancer, so the attending just closed him up. I was there when he handed the old man his death sentence. But the shoemaker wouldn't take it, Stevie, he wouldn't take the death sentence, even though it was delivered by someone with years of education and a wallful of credentials. I don't mind telling you, the old man's courage just knocked me out. I admired the hell out of him, and my heart went out to him for having to fight a losing battle."

"He died . . . ?" Stevie asked.

"That's what I kept asking the attending every couple of weeks. That guy thought I was an idiot to keep bringing up the obvious. I asked again at the end of the rotation. 'Look, Hawkins,' he said, 'Mr. Hoffman is probably dead and buried now. So pay attention to the patients who aren't beyond help.' I had to admit he was probably right. . . . I figured the old shoemaker had gone to another doctor. I hoped he was lucky, and that the end hadn't been too bad for him. . . ."

Stevie waited expectantly for more.

Ben smiled. "I was doing my training in plastic surgery when I bumped into my old mentor. When he saw me, he got this sheepish look and asked if I remembered Mr. Hoffman. I'd never forgotten him. 'Damnedest thing happened,' he said. 'The guy came into my office for a checkup, demanding a new set of tests. Well, he'd already lived about three times longer than I'd expected, so I did them. There was no cancer, Ben, not a single trace.' My teacher didn't want to call it a miracle. . . . He wasn't a religious man, and neither was I. But I figured that if Hoffman could heal his own damaged body without any help from us, who's to say people can't heal the wounds we can't see?"

"I understand why you told me that story, Ben, but I'm not Mr. Hoffman. I just . . . wouldn't know where to begin."

"Begin by looking inside yourself, Stevie. Use your time at Bellevue to meditate."

"You mean like the Hare Krishnas?" She laughed.

"I mean like Stevie Knight. Clear your mind of clutter. And then take a fresh look at your own history, at the way you handled yourself, and the choices you made. Forgive your own mistakes . . . and maybe you'll be able to forgive other people's mistakes too. You've shown me a lot of anger, today, Stevie, and while I won't argue with your right to be angry, I want you to take the next step. Think of the anger as a dark, poisonous cloud. . . . Let it blow away from you instead of breathing it in. Can you do that?"

Stevie pondered the question and answered honestly. "I don't know." Then, wanting to say good-bye on a positive note, she added, "But I'll try."

For you, she was about to add. *I'll try for you.* But she was getting to know Ben; she could already anticipate his comeback: *No, don't do it for me but for yourself.*

So she would. Because she would do whatever he said.

2

When Stevie returned to Bellevue, the bed next to hers had a new occupant. "What happened to Kate?" she asked a nurse.

"Transferred," was the reply.

"Where?" Stevie pleaded. "Did her family take her home? Please tell me where she's gone. . . ."

The nurse saw the caring expression on Stevie's scarred face and relented. "I shouldn't be telling you," she said. "It's against regulations. . . . Kate was sent to Manhattan State. There was nothing else we could do for her here."

Manhattan State, Stevie thought with a shudder. The state hospital was located on Ward's Island in the East River. It wasn't so far away in distance, but for Kate, it was likely to be the end of the line, the place where she would grow old and die. She had a vision of Kate sitting in a chair all alone, staring into space and wearing the same sweet, resigned expression year after year. Then Stevie remembered that fateful day when she had seen a flicker of something in the empty eyes, when Kate had lurched childishly toward the television set.

It isn't right, Stevie wrote in her notebook. It isn't right to give up on people who can't help themselves. I know they're busy here, but someone should have made the time. Ben would have made the time.

In the days that followed, she tried to follow Ben's advice, to keep it with her even when he wasn't there to offer encouragement and support. She began meditating every morning, and then to follow that quiet time with a look at her own history. Sometimes the process made her wince, occasionally it made her smile, but always it left her with a greater determination to move forward.

One afternoon, she had a visitor. It was Lee Stone, his arms laden with flowers and candy and toiletries. Stevie felt a moment of shame and embarrassment—for her damaged beauty and for being helplessly locked up in this shabby place. When he saw her injured face, Lee dropped his packages on the bed without ceremony.

"Stevie . . . I'm sorry," he said. "I've been trying to find you for weeks. Finally I really bit the bullet . . . and called Samson. He told me you were here."

Stevie couldn't stop a rueful smile from touching her lips. So he had read her letters.

"God, Stevie, I blame myself. . . ."

She saw the expression of guilt on his face, the sorrow in his gray eyes—and for a moment she was glad. None of this would have happened if Lee hadn't walked away and left her. But a second later, Stevie heard herself say, "Talk about crazy, Lee—that takes the cake. Blame yourself? There's so much that came before and after. It wasn't your fault, none of it. . . ."

"I should have made sure you were all right," Lee insisted.

"No, that was my job," she replied, again surprising herself. Her time with Lee seemed a part of the history she was now trying to understand, and she felt like a different person from the woman who had needed him as protection from her own temptations.

He shifted awkwardly on his feet, unbalanced by the change he saw. "Stevie," he began again, "I want you to understand how it was for me. I was angry and jealous . . . I felt betrayed. I shouldn't have come down on you so hard. . . ."

Looking at Lee, she saw him from a distance of her own making. He was a man with a keen sense of responsibility, and now he was ready to accept a full measure for what had happened to her. But she didn't want a man to come to her as a kind of duty. That only made her anxious to send him away with a clear conscience.

"Hey, I know you didn't mean to hurt me," she said softly. "You put your faith in me—gave me a very valuable gift—and I misused it. I thought I loved you, Lee, but maybe I didn't know how. You said I needed to love myself first. That's what I'm working on now."

"I'm glad," he said. "Look, Stevie, maybe I have no right to say this now, but I did—I do—care for you. I only wanted . . ."

"You only wanted me to be a little closer to perfect," she cut in gently. "It's okay . . . you don't have to deny it." As she was speaking, Stevie thought of Ben, who didn't judge or demand, who didn't turn away from what was ugly in her past—or demand that she be better than she was.

"You told me you didn't want to be a crutch, Lee," she continued. "You said—"

"I remember what I said," Lee cut in, flinching from the echo of his own words, hearing in them now a message of rejection he hadn't intended. "I wish I could take it back. . . ."

"No," she said, "you were right. What we had . . . it was all lopsided, Lee. You were . . . you were like the white knight in the fairy stories. You wanted to rescue me from everything bad . . . and I wanted you to. I wanted you to fix everything that was wrong. And I didn't give enough back."

"But you did," he said. "You gave me yourself, Stevie."

She shook her head sadly. "You were right about that, too. I gave you my problems, that's all I had to give. I was Pretty Stevie Knight, someone Samson made up. She's gone now, Lee. . . . I'm still looking for plain Stevie Knight."

He nodded in acceptance and moved to the door. "When you find her, I hope I'll get a chance to meet her. . . ."

But Stevie could give no guarantees.

"At least promise you'll call if you need anything," Lee said. "No white knight this time, Stevie . . . just a man who cares about you."

"I know you were always that," she said.

He hesitated in the doorway, as though he wanted to add something else. But then he turned quickly and walked out.

As the reminders of her surgery began to heal, and she began to see the results of Ben's exquisite work, Stevie came to depend more and more on his constant presence. Not as a crutch the way she had done with Lee, but as a friend and a teacher, one who helped her to think objectively about her own history, to reach inside herself for the golden promise of self-knowledge. As Ben explained how childhood often sets the stage for the dramas of an entire life, Stevie realized for the first time that her childhood wounds, left untended, had festered and deepened, tainting her life with dismal expectations—which she had then made come true. This discovery, more than any other, brought with it enormous relief. If, she realized, the Admiral kept appearing in all her relationships with men, it wasn't fate that conjured him, but rather the unresolved fears of a vulnerable child.

Two things happened as Stevie became more comfortable inside her own skin. The days of her confinement passed more quickly, and she found it easier to cooperate with the staff psychiatrist who held the key to her release. Feeling freer, she became even more interested in other people, filling page after page in her notebook with observations and questions, which she discussed with Ben.

One evening, as Stevie waited eagerly for Ben's visit, bursting with the news that she would be leaving Bellevue in little more than a week, he failed to appear at his usual time. Feeling stronger than she had in a long time, Stevie provided for herself any number of reasonable explanations. But when another day went by and then another, she called his office, only to be informed that Dr. Hawkins was not available. Pressing for more information, she was given none and told instead to leave her name and telephone number. Stevie hung up frantic with worry, not for herself, but for Ben. Something was terribly wrong, she was sure of it; yet here she was, still locked up with no way of finding out if he was sick or hurt. And then she remembered: there was a way, after all. Quickly she dialed a number, feeling a rush of relief when the familiar voice answered.

"I need a favor," she said without preliminaries.

"Anything," Lee answered quickly, a glimmer of hope lighting his gray eyes.

"There's a man . . . I need to find out where he is."

"Oh." There was a silence, as the glimmer flickered and faded. "Does he mean something special to you?"

"Of course he's special," Stevie replied impatiently. "If it wasn't for Ben Hawkins, well . . . never mind."

"I see. . . ."

"I haven't seen him in days, Lee. I'm worried sick, and I can't get a straight answer from anyone at his clinic. . . . It's at Park and Sixty-third. Can you help? I need to know where he is, what's happened to him. You said you'd help . . ."

"I remember," Lee cut in, his voice flat and expressionless. "I won't let you down, Stevie . . . not this time."

Two days later, an envelope arrived. Inside was a clipping from the *New York Times*. "Surgeon Sued for Malpractice" said the headline. Then came the details of how Dr. Benjamin Hawkins, a prominent plastic surgeon, was being charged with operating while under the influence of alcohol, of leaving a sponge inside a patient's chest while performing a breast augmentation. The patient developed an abscess and required a second operation. She was demanding two million dollars in damages. Dr. Hawkins, the article said, was not available for comment.

How could that be? Stevie wondered. She'd never seen Ben anything but sober. Her own lovely face bore testimony to his skill as a surgeon, her own experiences testified to his decency as a human being. Why hadn't he told her he was in trouble?

Two days later, in her first moments of freedom, Stevie rushed to the clinic on Park Avenue and demanded to see Ben.

"Dr. Hawkins is not seeing patients today," the receptionist said.

"He'll see me," Stevie insisted grimly. "Tell him I'm not leaving until he does." And with that, she took a seat in the reception area, folded her arms across her chest, and prepared to wait.

The man who came out to greet her bore only a passing resemblance to the Ben she'd known. His silk tie was askew, his blazer rumpled, as if he had slept in it, his face gaunt and haggard, his carriage weary as he ushered Stevie into his private office.

"Why did you stop coming to see me?" she asked as

soon as they were alone. She waved the clipping in his face. "Was it because of this?"

"I thought it was better if I stayed away."

"Better for who?"

"For you, of course," he replied, surprised that she would ask. "You have your own problems, Stevie. I didn't think it was fair to burden you with mine. . . ."

"Isn't that for me to decide? Friends help each other, Ben. Was it fair for you to decide I couldn't help? To treat me like a charity case who had nothing to give?"

He picked up a glass paperweight, looked inside as if it were a crystal ball. "Maybe not," he said. "Anyway, there's nothing to be done. The insurance company will settle the case. . . . They won't go to trial, not after I told them I wouldn't defend myself."

"I'm not talking about the lawsuit, Ben. I'm talking about you!"

"That's pretty well settled too," he said wearily. "I thought I was sober when I did that operation. If I don't know the difference between drunk and sober, then it's time for me to stop practicing."

"But you did a wonderful job on me!" she argued. "I'm sure you did a wonderful job on hundreds, thousands of people, Ben. One mistake doesn't make you a bad surgeon!"

He leaned back in his leather chair and closed his eyes. "One mistake cancels out a thousand good operations. I'm a drunk, Stevie," he said. "I've been a drunk for more than five years, since Pat, my wife, died. I've been a careful drunk, mind you . . . a careful and solitary drunk. I always nurse my whiskey alone, and never in public. I have all kinds of hangover remedies, and if any of my colleagues ever noticed . . . well, doctors are great at covering up for one another. It's like a fraternity rule—a bad one, but the fraternity makes it stick. Up until now, I've been lucky.

But making the kind of stupid, careless mistake I wouldn't accept from a first-year resident is inexcusable, Stevie, criminal. I can only take this as a sign—from the patron saint of drunks, maybe—that I haven't the right to go on testing my luck on my patients. I'm only grateful I didn't do any lasting damage to a woman who trusted me."

Stevie kept shaking her head throughout Ben's recital, as if she couldn't believe any of it. In all the time she'd known him, she had never seen anything that reminded her in the least of Irene—the slurred speech, the glazed eyes, the telltale breath mints, nothing that would suggest Ben was not in full control of himself. "But what about all the advice you gave me . . . about healing myself? It was good advice, Ben. Why won't you use it to help yourself?"

"The oldest line in our book, isn't it?" he said sardonically. " 'Physician, heal thyself.' But even a doctor needs a sound mind to help himself, Stevie. My mind is a mess, at least the part of it that relates to me. . . ."

Stevie couldn't bear to hear Ben deride himself so. She jumped up from her chair and ran to his side, putting her arm around his shoulder. "Then I'll help you," she said without a moment's hesitation.

He smiled, as if she'd presented him with a lovely but inappropriate gift. "And how do you propose to manage that?"

"Damned if I know," she answered honestly. "But that's what I'm going to do. You helped me save my life, and now it's my turn to pay you back."

Instinctively, and out of her own experience, Stevie knew that this was not a time for Ben to be alone. "Let me move in with you," she said. "You need someone now, someone . . ."

He shook his head, and she could see that he was embarrassed. "Stevie," he said, "there's nothing in the world I'd like better than your company. But—"

"But what? Do you have a girlfriend?"

He laughed without merriment, as if the joke were on him. "No," he said. "A bottle of Johnny Walker is the only steady date I've had in a long time."

"Then what?" Remembering the moments of near-intimacy they'd shared, she thought that perhaps Ben's reluctance was a way of keeping her at arm's length. "I just want to be your friend," she offered. "I promise I won't put any moves on you. . . ."

A shadow came over his expression. "Well, that sure isn't very flattering."

Now it was Stevie's turn to be embarrassed. "You're getting me mixed up, Ben. Let's just concentrate on getting you back on your feet for now. Give me one really good reason I shouldn't pitch in. It just so happens the best way to do that is to be with you."

"The truth is," he began hesitantly, "the truth is that I don't trust myself to stay sober for any length of time . . . especially now, Stevie. And I don't want you to see me out of control. I don't want you to think any less of me than you already do."

"If you believe that," she said, meeting his tortured eyes with a fire in her own, "then you don't know me at all. I know what you're going through," she argued passionately, feeling as if she were fighting for Ben's very soul. "I know what it's like to be out of control, to give in to temptations that seem too strong to fight. Mine almost killed me, Ben —but you didn't turn away. You helped me find hope again. Don't turn away from me now. . . . We can help each other," she improvised, not realizing that she was saying something profoundly true. "I'm not going back to my old life . . . and I'm not going to let you slip away. We both have to move forward . . . can't you see that? Let's do it together . . . because we sure as hell can't do it alone!"

* * *

No sooner had Ben surrendered to Stevie's determination than she moved into action. Making a hasty trip back to her own apartment, she packed a single suitcase with her simplest clothes and a few basic necessities. And as she closed the door on the showplace that had surrounded her once with such sterile luxury, she knew she would not be back.

She picked up Ben at the clinic and returned with him to his town house around the corner. On the outside, the three-story red brick house resembled its neighbors; on the inside, it reflected the history of the man she had come to know. The furnishings were eclectic, all authentic, from the Chinese carpet on the dark, herringbone floor of the living room to the African tribal masks on the walls of his magnificent library. Every piece, from the Jacobean bench in the entry hall to the country French armoire in the kitchen, had been carefully selected over the years, not hastily assembled by an expensive decorator. She could imagine Ben and his late wife happily filling this home with things of beauty, imagining the years of joy ahead.

Yet as she continued her inspection of the house, Stevie could see the telltale signs she remembered so well from her life with Irene—the stains on the carpets, the piles of litter in every room, the imprint of damp glasses on furniture surfaces, the layers of dust and neglect.

Seeing his home through Stevie's eyes, Ben explained quietly, "I let the housekeeper go when this . . . this whole business started."

Stevie understood. The absence of another person, the solitude, made it easier for Ben to sink deeper into his private despair.

In the kitchen, she found the rest of the evidence—the empty bottles that had once held Ben's particular poison. "I've seen all this before," Stevie said, "more times than I want to remember. It's what happens from now on that counts," she added, striking an optimistic note that she hoped would ease his embarrassment. "Where do you keep the stuff?" she asked.

Silently Ben led the way to an antique English music cabinet that hid his rows of whiskey bottles from view. "You know what we have to do with all this, don't you?" she asked quietly.

The muscle in his jaw twitched. He forced a light tone. "Shit, Stevie, that stuff is liquid gold. I don't know if I can . . ."

She was tempted to coax and plead, but something stopped her, a memory of how she had once tried—and failed—to stop Irene's drinking by hiding her bottles. "It's up to you," she said, meeting his dark eyes. "I'm with you all the way . . . but it has to be your decision, your moves."

She waited for what seemed an eternity. The answer came in a hushed whisper. "All right, kid. God help me, I don't know if I'm up to this . . . but I'll give it a shot." He tossed her a playful glance. "No, not a shot—that's the one thing I don't need—just a good old 'college try.' "

He scooped up four bottles in his arms, carried them into the kitchen, and started emptying them into the sink one by one. Once Stevie saw that he had begun on his own, she joined in. She stood by his side at the sink and watched his face as the amber liquid swirled and then disappeared down the drain. He seemed so willing now. . . .

So was this all of it? she wondered. Or did he, like Irene, have his secret places—under the bed, behind books, on the top shelves of closets? One thing at a time, she told herself, feeling Ben's struggle as if it were her own.

She made a pot of strong coffee and set it out on the kitchen table along with two china mugs. "It's your turn now," she said to Ben. "You know everything there is to know about me . . . everything important. Now tell me how the hell you ended up here," she said, deliberately reprising the first words he'd ever said to her.

The smile on his face told Stevie he remembered. "My story isn't as good as yours. . . ."

"Good?" she cut in indignantly. "What's so good about my story?"

"Well," he said, choosing his words carefully, "I feel as if there are no excuses for me . . . except too much complacency. Life pitched me one home-run ball after another, Stevie. I expected it to be that way always. And then Pat got sick. . . . The prognosis was bad, but I was sure we could make a miracle together. We fought that disease, Stevie—Christ, how we fought it. But she died," he said, his deep voice cracking, "she died anyway. . . . Everything we did, it wasn't enough. I couldn't believe it . . . didn't want to believe it. The day I buried her, I felt like my life, at least the life I'd loved, was over. I came home and I got drunk. . . . That's how I paid my respects to Pat, Stevie. I came home and got roaring, stinking drunk."

"That isn't so terrible," she murmured. "You were in pain, Ben."

"I was," he said, his dark eyes reliving the memory of that pain. "I used the alcohol like medicine, to cut the pain, to ease the sadness and the loneliness. I don't know when that stopped, Stevie," he said, his voice dropping, "but the time came when I drank just to get drunk."

"It was the same with me, Ben," she said, remembering how she and Pip used to play the game of swallowing everything in sight, just to see who would blast off into oblivion first. "We don't have to do that anymore," she said, improvising again. "The longer we stay away from whatever tempts us, the better we'll feel. And the better we feel, the less we'll be tempted."

"You sound like a preacher," he said with a smile.

"I feel like one," she admitted. "I don't want to lose you

to the bottle . . . I've already lost too much to booze and pills. Don't let me lose you, too, Ben. Promise me . . ."

"I can't," he said gently, his face mirroring Stevie's disappointment. "And if I promised anything now, you shouldn't believe me."

Just as she was about to press him harder, she remembered how Lee had extracted the same kind of promise— and how readily she had broken it when confronted with temptation. "You're right," she said, "you're absolutely right. Let's just get through today, and we'll worry about tomorrow later. . . ."

Working on instinct, Stevie reached back into her childhood for the military discipline and routine she had once rebelled against. Where once it had imprisoned her, now she felt it would provide order and security for lives that had fallen apart.

In the days that followed, she saw to it that she and Ben did almost everything in tandem. They shopped for food, they prepared it together, they took long walks in Central Park, they made and consumed pots of dark coffee, and they talked for hours, sharing experiences they had once carried alone, either from shame or pride. Only when it was time to retire did Stevie go to her own room, leaving Ben with a reminder that she would wake him if she was troubled—and asking him to do the same.

Knowing how shamed Ben felt by his problem, Stevie tried to mend his damaged dignity by involving him in projects that reminded him of who he was. She created daily projects to clean and restore his home to its former beauty. She saw to it that his clothes went to the cleaner's, that he shaved every day, that his thick silver hair was trimmed. But most important, she involved him in searching out clues and signposts for this road they had chosen to travel together. And every day that Ben didn't drink was a victory, she felt, for both of them—a day they celebrated with a ceremonial red check on the calendar and an evening toast with sparkling water flavored with lemon.

Together they scoured the city's libraries for any material that related to alcohol and addiction, adding it to the collection of books and medical journals in Ben's study. Almost religiously, they read for at least three or four hours every day, sometimes silently, sometimes sharing information aloud. Whatever Stevie didn't understand, she asked Ben to explain; after all, this was his fight too.

"It says here that alcoholism is a disease," she said one evening. "If that's true, how come alcoholics aren't treated like . . . like diabetics?"

"Good question," Ben replied with a smile. "Medical men have been trying to come up with a good answer for a long time. A very long time." He got up and scanned a row of carefully arranged books with his fingertips, then pulled out one. "Here," he said, finding the page he wanted. "Read this. . . . It was written in 1784 by Dr. Benjamin Rush, one of the signers of the Declaration of Independence."

Stevie read the tract, which was titled "An Inquiry Into the Effects of Ardent Spirits on the Human Mind and Body." It identified alcohol as addictive and stated that once an appetite for it was established, the drinker lost all control over his drinking. What Dr. Rush claimed was that drunkenness is the fault of the drinker only in the early stages of the disease, before alcohol took control. "This makes sense," Stevie said, remembering with a pang of guilt Irene's tearful admission of helplessness. "But if alcoholics are sick, why is it so hard to cure them?"

"That," Ben said with a sigh, "is the million-dollar question." He thought for a long while. "Your comparison with diabetics isn't bad, Stevie. . . . There isn't a real 'cure' for them either, yet there are ways to live with the disease, treatments to keep it in check."

"But people who have that disease have to do what's good for them," Stevie jumped in. "Otherwise, they get sicker and die, right?"

Ben laughed in spite of himself. "You don't leave a man any loopholes, do you?"

"No," she said. "No loopholes and no excuses."

As Stevie groped her way through the maze of facts intertwined with myths, luck or fate took her to the story of Alcoholics Anonymous. It was a story that excited her imagination . . . of a fateful meeting between Bill Wilson, a stockbroker with no medical education, and Dr. Bob Smith, an alcoholic physician. Of how they came together in Akron, Ohio, in 1935, with nothing more than the determination to mend their own alcohol-ravaged lives. As she read on, she felt that the same kind of destiny had brought her and Ben Hawkins together.

Limited though her education was—or perhaps because her mind wasn't cluttered with elaborate theories—Stevie grasped one important principle: It can't be done alone. Remembering how she'd felt when Lee had left, how helpless she'd felt in the face of temptation and how much easier it was to reach for the devil she knew, she realized that Ben needed the support of someone who understood the nature of his struggle. More than ever, she wanted to be that person. Yet as Stevie reflected on the successful dynamics of AA, a new idea began to form in her head. Now it was the Admiral who was her source of inspiration: "Decide your objective," he said, "and your strategy must fall into place."

"How would you feel about getting out of the city?" Stevie asked Ben.

"You mean a vacation?"

"No. I mean . . . a retreat. Someplace close to nature."

"I have a big house on Shelter Island," Ben said, "but at this time of year, it's going to be pretty deserted. . . ."

"It sounds perfect," Stevie said. "But first, there's something I have to do right here."

The party at Samson's town house was in full swing. The surroundings were different from the Wherehouse, more uptown and more luxurious, but the music was just as loud and the atmosphere just as decadent. After all she had been through, Stevie wondered how she had ever thought it fun to get as wasted as the people she saw now.

"Pretty Stevie! What a pleasant surprise," Samson said, as if she'd never been away. But she had—and that made all the difference in the world. "You look wonderful," he gushed, "better than ever! Your face . . ."

"I was lucky. . . . I'm not pushing my luck anymore," she said quietly. "I've been straight for a long time. I know you probably think that's just too, too quaint . . ."

Samson gave the boyish smile she had always found so endearing, yet now, with the darkening shadows under his eyes, his face looked incongruously older. "No . . ." he said slowly, "I don't think it's quaint. But how did you do it, Stevie?"

"I got a good look at the end of the road, Samson. It wasn't pretty . . . just like none of this is pretty," she said with a gesture that took in the party and a way of life. "I decided to stop dropping out," she continued, "to be a real person. . . ."

"Oh, that." He sighed, rolling his eyes. "Well, you already know how I feel about reality, Pretty Stevie. It's highly overrated, so if you've come to convert me, you're just wasting—"

Suddenly and without warning, someone came up behind Stevie and gave her a hard push that almost knocked her down. She turned to face her attacker—it was a young woman with purple hair and wild eyes. "I know what you're up to!" she raved. "You want him to dump me and take you back, but that's not gonna happen, Stevie Knight! You better get your ass out of here, and pretty damn fast—before I fix that pretty face once and for all!" And with that, she pulled a switchblade from her thigh-high boots. Stevie froze, and a scream of horror escaped her lips.

Quickly Samson stepped between the two women. "Back off, Baby Jean," he snapped. "I said back off right now—or you're history! I'm fed up with your tantrums—fed up, do you hear?"

Stevie stared in disbelief. Was this the Baby Jean she had met before, the innocent-looking teenager who had replaced her in Samson's affections . . . this wild-looking creature who was now crumpling under his attack?

"Baby Jean's harmless," he explained as the girl slunk away. "She likes to play at being the wild one, but she's too stupid to make the role truly convincing. . . ."

Stevie wasn't at all sure that the girl was harmless, any more than she believed that Samson's games were harmless. "You can tell Baby Jean not to worry," she said. "I didn't come here to stay." She turned to face the group of partygoers that clustered around them after witnessing Baby Jean's scene.

"What I came for," she said, raising her voice, "was to remind you all that Philippa Mason—Pip to us—died four months ago. She was beautiful, she was talented, she was rich, just like most of you . . . and her life was wasted. Nobody can bring her back . . . just like nobody can give me back the years I threw away. We thought we were cool and sophisticated, Pip and I . . . so cool that she's dead and I ended up in Bellevue.

"I'm here because I thought that maybe, just maybe, some of you were tired of living like parasites, of being sick and messed up all the time. I thought there might be someone here who doesn't want to end up dead or crazy ... who needs help and doesn't want to go into a hospital. I'm asking you to come with me right now. I give you my word, you won't be sorry."

There was a long silence, then murmurs of muted conversation. Was Stevie Knight serious with this new routine —or was this yet another of Samson's games? A woman giggled drunkenly, but Stevie stood her ground, searching the faces one by one. And in the end, she did not leave alone. First came Johnny London, the rock star, with his girlfriend, Nancy, in tow. Photographer Mary Carstairs followed, and so did actor Bobby Reese. That was all, but it was enough to make a group, a surrogate family—one that would help its members grow, instead of joining in their destruction.

"Well, well," Samson mused as the little group left his house, "Pretty Stevie Knight playing the Pied Piper.... Interesting, but will it ever open on Broadway, I wonder?"

3

As the small band boarded the ferry that would take them across a small stretch of Atlantic waters to Ben's retreat on Shelter Island, Stevie felt as if they were all pilgrims, embarking on a journey through unknown waters and uncharted territories. She had made herself their leader, and she felt the awesome weight of that responsibility now. Yet as all travelers through life must do, she carried with her a faith in something beyond herself. For some it was religion; for Stevie it was a powerful conviction that where there was a desire to travel a new and different road, there had to be a way to find it.

The March sky was nearly white with clouds, the air bitingly cold with the last reminders of winter. As Ben had predicted, Shelter Island was quiet and nearly deserted. His weathered gray clapboard colonial with white shutters and black trim beckoned a welcome to the small band.

Even before the heat was turned on, Stevie felt the warmth of the place. The furnishings were sturdy and simple, burnished by generations of use and polishing; the collection of quilts, the copper pots, and the primitive earthenware reflected the late Pat Hawkins's passion for flea markets and fairs.

The boxes and bags of provisions were stowed in the big country kitchen, and a light meal was prepared and consumed. A fire was lit in the living room's floor-to-ceiling fireplace. Pots of coffee and tea were set out, and Stevie gathered her group around the fire. Sitting cross-legged, her lovely face illuminated by the flickering flames, she said, "I'm not going to make any big speeches. We have a chance at life, it's as simple as that. Anyone who doesn't really want to take it, anyone who's having second thoughts, you can either talk them out with the rest of us—or leave on the next ferry back." She paused for a moment and looked around, but no one spoke. "Okay, then," she continued, "why don't we start by having each of you tell the group why you came?" There was another silence, and Stevie saw that she would have to give more direction. "Johnny," she said, choosing a man who performed publicly for tens of thousands of people to start, "you were the first to leave Samson's party. . . . Tell me why."

Johnny London reached for his coffee as he had so often reached for more powerful stimulants, and took a swallow. "Jesus," he said, "I could do with a little something to sweeten this . . . and I don't mean sugar!"

There was a burst of nervous laughter. Stevie was about to jump on Johnny for reminding the others of what they were giving up when instinct took over and held her back. Johnny was being honest, she realized, and that was better than pretending to be strong when you weren't. "Okay," she said, "Johnny gets points for telling the truth. Now, talk to us some more, Johnny. . . . We're all friends here, and we all know what it's like to want a drink or a pill or a snort."

Johnny gave the trademark grin that had graced his album covers. "You want to know why I came with you, Stevie?"

"I'm glad you did," she said.

"I've been a pretty good drinker since I was sixteen," he said. "When I started out working the small clubs on the Jersey Shore, me and my band, we used to get maybe a hundred bucks, tops—and free booze all night long. Hell, we thought that was a terrific deal—a chance to be famous, a chance to pick up the prettiest girls . . . *and* all the liquor we could handle.

"After a while, the money got better . . . and so did the girls . . . and the bennies. Me and the band, we were wasted all the time. Now the guys from the record companies were giving us anything we wanted, just so we'd put our names on the dotted line. Man, it was heaven . . . sex and drugs and rock and roll!"

"If it was heaven," Stevie cut in, "then how come you're here?"

Johnny's grin faded. "But it was," he insisted, "at least for a couple of years. I started having blackouts on our last European tour, so I cut back on the booze, and everything seemed to be copacetic. Well, last month, we were winding up a ten-week tour of the States in L.A. I had some time to kill, so I rented a car and drove down to Baja. One night I went into this little cantina and put away a few shots of tequila. I wasn't drunk . . . just feeling good. Nobody in the place recognized me, and I started shooting the breeze with the bartender. So he asks my name . . . and you know what? I sat there on that barstool like a jerk, and for the life of me, I couldn't come up with a name . . . not the Johnny London thing, not even the name my mother gave me. That scared the hell out of me, Stevie. . . . That night you came into Samson's place, it was like . . . hell, this is gonna sound ridiculous, but it was like a sign from somewhere."

"Maybe it was," Mary Carstairs chimed in. "And I know exactly how Johnny was feeling. I used to have a great career, photographing the top models in the world . . . even

Pretty Stevie Knight, remember? That was before I started losing things . . . pieces of my life, friends, even my work. I'd shoot rolls of film when I was stoned, thinking they were gonna be just brilliant . . . better than Avedon, better than anybody. But when I developed the stuff, it turned out to be junk. And the worse my work got, the more I needed to be stoned."

Once the walls of reserve had been broken, it seemed that everyone wanted to speak, and it was all that Stevie could do to maintain order. As the hours flew by, ashtrays filled with cigarettes, coffee gave way to warm milk—and Stevie remembered the need for discipline and routine.

"Let's hear from Bobby," she said, pointing to the young, blond actor, "and then we'll all turn in. Reveille's at oh seven hundred hours . . . no exceptions!"

There was a good-natured groan of protest, the loudest being from Johnny, who often tumbled into bed at sunrise.

"I've been listening to all of you," Bobby Reese began, "and what I've been hearing is that at some point, you all felt scared or ashamed of the way your lives were turning out. I've been ashamed all my life . . . at least ever since I realized I was gay. . . ." He stopped and searched the faces around him for signs of disapproval—or worse.

"Go on," Stevie encouraged.

"When I came to New York," he continued, "it didn't seem so bad, being gay, not like it had been at home in Utah. I got a running part on a soap and enough money to party every night. When I cruised the bars, there was always someone who wanted to come home with me. I had an experience something like Johnny's . . . I woke up in a hotel room with a guy. I couldn't remember his name or even where I'd picked him up. And suddenly it seemed like the most important thing in the world to know who I'd slept with. So I got out of bed, picked up his pants, and reached for his wallet, figuring I'd see some ID there. Next thing I knew, I was flat on the floor and my nose was bleeding. The guy thought I was trying to rob him, just like some cheap trick. You know what? I didn't blame him. He almost broke my face, and I didn't blame him. I went on a six-day bender . . . and lost my job. You see," he said, his voice cracking, "I thought I'd put the shame behind me, but it was still there, waiting to come out. . . ."

Impulsively, Stevie got to her feet and put her arms around Bobby. "It's okay," she said softly. "It's going to be okay . . . you don't have to be ashamed here, not with us."

In the days that followed, Stevie tried to keep one step ahead of the group, drawing up rules and then observing them in operation.

Everyone here was equal. She made that clear; by virtue of their common problems, no one was better than the rest, no one worse. Yet someone had to lead and direct, else it was certain the group would founder.

The day's routine began at seven, with a brisk walk on the deserted beach, followed by breakfast, prepared as all meals were, by teams of two in rotation. The group would meet until it was time for lunch, and after that, anyone who had a medical problem would see Ben. The afternoon began with an exercise session, anything from U.S. Navy calisthenics to relay races, followed by a half hour of quiet meditation and a round of chores, such as cleaning the house, doing laundry or shopping for groceries. New rules were made up as needed. When, for example, it seemed that people were spending hours on the telephone talking to friends, Stevie put a limit of one five-minute call per day. When it seemed that too much time was spent watching television, Stevie added another group session before dinner and daily homework assignments to be completed before bedtime. Each member was invited to use the library, which, although more modest than the one in Ben's town house, was filled with books and journals on holistic medicine, psychology, and the history of healing.

As the small band of pilgrims came to know one another, they came also to know more about the nature of their problems. It was Ben who suggested that they spend at least part of every group discussion sharing information and educating themselves about drugs and alcohol. And it was Ben who volunteered to get the ball rolling.

"Think about this," he said, "whenever you're tempted to take another drink or do another line. You're born with ten billion brain cells . . . it sounds like a lot, but that's all you get. Some of these guys wear out and die as you get older; that's natural. But when you abuse alcohol or do a lot of drugs, they start dying off a helluva lot faster, maybe two or three times faster.

"The bad news is that even when you clean up your act, there's no way you can bring back those dead brain cells. The good news is that after three to six months of sobriety, brain function returns. In plain English, that means that the undamaged areas of the brain seem to take over the work of areas that were destroyed . . . like when an employee takes over the job of somebody who quit, in addition to his own work. In an alcoholic or drug addict, this doesn't happen—and pretty soon, the whole damn factory is out to lunch."

There was a moment of silence as all considered the personal implications of this news. "So if you know all that, Doc," said Johnny London, "how come you kept on drinking?"

Ben laughed. "That's a good question, Johnny . . . and the only answer I have is that it's hard to think clearly when your brain is messed up with alcohol."

Nancy came to his defense. "Don't feel bad," she said. "My folks wanted to get me off liquor so bad they paid out fifty bucks an hour for a shrink. He told me that my drinking was only a symptom of my underlying problems. I said, 'Okay, let's get to it.' Three years later, my problems were resolved—and I was still drinking like a fish!"

Everyone laughed, not the laughter of ridicule, but the sound of deep understanding, of knowing someone else's pain and for a moment rising above it.

"My opinion, if it's worth anything—" Ben began.

"Cut that out!" Stevie interrupted. "Your opinion is worth plenty, and no damn lawsuit is going to change that."

"Okay," Ben smiled, "my opinion is that it's better to stop using before you even try to figure out the whys and wherefores. After all, you don't look for the cause of the fire when the building is burning, and you don't try to navigate a sinking ship."

After the group had been at Ben's home for two weeks, there began a trickle of new arrivals—friends and relatives—raising their ranks to an even dozen, and making it necessary to form two separate discussion groups.

Stevie welcomed each newcomer with open arms. But when she called reveille one morning and found the remnants of a pill-and-booze party in one of the rooms, she was reminded of the harsh truth that addicts of any kind couldn't be trusted. She made another rule on the spot. Any newcomer to the Hawkins house would have to turn his bags and his clothing inside out. "Just this once, we'll let it go," she said, "because I should have known better. But from here on in, anyone who uses is out. We can all help each other—but only if we're straight."

"What happens when we leave here?" Mary asked. "What happens in the real world?"

"What do you want to happen, Mary?" Stevie countered. "Close your eyes . . . take as long as you need and make a picture. See yourself exactly the way you want to be. What are you doing in the picture?"

Mary closed her eyes and assumed a lotus position, breathing rhythmically in and out. Soon her face was transformed by an expression of serenity. "I want my work to be good again . . . better than good. I want to get married. I want kids. I want someone to love me for keeps." She opened her eyes.

"Hang on to that picture," Stevie urged. "Fix it in your mind and remember it when you're back in the real world. And if the temptations outside ever get too strong, just pick up the phone and call one of us. . . . We'll remind you."

Stevie repeated the exercise, working her way around the room. When she came to Ben, she was sure she knew what his answer would be, yet when he closed his eyes, he had no answer at all. "I don't know," he said finally. "I just don't know. All I can tell you is that I'm not going back to my practice."

"But why?" Stevie asked. "The lawsuit's going to be settled soon. . . . People will forget in time. You haven't taken a drink in weeks. . . . You can be better than ever."

He shook his head. "That part of my life is over," he said. "Drunk or sober, I know that. Now," he added, "I think I need to find something to care about again."

"What about you, Stevie?" Johnny asked. "Where do you want to be a year from now?"

Stevie was startled by the question. She'd been so intent on getting everyone else focused that she hadn't even thought about herself. She closed her eyes, relaxing first and then concentrating on a tiny dot of light in the center of her mind. The tiny dot burst into a beautiful scene, a place of warmth and clear blue skies. She was surrounded by people, just as she was now, and she was happy. "I want to do this," she said clearly and with the most conviction she'd ever known in her life. "I want to do exactly what I'm doing now."

It was after her vision that Stevie decided on a date—a month from the date of arrival—when her first group of pilgrims would go home. A retreat had to have a beginning and an end, she realized, or else it could easily become a substitute for living.

Resisting all attempts to find out what she was up to, she made several mysterious trips into town, returning with an assortment of bags and boxes.

On the last day that they would all be together, Stevie took Ben into her confidence and asked his help. Closing the door of the living room behind them, they worked together for two hours, blowing up balloons and stringing garlands of brightly colored crepe paper. And when they were finished, Stevie asked Ben to "assemble the troops" and bring them in. She put a recording of "Pomp and Circumstance" on the record player, feeling a rush of tenderness and pride as her "graduates" filed into the room, heads held high, forming a circle. In the center, on a table covered with a bright red cloth, was an enormous white cake. Written in red icing was "Happy Graduation Day," followed by the names of every member of the group. A candle stood by each name.

Stevie lit the candles. "Everyone hold hands. . . . Now make your wishes and blow out the candles!"

Soon they were all laughing and clapping. "I'm proud of us," Stevie said. "I'm proud of all of us. You've all worked hard . . . and you all deserve medals. Mary, will you step forward and collect yours. . . ."

Solemnly, she pinned on the young woman's chest a bronze medal, engraved with her name, the date, and "Shelter Island, U.S.A." "Be happy, Mary," she said, her eyes welling with tears, "and for God's sake, be straight."

By the time she had given out all the medals, Stevie was crying openly. Now that the time had come to say good-bye, she realized how much she would miss her group and how much she had come to care for each and every one of them. Once the cake had been sampled, once hugs and kisses and promises to keep in touch had been exchanged, Stevie walked her graduates outside. In front of Ben's house, the trees were bursting with buds, the forsythia already golden yellow—a fitting reminder that for these alumni there would be another spring and a time of blooming and growth.

4

It was Stevie who had the dream, but it was Ben who helped make it reality. It was Stevie who chose the place, but it was Ben who liquidated his stocks and bonds in order to buy the eighty acres outside of Taos and to build the adobe structure that would become the heart and nerve center of those that followed. She had read in a book on folk medicine that New Mexico was once believed to be the center of the universe; it seemed fitting that their pilgrimage to redeem lost souls would journey there.

"This is just a loan," Stevie insisted. "I'll find a way to pay you back someday, I promise."

"I think of it as an investment. We're supposed to be in this together, remember . . . partner?" he said, ruffling her hair affectionately.

How could she ever forget? Were it not for Ben, she might still be stumbling along in the dark, still in search of a life and an identity.

"That works both ways," Ben said as if he knew what she was thinking. "You helped me find a lot of good reasons for staying sober, Stevie . . . something to care about."

As they pondered the question of what to call the place, Ben suggested "The Haven."

Stevie shook her head. "Haven sounds like a place to hide. . . . you tried that and so did I. No," she concluded, "you can't hide, but you can get the help you need to go on."

And so The Oasis was born, in the New Mexico desert, and those who came to renew themselves were to be called "Travelers."

"There's just one more thing," Stevie said hesitantly. "I think The Oasis should be a place just for women. . . ."

"Hey, where the hell did that come from?" Ben asked, incredulity giving way to suspicion. "I never figured you for a sexist."

"I'm not. Women may be equal—and I say *may be*— but they're not the same as men, and when it comes to treatment of addictions, no one seems to notice—or care. Look at these reports," she said, dumping a pile of papers on Ben's lap. "Just look at these numbers! Women represent fifty percent of the country's alcoholics, eighty percent of prescription drug users, one third of cocaine addicts. Addicted women become social outcasts. . . . We may have come a long way, Ben, but it's still more okay for a man to get drunk than it is for a woman!"

Ben waited until Stevie's passionate outburst wound down. "I can see you've done your homework," he said thoughtfully, noting the determined set of her jaw, the combative stance of her body. "Tell me what prompted it, Stevie. Is this about women in general . . . or one woman in particular?"

"I don't understand," she said, taken by surprise.

"I think you do," he insisted. "Look, Stevie, there's nothing wrong with feeling sad because you couldn't help your mother. And you may be absolutely right in choosing to help women like her," he said, handing back the sheaf of papers. "I just want you to be honest and clear with yourself, that's all."

"That's a lot," she said quietly. "But if I can count on you to keep me honest . . ."

"For as long as you need me," he said, taking her hands and holding them, a silent question in his eyes.

Together Stevie and Ben made The Oasis bloom with life, often working side by side with the landscape artists they commissioned, creating tranquil gardens and pools to soften and enhance the rugged natural beauty of the terrain.

Together they searched the workrooms and factories of New Mexico for furnishings that represented the best work of regional craftsmen. Never forgetting her Bellevue experience, Stevie was determined to create an atmosphere of beauty and serenity that would speed the healing process.

Together, she and Ben interviewed prospective staff members, looking for a balance of formal training and compassion, but more than that, a willingness to learn and grow with the people they would be treating. More than once they rejected a candidate who simply offered impeccable credentials from good universities in favor of one who possessed an explorer's curiosity and a readiness to break new ground.

And as their preparations neared completion, Stevie decided to hold a press conference. "We should show the people who live in the towns nearby what we are," she told Ben. "We're going to need their cooperation and their support." Together they drafted a simple press release, stating that The Oasis would be dedicated to the treatment of addictions.

She had expected only a handful of local press and officials to show up at the press conference. To her surprise, the auditorium was nearly filled with reporters and photographers. For a moment, Stevie felt panic. She had planned an informal get-together over coffee and Danish in one of the dayrooms, and now it seemed she had a full-blown media circus on her hands—practically the kind Samson used to love.

"You can do it," Ben said. "Just remember all those times you worked in front of the cameras . . . only this time it's for something real, not make-believe."

"That's why I'm so scared," she protested. "This is too important to mess up."

"You won't mess up," he said, giving her a good-luck kiss. "Now go on out there and knock 'em dead."

The buzz of conversation intensified as Stevie appeared. She raised her hands asking for silence, then pressed against the podium; it was an exercise that relieved tension. "Ladies and gentlemen," she began, "welcome to The Oasis. You already know why we're here, so let me tell you something about our basic principles, which are very simple. The first is to recognize that the addiction is in control and we can't recover on our own. The second is to get honest, first with ourselves and then with others. The third is to talk it out with others and to gain truth in the process. This is a crucial part of recovery," she continued, "because the addict's life is a monologue—he connects with his addicted self and that is all. The recovering addict is one who understands and uses dialogue."

"Miz Knight . . ." A male reporter rose to his feet, waving his arm.

"Yes? You have a question?"

"Yeah," he said, grinning broadly. "I hear you using the word 'he' when you talk about addicts, but according to my information, The Oasis is gonna be a club for ladies only. How do you justify that?" There was a deep collective rumble, and Stevie was suddenly afraid that this was why so many of the press were here, to mine out—if not stir up—controversy.

"I don't have to justify it," Stevie replied quickly. Then, regretting her haste, she amended herself. "What I mean is that we intend The Oasis to fill a need that isn't being met anywhere else. Female addicts suffer depression, low self-esteem, sexual problems far more than men do. Female alcoholics suffer more serious physical damage because their bodies have a lower percentage of water than those of men. Alcohol isn't diluted as quickly—it takes smaller amounts to push blood alcohol levels to the point where you get serious damage to the body and the mind. Organ damage, especially to the kidneys, is a lot more severe in women than in men."

Still on his feet, the reporter fired another question. "Isn't it true that you're a junkie yourself? Isn't that the real reason why you're interested in treating women only?"

"Yes, I'm a junkie," Stevie answered, her voice quivering with indignation, her eyes burning with what Ben called messianic zeal. "I'm a junkie who doesn't use, but if you've come here looking for dirt on my personal life, you're wasting your time. I will tell you, though, that being a junkie has taught me a lot about women. Pregnant addicts or alcoholics are afraid to get help, afraid their babies will be taken away. So they avoid medical care altogether—jeopardizing their babies and often giving birth to a new-generation addict.

"If guilt and shame and fear aren't enough, when women do seek help, and they go to a coed facility, there they face sexual harassment from male patients.

"This would be difficult enough for strong, healthy people, but most of the women we're talking about have real problems with men to begin with—either because of incest, sexual abuse, or bad marriages. Now . . . does anyone else want to tell me why The Oasis shouldn't be a treatment center for women?"

The room was very still. Then there was a burst of applause from one corner, joined by another and yet another, until people were standing and clapping hands in unison.

Working on adrenaline, Stevie went on answering the questions that were put to her for a full hour. "My staff will show you around," she said then, and rushed out past the crowd to find Ben. It was his opinion she wanted.

"You were great," he said, but his expression didn't match the words.

"Did I leave something out? Tell me, Ben. I can't even remember half the things I said—"

"Stevie," he cut in, "there's someone here to see you. . . ." Ben indicated a tall young naval officer in dress uniform standing in the corridor.

Could it be? she wondered. Could it be that the Admiral had actually sent a message . . . or even come here himself?

As she approached the officer, he saluted smartly. "Miss Stephanie Knight?"

"Yes. . . ."

"Ma'am," he said quietly. "I regret to inform you that your mother, Irene Knight, passed away last month."

The shock hit Stevie like a physical blow. Her knees buckled, and she might have fallen, had not Ben steadied her with his strong arms. All the excitement of the day dissolved into ashes.

"How?" she asked, groping for reality through a haze of disbelief.

"It's all here, ma'am," the officer said, his eyes filled with compassion as he handed over a printed document. It was a copy of Irene's death certificate, duly signed by a Navy doctor. The primary cause of death was given as cirrhosis of the liver. A list of contributing complications was given . . . all the euphemisms the Admiral would insist on. But Stevie knew all too well what had killed her mother.

"I have something else for you, ma'am," the officer said, reaching into his pocket for a small package. "Your mother left you this in her will. Admiral Knight instructed me to deliver it."

Stevie recognized the old crimson velvet jeweler's box at once. It held the garnet brooch that had been given to Irene by her mother on the day of her wedding. "Thank you," she whispered, fighting not to break down. The officer saluted again, turned on his heel, and left.

Ben led Stevie outside, into the shelter of a secluded "meditation garden," and held her in his arms. "How could he?" she began to cry. "How could he just let her die without telling me? Not even to say good-bye, Ben, not even a good-bye. . . . How could he be so cruel? Why does a man like that have children, Ben?"

"I don't know," Ben murmured against her hair. "He must be a miserable, lonely man."

But Stevie didn't hear. Clinging to Ben for comfort, all she could think of was her own loss. "It isn't fair," she sobbed brokenly, "it just isn't fair. I kept hoping . . . Oh, Ben, I was so awful to her, and every time I wrote to say I was sorry, he sent the letters back. She never knew, Ben, she never even knew I was sorry—"

"You can't be sure of that," he cut in. "Maybe she did know, Stevie. Maybe she understood that your work here had everything to do with her."

"Do you think so?" Stevie asked, a tiny glimmer of hope in her swollen red eyes. "Do you really think so?"

Ben nodded. "I think she loved you as best she could, Stevie. Maybe she couldn't be the mother you needed, but if you can forgive her now, then maybe you can forgive yourself too."

Stevie burrowed deeper into the shelter of Ben's arms. They remained outside in the shaded seclusion of the garden for a long time. And when a chill in the air signaled the setting sun, Ben took Stevie into her private quarters, tucked her into bed, and made her a cup of herbal tea.

He sat beside her throughout the long, dark hours of night, holding her when she cried, murmuring words of comfort, taking care of her as he had done before. When there were no more tears left, Ben was simply there, as he had been since the day they'd met.

As the thin, early light of dawn streamed through the windows, Stevie was awake, tired to the point of exhaustion, yet at the same time curiously strengthened by the power of Ben's caring.

She touched his face, relaxed in sleep, with her fingertips, tracing the aristocratic features that had become almost as familiar as her own. Ben's dark eyes flew open in surprise, melted with love at the sight of Stevie, her tousled blond hair framed with a golden halo of sunlight. He kissed the dried tears that stained her cheeks. Her arms went around his neck, drawing him close. Her mouth found his in a long, sweet kiss.

"I love you, Stevie," he whispered, "since the first . . ."

"I love you. . . ." The words seemed natural and right, as did the love that blossomed in the morning of a new day, affirming life in the midst of the dark shadow of death.

Where once Stevie had sought relief from sorrow and pain in the magic elixirs of forgetfulness, now there was work—hard, demanding, consuming work. And there was Ben, a vital partner in that work. They had traveled so far together, leading one another from the darkness into the light. He had been friend and mentor; now he was both lover and the father she'd never had.

The press conference produced a wave of stories; some were laudatory, some were skeptical. One described her as the patron saint of fallen women, suggesting that she was qualified for the role because she had been one herself.

The stories in turn produced an avalanche of mail, some

of it from the women's advocacy groups that were springing up all over the country, most of it from addicts and
their families. For each of the first fifty beds of The Oasis,
there were dozens of applications. Faced with such over-
whelming need, Stevie hired a local fund-raiser to seek
endowments and grants from major corporations, in the
hope of one day expanding the space that seemed far too
small from the very first day.

Two weeks after she admitted her first group of Travelers, Stevie received an early-morning phone call. The
voice on the line was Samson's, stirring memories of a past
that now seemed strange and surreal. "I've been reading all
about you," he said. "I never thought Pretty Stevie Knight
would turn into a savior of lost souls. Congratulations—or
commiserations—whatever seems most appropriate. . . ."
Though his manner was light and flip, to Stevie his voice
sounded tired and forced.

"Why don't you come and see for yourself," she said.
"It's beautiful here, Samson. . . . You could rest and—"

"Are you inviting me to take the cure, Pretty Stevie? I
thought your doors were open only to women."

"Come as a friend," she urged, wanting for Samson
what she had found for herself, what she had not been able
to give Irene—strength against temptation. "Let me show
you what we're doing at The Oasis. Just give it a chance,
Samson. Give *yourself* a chance."

"Perhaps I will," he said with a sigh. "Perhaps one day I
will. But you know how it is . . . so many places to go, so
many people to see. . . ."

Samson didn't come, but instead sent a package, air express. It was a small portrait, curiously old-fashioned and
painted from memory, of a beautiful young woman with
sad, haunted eyes, clad in the classical robes of a Roman
goddess, brandishing a sword against a demonic figure
whose face bore a striking resemblance to his own. How

strange, she thought. Did Samson really imagine himself to be a prince of darkness and nothing more? And did he really see her as a kind of nemesis, when she wanted nothing more than to be a real friend?

Prompted by her sad and bitter experience with Irene, Stevie sat down immediately and wrote a long letter to Samson. As she had not been able to do with her mother, she talked of what had been good in their relationship. Remembering the frightened boy he had shown her, she reached out, saying he only had to call and she would be there. She signed the letter with love and sent it off, in the hope that one day Samson would accept what she had to offer.

With Ben at her side, she gave herself to those who were ready to be helped. And in the years that followed, she often felt akin to the mythical figure in Samson's painting, struggling to exorcise the demons that held her Travelers hostage, consuming their lives—and frequently those of their loved ones.

The Oasis was without pretensions or dogmatic philosophies, and yet, like Alcoholics Anonymous—which had been founded by people themselves in desperate need of help—it worked.

Though her rewards were rich, Stevie never had the luxury of complacency. As her dedication grew, she realized that her education would never end, and that she would have to continue learning for the rest of her life.

Sometimes her education came from books and journals, and sometimes it came, in unexpectedly painful ways, from the very women she sought to help.

From Virginia Folsom, the wife of a Denver billionaire who came to New Mexico in the midst of a highly publicized divorce battle, and following a dramatic failed suicide attempt, Stevie learned that Travelers sometimes came to The Oasis with a hidden agenda, one that was destructive as well as deceitful. No sooner had Virginia settled in than reports began to appear in the press, detailing her mental sufferings at the hands of her husband and her anguished attempts to overcome the problems. When confronted, Virginia tearfully and adamantly denied having anything to do with the stories. But after a careful investigation, Stevie discovered that, in an attempt to increase the size of her divorce settlement, the woman had bribed a dining-room employee to carry out rambling, hysterical denunciations of her husband and fabricated descriptions of her own treatment. Stevie dismissed the employee and, with enormous sadness, sent Virginia home.

"I feel like I failed somehow," she said to Ben. "I feel like I should have spotted whatever was wrong with Virginia from the start. I should have—"

"You're not a mindreader," he cut in firmly. "You've got damn good instincts, but you'll drive yourself crazy if you try to second-guess every person who comes through these doors. You're bound to make mistakes, Stevie. . . . Just accept that and try to learn."

Though Ben's advice was sound, Stevie could accept it only in part. She took each and every mistake as a personal failure, and though it was painful to do so, she was forced to recognize that there might be people who could not be helped at The Oasis. By experience, she learned the danger signals that would help identify them: women who were isolated and closed off, even when not drinking or using drugs; who persisted in seeing themselves as different from everyone else; who could not or would not give up destructive behavior and who were unable to hear anything that would help them do so; women who were persistently angry or paranoid.

Though her work involved constant struggle, Stevie found in it peace and fulfillment, a reason for living. Her relationship with Ben provided the kind of security she had longed for but never known. For once in her life, it seemed there was nothing missing.

Believing that she and Ben were like two parts of a single unit, operating in perfect harmony, she was surprised when, in the middle of a weekly evaluation conference, she caught him staring out the window. She stopped speaking, but he didn't seem to notice, not for a long while.

Suddenly he turned and, with an intensity she hadn't before seen, blurted out, "Marry me, Stevie . . . right now."

She stared it him in disbelief. Where was this coming from? she wondered. And why the urgency?

He smiled belatedly and took her hand. "I know this isn't the most romantic proposal in the world, but I'll make it up to you, I promise. Just say you'll marry me. . . ."

"I don't understand," she said. "Things are going so well, Ben. Why do you want to get married all of a sudden?"

"It isn't all of a sudden. . . . If you cared about me you'd have noticed."

The reproach in his voice was as startling as the proposal. She pushed the papers aside in an apologetic gesture. "All right," she said, "I'm sorry if I've been preoccupied. Talk to me, Ben. Tell me what this is about."

He ran a hand through his silver hair, looking flustered and boyish. "I need some definition in my life, Stevie. I don't want to go on like this . . . just drifting."

"How can you say you're drifting, Ben? I thought we were making a life together."

He shook his head. "The Oasis . . . it's your life, Stevie. I've just been your ally . . . your consort," he added with a trace of disappointment.

"No," she cut in. "You've been vital from the beginning."

"I don't want to argue," he said. "It isn't enough for me,

Stevie. I want a real marriage, not just . . . an arrangement. I want us to be a family . . . maybe even have a child. . . ."

Stevie's disbelief mounted with every word. What Ben was suggesting . . . it was all so different from what had been perfect for her. "Will you give me some time to think about it?" she asked. "I need—"

"Time. . . ." he said softly. "I guess that's an answer."

"Don't be like that," she pleaded, unable to understand Ben's urgency. After all the years of patience and understanding, why was he acting this way?

When the administrator of the Walsh Foundation called and asked Stevie if she could come to Washington to discuss next year's funding for The Oasis, she agreed at once, relieved to have a legitimate excuse for postponing her answer to Ben. His proposal had been profoundly unsettling; not only did Stevie begin to suspect that she didn't know Ben as well as she had believed, she also felt pressured by the revelation that he wanted and hoped for fundamental changes in their relationship.

The trip to Washington was necessary, she told Ben, just as it was necessary for him to stay behind and to supervise The Oasis in her absence. Did he believe her? she wondered, or did he realize that he had upset her fragile sense of life being all that it could be?

Yet no sooner was she on the plane than guilt overtook her. Ben's yearning for a real home and family touched Stevie deeply. He deserved better than evasions and equivocations, and she could see how she'd hurt him when she failed to respond with a spontaneous and joyous "yes." How could she expect him to understand her hesitation when she didn't quite understand it herself? Was it only because Ben's proposal had caught her unprepared—or was it something that would hurt Ben even more . . . the dream that had been put aside but never truly forgotten, the dream of another man's love?

When Stevie reached Washington, she was met at the airport by Vincent Sutherland, the administrator of the Walsh Foundation, and ushered into a waiting limousine. "I hope you don't mind," he said, "but I've taken the liberty of including your name on the list of guests at tonight's Walsh Foundation banquet."

"Of course not," she answered graciously, though in fact she had hoped for the chance of a good night's rest before she faced the long and tedious business of going over her projected allocation of Walsh funds item-by-item tomorrow morning.

"Good," he said. "My wife is looking forward to meeting you. And so, I might add, are the other members of the board. It's strictly a matter of public relations," he added with an apologetic laugh. "As long as you have Mrs. Walsh's support, the board is more or less obliged to approve next year's grant, but . . ."

"I understand," she said. "The board wants to get a look at the person behind Mrs. Walsh's favorite charity. I can't say I blame them, Mr. Sutherland. I probably should have made this trip before, but there never seemed to be enough time."

"You're here now," Sutherland cut in smoothly. "I hope we can make your stay in Washington pleasant enough so that you'll come back to see us again."

Sutherland dropped Stevie off at the Mayflower Hotel, with a promise to return in three hours. It was only after she checked in and started to unpack that she realized she had brought nothing remotely suitable to wear to a formal party. Somehow she had discarded the habit of dressing up along with the lifestyle that had nearly destroyed her. Quickly she went back downstairs, hailed a taxi, and asked the driver to take her to the nearest department store.

Ten minutes later, she was wandering through the formal-wear boutique at Garfinckel's. It had been years since she'd shopped for anything more elaborate than shirts and trousers, and much as she wanted to make a favorable impression on the Walsh board, nothing on the racks seemed to be right for the woman she had become.

At the urging of an eager saleswoman, she halfheartedly tried on and rejected a half dozen items—and what they represented—startling confections in Dayglo colors, elaborately beaded gowns that seemed to weigh more than she did, cocktail dresses in provocative see-through fabrics.

"Don't you have anything else?" she asked in desperation. "I'm not looking for a costume . . . just something to wear to a grownup party."

The salesgirl disappeared into the stockroom and returned with a simple cream-colored strapless dress with a matching jacket. Though it was a perfect fit and set off Stevie's year-round tan, it also drew attention to her flyaway sun-streaked hair. After paying for the dress, she stopped at the cosmetics counter and bought a rinse that promised to produce "dazzling highlights and instant manageability."

When she returned to the hotel, she washed her hair, then soaked for a luxurious twenty mintues in a scented bath, thinking how long it had been since she'd indulged in any kind of feminine vanity—and how the fussing and primping that had been an important part of her life as a mannequin had all but disappeared.

As she made up her face and slipped into her new dress, the woman reflected in the mirror was unmistakably lovely . . . and yet, something was missing, something remembered and never quite forgotten. It was, Stevie thought with a pang of nostalgia, the glow of anticipation, the eagerness of a woman to see herself mirrored in the eyes of a man who loved her. She had such a man at home, she reminded herself, a man who loved her in blue jeans and work clothes. Why couldn't that be enough? she asked herself. Why couldn't she embrace with all her heart the gift of Ben's love?

The party at Walsh Foundation headquarters on Embassy Row was just getting underway when the foundation limousine dropped Stevie, along with Mr. and Mrs. Sutherland, at the front entrance. White-jacketed waiters were serving canapés and champagne while a small orchestra played dance music in the main gallery.

The Sutherlands introduced Stevie to each of the five foundation board members, and though diplomacy had never been her strong suit, she made a point of voicing her appreciation for their continued support. Sipping a club soda, she dutifully engaged in the kind of light party conversation she'd all but forgotten. Smiling graciously, she danced with the unmarried board members—and hoped she was giving a good impersonation of a woman who was happy, contented, and at peace with herself.

As soon as she could politely excuse herself, Stevie left the Sutherlands and went to look for a telephone. Though she had left The Oasis in Ben's capable hands, she still needed to assure herself that all was well in her absence.

As she passed what seemed to be a library, she saw a familiar figure emerge from a dimly lit corner. Her heart gave a lurch of recognition, her body moved forward, a radiant smile on her face. It's fate, she thought, it's fate that brought him here, now.

A moment later Stevie stopped in her tracks, the smile frozen into a grimace of pain. Lee wasn't alone . . . he was with a woman, a beautiful woman wearing a stunning gown. She was looking into his eyes with that kind of secret confidence that lovers share. Her arm slipped into his possessively, as she waited expectantly to be kissed.

Stevie turned away quickly. She didn't want to see any more—nor could she bear to be seen. She couldn't pretend they were nothing more than old friends, not when her heart was saying: That could have been you, that should have been you . . . if only.

Stevie told herself it was all for the best, seeing Lee again and knowing that he was a closed chapter. She couldn't forget him; that would be asking too much. But she could try to practice what she preached: live in the present, and do it one day at a time.

Yet she could not seem to give Ben the answer he wanted. Nor could she explain to his satisfaction why she couldn't agree to be his wife.

The relationship that had once worked so smoothly began to change. Where once they had been relaxed partners, now Stevie felt she could scarcely turn around without running into a wall of reproach.

"I can't work like this," she said finally. "Every time we're together, you keep giving me those hangdog looks. What's going on, Ben? I know you . . . there has to be something going on."

Ben simply shook his head. "Nothing's going on. . . . I'm just crazy about you, that's all."

She was almost certain that Ben was hiding something. Why else would he act so strangely? Her own heart suggested an answer: people in love didn't always behave the way normal people did.

In a gesture of reconciliation, Stevie tried to give Ben the kind of love it was in her power to give. She made a point of spending more time with him, of being more attentive. But when she suggested they take a weekend holiday away from The Oasis, Ben simply refused.

"That's not good enough," he said. "I see what you're doing, Stevie, and it's just not good enough. Unless you're ready for more than a vacation—"

"That sounds like an ultimatum," she cut in, scarcely believing her ears.

His face was rigid. "Yes . . . that's what it is . . . an ultimatum."

She was silent. How could Ben do this to her after all his talk of love and commitment?

"I'll be leaving here next week."

Disbelief gave way to shock. "Leave? Ben, you can't be serious. . . ."

Even after she watched Ben pack his belongings into his Jeep, even after he started the motor, Stevie couldn't believe he wouldn't somehow change his mind. She told him she loved him, she told him she needed him, but that didn't seem to make a difference. To Stevie it seemed that either she had never known Ben Hawkins at all—or else he had changed into someone else.

When he left, he took with him all the warmth and humanity that had softened the rigorous, military discipline of Stevie's life. Was she always to be one of life's orphans? she wondered sadly. To reach out for love and then to have it snatched away?

In the two years that followed, The Oasis grew and prospered. Stevie's unorthodox methods became celebrated worldwide. She was invited to speak at seminars on addiction in Europe and Asia. And yet as her professional star burned ever more brightly, Stevie Knight the woman seemed almost to disappear, and always it seemed that with each step forward for The Oasis, Stevie suffered another personal loss.

There was, for example, the day she received the news that her grant from the Walsh Foundation was to be doubled. As she waited to meet with her administrative staff to plan a badly needed new wing, she rang the dining room and asked for a carafe of coffee. She glanced idly through her morning paper—only to be confronted with a garish, screaming headline: "Drug-Crazed Porno Star Stabs Pop Artist Samson Love!"

The story that followed was pieced together from the deranged ramblings of "Baby Jean" Cooper and anecdotes from a coterie of famous people, all claiming to be Samson's close friends. It was a story much like Stevie's, but with some terrible differences. After Baby Jean's ten minutes in the spotlight were over, after her banishment from Samson's inner circle, she had threatened revenge with pleas that he take her back. Samson had not heeded her request. Had he believed so much in his own immortality? Or had he simply been too afraid to acknowledge the reality of death? Stevie's heart ached for the child-man she had known, the boy who had wanted so much to believe he was immortal that he had died such a horrible death—at the hands of one of his own artistic creations.

She felt the slender threads of her own history were breaking one by one. The theme of loss, so resonant in her life, now seemed to Stevie to be her destiny.

A year later, Marianne Forman, a distinguished author whose career had been all but destroyed by alcohol, wrote a book called *Six Weeks to Salvation*, describing her treatment at The Oasis. Dedicated "To Stevie Knight, who showed me that miracles are possible," the book became a best-seller, generating a fresh new wave of acclaim for Stevie's work.

Stevie was awarded an honorary doctoral degree from Columbia University, but before she could fully savor the honor, she received a letter from Ben with a Santa Fe return address.

"Dearest Stevie," it began, "I know I hurt you when I left. Forgive me for that, as I've forgiven you for loving The Oasis more than you loved me. I've been fighting the battle of my life, Stevie . . . and doing a damn good job of it, even if I do say so myself. I want to see you again, old friend. . . . We've been through too much together to leave it like this. All my love, Ben."

Dear God, she thought, what did Ben mean? Was he drinking again? Whatever he was going through, he shouldn't be doing it alone. She stuffed his letter into her pocket and made several quick phone calls in succession, informing her staff that she had a personal emergency and asking them to take over her duties while she was gone. Within the hour, Stevie was in her car headed for Santa Fe.

The cream-colored adobe house was set on a small bluff overlooking a peaceful valley. She rang the doorbell. A housekeeper opened the door, and when Stevie gave her name, the woman nodded and led her to the back of the house, where Ben was working in the garden.

When he saw Stevie, he held out his arms and she ran to him. "Ben! Oh, Ben," she called out, laughing with relief at the sight of him, fit and tan and obviously healthy.

"Thank you for coming," he said with a formality that tore at her heart.

"Did you imagine I wouldn't? Even for a minute?"

"No," he said with a sad smile, "I didn't. Not when I invited you as a friend in need. Sit down," he said, showing her to a shaded nook where a wrought-iron table and chairs had been placed. The housekeeper brought a pitcher of lemonade and two glasses, and as Ben poured, Stevie noticed a tremor in his hands. Was he nervous about seeing her again . . . or had he been drinking after all?

"Ben," she said, "your letter. . . . What did you mean when you—"

"Not now," he cut in. "First tell me about you . . . not the stuff I read in the newspapers. Tell me about the Stevie I love."

"That's all there is," she answered lightly, "what you see

in the newspapers. Ben, I want to know about that letter." She hesitated for a moment. "Are you drinking again? Is that what you meant?"

There was a long silence, then a sigh. "I wish it were that, Stevie. I never thought I'd say such a thing, but I wish it were just the alcohol. It's . . . it's something a lot tougher to beat. It's called amyotrophic lateral sclerosis— 'Lou Gehrig's disease,' to most people. What it does, Stevie, is try to kill you just a little bit at a time. It starts to attack your muscles, little ones first. . . ."

Stevie found herself scarcely breathing as she listened with growing horror to Ben's matter-of-fact description of the wasting away of every muscle function . . . until nothing was left but an active mind imprisoned within a helpless body. "No . . . " she whispered, "no, it can't be. . . ."

"My reaction exactly . . . at first. Now that I've had a few years to live with it, I know—"

"A few years? Ben! Are you saying you knew about . . . this thing when you were with me? But . . . why did you just go away without telling me, without giving me the chance—"

"Because I wouldn't have found out what I needed to know—if you loved me enough to marry me. And when I did find out . . . well, I didn't want you with me out of pity. I wanted a wife, Stevie, not a nursemaid."

"Come back with me now," she said without hesitation. "We'll be together. It's better than being alone."

"I don't know if I'm going to be around that long. . . ."

"What do you mean?" she asked, afraid to hear his answer.

"My plan is to go on fighting every way I know how, Stevie—exercise, diet, vitamin therapy, the works. Hell, my doctor is amazed at the shape I'm in. But if I ever start losing this fight, well . . . I'm not sure what I'll do then. I don't think I'll stick around long enough to say 'uncle'. . . ."

"Ben, you can't mean that. . . . You're a doctor, for God's sake!"

"I mean exactly that. You know, Stevie, for some people, life itself can be an addiction. They stay in it long after it stops having any meaning because they just don't know how to quit."

With all her heart, Stevie wanted to argue with him, to plead for every minute of Ben's precious life. And yet, seeing him now, loving him beyond words for his goodness and decency, she wondered if she had the right to ask him to endure what seemed to her unendurable.

"I didn't ask you here to make you sad, Stevie," he said, taking her hand and trying to squeeze it. She could feel the tremor now, the weakness of his grip.

"Take my advice, Stevie . . . one last time?"

She nodded silently, not trusting herself to speak.

"You know," he said, "I'm proud of everything we've done together. I'll never forget that . . . or you. In some ways, you're the most honest person I know. Except when it comes to love. That's when you cheat."

"Cheat?" she repeated.

"Exactly. Lots of people have demanding, fulfilling, important careers—and a personal life too."

"But I . . ."

"Let me finish . . . please, Stevie, it's important to me. I couldn't make you understand when we were lovers. I hope you'll listen to me now. . . . I know how much you care about The Oasis. I know how much you care about each and every woman who walks through those doors. But I think for you The Oasis is more than a life's work. I even think it's more than a mission. I think for you, The Oasis has become a fortress, a place to hide, a defense against giving yourself. Don't shake your head like that, Stevie. . . . I was there, remember?

"Yes," she said, tears spilling onto her cheeks, "I remember." She wanted to be brave for Ben's sake, but the pain of knowing he was trying to help her, even while his own life was ebbing away, was unbearable.

"I've seen you work eighteen hours a day, seven days a week. I've watched you do jobs that other people could do. I've seen you act as if The Oasis would go up in smoke if you took a vacation. Stevie, it just isn't true. If you were to die tomorrow, The Oasis would go on. Other people would carry on. But Stevie . . . there's one job no one else can do the way you could. Promise me you'll take care of it. Give me your word."

"Anything. . . ."

"Fill your life with love," he said, "a complete love. Don't make The Oasis a substitute. Promise. Grant me that one wish. . . ."

Grant the dying man a last wish. She could almost hear the missing words. But without Ben, how could the promise be kept? Once there had been Lee . . . and now he had someone else.

Yet she nodded to Ben, giving him the promise he sought.

When she left him, he raised it again and made her repeat the vow. "Be loved, let yourself be loved," he said— and she answered, "I will."

She had wanted never to let him down; now she felt she might, despite her best intentions. She felt a lie had finally passed between them.

Book Six

1

Anne gave her thick black hair a final stroke of the brush, then swept it back with a ribbon. The effect was youthful and becoming, yet somehow incongruous with the clothes she wore—the expensive silk blouse and well-tailored gabardine slacks that had been the most casual items in her wardrobe.

Would Hal notice? she wondered, as she applied a bit of lip gloss to her otherwise unmade-up face. Would he see that the tension lines around her mouth had eased, that her skin glowed and her eyes sparkled without benefit of artifice or drugs?

She left her room and hurried towards Stevie's office . . . it was all she could do not to run. She had missed Hal terribly, and when he'd sent word that he was meeting with the governor in Santa Fe, and that there would be time for a brief stopover at The Oasis, Anne had been beside herself with happiness. She was grateful to Stevie for allowing Hal to bypass the usual visiting procedures—and for giving them the use of her office, so they could have some privacy, away from prying eyes and wagging tongues.

Anne settled herself in Stevie's chair and looked outside the picture window that framed the mountains. She felt as if she'd climbed them all and was still reaching for the top. No pain, no gain, Stevie often said, whenever one of her Travelers complained that it was hard to make real changes, the kind that endured. As Anne had rediscovered the passionate and caring young woman who had fallen in love with young Hal Garretson, she realized just how hard it would be to hold onto her newfound sense of self, to protect it from being fragmented by the demands of Hal's political career. Those pressures weren't going to disappear; she could, in fact, count on them to get worse. But of one thing she was certain: if she allowed herself to be swallowed up again, she would have no one to blame but herself.

Alone in Stevie's office, Anne waited, watching the minutes on the clock tick away, feeling the kind of disappointment that drugs had once helped her ignore. Hal wouldn't break his promise, would he? He wouldn't say he was coming—and then just not appear? Only if something really important came up, she answered herself, knowing all too well the priorities of a man who had both eyes fixed firmly on the White House.

When, finally, Hal did appear, Anne rushed into his arms eagerly, needing the reassurance of a love that had been too long neglected. "I've missed you," she murmured, "I've missed you so much."

"I've missed you, too, hon," Hal said, but it was he who broke the embrace. "You look different," he observed with a frown, holding Anne at arm's length.

"Is that a compliment or a complaint?" she asked more sharply than she'd intended.

Hal looked startled. "A compliment," he answered, recovering quickly.

"Good," she said, "because the way I look now . . . well, that's me, too . . ."

"How have you been?" he asked heartily in that way that

healthy people have around the sick. Had she become something strange and alien, Anne wondered, simply by the act of trying to become well?

"Better than I have been in years," she answered. "I'm starting to enjoy things I stopped noticing a long time ago. I'm learning how to work with my body instead of against it. I can't wait to share some of the things I've learned with you, Hal. We had a seminar last week on combatting drug use among teenagers," she continued and started to describe how the new methods could be used in inner-city programs. Then suddenly she stopped—when she noticed Hal glance ever so surreptitiously at his watch. Once she might have ignored the gesture, or even apologized for keeping him, but now she said: "You just got here a few minutes ago."

"I know, sweetheart, and I could kick myself for that, but I have a plane to catch in forty minutes. My meeting with the governor ran longer than I expected, and I couldn't very well cut him off, not when I'm counting on his support. I . . . you know how it is, Anne, I don't have to tell you."

"Yes," she said slowly, "I do know how it is. But I also know that you're the one who chooses your priorities, not the governor or anyone else."

He looked surprised again, shook his head as if he couldn't believe what he was hearing. "You've changed, Anne."

She nodded. "And I intend to go on changing," she added with a determination she hadn't shown him in a very long time. "I love you, Hal, and I want you to be president. I'm ready to make sacrifices, but I expect something in return. You have to make some changes, too."

"What kind of changes?" Hal asked, a puzzled expression on his face. "You know I love you . . . I don't understand."

"I can see that," she said, "and I can also see that we have some important decisions to make about what our life is going to be like in the future. I won't be put on hold until after you're elected, and I won't go on acting as window dressing for your campaign." Deliberately she looked at the clock on the wall. "As it happens, I have an important meeting, too. My group begins in five minutes, and I can't be late."

Anne gave her husband a kiss, and for the first time in years she felt that he was the one who was holding on for just an extra moment before she slipped away. It was a good feeling, no, it was a wonderful feeling. Maybe, she thought, just maybe if we both try hard, we can start all over again. . . .

Part of the therapy for those at The Oasis was the performance of daily tasks, simple tasks that reminded them of the basic elements of life. This was true even for those who had risen to enjoy lives of great wealth and privilege.

This was how Anne Garretson and Kanda Lyons came to be working in The Oasis kitchen on a Saturday morning, preparing dozens of sandwiches for an afternoon picnic.

As Kanda sliced her way through what seemed like a mountain of tomatoes, she wondered what her fans would say if they could see her now, looking like a plain kitchen maid, without the flash and glitz that had become her trademark, dressed in jeans and a plain white T-shirt, her hair tied back in pigtails.

In her mind's eye, she conjured up a fantasy interview on *Lifestyles of the Rich and Famous*. "Ladies and gentlemen," Robin Leach was crowing, "we have with us today none other than recording star and Academy Award winner Kanda Lyons, one of Hollywood's most glamorous stars. Tell our viewers what you've been doing this week, Miz Lyons." Why, Robin, you wouldn't believe how busy I've been . . . so much to do, you know, trying to figure out how to get past my problem with self-esteem. "Fascinating, Kanda. I'm sure all your fans would love to know what exciting things you have planned for the future." Well, I'll have my hands full, Robin, making sandwiches and trying to decide whether to put butter or mayonnaise on this next batch of bread.

Kanda smiled at the working of her own imagination. Strange, she thought, how she'd come here prepared to hate everything about The Oasis. Yet as her craving for the white powder subsided, as she began to examine—however reluctantly—her own history, some of her strongest prejudices had begun to waver. Especially after finding a woman like Anne Garretson, a woman she'd admired more than Jackie Kennedy, was stuck here too, going through the same kind of changes.

"Would you believe it?" Kanda griped, half bemused as she grabbed a loaf of freshly baked whole grain bread. "I spent half my life trying to get away from the fact that my mother was a maid . . . and here I am, doing just what that poor old black woman used to do."

Anne looked up from the breast of turkey she was slicing. She got a kick out of Kanda's gritty abrasiveness, secretly admired her ability to give as good as she got in the most heated of group sessions. And curiously, it was at those moments when the singer seemed most defensive that Anne's heart, sensing the pain and turmoil underneath, went out to her. "My grandmother was a cook," Anne said matter-of-factly. "And my grandfather was a bricklayer . . . until he broke his back on a construction job. Then it was my grandmother who brought home the bacon—sometimes literally—by working in other people's kitchens. If you look back far enough, Kanda, we all come from hardworking people who had to struggle. That's what this country is all about, isn't it?"

"But we weren't all slaves, were we?" Kanda's rejoinder was quick and automatic.

Anne passed a plate of turkey over to Kanda. "When are you going to give that one up? It makes you sound like a couple of politicians I know. They keep making the same old tired speeches every time they get stuck for something to say."

"You're talking pretty tough these days," Kanda remarked, then struck the sassy pose that had graced her last album cover—the only difference being she had a kitchen knife propped on her shoulder, instead of a Fendi white sable cape draped over it to the floor. "But you better watch out when you mess with this bad-assed lady from Chicago. Because I sure could teach you a thing or two about being tough even on one of my bad days."

Anne smiled wistfully. "I'll bet you could. Matter of fact, I wish you would."

Before Kanda had a chance to reply, Deni Vickers came into the kitchen to pick up the tray of sandwiches. "Hey, Anne," she said breezily, "you sure look good in the kitchen. I'll bet all those blue-collar constituents of Hal's would be impressed if they could see you now."

Anne smiled politely, but Kanda saw the smile fade quickly as soon as Deni left the room.

"Has *that* mama been giving you a hard time?" Kanda said.

Anne sighed and leaned against the oak worktable. "That 'mama,' Kanda dear, scares the bejesus out of me. The way she looks at me, I feel so . . . so naked."

"Hell," Kanda said mockingly, "she just thinks she's some kind of media superstar. But don't let her bust your butt, Annie. You've got real class. You and the senator, you are one dynamite team."

"Thanks, hon," Anne said quietly. "I was just starting to believe that, too—and to think I could be myself, not just a piece of pretty window dressing for Hal's campaigns and Washington parties, but be . . . someone who could advise him, and help him, and even make a difference on my own." She bit her lip. "And now. . ."

"What about now?" Kanda probed.

"My new outlook may not matter."

"Sounds to me like you're feeling sorry for yourself," Kanda said, shaking the knife at Anne in mock reproach. "I didn't have you figured for a quitter."

Anne shook her head. "I don't want to quit! My choice was to beat my own problem, and then get out there and fight again to solve other people's. Unfortunately, I may not have a choice. . . ." She hesitated for a moment, then, deciding to share her burden with Kanda, described the sword that had been held over her head by Livy Walsh. "It looks like Livy's backed off," Anne concluded. "But now I've got Deni Vickers to worry about. Is she going to give me a break? That little dig she made—about the voters in Hal's district 'seeing me now' may be a tip-off."

"Goddamn," Kanda declared, "that's dirty pool!" She surprised herself with the heat in her response. It had been a long time since she'd cared at all about anyone else's problems; where a privileged white woman was concerned, she didn't think she'd ever given a damn before. It struck Kanda now that here, for the first time, she'd become color-blind. The Travelers weren't divided into black and white; she wasn't keeping a count of who was who, which was which. They were all just women with dangerous and deadly cravings. And along with not keeping track of color, she'd become more tolerant of herself. Since she had stopped being so acutely conscious of the "whiteness" of others, she no longer felt a deep-seated hatred of herself for being black.

"Dirty or not," Anne said, "I don't see much I can do about it. I have to keep my fingers crossed that Deni

Vickers will give me a break. Stevie seems to think it'll be okay." Anne shrugged. "It better be. You know as well as I do what the media could make out of my problems."

Yes, Kanda thought, she knew only too well—the media could make you a star one day and a has-been the next. Of course, she had given them more than a little help, flaunted her bad-girl behavior. But Anne's was a far different case. She didn't deserve to be tarred and feathered for the sake of building someone's TV ratings or magazine circulation. Hal Garretson was a man who wanted to help others, and so was his wife. Kanda hadn't much use for politicians, but Garretson was more than hot air and phony promises. Hell, he was still fighting for civil rights, even after everybody else in Washington acted like the battle was over.

"Anne," Kanda said, "if Deni Vickers does open her big mouth, you have to fight back. Don't just lie down and take it."

"I don't think I would. But when you take on the media, it's a losing battle."

"The only battles that get lost before they even start are the ones where one side just gives up. Doesn't matter how the odds are stacked. Didn't your mother ever tell you the story of David and Goliath?"

Anne smiled in spite of her anxiety, picturing herself with a slingshot aimed directly at the cold, gray eye of Deni's all-seeing camera. "If my mother didn't . . . Hal has," Anne said, shredding a new head of lettuce. "I hear it from him every time he has to go up on the hill and fight for some new bill that's going to cost money to create low-cost housing, or feed the poor. But let's not worry about Deni for now. Maybe that'll work out. Tell me how you're doing. I know it was rough your first week here. If there's anything I can do . . ."

Kanda nodded an acknowledgment of Anne's offer. She

knew it was sincere and real, like Anne Garretson herself. "Things are lookin' up a little." Kanda paused, staring off into a memory of a thousand ruined opportunities. "But we never know how the movie ends till the last reel, do we? And I ain't there yet."

Anne laid down her knife and looked at Kanda. "Stop me if I'm out of line," she said, "but maybe you're further along than you think. I've seen some good changes in you."

"Really?" Kanda asked shyly, surprised that someone other than staff had been watching her. "Like what?"

"Like . . . you don't seem so shut down anymore. The first day you came into the group, you acted like you couldn't be bothered to talk, let alone listen. But after a while, I could see that you were listening, even when you didn't say anything. You even look different now. Your face has lost the tension. You just don't look . . . angry all the time."

"Stevie keeps us so tired workin' and talkin' and hikin', who's got a cotton-pickin' minute to be pissed?"

Anne laughed . . . and Kanda with her.

"And you do that, too," Anne said, remarking on Kanda's laugh. "Makes you look so much more beautiful."

"You mean beautiful for a black woman," Kanda replied, the old defensiveness springing up by reflex. She didn't like compliments. She'd heard too many, and too many had been used against her by people who wanted to steal her money, her talent . . . or her soul.

"That's not what I meant at all," Anne said firmly.

Kanda still shrugged it off. "I don't want none of that shit, Anne."

"What shit?" The word didn't come easy to Anne, who had spent so many years guarding her language for the sake of image. But it felt good to talk honestly with Kanda.

"You're just layin' it on to make me feel good."

"Bet your ass," Anne said. "And what the hell's wrong with that? Sure I want you to feel good. Kanda, I like you. I could even use a friend like you... someone who'll always tell me the way it really is. What put me here is having too many people around who only want to see it one way—who wouldn't let me be even the least bit less than perfect. Well, I'd have an easier time keeping up my political image—if I'm lucky enough to go on needing one—if I had someone in my corner to tell me how to... to get real."

Kanda looked startled—and then she started to laugh. "I sure could do that, honey. I'd keep your feet on the ground even if I had to nail 'em there." She breathed deeply, as though gathering herself to make an enormous physical effort. "And I wouldn't mind having someone around... to say the things I need to hear to make me feel good."

"Someone you can *trust*," Anne amended. "You don't want to hear pretty things from people who are just out to take you. . . ."

"Amen, sister Anne," Kanda said, rolling her eyes. "Not like my second husband, for example—that sweetheart who ran off to South America with my money? Hell, half the stars in Hollywood trusted him. . . . Guess they can kiss all those millions good-bye." She laughed, then stopped abruptly. "Hey, what am I laughing about? I'm broke... my life is a mess... and the IRS is busy picking over whatever that rat didn't steal."

Anne reached across the table and took Kanda's hand. "Maybe I can help," she said. "Hal knows some good tax lawyers in Washington, people you can trust. Maybe they can untangle the mess, make some kind of a deal with the IRS. . . ."

"You'd really stick your neck out for me... ?"

Anne shrugged. "Doesn't seem like such a big risk. I know you can earn more money, Kanda. You can be better than ever if you stay away from the drugs. All the world loves a comeback, and you can do it. But as they love to remind us in the groups, nobody does it alone. I just want you to know that I'd like to be your friend—now . . . and when you get out of here."

"Hell," Kanda said, dimpling mischievously, "if you mean that, then you better make sure you get yourself into the White House. Because that sure would make one big mother of a place to start my comeback!"

For Stevie, the chore at hand was more complex and difficult. Saturday night was often a time when she reviewed the files of the Travelers, evaluating their progress during the past week, and she had been at it since after supper.

Now only two folders remained on the desk before her. Stevie hesitated, and almost reached for the lamp to switch it off: these two could wait. But then she admitted to herself that they couldn't. She had already avoided dealing with these Travelers in too many ways. Choosing the easier of the two tasks first, Stevie opened the folder marked "Lyons, Kanda."

In show-business terms, it was a mixed review. On the one hand, there were still reports of uncooperative or disruptive behavior, particularly when it came to certain rules and regulations; Stevie noted that Kanda was still denouncing the seven A.M. wakeup and the ten P.M. lights out as "cruel and inhuman punishment." Though the language made Stevie smile, she was genuinely troubled by the singer's struggle against discipline and routine—elements that had been missing from her life too long, and which she now needed if there was to be any hope of restoring order to a badly disrupted life.

On the other hand, Kanda had fulfilled a most important homework assignment: listing the people—other than herself—to whom she had caused injury or pain. Without making excuses, she had stood up in front of her group and described how she had dumped the Wonders and abdicated the care of her own children to hired help. And she had listened to Stevie's reminder that an important part of recovery was in making amends. Was she ready to take the next step?

Stevie made some notes to herself: "Talk to K. about arranging visit with children? Talk to Miranda about arranging family therapy sessions after K. graduates?"

Reluctantly, Stevie turned her attention to the folder containing all the material on Deni Vickers. The staff comments ranged from guardedly neutral to somewhat positive. Deni appeared to be cooperative, almost a model resident in matters of discipline and routine.

But when Stevie reviewed Deni's own notes—so many of them half begun and then scratched out and revised—they seemed to bear eloquent testimony to her own confusion, rather than to hopeful progress. Maybe someone should be evaluating *my* performance, she thought, because I sure as hell can't seem to get it right.

Recognizing her personal dislike of Deni, Stevie bent over backward to be fair, whatever that was. And though she was known for her bluntness and candor, for using drill-sergeant tactics even with some of the most celebrated and powerful women in America, when it came to Deni, Stevie often found herself pulling her punches.

How else could she explain, for example, the difference in the way she treated Livy's threat to expose Anne's addiction, and the way she responded to the possibility that Deni might break the very same story? She hadn't hesitated to strong-arm Livy, but she had yet to even ask for the promise of Deni's silence. Was it only a wish to be fair and to give Deni the benefit of every doubt? Or did she see, in Deni's lifetime obsession with her father, a mirror image of confusions of her own that made her feel to talk with Deni was, in a way, too much unfinished business within herself?

Or was she kept back by something much less complicated? By jealousy. By a fear of her own vulnerability. By an unwillingness to tempt her heart with a situation in which she was no longer the savior but the supplicant. Would she ask Deni to release Lee . . . reveal that she had known him long ago—known him first—and bare the heartbreak that came from losing him?

She would have liked to think that she was above such weakness, that she would not compromise her responsibility to any of the Travelers. But, as with the heavy drinkers who gave up liquor and yet never spoke of "cured," only of "recovering," Stevie had learned that you had always had to be on guard against temptations.

Being on guard didn't help when Lee arrived in Taos and called to ask if he could take her to dinner. It was supposed to be about helping Deni Vickers, at least that was what he said—and what she tricked herself into believing. How could she know that the night would be so beautiful, that Lee would take her to the most romantic restaurant in town?

At first, she listened to the story of how he had gotten caught up with Deni. He had been alone, unable to connect for very long with any woman since . . . but he left that part not quite finished. Anyway, she was an undeniably beautiful and exciting woman, and in the beginning of their own involvement, he'd had no idea of how deep her problems went. And of course, when he found out, he couldn't walk away.

"Not you," Stevie said. "You'd have to stick around and try to make it better."

"There was a time once," he answered, "when I walked

away from someone too soon. I didn't want to make that mistake again."

"Maybe you didn't make a mistake, Lee. Maybe you did exactly the right thing. I went through some rough times, but here I am. I had to put myself together because I lost so much when you left that I knew I could never let it happen to me again. If ever someone like you came along, I . . ." She trailed off then, giving herself the excuse that she mustn't open old wounds—but knowing, really, that she couldn't finish the lie. She couldn't speak of someone like him coming along, because there could be no one like him. And he was here right now.

The mood of memory shifted then into something else —an underlying refusal to accept regrets on both sides, a palpable shared wish to go back and start over. Whatever resolve they had both come with that night, the wine . . . and the arrival at their table of the strolling guitarist . . . and all the alchemy of romance turned regrets into hopes.

From dinner, they went to his hotel. She fell into his arms as if her body had a mind of its own. She kissed him hungrily, consumed by the longings she'd denied for so long. "Stevie, oh, Stevie," he murmured against her throat, his voice husky with passion, "I've missed you so much."

She tore at his clothes, her flesh quickening with arousal. Moaning softly as he caressed her breasts, twining her fingers in his hair, she wrapped herself around him, filling herself with the hard maleness of him, remembering at last what it was like to be a woman. All boundaries between them dissolved, all sense of time and place were gone as they melted together, moving as one, reaching for the sweet fulfillment of their deepest desires.

She clung to him, calling out his name, her back arching to meet him, to ride the crest of passion that engulfed her, erasing doubt and reason and common sense.

But when their passion was spent, the sweet afterglow

was very brief, and there were no tender reassurances of love—only a long, eloquent silence.

At last, Lee spoke. "What are we going to do, Stevie?"

Stevie's answer was wrenched from her very soul: "There's nothing we can do. . . ."

Filled with remorse, she tore herself from his arms and rushed back to the safety of The Oasis. She knew then that Ben had been right all along. The Oasis was her fortress—the place where she helped other women confront their feelings while she hid from her own.

For a day she sat vigil for her lost love. But then Lee called. Unwilling to accept the finality—all the more because he had let a wrong decision stand once before—he begged for a chance to see her again. And out of weakness, she said yes.

She waited for him, alone in her office, listening to the silence that was broken only by the sound of crickets and night birds. And when she heard the footsteps that heralded his arrival, she ran to the window and looked. The full moon lit his face, strong and clean in outline, his broad shoulders, his easy, confident walk.

Why had it taken so long? she asked herself. Why, when they finally knew they were right for each other, why did it have to be too late?

A moment later he was in her office. She flicked on the lights and stood, swaying behind the protection of her desk, wanting nothing more than to rush back into his arms. He stood in the doorway as if he was struggling with the same feelings.

"Thanks for seeing me," he said.

"How could I refuse?" How much more she wanted to say. . . . But what was the use of torturing herself with what couldn't be?

He dropped into the chair facing her desk, his handsome face creased with worry and pain. He reached across the desk and took her hand. "Stevie," he began hoarsely, "I've been up all night, going over it and over it."

For a while, they went through the motions of talking, of pretending they had choices, when, being who they were, there was only one choice. They talked to postpone it, the inevitable moment of good-bye.

He stood up and walked to the door, very slowly, as if hoping she might call him back. He turned for a last look, and she gripped her desk as hard as she could, fighting to stay in place. But then her will broke and she ran to him, burying her face against his chest, clinging like a child, knowing that this one embrace would have to last forever.

Finally she tore herself away. "I love you," she said. But that changed nothing. A moment later he was gone.

If there was one single reflection of how spartan Stevie's personal life had become, it was to be found in the way she spent her Sundays. Provided no one else needed her attention, her time, or her energy, the day began with a swim —uninterrupted by any emergency, she always hoped— followed by the luxury of a leisurely breakfast.

On one Sunday, while she sipped her fresh orange juice and read the paper, her attention was captured by an article on the increasing use of amyl nitrate—nicknamed "Rush" —among teenagers to heighten sexual stimulation, and the growing popularity of a more recently invented psychedelic drug called "Ecstacy." Stevie shuddered at the very name, the blatant promise of dreams supplied by a chemical combination of amphetamines with synthetic mescaline. Didn't they know that always, at the end of the dream, came the nightmare?

She tore the article from the paper, marked the key passages with a red pencil, and made a note reminding herself to research the subject more fully. A day would inevitably come when she would have to deal with someone whose life had been destroyed by it, and Stevie wanted to be prepared. It never ended, she thought, the search for bigger and better thrills; only the names of the potions and poisons seemed to change.

She poured a second cup of coffee, indulging the one addiction she still allowed herself, and drank it slowly, savoring the taste of the freshly ground Hawaiian Kona that her kitchen staff kept replenished at all times.

The sports watch on her wrist said it was nearly ten o'clock, reminding Stevie it was time to be on her way. She went to the closet that contained her simple wardrobe and pulled out a western-style cotton shirt and a pair of neatly pressed jeans. How different these clothes were from the lavish furs and silks of her New York days, yet how accurately they, too, reflected what her life had become.

When she finished dressing, she put some things into a small shopping bag—a new historical novel, a few scientific journals, and a new computer game—and went out to her car.

Pulling out of the driveway, she waved to the gardeners who kept The Oasis green and beautiful, and then headed for Santa Fe. She had been making this trip every Sunday for almost two years, ever since she'd learned of Ben's illness. At first their time together had been like the weekly reunion of two old and dear friends. They had picnicked in Ben's garden, strolled through the State Art Museum, and visited the archaeological center at the three-hundred-year-old Palace of Governors.

As Ben had grown weaker, the boundaries of his physical world had shrunk, limiting him first to the confines of his home, then to a wheelchair, and finally to his bed. As his muscles had wasted away, as normal conversation had become impossible, Stevie had found for him a computer system that could be run by the impulses of a mouth-held control.

Always her teacher and mentor, Ben had become her unfailing source of courage, for when she saw how valiantly he struggled against his disabling disease, she felt she could do no less than her best.

When she reached the simple adobe house on the bluff, Stevie parked her car quickly, bounded up the steps, and rapped on the door. Seeing Stevie, the housekeeper began to cry.

"What's wrong, Rosa?" Stevie asked, not wanting to hear the answer, not wanting to know that Ben was worse.

"He's gone," Rosa said. "Dr. Ben is gone. . . ."

Even as Stevie's composure cracked, she reached for a final bit of hope. "You took him to the hospital in Santa Fe?"

Rosa shook her head. Dr. Ben was beyond hospitals and beyond hope.

"But why didn't you call me?" she asked brokenly. "You promised, Rosa, you promised you'd let me know if—"

"He told me no, Miss Stevie. He said call the doctor and that's all. . . ." As if to show she was hiding nothing, Rosa walked Stevie into Ben's room. The hospital bed was still there, the computer, the bedside tray, even the vitamins he took intravenously when he was no longer able to swallow.

But Ben was no longer there.

Rosa handed over an envelope. "He told me to give you this, Miss Stevie."

Stevie sank into the big overstuffed chair that had been her place, opened the envelope, and began to read the computer printout. She could almost hear Ben's voice talking to her as he had in the old days, when they'd first met.

"I know you'll think this is a dirty trick, Stevie, but the last leg of the journey is mine alone, so I guess I should be able to decide how it goes. Call it an old man's vanity, but enough is enough. I've let you share every indignity this disease has hit me with, so you'd better understand that when I meet my maker, I intend to do it without you holding my hand.

"It goes without saying that you've been my best friend and that my work at The Oasis was the best of my best. Whatever I leave behind is yours. Use it any way you like, but please look after Rosa and see to it that she has a job. And that's it. No tears, Stevie, I did the hard part your way and hung around a lot longer than I meant to. Now you do your part and deliver on the promise I asked for. All my love, Ben."

As she finished the letter, she brushed the tears from her face, just as if Ben could see her. She walked through the rooms of the house one by one. Even in death, his generous heart sustained her. It was here in the books he loved, the knowledge he sought and pursued throughout the final months of his life, the kindnesses he had shown her even while he was in need of kindness himself.

Yet knowing how much he loved her, Stevie had never been able to tell Ben why she could not keep the promise he'd sought. In the years they'd been friends, Stevie had shared all kinds of intimacies with Ben, revealed her secret self—all save the part that belonged to Lee. She'd told herself she was protecting Ben's feelings, but perhaps she'd been protecting herself. Ever since Deni had come to her for help, ever since she'd learned of Lee's involvement with her, Stevie had been shamed by her treasonous feelings, by the constant reminders that underneath what Ben laughingly called her "missionary zeal," she was, after all, a woman.

Do you understand now, Ben? she asked the silence that surrounded her. Do you understand now why I can't keep the promise I made you to let myself be loved?

2

After the rugged emptiness of the New Mexico desert, the streets of Washington seemed cacophonous and chaotic. Was it simply the din of automobile horns and the poisonous vapor from thousands of exhausts that added the final ebb of fatigue to Stevie's long journey? Or was it the turbulence she felt within?

As her taxi inched its way toward the Willard Hotel, her luminous hazel eyes were troubled, unseeing of the beauty of cherry trees bursting with pink and white blooms, oblivious to the symbolism of spring. Of all the difficult times in her career, these past weeks had been perhaps the worst. After long years of experience had honed her instincts and reflexes to a fine professionalism, she now found herself constantly questioning both her objectivity and her judgment, at least as they related to Deni Vickers. How ironic, she thought, to be receiving this highest of awards at the very moment she doubted herself most, to be given what would seem like a consolation prize compared with the kisses of the man she couldn't stop loving.

As Stevie checked into the superbly restored landmark hotel, the reception clerk handed over several message slips. "For you, Miss Knight. . . . These all came in today."

She scanned them quickly, fearing there might have been some emergency at The Oasis. But they all gave a local number to call back. And then she noticed that the top slip had a more detailed notation: "Pentagon Operator No. 4452." Automatically her hand closed around the slips of papers, crushing them in a fist, like a stranglehold. Then she thrust them deep into a pocket. As far away as she had stayed from the Admiral, she knew that there had been promotions over the years; she guessed that he might be at the Pentagon now. Two or three years ago, in fact, the wife of a high-ranking Army general who was at The Oasis had asked Stevie if she was related to "Fleet Admiral Custer Knight." Stevie had cut the conversation short with an ambiguous answer: "Related," she said, "but only very distantly."

Now just the thought that he might be trying to make contact made her heart start to pound.

Not until she was alone in her room did Stevie reconsider the possibility of returning the calls. Could she ever truly grow up if she didn't settle things with the Admiral?

She retrieved the sheaf of slips from her coat pocket and smoothed them out on the writing desk. And, as she examined them more carefully, she could smile bitterly at her own foolishness. The Admiral try to contact her? Of course not. Never. The name given on the first-received of the several calls was "Rear Admiral Sanford Graystone." *Sandy.* Good for him; he had finally gotten his own promotion, cut the lines that kept him tied up in Cus Knight's wake like a rowboat towed by a battleship.

His name, the memory of their clandestine meetings at the Dreamland Motel, evoked feelings of shame, but something else, too—a curious pleasure in knowing that there was someone who remembered and had been fond of that unhappy, troubled teenager, young Stevie Knight.

She dialed the Pentagon number without further hesitation.

"Stevie," he said, sounding almost as eager as he had twenty years ago. "I need to see you."

"I'm only here until tomorrow, Sandy. I'm supposed to—"

"I know, kid," he cut in, "I saw it in the papers."

"Hey, I'm not a kid anymore," she said, not altogether lightly.

"No, of course—you're anything but. Pardon me, Stevie. Being given an award at the White House, that's big stuff. I'm proud to have known you."

He paused. Stevie felt edgy. Obviously he was calling for something more than to congratulate her. Did he think she might still be accessible—

His voice broke into her thoughts. "Stevie, I'd like to see you. I know you're busy, and you've got this luncheon with the President at noon, and God knows what else. That's why I tried so hard so reach you today. Let me come over now. . . . I can be there in ten minutes."

"Sandy, it's wonderful to hear your voice again. But we've both come a long way—"

"Hey, Stevie. I'm happily married with four kids, the oldest going off to college next year. You're right when you said we've come a long way. In fact, when I think of the past—the way you and I . . . Well, I'm ashamed. I figure I owe you an apology."

If he were there, she would have hugged him. It was never too late for apologies. She didn't need Sandy's to regain any part of her self-respect; she'd done that on her own. But it put the final polish on an area of memory that had remained tarnished.

"Thanks, Sandy. But I know it took two to make anything happen."

"So will you see me?" he persisted. "Just give me twenty minutes, Stevie. . . ."

Could it be that his wife—or one of his children—needed help? She detected a troubled edge in his plea.

"All right," she agreed wearily, though she desperately needed to rest. After hanging up the telephone, she went into the bathroom and splashed some cold water on her face. The woman in the mirror still looked remarkably youthful in spite of her never-ending battle with armies of demons that came in the most treacherous disguises; the features that had graced glossy magazine covers the world over, even more beautiful now, were more clearly defined by the wars that had been so hard won over the years. Yet when Stevie looked at the reflection, she saw only the dark smudges of fatigue around her eyes, compounded by a frown of self-doubt.

When Sandy arrived a short time later, Stevie saw that her anxiety about him had been groundless. His greeting was warm, but militarily correct.

"You look wonderful," he said, "just the way I remember you."

"Thanks," she said, taking the compliment as he meant it. "You look . . . more distinguished," she added, for Sandy was now the very picture of high-ranking privilege. "What are you doing in Washington?"

"Cus . . . your father got me assigned to the Navy Department. I don't know if you remember, but I was always best at administration."

She smiled in spite of herself, for she had seen Sandy only as the Admiral's personal slave.

"Stevie . . . " he said hesitantly, "it's your father I'm here about. Have you seen him at all lately?"

"No." Her answer was grim and unequivocal, but Sandy pressed on.

"Then you don't know—"

"Don't know what?" she cut in impatiently. The last thing in the world she wanted now was to talk about the Admiral.

"Stevie," he said, "I know you have reasons to be angry with Cus. Hell, there were times I felt like blowing his head off myself. . . ."

"It isn't the same," she interrupted, "and you don't know what it was like. Sure, he may have made your life hell on the job, but it wasn't the same as what he did to me."

Sandy nodded. "Okay . . . maybe you're right, but hear me out anyway. Stevie, your father had one great love in his life, and that was the Navy. Maybe that was wrong, but that's what he was—one hundred percent Navy. Custer Knight might have been one of the great ones, Stevie, like "Bull" Halsey or Chester Nimitz. But there was something in him . . . it was worse than anger, it was like a volcano. He tried to control it, but it was stronger than he was . . . and after your mother died . . ."

Stevie gave a small wounded cry. "Sandy, why are you telling me all this? Am I supposed to care after . . . ?"

"You decide," he said. "Just let me finish. Stevie, they passed him over, time after time. On the Navy side—as a man with ideas, a tactician, a theoretician in where the Navy should plan to go—he would have been a brilliant addition to the Joint Chiefs. But he was his own worst enemy. And he never recognized that . . . he just got angrier and more bitter. One day he just exploded. It was over some small, chickenshit thing . . . his driver was late picking him up for an appointment, the car wasn't the way he liked it, all spit-and-polish. The driver was a new guy . . . he made the mistake of opening his mouth, and Cus went nuts. He beat the hell out of the guy, put him in the hospital for a week."

"That doesn't sound like anything new to me," Stevie said quietly.

"Maybe it isn't," Sandy agreed, "but times have changed, and so has the Navy. The driver's folks called their congressman, and he went straight to the Navy Department. They had Cus dead to rights. . . . At least a dozen people saw him do it. The Navy couldn't let it go, Stevie, not this time. They gave Cus two choices—retire or face a court-martial. He retired. Do you know what that meant to Cus Knight? He's lost everything. . . ." He waited for Stevie to react, but she remained silent.

"Well," he said finally, rising to his feet, "I thought you should know . . . for your own sake, if not for his."

"Thanks for coming, Sandy. I know you meant well. I just . . . I just don't know."

As she closed the door behind the man who had been her ally and also her pawn in a different kind of struggle, Stevie pressed her palms against her eyes and slumped against the door frame. Why should I care? she asked herself. Why should I? Her emotions were already raw and battered, so why the hell should she even try to dig deep inside for a bit of compassion for the man who had nearly destroyed her?

The White House staff had outdone itself, surrounding the awards banquet with all the pomp and circumstance of the nation's highest office. An honor guard representing the three branches of the service stood at attention, as guests, members of the Washington press, and the diplomatic corps presented their coveted invitations to a dark-suited contingent of FBI men and then passed into the reception room, where musicians from the Washington Symphony played selections from Broadway shows.

Inside, there was a horseshoe arrangement of round tables, covered in blue linen, set with the French china that had been a legacy of the Kennedy presidency, and decorated with silver baskets of red, white, and blue flowers. In the center were two tables, one occupied by the President of the United States and his family, the other by those to be honored. Stevie sat with the four other men and women to be similarly honored: a distinguished scientist who had done breakthrough work in the field of AIDS research; a venerable author who had spent twenty years writing a brilliant ten-volume history of the United States; a black mayor who had made his city a model of racial harmony; a chief executive officer who had rescued an automobile-manufacturing company from bankruptcy, saving tens of thousands of jobs.

Yet even surrounded by such distinguished company, Stevie found it difficult to concentrate, to make conversation. There was a confusion of voices speaking inside her own head, demanding her attention and pulling her this way and that. And in the midst of it all the echo of the story Sandy had told, the vivid picture he'd painted of the Admiral's final mistake.

She picked at the lunch that had been prepared by the White House chef, smiled mechanically when she was spoken to, and tried to answer the questions that were put to her about the work of The Oasis. She watched when the President left his table, walked to the podium that had been set up, and positioned himself before the microphone, the large facsimile of the presidential seal at his back.

She applauded politely as the achievements of the other honorees were lauded and their medals were presented. Then she heard the words that snapped her to attention:

"... and it is with great pleasure," the President was saying, "that I present this next Medal of Freedom, to a woman whose efforts in the battle against addiction have been nothing short of heroic, whose tireless work and unending fund of compassion are an inspiration to us all ... Miss Stephanie Knight!"

Applause rippled through the room as Stevie got up from her table and walked to the podium. Shaking hands with the President, she accepted her medal. She fumbled for a moment with the index cards on which she'd made a few notes, then shook her head imperceptibly and put them aside. "The President has spoken of my compassion," she said, "but I want to take this opportunity to ask for yours. I want to tell you what it's like for tens of millions of Americans who struggle with addictions.

"I'm the daughter of an alcoholic," she continued. "There are more than twenty-eight million of us in this country. Most of us were brought up in a code of silence.

"People like me were never children. We grew up believing we weren't good enough to be happy. We never confronted our reality, so even when we leave home, our new lives are a lie. I was so ashamed of who I was, I tried to become someone I was not. I became an addict myself, as so many children of addicts do. My fantasy became reality . . . and so it was impossible for me to love or be loved.

"I count myself among the lucky ones. I survived, as many do not," she went on, her voice cracking with emotion as she silently counted her own honor roll of dead. "I escaped the fantasy that nearly destroyed me . . . and found an identity based on truth." Stevie paused, thinking she had nothing more to say, and then, as if hearing a voice she'd never quite heard before, she began to speak again. "Truth," she said, "brings freedom from pain and from anger. It finally brings forgiveness, and only then can we heal our damaged souls. . . ."

As she acknowledged the applause and acclamation that surrounded her, she felt the awesome weight of the medal she held in her hand, the symbol of what The Oasis and what Stevie Knight were all about. If she was truly to live up to the honor that had been given her, there was something she had yet to do.

* * *

As she hurried through the White House's South Portico, she heard someone call her name. She turned to see an attractive man with dark hair and piercing blue eyes, a stranger as far as she knew, yet somehow familiar.

"Miss Knight... I'm Carey Walsh. Congratulations on your award. From everything I've heard about you, it's long overdue," he said. With a somewhat embarrassed expression, he went on to explain, "My mother was the one the White House invited.... You might say I just stepped in and took her place. That seems to be the Walsh story, but I suppose you've already heard it?"

Stevie heard the question. "Carey, I do know what's going on between you and your mother. It isn't exactly the world's best-kept secret.... I think it's a damn shame, all of it."

"I do, too, but—"

"But nothing," she cut in. "Livy Walsh is one of the most decent people I've ever met. Sure, she's got her blind spots, like everyone else, but she's trying—damn hard—to work through them. I think she's ready to meet you halfway."

Carey Walsh gave an ironic smile, and in his face, Stevie could imagine the face of Ken Walsh, the man Livy had loved with all her heart and still mourned after so many years. "That story sounds familiar," he said. "Livy came home from The Oasis full of good intentions once before...."

"People change," she said with a smile. "Sometimes they need a little practice before they get it right." She looked at her watch. "I have a plane to catch, Carey, and it can't wait... not any longer. But I'll make you a promise. You'll be hearing from Livy... and soon. When you do, try to remember that she's the only mother you'll ever have. It's damn lonely being an orphan," she added quietly. "Take it from someone who knows."

It was late in the day when the taxi dropped Stevie off in front of 128 Shady Lane. In the soft hues of twilight, the house was as she remembered it—an all-American house that might have sheltered an all-American family. Once it had seemed like the grimmest of prisons, but the years had erased the aura of menace and fear that Stevie had always felt as a child.

She rang the bell, and when no one answered, she stepped inside, unconsciously inhaling deeply, as if she might catch some familiar scent, some evocation of time and place. The air was still, almost antiseptic, devoid of clues as to who lived within, making Stevie feel as if she had wandered into unknown territory.

"Is anyone here?" she called out, and as she turned to go into the living room, suddenly a form loomed before her. It was the Admiral—yet it wasn't. He was dressed in the uniform he was no longer entitled to wear. It was clean and well-pressed, yet it no longer seemed to fit. It seemed now like a costume, draping the body of an old man.

He showed little surprise at her presence. Or was there perhaps a slight flicker in his eyes? For a moment she thought he might send her away, but he grudgingly stepped aside, allowing her to enter the living room. "I suppose you'd better come in, now that you're here," he said gruffly. He waited until she perched, somewhat tentatively, on the edge of a chair, and then he took a seat across the room. They stared at one another across the distance that was far greater than a width of carpet.

"I suppose you've come to gloat," he said finally.

"No, that's not why I came." Her response was quick and sure. Yes, there had been a time when she would have delighted in his misfortune, rejoiced in his punishment. But now . . . "I came . . . I came because I want to make peace with you," she said.

A smile played around the corners of his mouth. "It's late for peace," he said gruffly. Yet he didn't get up from his chair and throw her out. That was at least something, she thought, especially after their last meeting.

"I . . . I'm sorry about what happened to you," she said, to her own surprise. "What will you do now?"

"Write my memoirs." He laughed bitterly. "I'm not ready to die. . . . Not yet."

She heard the echo of Sandy's words: "Custer Knight might have been one of the great ones . . ." And in that moment, Stevie felt touched by a miracle. She pitied her father. She had told so many damaged women that parents do the best they can, yet she had never imagined the same to be true of the Admiral. And now, for the first time, she suspected that the cruel tyrant she remembered masked a frightened, crippled man, isolated and cut off from human warmth.

"I saw you on television this morning," he said, looking past her shoulders and out the window, as if he couldn't bring himself to meet her eyes. "I hope you appreciate the honor, Stephanie. . . ."

For a second she felt something like anger. Did he have to put her down, even now? And then she reminded herself: he doesn't know any better. If he did, he wouldn't be sitting in this empty house with no one to care. "I do," she answered. "Would you like to see it . . . the medal?"

Now he met her eyes. "Yes," he said, "I'd like that." She handed over the medal in its velvet presentation case, watched him pick it up reverently, turn it over to read the inscription—this man who had built his whole life around rituals of authority, only to be destroyed by them.

She took a deep breath. "Look," she said, "I've hated

you for a long time. But it doesn't make sense to me, not anymore. I'd be lying if I said the past didn't matter, but ... you're the only father I'll ever have," she went on, echoing what she had told Carey, "and ... and if it's all right with you, maybe we can start over."

She paused and waited for what seemed like a very long time. Was this journey, then, to have been in vain? she wondered. Did Custer Knight hate his only child so much that he would reject even the olive branch of peace?

The sun had all but disappeared outside, leaving only a thin gray light in the room. Stevie strained to see her father's face in the shadows. What was he thinking so silently, his shoulders moving with what seemed to be a sigh?

"Your mother ..." said a deep, low voice that seemed to float across the room, "your mother was thinking of you at the end. She loved you."

Stevie rose to her feet and crossed the width of carpet that separated them. "Thank you," she said, putting a hand on her father's shoulder. "Thank you for that."

As Custer Knight sighed and closed his eyes, Stevie thought she saw the glisten of a tear on his cheek. "I'm tired," he said heavily, and she understood it was time to leave.

"I'll come back to see you again," she said.

He simply nodded. All right, she thought, it was a beginning.

It was very late at night when Stevie reached The Oasis. She was physically exhausted and emotionally drained, craving nothing more than to collapse, fully clothed, onto her bed. But she couldn't allow herself to rest, not just yet.

After depositing her suitcase in her private quarters, she went out into the quiet and dimly lit corridors of The Oasis, hurrying along until she reached Room 118. She tapped, very lightly, stepped into the darkened room, and tiptoed to the bed nearest the window. Gently she shook the sleeping woman.

Livy Walsh sat up, rubbing her eyes. "What . . . what's wrong?" she asked.

Stevie put a finger to her lips, then motioned Livy outside the room. "Sorry I broke curfew," she apologized, "but I just couldn't wait to tell you . . . I saw Carey in Washington."

"Carey?" Livy was wide awake in an instant. "Did you talk to him, Stevie? Did he say anything . . . ?"

"I did . . . and he did. Oh, Livy, Carey loves you. . . . He's as much your son as he ever was Ken's . . . and doesn't want this war any more than you do. He's hurting, Liv . . . he's a grown man, and he's still hurting from whatever went wrong between you. Make peace with him . . . don't waste any more precious years."

Livy threw her arms around Stevie. "I'll try," she said fervently, "I promise I'll try."

Stevie drew away and looked into her friend's soft brown eyes. "You can do better than that," she said with a smile. "If I know anything at all about Livy Walsh, it's that you can make it happen."

A short distance away, in Stevie's office, there was yet another Traveler who was not asleep. It was Deni Vickers, speaking into the telephone in Stevie's office under cover of darkness. "I'll bet you all thought I was crazy," she was saying, her eyes glittering with excitement. "I'll bet you thought the network was ready to dump me . . . I guess you know different now. I guess you could say I've been undercover." She laughed triumphantly. "What do I have? I have stories you'd kill for, Frank . . . and they're all mine. You want a for-instance? Okay, how about this . . . a couple of months before she checked into this jail, Anne was so whacked out she was thinking about killing herself... what do you mean, how do I know? I heard it from the lady herself, right in group. And that's just part of it, Frank... I have the kind of dirt *nobody* else has...."

Deni paused, giving Frank Lester time to take it all in. She knew that Frank had a hard-on for her job. Hell, it didn't take a genius to figure that out, but Frank just didn't have the killer instinct, and that, in Deni's book, made him a permanent second banana. "Here's what I want you to do," she continued, "get my team down here tomorrow. I'm going to break the story on location, right here—just before I get the hell out. What? Are you crazy, Frank? I need The Oasis like I need twenty years in Sing-Sing."

Ready to rest at last, Stevie made a final sweep through her private world. Brief though her absence had been, she was like an overzealous parent, needing to reassure herself that all had been well in her absence. As she passed her office, she paused, then gave way to the temptation to check for important messages.

As she turned the handle of the door, Stevie heard a voice from within: instinctively she stopped to listen. The room was dark, but the deep, throaty voice was unmistakably Deni's. "... you just do what you're told and leave the thinking to me. That business in Afghanistan? Hell, I was just tired, Frank... you would have been tired, too, if you'd gone without sleep for seventy-two hours. Listen, I don't have time to bullshit with you... anyone who thinks Deni Vickers is nuts is gonna sit up and take notice. Just wait till I blow the whistle on Garretson," she laughed, "she won't know what hit her."

Stevie couldn't stand it any longer. She switched on the light and stormed into the office. Brimming with anger, she grabbed the phone from Deni's hand and slammed it down.

"What the hell do you think you're doing?" she demanded, her voice cold as steel.

"Doing my job, boss lady," Deni shot back, not moving a muscle from where she sat in Stevie's chair, her long legs draped on Stevie's desk, just as if she owned the place.

"Your job..." Stevie echoed in disgust, fighting the protest that came to her lips: I gave him up for you, dammit, I gave up the man I love for you!

"That's right," Deni smiled mockingly, "you said you wanted to help me, and you have... more than you know. You've given me a ticket back, Stevie, and I'm very, very grateful."

"That's it, Deni! You're out of here... first thing tomorrow morning!" With a strength born of consuming anger, Stevie grabbed Deni by the arm, yanked her from the chair, and dragged her out of the office.

"Let go!" Deni shouted, fighting all the way, "I said let go, dammit! I'll sue the hell out of you, Stevie! I'll tell the world what a goddamn Nazi you are!"

But Stevie was beyond hearing as she propelled Deni along the corridor, letting her go only when they reached the staff room Deni had occupied. Grabbing the carryall from the closet and throwing it on the bed, Stevie began pulling Deni's things from the drawers and shelves, stuffing them into the bag. Slow down, said the quiet voice of reason, take it easy, you're out of control, but Stevie just couldn't seem to help herself. In her haste she dropped Deni's notebook, and as she went to pick it up, she saw the name of Kanda Lyons.

Deni tried to grab it back; that was reason enough for Stevie to push her away—and to look at its contents. The notes had been scribbled hastily, the handwriting tiny and cramped or broad and sprawling... but Stevie could read it well enough... the ugly innuendos, the sordid, cheap journalism she detested, wrapped around not only Anne's most private secrets, but those of half a dozen well-known women, including Livy and Kanda.

"You have no right to look at my notes," Deni said defiantly, hands on hips in an attitude of challenge.

"I have every right! And I intend to destroy this garbage the minute . . ."

"Go ahead, boss lady, I've got everything I need up here," Deni laughed, tapping her forehead. "I've got everything I need to break the biggest stories of my career . . . hell, when I finish, nobody's going to remember why I came here . . . not after they hear all about your precious Travelers."

Stevie listened with growing horror as Deni raved on, about how she would have not one but an entire series of scandalous stories. "Maybe I'll lay off Livy Walsh . . . that's a lady I don't want for an enemy . . . everybody knows she's a drunk anyway . . . but the rest, I figure they're all fair game."

"My God," Stevie said, "you haven't learned a thing, not a damn thing! Not about yourself or anything else!"

"Sure, I have . . . I've learned who I am, boss lady. I'm Deni Vickers, and I intend to see to it that the world never forgets that name, not for a single minute!"

Against the knife edge of danger, Stevie fought back blindly. "If you use this filth," she said, waving the notebook in Deni's face, "if you use any of it, I . . ."

"You'll what, boss lady?" Deni mocked. "Slap my wrist with your ruler? Send me to bed without any dinner? Face it, Stevie, you're a loser . . . and so are all those other women I intend to expose."

"Then you'll expose yourself, too! If you dare to harm anyone here, Deni, you'll ruin yourself . . . I'll see to it!"

"You wouldn't," Deni said, her smile fading as she appraised her adversary. "Lee said you could be trusted . . . I guess the bastard lied."

"Don't you dare talk about Lee that way," Stevie blurted out, "he's better than you deserve . . . He's . . ." she caught herself quickly, but the damage was done.

Deni's topaz eyes narrowed, and for a moment she looked like a tiger ready to spring. "You," she hissed, "you're the one . . . the woman he'd never talk about . . ."

Stevie couldn't deny it.

"You've been making a fool of me," Deni accused, her voice redolent with anger, "both of you . . . pretending you wanted to help, when all the time you wanted him for yourself. Were you gonna try to get me locked up permanently, Boss Lady? Is that what you—?"

"It isn't like that," Stevie cut in. "Lee cares about you—"

"Shut up!" Deni shouted, "shut your lying mouth and get the hell out of my room!" She pushed Stevie through the door and slammed it behind her. A moment later Deni's expression of rage was replaced by a Cheshire Cat smile. Just wait, she thought, just wait until tomorrow. Let the bitch think she's throwing me out . . . I'll have my revenge on Miss High-and-Mighty Stevie Knight tomorrow. When Deni Vickers got through with The Oasis, no one who mattered would ever come here again.

Stevie's anger dissipated even before she reached her quarters, a sense of personal failure taking its place. She collapsed on the bed and tried desperately to think. No matter how she felt about Deni, she had no right to lose control, to expel her in the heat of anger, to threaten her for God's sake! Yet what was she to do now, when much more was at stake than her own happiness? If Deni's past record was any indicator, she would do exactly what she had promised—and destroy the lives of women who had put their trust in the sanctity of The Oasis. She would advance herself at any cost, she would build her ratings on the heartbreak of others without a second thought.

But didn't that prove how desperately troubled Deni was? Stevie asked herself. She could remember all too well a time when she had been angry and troubled, ready to strike out at anyone who came within striking distance. I have to hang onto her, Stevie thought. There has to be a way to reach her, even if I haven't found it yet.

By ten o'clock the following morning, The Oasis was under siege—surrounded by hordes of television reporters and print journalists, their automobiles and vans clogging the driveway, their cameras and equipment planted firmly outside the entrances, making it impossible for anyone to enter or leave without being bombarded with questions.

Instantly mobilized by the threat of danger, Stevie fought them off. Like a pioneer settler in days of yore, she faced her attackers bravely and tried to run them off. "This is private property," she said, "and you have no right to be here. There will be no statements and no interviews... now pack your gear and get out!"

"Is it true that Anne Garretson is one of your patients?" one reporter called out.

"I'm not going to discuss any of my Travelers with you. If you don't leave in fifteen minutes, I'm calling the police."

The threat fell on deaf ears. It was one that seasoned journalists had learned to ignore. A television mini-cam zoomed in on Stevie. "Is it true that Anne Garretson tried to kill herself before she came here?" asked Frank Lester. "Is it true her marriage is on the rocks?"

Lurking in the shelter of a nearby gazebo, Deni Vickers trembled with rage, choking over the bitter taste of betrayal. This should have been her moment, her show, and now it had turned into a media circus, with Frank Lester, that dirty, double-dealing bastard, leading the pack. All right, she thought, maybe she'd made a mistake in cutting him off at the knees once too often, but now it looked like she'd have to finish the job. Without Deni Vickers, without her inside information, Frank had nothing. She could grab the next plane back to New York . . . leave all these clowns in the dust, while she alone broke the story. Deni Vickers would be on top again . . . and Frank would be on the unemployment line.

From her sanctuary inside The Oasis, Anne watched with growing horror as her worst nightmare came to life. Stevie seemed to be fighting a losing battle. Against her pleas and her threats, the reporters were like a pack of wild dogs, smelling blood . . . Hal's blood, and they were going to tear at him, at her, until there was nothing left. "They're not leaving," she said to Kanda. "They're never going to leave me alone."

"Then get yourself out there, girl," Kanda urged. "Quit hiding here like a scared rabbit."

"But then they'll know . . ." Anne said, her voice barely a whisper. "They'll know everything . . ."

"They don't know shit," Kanda said with disgust, "but they're sure as hell gonna fake it, whether you talk to them or not. Show 'em who you are, Anne. Be proud of it," she urged, throwing her arm around Anne's shoulder.

The gesture struck a chord of remembrance . . . of another woman, an important and powerful woman who had tried to share her strength, who had urged Anne to fight the addiction that had ruled her life.

"Don't be ashamed of who you are," Kanda went on. "I know what that's like . . . it eats you up inside, makes you feel like you're nothing at all . . . don't do that to yourself, Anne. Get on out there, show those people what a *real* First Lady is all about."

"I don't know if I can."

"Sure you can. You just put one foot in front of the other, one step at a time."

And for the first time since Hal's political career had been launched, Anne Garretson made a political decision of her own. She would face the press—alone.

The two women marched through the arched doorway and out into the merciless scrutiny of a hundred camera eyes. When Stevie saw Anne, she threw out a protective arm, as if to shield her from the explosion of flashbulbs, the clamor of demanding voices. "It's all right, Stevie," Anne said with a calm that belied the cold knot of fear in her gut. "It's me these people came to see . . . now let's give them their story and send them home."

Her appearance unleashed a barrage of questions. Anne put her up her hand, as she had seen Hal do so often. The gesture commanded silence, and Anne made it clear she would not speak until she had it. Miraculously the clamoring voices were stilled.

"Ladies and gentlemen of the press," she said, "my name is Anne Farrell Garretson, and I am an addict . . . a recovering addict, thanks to Stevie Knight and The Oasis. That makes me like tens of millions of other Americans, but with a difference . . . my husband is a public servant. In the past, many of you have reported his achievements. I hope you won't yield now to the temptation to smear his good name for the sake of a story.

"But if you do," she continued, her voice growing stronger, "I hope the American public will prove you wrong. Senator Hal Garretson will go on fighting for what he believes in—and so will I! My battle against drugs is just beginning," she said, voicing an idea that had been recently born. "I intend to mount a campaign of my own, against an epidemic that destroys lives and entire families. I intend to share my experience with the American people

. . . to establish educational programs in schools and colleges . . ."

When Anne finished her statement, she answered a half dozen questions, declared the press conference over—and returned to the sanctuary of The Oasis. She did not look back. She had said her marriage was strong and healthy; she hoped that was true. She hoped Hal would be proud of her, but if he wasn't . . . well, she would have to deal with that problem, too.

"Anne . . ." a voice called out. It was Livy, holding out her hand. "My hat's off to you," she said. "Whatever those people out there do or say, I promise the *Chronicle* will be behind you one hundred percent."

"Thank you, Livy," Anne said, taking the proffered hand. "I appreciate your support . . . and I'm sure Hal will, too."

"No thanks necessary. You did the hard part yourself, Anne. All I'm going to do is report it fairly."

Alone in the shadows, her beautiful face twisted by an all-consuming rage, Deni watched her hopes for a comeback turn to dust. They had made a fool of her . . . those losers at The Oasis had made a fool of her, stealing her story, ruining her chance to show that Deni Vickers hadn't lost her touch. Black Jack would be ashamed of her now, for letting that bitch, Stevie Knight, walk off with the laurels . . . after she'd stolen her man. Nobody had ever made a fool of Black Jack Vickers . . . and by God, nobody was going to make a fool of his daughter.

Thank God it's over, Stevie thought, as she kicked off her shoes and stretched out on her bed. She felt as if she'd been run over by an entire tank division . . . yet Deni had done her worst and Anne Garretson had survived. So would The Oasis, though Stevie had spent hours trying to calm and reassure the other anxious Travelers, who now feared that their most personal secrets would be splashed all over the scandal sheets—or aired on the 6 o'clock news. But it isn't really over, Stevie reminded herself. She had lost Deni.

There was a knock on the door, and when she opened it, she was swept up by a strong pair of arms and kissed until she was breathless. "Lee," she whispered, disbelieving her senses. "What on earth are you doing here? I thought—"

"You thought wrong," he said, a determined set to his jaw, "we both thought wrong. Ever since you sent me away, I've been trying to imagine a life without you. When I saw what was happening at The Oasis today, I took the first plane out. I figured you needed me, and for once, I wasn't going to let you down. How the hell did that happen, Stevie? Was it Deni?"

Stevie nodded.

"I'm so sorry, Stevie. I feel like it was all my fault for bringing her here."

"It isn't your fault . . . I'm supposed to help people like Deni. If anyone's to blame, it's me . . . I didn't do my job this time, it's as simple as that. I had a terrible scene with her. I . . . I lost control, and—"

"There must have been a reason," he cut in. "I know you, Stevie . . . there must have been a reason."

"It doesn't matter," she said, reluctant even now to reveal how badly she'd been provoked. "What matters is that I've got to find a way to get her back. I've got to start over—"

"Stop it," he commanded quietly. "I came here to talk about us, not about Deni. It's taken us so long to find each other. Why are we still allowing our lives to be ruled by someone who can't be helped?"

Stevie shook her head. "I can't accept that, Lee. If I give up on Deni, it would be like . . . like saying she was hopeless, after I've spent my whole life trying to prove that *nobody's* hopeless. I just have to keep trying until I find a way to reach her. I have to—" She paused in midsentence, her senses suddenly alerted by the presence of something that shouldn't be.

A moment later, the stillness of the night was broken by the sharp, keening wail of a smoke detector. Instantly mobilized by the threat of a physical danger, Stevie picked up the telephone and dialed the local emergency number. "We have a fire at the The Oasis, in the west wing, as far as I know. I'm on my way to investigate, but you'd better send help right away.

"You stay here," she said to Lee.

"Not a chance. . . . I'm coming with you."

"No, dammit, I need you here. My staff will be here any minute . . . Tell them to form three teams and do a reconnaisance on the north, south, and east wings . . . to evacuate all Travelers if they find even a trace of fire." And with that, Stevie tore out of her quarters, racing toward the wailing siren sound. Let it be just a burning cigarette in a wastebasket, she prayed. Please, God, nothing worse than that.

Doors began to open, disgorging sleepy women into the corridor. "What the hell's going on?" demanded movie star Jennifer Halliday, clutching her maribou-trimmed negligee around her slender body. "A fire drill in the middle of the—"

"This isn't a drill," Stevie cut in. "We do have a fire in this wing, and we'll have it out very soon. I want you all to keep calm. Take something warm to cover yourselves and walk to the nearest exit."

Spotting Livy Walsh, Stevie took the older woman aside. "I don't know how bad the fire is, Livy. . . . I want you to make sure all the rooms in this wing are empty. Don't let anyone waste time packing personal belongings."

"Got it," Livy said, her parochial-school discipline matching Stevie's own. And without a second's hesitation, she was on her way, throwing open doors, bundling the half-asleep occupants into sweaters and jackets . . . and pointing them toward the nearest exit.

As Stevie ran past the gymnasium, the burning smell grew stronger and sharper, and by the time she reached the kitchen, she was confronted by black, billowing clouds of smoke and the powerful smell of grease. She pulled a fire extinguisher from the wall, then yanked open the door that led to the cooking area. A wall of flames, blazing out of control, threw her back choking and gasping for air. How could this have happened? It was as if the place had been drenched in cooking oil.

A moment later, Stevie was surrounded by a trio of dining-room workers in various stages of undress, all prepared to help fight the fire. "No," she said, "it's too dangerous. . . . Just cordon the area off until the fire department gets here. And for God's sake, keep away from the kitchen."

Suddenly another alarm went off in the adjoining wing, its high-pitched wail filling Stevie with dread. As she rushed toward the sound, she glimpsed through the clouds of smoke a wraithlike figure with a nimbus of red hair streaming behind. Stevie rubbed her burning eyes, trying to see more clearly, but the figure had disappeared. As she turned the corner, Stevie ran into another wall of flames, a bonfire of mattresses and linens spilling out from a storage room and blocking the corridor, filling the air with the acrid stench of burning cooking oil. Forced into taking a detour, Stevie reversed her steps, nearly colliding with Kanda Lyons, who was running in the direction of the fire, wearing nothing but an oversize T-shirt. "Where do you think you're going?" Stevie shouted, grabbing the singer's arm. "I want you out of here, this minute!"

"Not without Anne," Kanda said, trying to shake herself loose.

"Anne's in no danger, dammit, she's in the south wing! Now don't stand here arguing with me. . . . Just get the hell out!" As if to belie her words, the alarm in the south wing went off. Kanda broke away and ran to save her friend, with Stevie in pursuit.

The distance to Anne's room was only a hundred yards or so, but it seemed like an eternity before they reached it, calling her name, shouting it through the din of the shrieking alarms.

"She isn't here!" Kanda screamed.

"She must be outside already!" Stevie screamed back. "Everybody must be outside by now!"

"I have to make sure!"

Stevie rushed into Anne's bathroom and soaked two towels with water. "Here," she said, handing one to Kanda, "cover your face, and we'll check all the rooms."

Fighting the smoke that threatened to envelop them, Kanda and Stevie worked their way down the corridor, calling Anne's name. "There's nobody here!" Stevie shouted—and then she saw the wraithlike figure again. Realization struck with the force of a sledgehammer to the chest. It was Deni! Her face blackened with smoke, she was racing through every corner of The Oasis like a dark angel, leaving destruction and fear in her wake. For an awful moment, Stevie nearly gave way under the force of the hatred that sought to consume all she had worked for. But there was no time for weakness now, not when the safety of her Travelers was at stake. Taking Kanda by the hand, Stevie moved unerringly toward an exit. Pushing the door open, she half fell outside, breathing the cool, clear desert air in great, ragged gulps. Then, before anyone could stop her, Stevie went back into the building.

She had to find Deni. But where? There were dozens of

storage rooms, packed with inflammable materials. . . . Where would Deni strike next? she asked herself, moving by memory through the blistering heat, holding the wet towel over her head. Her lungs were like sandpaper, her eyes swollen, but Stevie pressed on. And then she saw Deni, just a few feet away, carrying a metal container, moving purposefully toward a medical-supply closet as if she were superhuman, beyond the reach of fire and smoke.

Stevie stumbled forward, calling out her name, and for a moment Deni stopped. Stevie could hear the ring of her throaty laughter just before the container came hurtling through the air and knocked her unconscious.

As the clanging of bells signaled the arrival of the town fire brigade, Lee made his way through the ranks of Travelers and staff, desperately checking every face in search of the one that was most dear to him. Dear God, he thought, she isn't here, Stevie isn't here. The main entrance to The Oasis was choked with flames now, and as the firemen scrambled from their trucks, axes at the ready, Lee realized there wasn't a second to lose. Covering his head with his jacket, he threw himself against a window, ignoring the shards of glass that cut at his face. Praying as he had never prayed before, Lee fought his way through the inferno. It was like 'Nam, the heat and the smoke, but now it was more than a buddy he needed to save, it was the woman he loved as much as life itself.

Amid the din of sirens and shouted orders, the muffled calls for help that came from the supply closet went unnoticed. Amid the urgent battle to quell the flames, no one heard the pounding on the door, the frantic attempts to budge the lock that had jammed shut. As the air grew poisonous and deadly, the pounding grew weaker, and the calls for help became fainter . . . and then stopped forever.

* * *

Gray fingers of thin, acrid smoke smudged the desert dawn, a grim reminder of Deni's final madness. And even as she surveyed the destruction that Deni had wrought, Stevie felt a heart-wrenching pity, a strange kinship with the twisted soul that had consumed itself with hatred.

Wrapped in blankets against the chill morning air, the survivors clustered around Stevie as if she were still somehow their shepherd. Yet there was something more in the gesture, something protective and caring, for they all had come to know that The Oasis was more than a place of work to Stevie Knight, that it had been her entire life.

Seeing Stevie's haggard face, perhaps mistaking her desolate expression, Livy came up to her and murmured, "It looks worse than it is, Stevie. I've spoken to the firemen. . . . The basic structure is still intact. It shouldn't take more than a few months to rebuild. I can promise you a million and a half from the Walsh Foundation. I can have a check cut no later than next week. . . ."

"You can count on me too," said Lee, holding Stevie close, as if he'd never let her out of his sight again. "I know this place means everything to you. . . ."

Stevie looked into his eyes with a vision that had been born of regret and set with the clarity of truth. "No," she said quietly, "not everything. The Oasis is important, but it isn't everything to me, Lee . . . not ever again. We'll rebuild, we'll start over. But before I'll let myself get lost in being a missionary, I have a different kind of promise to keep. . . ."

His eyes asked the silent question.

"A promise of love," she said.

And when he gathered her into a long, tender kiss, she yielded to one more temptation—the temptation of her heart, one she knew there would never be any reason to regret.

ILLUSIONS

JESSICA MARCH

☐ (A30-272, $3.95, U.S.A.)
(A30-273, $4.95, Canada)

Set in the diamond-studded world of Palm Springs, a passionate novel about a daring young woman who seeks retribution against the one man who has wronged her.

345